BLACKOUT TRAIL

LINDA NAUGHTON

ISBN 979-8-9868525-5-3 (E-Book)
ISBN 979-8-9868525-6-0 (Paperback)
ISBN 979-8-9868525-8-4 (Audiobook)
ISBN 978-1-965187-04-3 (Hardcover)
Library of Congress Control Number 2022920086

Published 2022 by Wordsmyth Creations, LLC, Pittsburgh, Pennsylvania, USA.

Visit the author's website: www.lindanaughton.com

Cover design by Deranged Doctor Design: www.derangeddoctordesign.com

For B.B.

PART ONE

CHAPTER 1

THE WORLD AS I KNEW it ended just after 9:42am Eastern Standard Time, though I didn't realize it at the time. My phone had just buzzed with a call from my sister.

"Hey Jess," I said, brushing back some errant hair as I brought the phone up to my ear. I cupped my hand over the other ear as one of those golf-cart style vehicles puttered by, carrying someone to the opposite end of the cavernous airport terminal.

"Anna. You said you'd call when you got in. The website says your plane landed thirty minutes ago." The chiding words had an edge of mirth to them, ribbing me like always.

"I haven't even been gone twelve hours and you're already stalking me online?" I chuckled. "I was going to call as soon as I got my bag. What is it—like, before seven there? Go back to bed."

"The girls got me up early," Jess explained. I could hear the smile in her voice. "They miss you already. I wish you'd change your mind and look for a job out here."

I smiled through my impatience. "Jess, we've been over this. You know there's only so long I can pretend to be civil to Dad and that woman. It's better if we have a few zip codes between us." After a beat, I added, "I miss you guys too."

"Okay, okay," she said, dropping it until the next time we talked. "Anyway, how was your fli—"

There was a click and then silence. "Jess? Hello?" I lowered the phone and narrowed my eyes at the blank display. No indicators, no clock—nothing. How could it be dead already? I'd charged it before I left Jess' house last night, and the damn thing was barely a month old. I scowled. "Oh, come on."

The nearby baggage carousel ground to a shuddering halt. A collective groan from the other passengers drew my attention away from the useless brick in my hand. Snatches of disjointed conversation reached my ears.

"Can you hear me? I think we got cut off. Frank?"

"The hell? I had plenty of charge left."

"Moooommy! My movie stopped!"

A growing sense of dread pooled in my stomach. It wasn't just our baggage carousel that had stopped; they all had. Both the overhead lights and the computer screens showing the baggage carousel assignments had gone dark too. The only light streamed in from the floor-to-ceiling windows lining the perimeter of the baggage claim area. Why hadn't the emergency lights kicked on?

The automatic sliding doors had also stopped, confounding a gaggle of college kids trying to leave. Beyond the doors, an ominous stillness had replaced the constant bustle of parking shuttles, cars, and taxis creeping along the pickup lane. There should've been engine sounds. Horns. Something. Now there were just a bunch of confused and pissed-off people getting out of their vehicles.

Grumbling from the other passengers gave way to a stunned hush. Panic bubbled just beneath the surface. You couldn't set foot in an American airport these days without being bombarded with reminders of terrorism. Everyone looked at each other, the same question written on our faces: Was this some kind of attack? What should we do? I expected some sort of alert or explanation over the loudspeaker, telling everyone to remain calm, but none came.

A thunderous crash from the opposite end of the terminal had me ducking and covering my head. Metal screeched on metal, accompanied by the tinkle of shattered glass and an ear-splitting grinding sound. A chorus of terrified cries erupted around me. I'll admit it—I screamed too. I caught a glimpse of a plane fuselage crashing through the airport ceiling before plowing into the ground.

The plane flattened the south end of the building as casually as a child knocking over a stack of blocks, and the resulting fireball sent flaming debris flying in all directions. At the opposite end, the shock wave knocked me off my feet. A rush of hot air stung my face and hands.

People started picking themselves up off the ground. Dozens of survivors made a mad dash for the exits. Their screams sounded distant to my ringing ears. Non-functioning doors proved to be a mild hiccup for the exodus. The lucky ones smashed through or pried the doors open before they got smashed against the glass.

Catching my breath, I rose to a crouch. The putrid smell of aviation fuel mixed with acrid smoke tickled my throat and made my eyes water. Heart hammering, I surveyed the destruction in slack-jawed horror. The rectangular terminal stretched for the length of a football field, and nothing remained of the south half but fiery rubble. Between here and there was a wide stretch where it looked like a bomb had gone off.

A man shambled along, his clothes engulfed in flames. He made it a few steps before someone knocked him down and started beating out the flames with a jacket. Other lumps of former passengers smoldered on the ground. A woman staggered in a daze, her shirt a bloody mess.

"My God," I breathed, pushing the ghastly images to some back corner of my mind, where I could process them later.

A hefty chunk of ceiling crashed down in front of me just as I made it to my feet. I jumped backward with a startled cry. This end of the building was comparatively intact, but everyone knew what happened to buildings after planes crashed into them. My gut screamed at me to make a run for it, but there were still injured people on the ground.

An older man crouched on hands and knees in the blast zone, his tailored suit now singed and tattered in places. I hurried over to him and bent to touch his elbow. "Can you walk?"

He stared at me like I was from Mars before his brain seemed to catch up.

"Yes," he replied, sucking in big gulps of air. "Yes, I think I..." His eyes went wide as saucers when he registered the surrounding carnage, and he got so pale I worried he might faint.

I stepped in front of him to cut off his view. "Hey! Look at me." Tugging on his arms, I pulled him to his feet and pointed to the nearest exit. "Go outside. You'll be safe there. Go!" I gave him a nudge in the right direction and he started moving.

Someone grabbed my arm. It was a little girl, about seven or eight.

"My daddy needs help. Please help him!" Her eyes were wide and pleading, tears tracing lines through the soot on her face.

"Where? Show me." I offered my hand and let her lead the way. My stomach clenched as she took us closer to the wrecked half of the building. Survival instincts screamed at me to head away from the blaze. We were still some distance from the fire, but the heat pounded my face like a blast of hot air from an oven. The automatic sprinkler system soon drenched us both, but didn't make a dent in the inferno at the far end. Thick smoke blanketed the area, and I had the sudden impulse to scoop the kid up and carry her out of the building.

"There! Daddy!" The girl's urgent cry staved off any thoughts of flight. She pulled free of my hand, dashing over to a pile of rubble. It looked like the ceiling had come down. A man lay face-down, half-buried beneath the debris. Across his lower chest was a large, twisted metal frame that might once have been part of the baggage conveyor system. The girl fell to her knees beside him, and I followed suit.

"Sir, can you hear me? Sir?" The smoke made my voice hoarse. I coughed and shook his shoulder. Groaning, the man stirred.

"Daddy, wake up!" The girl tugged on his hand.

He turned his head and opened his eyes, squinting against the sprinkler mist. An instant later, alarm flooded his face.

"Lily!" He tried to push himself up, but the metal stopped him. He grimaced and then looked at the girl. "Lil, are you okay?"

Lily didn't answer, but just burst out crying, sprawling across her father's shoulder in an awkward hug. Only then did he seem to notice me, brow creasing in confusion.

"She's okay," I assured him, not wasting time on introductions. "Let's get you out."

I worked to get him free. The loose rubble came away easily—most of it was light ceiling tiles, insulation and chunks of mortar. The metal frame, slippery from the sprinklers, was a bigger problem. Even when I squatted down and used the full strength of my legs to lift it, the frame didn't budge an inch. The father tried to help, straining to push up from below, but we got nowhere. I fell back, breathless and frustrated, and the exertion brought on another coughing fit.

"You need to get her out of here." Agonized eyes pleaded with me.

Lily blubbered something unintelligible into his shoulder.

"No." I recoiled, horrified by the suggestion. I didn't want to admit I'd been thinking the same thing just before we found him. It was different now that I knew he was alive. "We'll figure something out. Can you breathe okay?" I worried he was being crushed by that giant thing on his chest.

"Yeah, most of the weight isn't on me. But my arm's pinned."

"Okay, hang in there." The terminal had mostly emptied, but I spotted a few people helping the wounded out at the other end. "Hey! We need some help over here! Hey!"

One man looked our way, but his wide eyes drifted past us to the fire. He ran off in the opposite direction. Everyone else either didn't hear, or was already busy dragging other people out. As I let out a frustrated curse, my eyes lit on an abandoned luggage cart. I ran over and grabbed the cart, unclipping the bungee cords and leaving suitcases in my wake.

"What are you doing?" The father squinted at me.

"I'm going to lever this off of you." I slid the cart under the edge of the metal frame, as if it were a suitcase to be lifted. Lily watched me with wide, tearful eyes. "OK, try to slide out on three. One... two... three." On 'three', I pushed down on the handle with all my might. It held there for a second and then the joint at the base of the cart snapped clean off, making me fall in an inelegant sprawl on the ground. "Shit!"

The father grimaced. "We need something stronger. There—what about those poles?" He pointed to the belted queue in front of a rental car desk. The explosion and panicked flight of the patrons had knocked most of them over, making a disorganized jumble.

"Let's try it." I hurried to grab a post, hunching over to stay out of the smoke. The crash had shattered many of the windows and sliding glass doors, providing some ventilation, but I shuddered to think what noxious crap we were all breathing in. And it was getting worse.

Lily yelled, "The fire's getting closer!" The concrete ceiling and walls might not burn, but the aviation gas, carpet and furnishings all fed the blaze.

I pushed the ruined suitcase cart aside and put the post in its place. "OK, here we go. Again on three..." This time when I pushed down on the makeshift lever, it just jammed there, stuck. "Damn it, what is this thing made of?" It was heavier than it looked.

"It's not going to work," the father muttered, grim desperation in his voice. "Go. Please. Get her out of here."

"NO!" Lily's shriek was heartrending. She clung to her father, babbling. He mumbled something I couldn't hear, nuzzling the top of her head.

"It'll work," I insisted, adding a silent prayer. The idea of carrying away a screaming Lily and leaving her dad to burn to death was almost as terrifying as the approaching flames. "Come on, please." This time, it moved. Just for a second—just a bit—but it moved. I coughed and tried again, grunting and straining with the effort, and finally the frame lifted a few inches. It wasn't much, but it was enough. "That's it! Go!" Lily's father started scooting out from under the frame. "Hurry!" I urged through gritted teeth. "I can't hold it."

"I'm out!" he gave a triumphant shout. Lily flung herself against him. He grimaced at the force of her hug. "It's okay," he reassured her, pulling her up with his good arm. He cradled the other against his chest.

"Come on, hurry!" I ushered them toward the nearest exit, just as another part of the ceiling came crashing down in a shower of sparks behind us.

CHAPTER 2

GLASS LITTERED THE GROUND IN front of the non-functioning automatic doors. We ducked past jagged shards still clinging to the empty frame and squeezed through. Outside, a tunnel-like pickup lane ran between the terminal building and a parking garage. The roof connecting the two buildings had collapsed. Smoldering debris and twisted bits of metal peeked through car-sized chunks of concrete.

Lily's father pointed up the road. "Up there. It should be clear." Weaving around stalled vehicles, we brought up the rear of the exodus from the terminal building.

The moment we cleared the roof overhanging the pickup lane and emerged into the open air, I let out the breath I'd been holding. But then I heard a clamor of shouts from people gathered in a small grassy area nearby. Several of them pointed at something in the air: another jetliner. It almost appeared to be gliding, but the angle was far too steep to be landing.

"Pull up! Pull up!" a woman screamed, as if the pilots could hear her.

The jet didn't pull up.

"Everyone get down!" shouted Lily's father, and we scrambled behind a stalled car nearby. He murmured reassurances to his daughter, telling her to curl up in front of him. I took cover beside him, but my eyes didn't leave the jet as it came closer and closer to the ground. It smashed into one of the distant parking lots like a missile, the resulting explosion spreading flaming pieces of plane and cars for hundreds of yards. Lily screamed. I ducked, covering my head, and felt a weight on my back as Lily's father used his body as a shield for both me and Lily. A piece of metal clanged against the opposite side of the car, far too close for comfort.

"Jesus! What the hell is going on?" Lily's dad yelled. With wide eyes locked on the wreckage, I had no answer for him.

The other group scattered in a panic. Some ran for their cars or the Hyatt hotel across the parking lot. Others cowered among the vehicles. A few hid under the overhang of the terminal's traffic lane.

Images of watching the Twin Towers collapsing on TV kept playing in my head, and I looked back at the terminal. "We need to get away from the building."

Lily's father followed my gaze and the slight widening of his eyes told me his thoughts were running along the same lines as mine. "Over there. That bus."

He pointed to a parking shuttle further down the access road, and I nodded. A bus wouldn't help if another 747 tried to land on our heads —what would?!—but it would at least provide some protection from flying debris. We ran over, ducking again at the sound of another explosion somewhere on the other side of the airport.

Climbing through the open bus doors, we found we weren't alone. The driver had fled for parts unknown, but a half-dozen people sat or crouched in the aisles and between the seats. We pushed some suitcases aside to make room to sit in the little luggage alcove. Collapsing into the space, I panted as though I'd run a marathon instead of a hundred yards. I didn't know whether that was from adrenaline or smoke inhalation. Maybe both. My hands tingled, and I clenched them into fists in a futile attempt to stop them from shaking.

Lily sobbed softly, her father murmuring soothing nonsense to calm her down. "It's going to be okay," he promised. For a fleeting moment, I wished someone would tell me that. I was not at all convinced it would be.

I heard snatches of conversation from the other passengers: hushed murmurings about ISIS and 9/11, a few desperate attempts to find a working cell phone, and one middle-aged man who was just moaning "Oh God" over and over again.

His mumblings weren't going over well with everyone. "God, just give it a rest already," snarked a young man—a college student, judging by his UCLA T-shirt.

"How 'bout you shut the hell up, jagoff," an older woman snapped at him, her raspy voice a testament to a three-pack-a-day habit.

Tuning out the ensuing argument, I crawled over to the moaning man. "Sir." I touched his arm, which seemed to snap him out of his daze. "Are you hurt?" I didn't bother asking if he was all right. Were any of us, right now?

"N… no. I don't think so."

I looked him up and down. He wasn't injured, just scared out of his mind. I could relate. "Okay, good. You're going to be fine," I assured him, then looked around at the other passengers. "Anyone else hurt?" A flurry of head shakes answered me.

"Are we under attack?" asked a girl who couldn't have been over eighteen. Wide eyes searched mine for answers, terror etched into her soot-streaked face.

She was asking me? "I don't know," I admitted. "But we're all right for now. Just sit tight and we'll figure this out."

I moved back to the luggage area, where a shell-shocked Lily curled up in her father's lap. There was a resemblance in their faces, and their hazel eyes might as well have been carbon copies of each other. Lily's hair was a sandy blonde, tied back in a braid reaching midway down her back. Her father's was short and a little darker, a shadow of stubble lining his jaw. He looked to be about my age, early forties. Very handsome. Also very married, judging by the gold band on his finger. He shifted positions, his face twisting in a wince.

"Why don't you let me look at that arm?" I suggested, scooting closer. When he gave me a puzzled frown, I clarified, "I'm a doctor."

He held out the injured arm for me to see. "It's fine. Just bruised, I think."

I probed the bone with gentle fingers, noting the red, swollen welts on his skin, and tested his range of motion. A tough-guy grimace on his face suggested he was putting on a brave front for Lily, but I didn't press him. If he could move it like that, it probably wasn't broken.

I released his arm. "Should get it X-rayed just in case, but it looks okay for now."

Lily's dad asked her if she was okay, and she gave a listless nod. He then turned his concerned glance on me. "How about you, Doc? You all right? You're bleeding." He gestured toward my face.

I'd felt the sting earlier when the plane crashed, but hadn't paid it much mind. Now I touched my cheek, feeling a shallow cut from flying glass. I checked over the rest of myself just to be sure adrenaline wasn't masking any other injuries and then concluded, "Just a few bumps and scrapes."

He nodded, then stared at me for a long moment, looking like he wanted to say something. Finally he got it out. "Hey… what you did back there? Thanks."

I nodded, feeling awkward. I saved lives all the time, but this was different somehow. "Sure. You're welcome." I realized I still didn't know his name. "I'm Anna. Anna Hastings."

Lily canted her head to look at me. "Like Anna from *Frozen*," she said. A cough punctuated the tearful, timid whisper.

Not the first thing that sprang to mind when I thought about my name, but who was I to quibble with a traumatized kid comparing me to a princess? "Yeah," I smiled faintly. "I guess it is."

"I'm Mark Ryan. And this is Lily."

The usual platitudes like "nice to meet you" seemed inappropriate under the circumstances, so I just offered a nod. I heard a distant rumble and wondered if it was another plane going down further away from the airport. Shuddering, I exchanged a worried look with Mark. I wanted to talk about what was going on, to share my suspicions, but a glance at the terrified Lily convinced me to keep silent. She needed comfort, not speculation. The arguments at the back of the bus were bad enough.

I risked popping my head up to look out the window and gasped at my first good glimpse of the terminal building's ruined exterior. It reminded me of the pictures I'd seen of the Oklahoma City bombing. The jet had carved a diagonal swath of destruction from the roof to the basement on the south side of the building, leaving part of the upper floors hanging by a thread. Flames sputtered from the windows, thick black smoke pouring out. A piece of the tail section was still intact enough to be recognizable, but the rest of the plane was in pieces. A gray haze hung over the entire area. I sat back down, head spinning.

What the hell was happening?

A cough from Lily seemed to trigger a sympathetic tickle in my throat. I coughed a few times to relieve it, but the scratchiness remained. Mark and Lily both bore the telltale soot marks from smoke inhalation around their noses, and I suspected I did too. I wished I had some oxygen to give her—hell, to give all of us.

The girl sat in her father's lap with a vacant expression, tears drying on her cheeks. "I'm scared, Daddy," she murmured. "I want Mommy."

Mark's brow creased in a pained look. "I know, princess. We'll get back to her just as soon as we can."

"Where is she? Is she…" I looked back towards the terminal, feeling a pang of alarm at the possibility she might be still back there.

"No, no, she's in Boston," Mark explained, and I breathed a sigh of relief. He didn't have the *'pahk the cah'* Boston brogue, but now that I knew what to listen for, I could detect a hint of the accent in his voice.

"She had to stay home for her work till Thursday," Lily added in a small voice. She buried her head against Mark's chest, and he patted her hair.

"At least she's safe there." I tried my best to sound reassuring, then a thought struck me. "Is your phone working?"

Mark contorted to get the phone out of his pocket while balancing Lily. He frowned at it, then thumbed the power button. "No, it's dead. Yours?"

"I dropped it back there." Along with my purse, I just now realized. "But it died too, right before this all started." Mark's frown deepened at the news, a line furrowing his brow. Did he know something I didn't?

Raising my head to window height, I squinted up at the sky. I had no idea how many flights would have been in a landing pattern on a Wednesday morning, but there couldn't have been that many. Pittsburgh wasn't a huge airport. People were emerging from their shelters around the parking lot, many battered and bloody.

"I have to go. There are people hurt." I got up, stiff legs protesting, and moved forward to the driver's area to see if the bus had a first aid kit. The paltry box contained only some aspirin packets and band-aids —not even a pair of exam gloves or gauze pads. I tossed aside the useless piece of junk with a frustrated sigh.

Behind me, I heard Mark say, "We'll go with you."

"No! I don't want to go back out there," Lily whined. Her eyes widened, little hands digging into his shoulder with a death grip.

"Doctor Hasting is right, princess. Those people need help." Mark tried to soothe her, but she was having none of it. Her muffled protests soon devolved into sobs, and Mark pulled her into a comforting embrace. "Sssh, it's all right." I could see how torn he was, wanting to help but also needing to take care of his girl.

I crouched down beside them. "Hey, I think I have an idea," I began gently. Lily sniffled and canted her tear-stained face in my direction. I flicked my eyes up to Mark, hoping I wasn't stepping out of line. "There's a nice, safe hotel on the other side of the parking lot over there. I need someone to go there and see if they can send over some supplies, so I can help the people who are hurt."

"Like Band-Aids?"

I nodded. "Yeah, like Band-Aids. Bandages, sheets, blankets, water —whatever they can spare."

"And pillows."

"Hmm?"

"To go along with the blankets."

"Oh." I couldn't help but crack a smile. "Sure, pillows would be great too. Anything you think might help. Do you think maybe you and your dad could do that for me?"

Lily cast an uncertain look at her dad, who nodded. "Okay. Long as we don't have to go back."

"Great. Thanks. That'll be a big help." A glance included both of them.

Mark gave me a grateful nod. "I'll see if I can get the bus started, and we'll drive over and load it up with the stuff."

"Yeah, that would be perfect—and bring some of the wounded to the hotel. See if they can set up one of the ballrooms as a treatment area until more help gets here."

He nodded and moved to the driver's seat. While he familiarized himself with the controls, Lily sticking close by his elbow, I looked back to the other passengers. "Mark's going to take the bus over to the hotel. You'll be safer there. I could use some help with the wounded here, if anyone's willing to come."

The others exchanged uncertain glances. I suppose I couldn't blame them for not jumping at the chance to help. It looked like a war zone out there. One passenger rose to his feet, a burly, bearded guy in his late fifties wearing a Steelers T-shirt. "I don't know shit about medicine, but I'll lend a pair of hands. You tell me what you need, Doc."

I thanked him and established that his name was Jerry. At the front of the bus, Mark cursed.

"Won't start," he mumbled, twisting the useless key again.

"Yeah, the engine died right before that first plane hit. Driver ran off," Jerry said.

My brow furled. That was the same time the cars in the pickup lane stopped and my phone died. Mark and I exchanged concerned frowns, but neither of us offered any theories.

Mark stood up. "All right folks, it doesn't look like this thing is starting. We'll have to walk it." He scooped up Lily, assuring her, "Don't worry, princess, it's not too far."

I followed him off the bus in soggy discomfort. Leaving our little bubble of safety, my eyes scanned the clouds before drifting over to the ruined terminal building. The windows still glowed orange, and a tower of black smoke rose from the roof. How many other bodies were trapped within? Hundreds? Between the terminal and the crashed jets, I could imagine a thousand lives had been lost in that instant. Maybe more. I stared at the wreckage, trying to process the magnitude of what I was seeing.

Mark's voice startled me. "We'll send over some help as soon as we can." He caught my eye for a moment, gratitude mingling with concern. "Be careful, Doc. And thanks."

"You too." I watched them go, feeling unexpectedly anxious at being separated from them. They were strangers, but still the only two people I knew here. The rest of the passengers trailed after them, all except Jerry. Smothering another cough, I nodded my thanks again to him.

"Okay. Let's go see what we've got," I said with a grim resolution. Together we started toward where the screams of the wounded beckoned.

CHAPTER 3

"HELP US! SOMEONE CALL 911!"

It became a familiar refrain, everyone hoping that someone else's phone was working. It soon became apparent nobody's was. Coupled with the cars all dying, the realization left a hollow fear gnawing at the pit of my stomach. I couldn't worry about the hows and whys right now, though. There were dozens of people injured, and so far not an ambulance in sight.

Most of the evacuees had congregated in a grassy area between the short-term parking garage and the open parking areas beyond. The flat, grassy stretch was criss-crossed with access roads and stalled cars. There had to be more injured in the terminal, and on the far side of the lot where the second plane had torpedoed the cars. Right now, though, I had my hands full just with the people I could see.

I knelt down beside the middle-aged woman who had called for help. She was with a man—her husband, judging by their matching rings. Leaning against the wheel of a car, he clutched at a bloody gash on his thigh. "I'm Anna, I'm a doctor. Let me see?"

He obliged, but as soon as he removed his hand, the wound spurted blood up into the air. It splattered my shirt, pulsing in time with his heartbeat. *Oh shit.* I managed to keep the exclamation to myself, clamping my hand over the wound.

Jerry recoiled. "Damn, that's a lot of blood."

Seeing the panicked look on the injured man's face, I shot Jerry a brief glare. "It's all right," I assured my patient. "I'm going to take care of you. Jerry, can you hold pressure here? Tight as you can." I guided his hands to the right spot, then looked at the wife. "Ma'am, I need your scarf." Trembling hands fumbled to oblige without question. "Do you have a pen or pencil in your purse?" While she looked, I wrapped the scarf around her husband's upper thigh, just below his hip.

"Here, will this work?"

She handed me a pen, which I slipped under the knotted scarf. I turned it like a winch, drawing the scarf tight around the leg. The husband groaned at the pressure. "I know, I'm sorry. It's not comfortable, but it's going to keep you from bleeding to death." I secured the makeshift tourniquet in place, then had Jerry remove his hands from the wound. The bleeding had slowed to a trickle. "Okay, that'll hold you till help arrives. Ma'am, you keep an eye on that. If it comes loose, you tighten it back again and come find me, okay?" I started to move off, then remembered something. "Oh, do you have any lipstick?"

"Lipstick?" She looked at me like I had two heads, asking for makeup at a time like this. Nevertheless, she obliged by pulling a tube out of her purse.

"Thanks." I uncapped the tube and inked a red "T" on the man's forehead—the universal sign for tourniquet. I went to write the time as well, then realized my fitness tracker watch was as dead as my phone.

Another oddity I didn't have time to dwell on. "Anyone know what time it is?"

"Just after ten." Jerry flashed me his watch, an analog wind-up model. Mumbling my thanks, I scrawled 10:00 on the man's head, hoping it was vaguely legible. Not easy to do with lipstick.

"Okay, I'll be back to check on him when I can." I moved on to find another victim.

Someone found me instead—a college-aged boy with a panicked, soot-streaked face. "Hey, they said you're a doctor? My friend needs help over here."

"Yeah. What happened?" I followed him to another car.

"We were inside when the plane crashed, and this big chunk of ceiling came down on him. I got him out, but he's pretty messed up." He stood by helplessly, his hand on his head.

His friend lay unconscious on the ground, and only groaned when I rubbed his chest and called to him. A bloody gash on his scalp explained him being out cold, but his rapid breathing and deviated windpipe hinted at a serious chest injury. A few ribs moved under my probing fingers in ways they shouldn't.

"He's got some broken ribs, maybe a collapsed lung," I told his friend, even as I scrawled a 'R' on his forehead with the lipstick. I sat back on my heels, chewing my lip. Without equipment, there wasn't much I could do for him. Hopefully an ambulance would turn up with the gear we needed before he took a turn for the worse. "He's holding his own for now. I need you to watch him. If his breathing gets worse, come get me, okay?"

The kid locked eyes with mine, widening in panic. "How the hell am I supposed to know?"

I gave him a quick run-down on some signs to watch out for, then clapped his arm. "You can do this." I waved over Jerry. "You two take him over with the others. Move him as gently as possible."

And so it went. At some point the horror of what was happening would hit me, but as long as I kept moving, I'd be all right. One patient at a time, like a shark that just needed to keep swimming to breathe. I'd been a part of mass casualty incidents before, but never anything of this magnitude. And never by myself, with no supplies beyond the tube of lipstick I carried. I did the best I could with what I had, grateful every time I encountered a "walking wounded" patient who could get to the hotel under their own power. For a few, it was already too late. I left them with an "X" in magenta lipstick on their forehead to mark my grim proclamation and left them where they lay. More arrived at my little patient area by the first guy's car, which was growing faster than I liked.

The minutes ticked on, and I wondered why no help had arrived. Even with the cell phones down, someone must've noticed the giant fucking plume of smoke wafting up over the airport. Where were the ambulances? The fire trucks? Hell, at this point I'd settle for a damn news helicopter.

The smoke from the terminal wafted over the area, making my coughing worse. I desperately wished for a drink to soothe my throat.

Eventually I ran into another doctor. Her name was Bindu, an Indian-American pediatrician. Out of her depth doing immediate triage, she was relieved when I suggested she take charge of the patient area. An off-duty firefighter soon joined us. He and Jerry became my transport crew, carrying the wounded to Bindu as I roamed the parking lot, doing initial assessments and interventions. The fire and ominous creaking from the half-collapsed pickup lane kept me well clear of the terminal building. There might be wounded inside, but I couldn't help anyone if I got pancaked by rubble.

"Doc! Hey, Doc—Bindu needs you." Jerry's voice distracted me from a young woman with a bloody but superficial head laceration. I directed her over to the hotel with a handkerchief clutched to her head, then followed Jerry back to the treatment area.

It was the collapsed lung guy. "He's not breathing right. You said to get you if he was in trouble," reported his frightened friend.

I nodded, surveying the patient's deteriorating condition. So much for waiting it out. "You did a good job." I looked around at the gaggle of patients and my little team. "Anybody have a knife? Scissors? Anything sharp?" I got a lot of blank stares and head shakes, and cursed airline security.

"Here you go, Doc." Jerry's gruff voice got my attention, holding out a pocketknife. He must have been coming to pick someone up, not traveling himself.

"Bless you, Jerry," I murmured. "I also need a straw or a pen or something—any kind of hollow tube. And hand sanitizer and a plastic baggie." This time it was the wife with the bottomless purse who came through, rummaging around and handing over everything else I needed. I thanked her and began slathering the alcohol cleanser all over it. Wasn't the greatest sterilization, but it was the best I could do.

"Are you gonna do that neck thing like on TV?" Jerry wondered, peering over my shoulder.

"Not exactly. There's a hole in his lung and the air is leaking out into his chest, preventing his lung from inflating. I need to let the air out so he can breathe." I wrapped part of the baggie around the end of the straw, improvising a flutter valve. It would keep more air from being sucked in with each breath.

Everyone watched me. No pressure or anything. I doused some more sanitizer on the knife and the man's chest, took a deep breath, and then made an incision above one of his ribs. Air bubbling from the cut told me I'd gone deep enough. I stuck the straw in and saw the baggie on top fluttering in and out in rhythmic response to his breathing.

"Hot damn. Look at you, Doc MacGyver," Jerry said, whistling through his teeth. "Bet they don't teach that in med school."

Relieved to see the man's breathing and color improving, I allowed myself a weak smile. "Not so much. I learned that trick in Africa."

"Africa?"

Before Jerry could pursue that line of questioning further, the guy's friend asked, "Is he gonna be okay?"

"He's still in bad shape, but this'll help him till we can get him to a hospital. I need you to hold this straw steady until we can figure out something to keep it in place. Bindu, can you see if you can find something?"

"Of course," she answered, her smooth accent sounding unruffled despite the stress.

Transferring care of the makeshift valve to the man's friend for now, I stood up and dragged the back of my arm across my face. Although I was drying out from the fire sprinklers, the humid summer air and exertion had me sweating up a storm. I wiped the knife on the injured guy's shirt and handed it back to Jerry.

He waved me off. "You keep it, Doc. Think you'll be needing it more than me today."

"Thanks." Great. A tube of lipstick and a pocketknife—now I could practically open my own clinic.

As if on cue, a strange clattering sound drew my attention to the access road. A hotel bellboy pushed a linen cart stacked with sheets and cases of bottled water and—as Lily had promised—a couple of pillows. His eyes tracked the ruined terminal building in abject terror, his steps halting. "Over here!" I called, waving him over.

"You're Doctor Hastings?" the bellhop asked in a trembling voice when he came near.

"Yeah. Thanks for bringing this stuff over." Bindu and I started unloading the cart. A first aid kit sat on top, this one larger and better-stocked than the one in the bus. I'd have to thank Mark and Lily later. I grabbed a bottle of water for myself, splashing some on my hands to wash the blood off and then guzzling down the rest. My throat felt better, but it didn't stop another coughing fit.

Jerry, my trusty shadow, clapped my shoulder from behind. "You okay, Doc? You don't sound too good. Maybe you should sit down and rest a minute. Ain't gonna do anybody any good if you keel over next."

I got the coughing under control and shook my head to him. "I'm all right." Seeing his skeptical fatherly concern, I said, "Really, I'll be fine. Thanks though. Come on, we've got people a hell of a lot worse off than me to worry about." I flashed him a grateful smile, and we got back to work.

Word spread about our makeshift field hospital, and people started bringing the injured to us instead of us having to go out and drag them back. We also accumulated an EMT and a nurse. I kept waiting for someone to challenge me and ask who'd put me in charge, but everyone seemed content to accept my authority. I suppose nobody else wanted the responsibility.

Lucky me.

As I tended to a patient, a man called from behind me, "Doctor Hastings?"

"Just a second." I bent over a woman with a probable skull fracture from a flying hunk of debris from the parking lot, performing a neurological assessment. She seemed stable for now, but we would need to monitor her for any signs of a brain bleed. Not that there would be much we could do if she had one. "You're doing all right, ma'am. We'll keep you here under observation just to be safe."

"Doctor Hastings?" There was that voice again, more impatient this time.

I sighed and turned, surprised to find a man in a firefighter's turnout gear standing a few feet behind me. His white helmet marked him as an officer, "Lieutenant" emblazoned across the front over his engine number. Soot streaked his sweaty face and clothes.

Finally. Help had arrived. I felt a jolt of relief. "Yeah, that's me." I brushed some errant hair back out of my face.

"I'm Lieutenant Gardner. We ran into some of your people over by the terminal. They told me you were organizing things here?"

My people. "Yeah, I suppose I am."

"What's your status?"

I took a breath and made an expansive gesture to encompass the treatment area, which now sprawled across the grassy expanse between the parking lots. "We've got about twenty we need to transport immediately; the rest can wait a bit. I've been sending the walking wounded over to the hotel. Sure are glad to see you, though. What help can you give us?"

"Not much right now," Gardner dashed my hopes. "There are still some people trapped in the elevators and the tram in the terminals. That's eating up all our manpower. We need everyone out before the fire guts the place. We haven't got much to throw at it."

"Hasn't anyone from the city turned up?"

Gardner's frown answered that question before he even said anything. "No. Communications are down."

"I've got to get these people to a hospital. There are, like... thousands of cars out there." I waved a hand to encompass the parking lot. "They can't all be dead."

"Do you see anyone driving away from here?" He had a point. "We've got someone trying to fix our truck. That's the best I can do for now."

Fists clenched in frustration, I stepped closer to him so I could lower my voice. "Lieutenant, if these critical cases don't get to a hospital soon, we're going to start losing them. They need surgery and they needed it an hour ago." I wracked my brain for options. "How far's the nearest hospital? Can we move them on foot? Get some volunteers for stretcher bearers?"

"To a trauma center? Twenty miles, give or take. There's a small hospital closer, but I doubt they're equipped for this. Listen, Doctor, I understand your position. But just sit tight and do what you can. Help will be here soon."

I didn't like it, but he was right. It would take hours to transport the patients that far. Even if they could handle the strain, we couldn't maintain their treatment on the way.

Gardner took my grim silence for agreement, and went on, "The chief has incident command set up over on the tarmac, just on the other side of this building here. Until we get the radios working, find us there if you need us."

"Okay. Any supplies you can get us?"

"I'll see what I can do, but I wouldn't hold my breath. Our supply room is in there." He pointed to the burning terminal.

I sighed, rubbing my face. Guess it was more sheet bandages and pillow splints for us then. "All right. I'm going to move these people over to the hotel. All this smoke isn't doing anyone any good, and baking in the sun is hell for our burn victims."

"Good idea. I'll keep in touch. Good luck, Doctor."

"You, too," I offered, watching him go with a frown.

Jerry came up alongside me. "Are they gonna get these people to the hospital?"

"No." I chewed my lip. "We're on our own for now."

CHAPTER 4

MOVING THE WOUNDED TO ONE of the hotel ballrooms took over an hour. My aching back and arms made me glad we only had to carry them across the parking lot and not all the way to the hospital. As we were lamenting our lack of supplies, an EMT remembered every jetliner carried an emergency medical kit. I sent some people over to scavenge from the planes parked on the tarmac. A few others went to the lobby to make a plea for blood donors and for whatever painkillers people could spare. We ended up with a limited stock of medication and equipment, and I felt less naked with a stethoscope around my neck.

My helpful shadow Jerry had disappeared for a while once we got everyone to the hotel, saying he needed to go look for someone. When he returned, he had a young man in a crew cut and Army uniform standing with them.

Jerry introduced the soldier as his son, then lowered his voice. "Whatever's going on here, it sure ain't good. Looks like you've got plenty of help here now, so we're going to hoof it back home."

I thanked him with a hug, telling his son, "Your dad helped a lot of people today."

Jerry waved off the praise, embarrassed. I waved and watched them go. Only later would I realize I still had Jerry's pocket knife tucked away in the back pocket of my jeans.

The deluge of critical patients slowed to a trickle; most of the people still being pulled from the rubble were beyond help. There were still scores of walking wounded, though. By lunch time, we had dozens of non-ambulatory patients in our makeshift infirmary, many in critical condition. Already we had lost some, lacking the trauma surgery or other definitive treatments to save them.

"Dr. Hastings!" The alarmed cry from a nurse drew me to a patient in the corner—it was the young woman with the skull fracture I had treated earlier. I rushed over and heard, "She's crashing."

We did fifteen minutes of CPR, hoping for a miracle, but knew from the start that we would not get her back. A CT scan and neurosurgeon might have saved her, but now it was too late. I glanced up at the wall clock to announce the time of death.

"We did everything we could," I told the solemn faces of the treatment team. I kept my voice even, resisting the urge to smash something in frustration.

"I need some air," I mumbled, excusing myself out to the hallway. Someone had propped open the door at the end of the hall, and the occasional breeze was a welcome change from the stifling ballroom.

"Doctor Anna!" The shout made me look up to see Lily rushing down the hall with a big smile on her face.

I straightened just in time for her to throw herself against me in a hug so exuberant it felt more like a hip check. I gave her back an awkward pat as she wrapped her tiny arms around my waist. "Oh... uh, hey there."

"Sorry," Mark said with an apologetic smile, trailing her down the hall. He seemed to register the strain on my face, and his voice took on a concerned edge. "How are you doing?"

"Oh, you know—crazy morning," I said, in an understatement-of-the-century kind of way.

"You can say that again." Mark opened his mouth to say something else, but then Lily interrupted.

"We brought you some lunch. There was a really, really long line, but they let us get some extra to bring to you, so actually you won't have to wait in it." She unslung her backpack, which was adorned with various Disney princesses and lots of glitter. It was still damp from the sprinklers. Rummaging around in it, she came up with a wrapped-up sandwich, a bag of cookies and a bottle of water. "They had cookies and chips," she continued, handing me the food. "I didn't know which one was your favorite, but cookies are my favorite, so that's why I picked cookies. And Daddy picked you a water. I had a juice box."

I smiled weakly at her enthusiasm, quite a change from the terrified, shell-shocked girl I'd met a few hours ago. It never ceased to amaze me how fast children could bounce back from tragedy. In Haiti, as part of the relief efforts after the big earthquake, I'd seen kids playing soccer amid the rubble. I wished I had their resilience.

"Thanks. That's really sweet. I love cookies." Her face fell with disappointment. "But, you know, I don't think I can eat all of them. Maybe we can share—if your Dad says it's ok?" I arched my eyebrows at him.

Lily's face brightened. "Pleeeeease, Daddy?"

Of course he agreed. He'd have to be some kind of barbarian to deprive a kid of cookies after the morning she'd had. I dumped a couple of them into my hand and gave her the bag with the rest. She replied with a grin and a thanks.

"Lily—could you take those down by the water bubbler there?" Mark said. "I need to talk to Dr. Hastings."

"But I want to stay with you." Lily's easy-going manner cracked for a second, revealing the anxiety that bubbled just beneath. Poor kid.

"It'll just be for a minute, promise. Stay where I can see you, okay?"

"Okay. Can I get a drink?"

"It's probably broken because the power's out, but you can try." Disappointed, she nodded and moved off, out of earshot. Mark's smile was strained as he watched her.

I squinted at his expression. "What is it?"

Rather than answering, he slanted me a concerned look. "You sure you're okay?"

"Wow, I must look like shit if you need to keep asking." My mouth twisted.

"Just a little," he replied good-naturedly, before turning more serious. "I heard them talking out in the lobby. About all the critical cases. That's gotta be rough."

I blew out a breath, torn between polite lies and painful truths. "We're doing our best—'desperate measures' stuff since we still can't get them to the hospital. But yeah, it sucks. We've lost too many."

He frowned in sympathy. "I'm sorry. Is there anything I can do?"

"Thanks. But no, unless you can find a working truck—I don't think there's anything anyone can do." Pulling these kinds of stunts was something I expected in a disaster area or war zone, but this was America. "It's not supposed to be like that here." I said the last bit aloud and damn it, my eyes were tearing up. I blinked to hold them back, not quite ready for that much honesty in front of a stranger.

"You're not likely to find a working truck," Mark murmured. "And I'm afraid this is only the beginning."

"What?" My brow creased. "Why? Do you know what's going on?"

"Yeah, I'm pretty sure I do." A frown twisted his lips. "Have you ever heard of an EMP?" I shook my head. "Electromagnetic pulse. It's a wave of radiation that can damage electronics."

"*Radiation?*" My alarmed voice raised in pitch, and Lily cocked her head in my direction. When I forced a weak smile to reassure her, she went back to eating her cookies and flipping through a brightly colored book. But then I stopped and thought about it for a second. "We haven't seen anything remotely resembling radiation sickness."

"Not that type of radiation. It doesn't hurt humans, just electronics. Kind of like how a static charge can fry a circuit board even though you can barely feel it."

I frowned. I'd never heard of such a thing. "You think that's what made all the jets crash? Some kind of giant static charge?"

"Not exactly, but yeah, it's about the best analogy. Planes, cars, phones, TVs, the water and power grid—they're all controlled by computers nowadays. They're all vulnerable to an EMP." Mark shook his head, his stubbled jaw set in a grim line. "In fact, it's the only thing that could have taken them all out at the same moment."

It sounded outlandish. I wasn't sure I believed it, but I could tell from the worry lines etched on his face that *he* believed it. "What about a computer virus? Something hitting the entire Internet? That would explain the phones and the computers. Maybe the building's electrical system. Our plane had wi-fi..." The more things I started listing, the less likely it sounded. Mark saw my frown forming and waited for me to reach the inevitable conclusion on my own. "But that wouldn't explain the cars, or the firefighter radios, or my watch. Shit."

He was right—the only thing they had in common was the electronics. There's no way anyone could've gotten a computer virus onto all of those things. Maybe he was onto something. "This EMP thing—it's some kind of weapon?" I asked.

"Most likely, yeah."

"But if it was an attack, why here? Why Pittsburgh and not somewhere big like DC or New York or LA? It doesn't make any sense."

Mark's jaw clenched. "These weapons—they don't just target cities. They say a nuke detonated high over the Atlantic could cause an EMP over the entire eastern seaboard. Detonate one over the Midwest and you could hit the entire country." He ran a hand through his short hair, not liking what he was saying any more than I did. "There are even some theories that a strong enough solar storm might trigger an EMP-like effect all over the globe."

The entire country? The world? Every time I started to buy into his story, it got harder to swallow. But much as I hated to admit it, he'd caused a kernel of doubt. "Okay, let's just say for a minute you're right. How long does it last?" His Adam's apple moved, his eyes drifting over to Lily. "A few days? A week? What?"

When he spoke, it was a hushed whisper, "Doc, the electronics aren't just *off*, they're *fried*. All those planes and cars? They're paperweights until someone replaces the microprocessors with new ones. And all the computers in the factories that make the processors? They're probably fried too." Eyebrows raised, his worried hazel eyes searched my face for understanding.

I didn't have to be a tech geek to connect the dots. I had seen what happened in a world without basic infrastructure. And for the first time since he started describing this mad theory of his, I felt a tug of fear. "Mark, what you're describing…"

"I know. It's a lot to take in. But I'm telling you, Doc—I'm an engineer. I know what I'm talking about. It's the only explanation for why all of these types of electronics would fail at the same moment."

I shook my head again. "Why are you telling me this?"

"The effects of a large-scale EMP? It's huge. We're talking a hundred times worse than 9/11 or Katrina. I think we should tell people what's going on. Try to organize an evacuation."

I arched an eyebrow at him. "We?"

A corner of his mouth quirked upward in a ghost of a grin. "I was hoping you'd help. I saw how good you were, dealing with the wounded, organizing everything. Public speaking isn't my thing."

"It's not really mine either," I admitted. I shook my head. "But evacuate what—the whole airport? Where would you take everyone?"

"I don't know. We'll have to figure that out." Mark waved a hand to encompass the airport. "But I know this much: we can't stay here.

Things are okay now, but once people realize what's happening, there's going to be panic."

I let out a soft sigh, rubbing my face. I still didn't know how much of this I believed, but it was too serious to just dismiss out of hand. "All right, but listen—you can't just stand up in front of a thousand people and yell 'Apocalypse'. You'll start a riot. Or get laughed out of the room." He frowned. "Let's talk to the hotel manager and the fire chief. Let them hear your theory and see where we stand."

"Sure. Let's go find them."

I pushed myself off the wall. Lunch would have to be 'to go'. I had lost my appetite, but I had a feeling I should eat anyway. Who knew when I'd get another chance.

I started with the cookies.

CHAPTER 5

TALKING TO LIEUTENANT GARDNER WENT about as well as I expected. We found him speaking to Eva, the hotel manager I'd met while setting up the treatment area in the ballroom earlier. Though no longer surrounded by a horde of demanding people, she still seemed harried. My mother had been a hotel concierge for a long time, so I knew working in hospitality was a thankless job under the best of circumstances. Today? I think her job sucked more than mine—and that was saying a lot.

They both listened to Mark's theory. Eva reacted to the idea of evacuation like Mark had suggested she fly to the moon. "Where would we even send everyone?"

Gardner just brushed him off. "She's right, Mr. Ryan, I appreciate your information. But right now I've got hundreds of stranded passengers, dozens of critically injured people, several major fires and no vehicles or equipment. We've sent runners to the city and the National Guard base. I'm sure help is on the way." Then he was back to business, asking me about the status of the wounded in our makeshift infirmary.

Even my fellow doctor, Bindu, was skeptical of Mark's theory. "It's possible what he says is true," Bindu contemplated. "However, it seems soon to jump to conclusions." She resolved to just stay in the infirmary and see how things panned out.

Having played the doomsday version of Paul Revere to what passed for the authorities, Mark and I regrouped in a small alcove near the conference rooms. The dull hum of conversation from the refugees in the lobby filtered back to us.

"Nobody wants to listen," Mark said with a frustrated grimace.

"Mark, even if they believed you, what can they do? Their hands are already full with the crisis right in front of them, and you want them to think five steps ahead."

He frowned. "There has to be something else we can do."

"Look, you tried," I told him. "You at least planted the seed. Maybe once things have settled down a bit, they'll be able to give it more thought. Until then, there's nothing more you can do without sparking a panic. All that's going to accomplish is getting more people hurt."

I could tell Mark didn't like my answer. His jaw worked, looking as though he'd eaten something sour, but finally he nodded.

About then, Lily came over from the bench she'd been coloring on and tugged his hand. "Daddy, can we go to Grammy and Pappy's now?" Sensing his hesitation, she whined, "You promised."

Running a hand over his face, Mark gave a defeated sigh. "Yeah. I guess there's nothing more we can do here."

The announcement jolted me. I suppose I had this idea in my head that they'd stick around until the crisis was over, but of course they'd go. Even without a warning about the EMP, I wondered how soon it would be before more people tired of waiting around and left the airport to get back to their families. I felt a pang at the thought that we might not cross paths again. They were strangers still, but it didn't feel that way after what we'd just been through.

I realized Mark was staring at me and wondered if he was thinking the same thing. "What about you, Doc? You got somewhere to go? Friends, family in town?"

I shook my head. "No. I'll figure something out." With all the focus on spreading the word, I hadn't internalized what all of this meant for me. "I'll stay and help until we figure out what to do with the patients here."

Mark squinted at me for a moment, then said, "You should come with us."

Lily beamed at the thought. "You totally should, Doctor Anna. You'll like my Grammy and Pappy. They're really nice."

I smiled at the invitation. "That's nice of you guys, but I wouldn't want to impose on your parents. And anyway, they need me here."

"My in-laws, actually. And it's not an imposition." Mark stepped closer and lowered his voice. "Listen, Doc, I know you want to help, but things are going to get bad here. You remember what happened at the Superdome during Katrina? It'll be like that, maybe worse. I'm going to get my in-laws and then get out of the city. Wait a few days and see how things shake out. You should do the same."

"I can't just leave everyone here."

"You said so yourself—there's not much you can do for them anyway, right? And there are a bunch of other doctors here." He paused, his gaze intent. "You saved my life; now I'm trying to return the favor. Just come with us to my in-laws. Maybe we'll be able to find out more about what's going on, and decide what to do from there."

He had a point. We had gotten through the initial wave of patients and were in maintenance mode now. It was an experience I'd dealt with enough times in my aid work, helping with an initial crisis and then moving on. And what if he was right? I was alone in a strange city with nothing but the clothes on my back, in the middle of what might be the biggest disaster of our time. Here was a nice family offering shelter.

"Please, Doctor Anna?" Lily's pleading eyes would put a puppy dog to shame.

It was the straw that broke the back of my reluctance. I let out a slow breath. "All right. Just for tonight, then we'll see how things are in the morning." With any luck, the power would come on and we'd all have a good laugh about how paranoid we'd been. I could always come back, or head for a hospital and volunteer my services.

"Yay!" Lily's face broke into a wide grin, which made me feel better about the whole thing. But then her smile faded into a perplexed frown. "How are we going to get there without a car?"

CHAPTER 6

AFTER BREAKING THE NEWS TO Lily that we had a long walk ahead of us, we left the hotel. The silence outside was deafening. No traffic. No roar of jet engines. Just the indistinct sound of distant voices and the crackle of flames from the burning terminal. Only a handful of other people were in sight, the others having fled by now. The fire at the terminal cast a thick column of black smoke up into the sky. More smoke trails—presumably from other crashed planes—dotted the horizon, and a foul-smelling haze hung everywhere. Heading across the parking lot, we soon came upon the area where the second jetliner had crashed.

"Don't look, baby," Mark urged Lily. He scooped her up and walked with her little arms around his neck and her head buried against his shoulder.

Debris stretched for a hundred yards, a twisted tangle of metal from the plane and the cars it had plowed into. Small fires burned here and there, but it was nothing like the inferno consuming the terminal. Only a few of the scattered pieces could be identified—a seat, a section of fuselage with the aircraft logo, and a loose tire. Unfortunately, the same could also be said for the passengers. There were remains, but nothing intact enough to be termed a "body." I blanched at the sight, but I'd seen worse. Mark walked with his eyes focused on the ground right in front of him, looking ill.

The airport road led us straight to the highway. The blackout had hit after rush hour, leaving a scattered patchwork of disabled vehicles. It surprised me to see so many people still waiting near their cars, even hours later. I wondered how long they would stay, hoping for their dead cell phones to come back to life to call roadside assistance.

In our soot-streaked (and in my case, blood-splattered) clothes, we attracted more than our share of attention. Some people just gave us wary looks as we passed. Others engaged us in conversation, asking what had happened. I half-expected Mark to want to warn everyone about the EMP, but the first time someone approached us, he just gave an evasive answer suggesting there'd been a terrorist attack at the airport.

"We decided to walk home," he told them. "Might think about doing the same."

"Do you really think this was an attack?" I asked after leaving one such conversation.

He shrugged. "It's as likely an explanation as any. I mean, it could be natural—like that solar storm I told you about. But I figure a terrorist attack's more likely to get their asses in gear."

I supposed it didn't matter what the cause was. Not to people like us. I had the unsettling thought that we might never know what caused it.

We soon became pretty practiced at delivering our abridged version of events to the people we passed. The breadth of reactions surprised me—shock, horror, indifference, disbelief, anger, and debate. Always debate. We never stuck around long enough to see if the debate ended with anyone taking to the road themselves.

The afternoon sun beat down on us, radiating up from the asphalt to cook us from both sides. With only stubby trees beside the highway, the only real shade to be had was from the occasional overpass. We tried walking along the grassy median for some relief, but uneven ground and knee-high weeds posed their own set of problems. A painful knot of tension in my neck conspired with the lingering effects of smoke inhalation to give me a bitch of a headache. I rubbed my sweaty forehead, trying to ease the ache behind my eyes.

We couldn't talk freely in front of Lily, and small talk felt strained after everything that had happened at the airport. We trudged along, hot and miserable, in a subdued silence punctuated by occasional grumblings from Lily. I didn't mind them; she was holding up far better than I would have expected from a seven-year-old.

"Are we almost there, Daddy?" she asked again, her plaintive voice just shy of a whine.

"About halfway, I think. We should be coming up to the mall soon."

"Only halfway? Arrgh." Lily let her head flop back. "This is taking for-ev-er."

"I know, sweetie, but you're doing great," Mark consoled her with a soft smile. She peppered him with questions about the blackout, which Mark deflected with vague answers. He kept his voice calm and controlled, but I could see the line of tension in his shoulders.

Steering the topic away from the power, I asked, "How far away did you say it was to your in-laws?"

"About ten miles, I think." Mark replied. "We would've been there by now if we were driving."

"I thought the airport was near the city?" I frowned at the desolate landscape. "It looks like we're in the middle of nowhere."

"Yeah. Lauren always says Pittsburgh is like the biggest small town in America." Mark waved and arm. "You can drive an hour in any direction and it's practically all like this—hills, forests, farms."

"Lauren's your wife?" I guessed. Mark nodded.

Lily cut in, "We come every summer to visit Grammy and Pappy. And usually always when I have spring break too, unless we go someplace special. One year we went to the beach! Mommy says next summer we might even go to Hawaii." Her smile was fleeting, giving way to a pensive frown. "Daddy, when's Mommy going to get here?"

Mark's expression clouded with worry, his jaw tightening. "I'm not sure, Lil."

Lily's little hands tugged on the excess length of her backpack straps. She cut in, "How will she get here if all the airplanes and cars are broken?"

Mark didn't answer right away. Her sooty face tilted up at him, big hazel eyes searching his for answers he couldn't give.

"Well, we don't know about the planes everywhere," I pointed out. Before she could pull on that thread with more questions, I tried to distract her. "Hey, you said you might get to go to Hawaii next summer? Have you ever been there before?" Mark caught my eye, shooting me a grateful look.

"No, but Mommy and Daddy have. They went there when they got married, but that was before I got born. But I've seen pictures though. Did you know they have actual real live volcanoes there?" She punctuated the words with emphatic gestures of her hands.

I smiled. "I did know that. It's pretty cool, isn't it?"

"Have you ever been there, Doctor Anna?" Lily wondered.

"Actually, yeah, that's where I grew up."

"You grew up in *Hawaii*?" From the amazement in her voice, I think she would have been only marginally less astonished if I'd told her I grew up on Mars.

Mark was more restrained with his surprise. He peered at me. "Really? You don't look Hawaiian. I'm surprised you lasted five minutes there without turning into a lobster."

I smiled at their disbelief, which I'd gotten a lot of as a pale redheaded kid on Oahu. "I'm not Hawaiian. My Dad's ship was stationed at Pearl Harbor, and we lived on the base there."

When the clouds rolled in, muting the sun, we all breathed a sigh of relief. When they opened up and doused us in rain, Lily danced in the puddles and Mark and I were just glad to get cooled off. I cupped my hands and slurped water to soothe my parched throat. But after an hour of slogging through the downpour, I'd had enough. It reminded me of the rainy season in central Africa.

The desolate highway eventually returned us to civilization. Mark's analog wristwatch still worked, so we knew it was about five hours after we left the airport when we reached the sleepy, wooded neighborhood where his in-laws lived. After one too many complaints about her legs being tired, Mark had picked Lily up to carry her the last mile or so. He must have legs of steel.

"This is it," Mark said at last, veering off the road and onto the front walk of a sturdy red brick house. Balancing Lily in one arm, Mark opened the screen door and rapped with the brass knocker.

The door opened in short order. "Oh, you made it!" exclaimed the woman standing in the doorway. Her white hair was pulled back into a bun, and wire-frame glasses sat on a friendly face etched with laugh lines. "You poor dears, you're soaked. Come in, come in. George! Get some towels—Mark and Lily are here." She ushered us into the foyer, where we made puddles on the slate floor.

Her eyes shifted past the pair to me, brow knitting in confusion, and I gave an awkward smile. But before Mark or I could perform introductions, Lily shimmied out of Mark's arms, hurling herself at her grandmother.

"Grammy!" Lily started babbling a mile a minute. "Grammy, you are not even going to believe it. A plane crashed into the airport." She wrapped her little arms around the older woman, as if clinging for dear life.

The grandmother gasped. "My God, are you all right?" Horrified eyes looked from Lily to Mark and back again.

"We're fine, Nancy," Mark assured her.

He might have said more, but Lily was off babbling at a mile a minute. "There was a super huge fire, and Daddy was stuck, and I thought the fire was going to get us! It was really scary. And it wasn't just one plane, Grammy, it was all of them." She kept rambling into the older woman's side, but it got unintelligible after that.

Nancy hugged Lily close. "You poor baby." In-between soothing, she looked up at Mark. "We could see the smoke from here. We thought it might have been a plane crash, but the TV and internet were both out so nobody knew for sure. Are you sure you're all right?" Mark nodded again.

"I tried to come out to get you, but nobody's car would start." A new voice came from the stairs, and a tall, stocky man I presumed was George made his way down with an armload of towels. Lily assaulted him with a hug next, which he returned with an awkward one-armed pat.

Mark then seemed to remember me, waving a hand in my direction. "We're all right. Oh, Nancy, George—this is Anna. She—uh—she actually saved my life at the airport." He shot me a grateful smile that had me dipping my head in embarrassment. "And she didn't have anywhere else to go—things were kind of a mess there. Is it okay if she stays with us till we figure out what's going on?"

"Of course she can," Nancy replied without hesitation, and I murmured my thanks. "Goodness, what a day you've all had." Nancy took one towel and wrapped it around Lily, her nose wrinkling in distaste. "You smell like smoke and gasoline. You girls come with me. George, take Mark and put out some of those extra bins to collect more water."

I caught Mark's eye, and he offered an encouraging smile as Nancy ushered Lily and me upstairs to get cleaned up.

46

CHAPTER 7

WITH THE WATER PRESSURE NEARLY gone, we rinsed off with rain water. Not quite the hot shower I'd been dying for, but it was still a relief to wash the blood off and get out of my soggy, stained clothes. The soap and shampoo almost masked the smell of soot and aviation fuel. Almost.

"Lauren kept some things here," Nancy had explained when she handed me the small bundle with jeans, a scoop-neck T-shirt and the requisite underthings. "I think you're about the same size."

In fact, Lauren appeared to be taller and bigger-chested than me, but beggars couldn't be choosers. Mark and Lily, at least, had the luxury of wearing their own clothes—spares they kept here for their regular visits. Lily cheered when she found that her grandmother had gotten her a cute new outfit with pink and purple flowers on the shirt and leggings.

After we were all cleaned up, I asked Lily to give me a grand tour of the house so Mark could talk to Nancy and George alone about the EMP. Happy to play tour guide, Lily proudly showed off a room decked out in butterflies, princesses and stuffed animals.

On our way back downstairs, we passed a group of photos hanging in the upstairs hallway. George had been in the army in his youth. I wondered if he was a career man like my dad. One photo was a family portrait of Lily, Mark and Lauren, revealing Lauren to be an attractive blonde about my age. Lily took more after her dad, I thought, but she had her mom's high cheekbones and warm smile.

"Doctor Anna, do you think the planes will still be working in Boston?"

"I hope so." Before Lily could follow up with more questions about the blackout I couldn't answer, I asked, "So how old were you in this picture?" And with that, I had her distracted, prattling on about her last birthday and being in second grade next year.

We returned downstairs to rejoin Mark and his in-laws in the living room. They all wore grim looks after Mark's bad news.

George gave Nancy's leg a fond little pat and then rose stiffly from the couch. "Let's go check out the radio. It's down the basement. I'll get a flashlight."

"Mind if I tag along?" I asked, getting a grunted assent from George.

"I want to go too," Lily announced. Mark frowned, but Nancy saved him from having to say no by diverting Lily to help her in the kitchen.

I followed George and Mark down into the musty, unfinished basement. George's hand-held camping lantern provided more than enough light for us to see by, illuminating a sizable room stuffed with odds and ends. In one corner stood a workbench strewn with electronics.

"Have a seat," George sat down and pointed me to a second stool at the bench. "Mark, can you get that battery?" It looked like an old car battery. Mark brought it over, and George started fiddling with connections, squinting through his thick glasses.

"Did you build all this yourself?" I wondered while he worked, studying the collection of components.

"Well, I cobbled the components together. I was a radioman in 'Nam. Got out when the war was over, but I kept this up." He finished fiddling with the wires and then flipped on a switch. "That oughta do it." A dial in the center of the radio illuminated and static squelched from the speaker.

I glanced between the men. "Why isn't this radio broken like all the rest of the electronics?"

"Analog, not digital," George said.

Seeing my blank look, Mark clarified, "There are no circuit boards in this. The EMP wouldn't have affected it."

George started adjusting the knobs, eliciting high-pitched electronic whines from the device until he got them the way he wanted. "Now let's see who else is out there."

His gnarled fingers settled on a big dial in the center, which he started turning slowly. The radio screeched with a god-awful static sound, and George winced and adjusted the volume. He kept turning the dial, but it was just more of the same. I didn't know much about ham radios, but it seemed like an ominous sign. I chewed my lip as the static continued.

"Never heard so much static on this band before. You think this EMP thing could be causing interference?" George asked Mark. Mark gave a baffled shrug. "Let's try a different band." George spun the dial several times, then began moving it more slowly. There was still some static, but nowhere near as bad as the first time. "That's strange. Usually we'd have picked up some chatter by now. Nobody's talking." He settled on a particular frequency, and we heard the tail end of a voice speaking, "… local broadcast stations for further information. This is not a test."

The message started over with the bone-chilling emergency alert tone every child of the eighties knew by heart, and my fingers dug into the edge of the table in anticipation.

"This is the activation of the Emergency Alert System. The President of the United States has issued the following alert: A disruption of the power grid may cause some areas to experience prolonged power outages. Citizens in affected areas are urged to stay in their homes and remain calm. Treat all water as contaminated and boil it for at least two minutes prior to drinking. Authorities are working to restore power as soon as possible. Armed Forces, National Guard and emergency personnel should report immediately to their duty stations. Stay tuned to this station or your local broadcast stations for further information. This is not a test."

George muted the signal before it repeated, and we all exchanged grim glances.

Mark spoke first, "Well, that was pretty vague. 'Some areas'? 'Prolonged'? They have to know it's an EMP. Why would they tell people to stay at home?" His frustration was palpable, and I could imagine him replaying the conversation with Garner in his head.

"They're the government. What are they going to say? 'The power's out for good—get the hell out of Dodge and good luck'?" George arched an eyebrow. "The fact that it's vague tells us a lot. And them recalling all the troops."

"If it was just an isolated area, they would've said where," I realized, and George nodded. "But we still don't know how big it is. Can you keep trying—see if we can pick up anything else?"

He turned the dial once more until a garbled noise like aliens talking broke the ominous silence. George fine-tuned the dial and the voices came in clearer, albeit not in English. George started to turn past it.

"Wait, that's French," I said, leaning forward on the stool.

"You speak French?" Mark asked.

I translated what I was hearing aloud for the guys, picking up the conversation in mid-sentence. "… saw a helicopter come down over the city. All the cars have stopped." My blood ran cold, and I stopped talking. *It's not just here.* Shaking off the pall of dread, I picked up the translation, "The other guy is saying it's the same where he is. The cars, the computers—all dead."

Mark's face had gone pale. "Where are they?"

"I don't know; they didn't say. How can I talk on this thing?" I asked George. He gave me a quick primer, and when there was a lull in the conversation between the two Frenchmen, I cut in. "This is K7QT3 in the United States, Pennsylvania," I said in French, "We are seeing the same thing here. Where are you located?" I added a clumsy, "Over," not knowing if the word translated into French. Hopefully they got the idea.

The replies came back in short order: Paris. Toulouse.

"My God," Mark breathed when I told him. "That's both ends of France."

The man from Paris described widespread panic and looting. In Toulouse things weren't so bad. Yet. We signed off with the Frenchmen and George kept tuning the dial. Eventually he found a channel where some operators were communicating in English, and it was more of the same. Kansas City. North Carolina.

My heart sank when someone mentioned Oregon. "My sister and her family are in Seattle," I whispered. "I just left them last night."

Even after hearing about France, I had clung to the belief that it was just the Atlantic coast; that they were safe. Assuming it hit there at the same time our call dropped, Jess and the girls would have been at home together. Would they have the foresight to get out of the city? I wrung my hands, a powerful wave of helplessness washing over me. I'd give anything just to send them a message. Tell them what to do.

Mark must have seen the look on my face, for he came over and put a comforting hand on my shoulder. He understood; he must be going crazy worrying about his wife. Much as he tried to hide it, it was there in his eyes. I looked up and gave him a grateful nod.

Eventually George turned off the radio, and we all sat in a stunned silence.

"Big chunk of the US that we know of. Across France, which probably means all of Europe too." Mark summarized what we knew, his voice soft and grim. Lacking a third chair, he was just sagging against the workbench behind me. "It's safe to assume it's global."

"You think it's that solar storm you were talking about?" George wondered.

"Maybe. Or a coordinated attack. One nuke to take out Europe, a couple for the Americas." Mark sighed, rubbing his face. "I guess we'll find out if Chinese paratroopers start landing tomorrow."

George snorted. "Or those ISIS bastards. Wouldn't put it past 'em to try to cripple the West."

"It could've been anybody. What does it matter? Either way, the result is the same," I pointed out.

"Yep," said George. "And we're all pretty well fucked."

CHAPTER 8

WE TRUDGED UPSTAIRS TO DISCOVER that Nancy and Lily had gotten dinner on the table. Seeing our faces, Nancy knew the gravity of the situation. George took her aside to catch her up while Lily prattled on to me and Mark about the stew and biscuits they'd made. I forced myself to pay attention.

Nancy insisted everyone take a few minutes to eat before making plans. "The apocalypse can wait half an hour," she said sternly to George when he protested. "We still have to eat." Frowning, he nodded and took his seat around the circular dinner table.

"What's an apoc-a-lip?" Lily asked, causing the adults to exchange grim looks. We couldn't keep her in the dark forever, but nobody was ready to broach the subject. Mark brushed off her question with an answer I couldn't quite hear.

My stomach rumbled upon seeing the food; I hadn't realized how hungry I was. I joined them in saying grace, George adding an extra plea to protect our families in the times ahead. Then we began to eat. "Enjoy it while it lasts," George remarked. "It'll all go bad soon enough."

"We can preserve some of it," Nancy suggested. "Ruth is into canning." This led to some back-and-forth about various types of food preservation, but I spaced out of the conversation. My mind was still spinning over the implications of what we had heard on the radio.

At some point, I realized that Nancy had said my name and was now looking at me expectantly. "I'm sorry, what was that?"

Nancy smiled, not put off by my atrocious houseguest manners. "Lily said you're from Hawaii? What brings you to Pittsburgh? Usually people go the other way around." She and George both gave strained smiles at that. I guessed the small-talk was an attempt to cling to some semblance of normalcy in the face of disaster.

"Oh, I was born there, but I haven't lived there since high school. I was supposed to have a job interview tomorrow." I sipped at my iced tea (without ice) and remarked dryly, "Don't think that's going to work out."

"Where were you working before?" Mark wondered.

"I was in Africa, working with MSF. Before that, San Diego."

Lily sat up and leaned forward with keen interest. "We learned about Africa in school. Did you get to see any *wild* lions? Or elephants? And what's M.S.F.?"

I smiled at the rapid-fire questions. "A couple, but they were pretty far away." Lily gave a quiet, awe-struck "wow". "MSF is Médecins Sans Frontières." I translated it to the more widely known English name. "Doctors Without Borders."

George tilted his head at me. "Humanitarian work, right?"

"Yeah." I then gave the confused-looking Lily a more elaborate answer. "They send doctors to places where they don't have enough.

Especially when there's an emergency, like a big storm or a war." The girl gave a soft 'oooh' sound, nodding.

"How long were you in Africa?" Mark wondered.

"I did a few missions there over the last ten years or so. Central African Republic and South Sudan mostly. Also Haiti, after the earthquake."

Nancy passed George the peas. "I've heard of Sudan, at least. George Clooney was always on the news talking about the genocide there. So awful."

Talk about a colossal understatement. My face sobered. "Yeah." Storm clouds of bad memories loomed, making me tense up, but I forced a fake smile and steered away from them. "I got to meet him once—Clooney. Well, sort of. We were doing vaccinations in one of the refugee camps he was visiting. I said hi, and he smiled as he walked by." Lily asked who Clooney was, and Mark mumbled something to her about 'grown up movies'.

George took advantage of the lull in conversation that followed. "I'm going to go to the neighbors after dinner and ask them to come over so we can start making plans."

"Plans for what, Pappy?" Lily asked, her voice muffled by food.

Before George could say anything, Nancy answered for him. "For what we're going to do while the power's out. But we can talk about that later." She gave George a pointed look, and he grunted in agreement.

Mark frowned down at his plate. I wondered how he was going to break all this to Lily. She was a very resilient little girl who was handling everything else remarkably well, but still... as someone who'd delivered more than my share of bad news, I didn't envy him that conversation.

Dinner wore down, Nancy doing the job of grandmas everywhere by asking if we were sure we had enough to eat. I got up to help her clear the dishes away and realized Lily had dozed off in her chair.

"Someone had a long day," I observed with a soft smile. I was feeling pretty ragged myself.

Mark smiled. "I'll take her upstairs." He scooped her up, pressing a kiss to her forehead when she briefly stirred, and then disappeared up the stairs with ginger steps.

"Maybe you should wait until morning to talk to everyone," Nancy suggested after George had brought in a bin full of water from outside for the dishes. "It's getting dark and it's still raining."

George shook his head, adamant. "Sooner we get organized, the better off we'll be. Once more people start to realize what's happened, things are going to get bad fast." They started talking about who they were going to round up for the meeting, but the names meant nothing to me. George asked, "Anna, is it all right if we tell people you're here? In case anyone's sick or hurt?"

I looked up from the dish I was drying. "Sure. But I don't know how long we'll be here. Mark was talking about heading out of the city ASAP." A frown touched my lips, not sure if I was included in that plan. He'd invited me here, but was vague on the rest of it. At any rate, I wasn't planning on staying for long. I'd figure something out.

Soon after that, we finished the dishes, and Mark and George ventured out into the rain to round up the neighbors. While they were gone, Nancy and I chatted as we took stock of supplies in the kitchen. The sun had gone down, plunging the house into darkness, but she had a stock of candles and even an old oil lantern she put to good use. Having had my share of interrogation at dinner, I tried to steer the conversation to Nancy's family.

She and George had both lived their whole lives in Pittsburgh, except for George's tour in Vietnam. Nancy prattled on about how proud she was of Lauren. Successful career woman, awesome mom, awesome daughter—she sounded pretty great. And like any proud grandma, Nancy was all-too-happy to tell me what a great kid Lily was.

"You'd have been proud of her, the way she kept it together at the airport," I told her. "Helping to rescue Mark. She was amazing." Nancy peppered me for details about what had happened. I answered her questions politely, but she got the hint that I didn't want to talk about it and changed the subject. But the damage had been done, and the stress I had been trying to dodge all day came crashing down.

"Are you all right?" Nancy asked, eyeing me in concern.

"I'm just tired," I lied. "I took the red-eye last night, and today was kind of crazy. Could I just lie down on the couch?"

"You poor dear, you must be exhausted. You can have the guest room. It was all ready for Mark and Lauren. I'll show you up to it."

"No, really, it's okay—I can take the couch. Mark might want to be closer to Lily."

Nancy fetched a lantern and a flashlight from the kitchen, pressing the latter into my hand. "Don't be silly, you're our guest. Mark will be fine on the couch. He would insist on it himself if he was here."

That didn't surprise me at all—he struck me as pretty old-fashioned on that front—and I was too tired to argue. "All right. Thank you. I appreciate you all taking me in," I said, as I followed her up the dark and creaky stairs. "You have a lovely family."

"Thank you, dear. It's the least we can do after what you did for Mark and Lily. Here's the guest room," she said, opening the door to one of the rooms Lily showed me earlier. "We'll be downstairs if you need anything."

I thanked her once more and went into the room, where I fell onto the bed and tried not to think about all the lives lost today, all the families separated, and a world that would never be the same.

CHAPTER 9

SLEEP DIDN'T COME EASILY, BUT eventually I drifted off. I awakened in the middle of the night, not sure what time it was or what had woken me up. Disoriented in the pitch-black room, I fumbled for the nightstand until my fingers found the flashlight Nancy had given me. I clicked it on, reassured by its little beam of light. Straining my ears to listen for anything unusual, all I heard were cicadas chirping, or buzzing, or whatever the hell you called that god-awful noise they made.

Then came a soft, plaintive cry. "Daddy!"

I was up and out of the bed in a heartbeat, moving toward the door. A quick glance at my watch reminded me that it was dead. I don't know why I was even still wearing it. Standing in the doorway, I waited a moment to see if Mark was coming upstairs. When he didn't appear, I crossed the hall to Lily's bedroom.

"Lily, are you all right?" I panned my flashlight over the bed.

Lily sat up, wide-eyed, her lower lip trembling. Tears streamed down her face, and she whimpered quietly. I stood there for a second, uncertain, and then crossed over to the bed.

"Hey, it's okay." I sat down and laid a hand on her shoulder, and she surprised me by latching onto my side in a fierce hug. I patted her back, murmuring soft assurances that everything was going to be okay. "Did you have a bad dream?"

Her head bobbed against my shoulder, calmer now. "And then I woke up and it was really dark and scary. Mommy usually always leaves the hall light on."

"Oh. Yeah. The power's still off, so none of the lights are working." I had a flash of inspiration. "Here, I'll tell you what—I'll put my flashlight right here. That way if you wake up again, you can just turn it on and you won't be scared. Okay?"

She gave a tiny nod, and I shifted the light towards her nightstand. A pink stuffed animal lay on the floor next to the bed. "I think you dropped someone." I scooped it up and handed it to her.

Lily clutched it tightly. "That's Beauty," she said. "She's Sleeping Beauty's cat."

"Oh, is she?" I smiled. I didn't remember Sleeping Beauty having a cat, but it had been ages since I'd seen the movie. "She's cute. Here's the flashlight, right here where you can reach it." I set it on the nightstand, pointing up at the ceiling. "Did you need anything else?"

"Will you stay until I go back asleep?"

"Umm… how about I go get your Dad…" I started to rise, only to have her grab my arm in a panic.

"Don't go," she cried.

"Don't worry, I'll just call down to him." I didn't want to say no to those big, scared eyes, but it felt like overstepping to stay without getting Mark. It turned out to be a moot point, as another flashlight bobbed up the stairs. "Oh, see? Here he comes."

I hung out in the doorway while Mark got Lily settled. She fell asleep faster than I would have thought possible. Mark clicked off the flashlight on the nightstand and joined me. "Thanks for your help. She was glad you came right over."

"Sure, no problem."

Mark smiled. "You heading back to sleep?"

Rubbing my face, I sighed and said, "I should, but I'm wide awake now. What time is it?"

He checked his watch, tilting it so the glare from the flashlight didn't wash out the glass face. "Little after three. Long as we're both awake, you want to come downstairs? I wanted to talk to you about something."

I arched an eyebrow. "That sounds ominous. But okay, sure." I motioned for him to lead the way.

CHAPTER 10

MARK SAID NOTHING ELSE UNTIL we had moved to the kitchen, not wanting to disturb Nancy and George asleep in the downstairs bedroom. As he lit one of Nancy's candles on the table, Mark asked, "Want a drink? There's still some scotch left. George busted it out after the meeting earlier."

"Just a little, thanks." I watched him fetch a pair of short juice glasses from the cupboard, and he poured us each a dram. "How'd the meeting go?" He handed me a glass and we both sat down. Mark just scowled. "That well, huh?"

He sighed, sipping scotch before speaking. "A lot of them decided to stay. They think it'll just be temporary, that the government's going to swoop in and save the day. That BS emergency message on the radio didn't help."

"What about Nancy and George? Are they staying?"

"No," Mark said, the relief evident in his voice. "They believe me, at least. So did one other couple—the Millers. George's sister has a farm out in the country. They're going to head out there tomorrow. Well, later today, I guess."

"On foot?" I asked, eyebrows raised at the image. Nancy and George seemed fit for their age, but I had a hard time imagining them trekking out to "the country", however far that was.

"The Millers have an old truck that still runs. Vintage cars don't have any electronics in them," he explained, cradling the glass between both hands and staring at it thoughtfully.

"Well, that's good." I couldn't help but wonder if I was included in the plan to head out to the farm, or if this was the end of the line for us. I was loath to broach the subject. Instead, I tasted the scotch, my nose wrinkling at the taste. "I can't blame them for wanting to stay. I still don't want to believe it."

"It's hard to take it all in. But believing it is what's going to save us." He paused. "You said your sister's in Seattle?"

"Yeah. Well, I guess technically it's Tacoma. She's stationed at the air base there. They let me crash with them when I got back from Africa." I frowned and took another drink to see if it tasted better the second time around. It didn't, but that was only half the reason for my frown. "All those times I was overseas, the years we lived apart—it was no big deal. I missed her sometimes, but we'd talk, and I knew I'd see her again eventually. Now…" I let that thought trail off, worry gnawing at me. "I keep thinking… if I'd just taken another flight, left later, I'd still be there with them."

Mark nodded, his expression somber. "I know. I feel the same way about Lauren. We were just trying to save on ticket fees, you know? Why reschedule all three when she could just meet us here in a couple days?" He snorted. "Seems so stupid now. So petty." He knocked back his scotch, but didn't go to pour himself more. "What about the rest of your family?"

"My mom's still in Hawaii. My dad lives near my sister. He's retired Navy, so he should be able to make it onto the base with her." I didn't list my stepmom, who was also with them. She could be under a 747 for all I cared. No, that wasn't fair. Much as I despised the woman, I wouldn't wish her harm. Well, not serious harm. "How about you?"

"Just Lauren and Lily," Mark said. He turned his empty glass in a slow circle, considering, before he ventured in a soft, serious tone, "Lauren's going to know it's an EMP too. She's the one who told me about it. She'll recognize the signs, and she'll know to get out of the city."

"That's good, though, right? She sounds like a smart woman. I'm sure she can take care of herself, and you can find her when things have settled down."

Mark got up from the table, startling me with the sudden motion. He paced over to the sink, staring out the window into the pitch blackness for a long moment before he turned back to face me. "Things might not 'settle down' for years, Anna. I need my family together."

I squinted at him in bafflement. "Sure, we all want to be with our families right now, but…" My brain got stuck on the 'but', unable to articulate the million ways in which that was impossible. "We can't. I mean, yesterday I could have flown to Seattle and been back with my sister in a few hours. Now they might as well be on the moon."

"We have a cabin," Mark continued, as if I hadn't said anything. He leaned backward against the counter, resting on his hands. "It used to belong to my granddad. We go up there every year. It's in the backcountry in Maine, hell and gone from anywhere. It's got fresh water, fish, game—it's a perfect place to ride out this mess. That's where Lauren would go." There was a determined set to his jaw. "I'm going to meet her there."

I blinked several times, staring at him and thinking I couldn't possibly have heard him right. "But…" Again I was hung up on that word, but this time I stammered on to, "How? You can't drive some ancient truck all the way to Maine in the middle of a disaster. You'll be lucky to make it a hundred miles." Visions of him and Lily broken down on the side of the road, or carjacked for one of the world's few working cars, filled my head.

Shaking his head, Mark said, "No, I know we wouldn't get far in a vehicle. Besides, Nancy and George and the Millers will be taking the truck in the opposite direction. But there's a trail—a backwoods trail, off the beaten path."

I chuckled. "So you and your seven-year-old daughter are going to walk, through the woods, all the way to Maine? I think you need to lay off the scotch." He met my eyes, and I was struck by the conviction there. "God, you're serious, aren't you?" He said nothing. "Mark, come on—do you realize how insane that sounds?"

"Says the woman who traveled around the world to take care of strangers in a war zone." Mark arched his eyebrows at me.

I blew out a frustrated breath. He kind of had me on that one. "I don't have a kid to worry about." Running a finger along the lip of my glass, I asked, "Is this what Lauren would want? For you to drag Lily off into the wilderness on some mad quest to find her? You said so yourself—things are going to get really bad out there. You'd be better off just going with your in-laws."

"All the more reason I want us all together," Mark retorted, undeterred by my skepticism. He returned to his seat at the table, fixing me with a determined stare. "I want you to come with us."

Knock me over with a feather. I stared at him, speechless, for several seconds. "Okay, now I *know* you're crazy. You want me to walk halfway across the country with you and your daughter? Mark, you hardly know me."

"I know enough that I'm willing to take a chance." Mark shrugged. "You saved my life. You helped all those people. Lily likes you, and you're good with her. It's going to be hard for her without Lauren. I think it would help her—you know, a woman's touch."

That made me squint at him. "A woman's touch?" I echoed, my voice stern and flat. "For her or for you?" I didn't *think* that was his angle, but we barely knew each other. Why it mattered, I didn't know. There was no way in hell I was doing this.

He surprised me by letting out a bark of laughter, as if the idea of being interested in me was preposterous. I wasn't sure whether to be relieved or insulted. "Come on, I didn't mean it like that. I'll be a perfect gentleman, I swear." Then his mirth faded to a more serious look, lips thinning. "Look, I'm not an idiot. I know this is going to be hard and dangerous."

"You think?" I made a scoffing sound at his understatement-of-the-century. "Mark, even if you get there—and that's a big damn 'if'—what then? You just live in a log cabin in the middle of nowhere forever? What are you going to do once winter comes?"

"Lauren's got some food stored up there already, and we'll get there in time to gather more before winter. And we won't have to stay there forever. Just long enough to ride out the worst of it. Besides, there are other cabins up there too. We wouldn't be *completely* alone."

He must have seen my dubious expression, but he ignored it. "Lil and I will have a better chance with another adult along. And I think you'll be better off, too. When things start falling apart, it's going to be pretty dangerous out there for a woman alone."

"Or a man and kid alone."

"Sure, anyone alone." The tone in the words made me wonder if he really believed that or was just saying it to placate me. "We team up, we can watch each other's backs. And when we get to Maine, you can stay with us as long as you want."

"I'm sure your wife would be thrilled with that," I said dryly. I frowned, wondering just how long he'd been working up to this spiel. He seemed to have it all figured out. "What if she's not there?"

He stiffened. "She'll be there."

I could see him clinging to that desperate thread of hope. I leaned back in my chair with a sigh, not wanting to be the one to take it from him. "Mark, you don't know that. Be realistic. She might end up somewhere closer to Boston. She might come *here*, for God's sake. She knows you and Lily are here, and her parents. You could risk everything, go all that way, and have it all be for nothing."

"I know Lauren better than anyone. She'll be there." Mark insisted, a fierce set to his jaw.

Frustrated, I gritted my teeth for a moment and then tried a different tack. "Do you even know anything about cross-country hiking? Camping? Living off the land? Any of it?"

That one made an impact, and a frown crept across his face. "I've been camping before." The defensive reply was less than inspiring.

"And I've gone on a couple day-hikes. That hardly compares to walking hundreds of miles."

"We'll get some books; talk to George. He was in the army, and he likes to go hunting. You're a doctor; I'm an engineer—I'm sure we can figure it out. It's not rocket science." He scowled at my obvious skepticism. "Look, Anna, you're not going to talk me out of it. Lily and I are going. I'd rather you went with us. We can do this."

I don't know why I didn't just tell him *no* right then and there. His plan was ridiculous—borderline suicidal. And yet, I couldn't help but be moved by his conviction and his devotion to his family. Finally I sighed. "I'll think about it."

He grinned, then refilled his glass and held it up like he was toasting. To what, exactly, I don't know, since I hadn't agreed to anything. But I clinked my glass against his anyway, squinting at him.

This felt like the beginning of a terrible decision.

CHAPTER 11

MORNING CAME TOO SOON. I'D turned in not long after Mark proposed his crazy scheme. Reason and logic told me it was insane, but I kept coming back to one thought: *They won't make it on their own.* Despite them being barely more than strangers, I didn't want anything bad to happen to them. Still, that didn't mean I had to join them on the crazy train. Maybe Nancy and George could help talk him out of it.

I dozed in fits and spurts until the smell of sausage wafting up from downstairs finally dragged my tired ass out of bed. Stiff legs protested the movement, sore after all the walking we did yesterday. Like I told Mark, I'd only ever been on a couple of short hikes before. In college in San Diego, I joined a couple friends on a lark to hit the trail in Los Penasquitos Canyon. It was maybe ten miles, round-trip, and we were back in our cars in time to grab dinner and beers afterward. We'd done a couple other day hikes in and around the city, and I'd walked a fair bit in Africa and Haiti when the roads were bad. I didn't mind it, but it hardly qualified me as a long-distance hiker.

What would it be like to walk hundreds of miles?

More importantly—why wouldn't my brain let go of the idea?

I trudged to the bathroom, forgetting for a moment that there was no water. George and Nancy had left a bucket of rainwater next to the toilet for flushing, but I'd lay odds everyone would be digging slit trenches within a day once they realized what a waste of water this was. Borrowing a hairbrush from the medicine cabinet, I tried to make myself presentable. Worried eyes stared back at me in the mirror, ringed with dark circles. What I'd give for a shower, a toothbrush, and a change of clothes.

Sighing, I ventured downstairs. I found Nancy in the living room, tucking some pictures and knick-knacks into a suitcase. "Morning," I greeted.

She returned the greeting with a subdued smile but didn't ask me how I'd slept or anything. It was probably obvious. "Breakfast is almost ready," she said.

"Do you need any help?" I wondered.

"No, thanks anyway," she answered with a frown. "We can't bring much so it won't take too long to pack." She looked around the living room, tears springing to her eyes. "We've spent thirty years in this house." She sniffled and turned away, fussing with something in the suitcase.

I'd been rootless for so long, the idea of getting attached to a house was a foreign concept to me. But I still felt for her; I hated to see anyone in pain. I stepped up behind her and laid a hand on her shoulder. She patted it once to acknowledge it but didn't turn around.

Sparing her a sympathetic look, I left her alone and headed into the kitchen. Mark leaned against the counter, sipping a glass of orange juice, while George stirred what looked like scrambled eggs in a frying pan. Bacon and sausage cooked in another pan, making my stomach rumble.

George and Mark offered quiet greetings, then George said. "Mark, you want to go wake Lily up?"

"No, let her sleep. She had a rough day."

Before long, we were all sitting down to a hearty breakfast in the dining room. "Frank said he'd bring the truck over around noon, so that gives us a couple hours to get ready," George said. "Don't know what the roads will be like. The bridges and tunnels are probably a mess, but we can avoid the city. With a bit of luck, we can be at Ruth's farm by dinner time." Nancy gave a somber nod, but didn't say anything.

I caught Mark's eye and arched my eyebrows. His head dipped with a frown. We both knew it was time to tell them. George caught our exchange, and his lips drew together in a puzzled look before he took a bite of eggs.

Mark cleared his throat and blurted, "We're not going with you."

George and Nancy looked at each other, then at Mark, baffled. "What do you mean, you're not coming with us?" Nancy let out a nervous laugh. "Where else would you go? You can't stay here."

"No, we're not staying," Mark assured them. He shifted in his chair. "I'm going to find Lauren."

Nobody said a word. George and Nancy didn't even move—they just stared at their son-in-law. Nancy's jaw hung open in a mix of shock and dismay. George's gruff stare was harder to read, but he didn't look happy. I tried to stay as unobtrusive as possible, not wanting to be drawn into the family drama.

Nancy broke the silence first. "In Boston? How on earth are you planning to get there?"

"Lauren won't stay in Boston. She's too smart for that. She'll head for the cabin, so that's where we're going to go." Mark met their incredulous stares without faltering. "There's a cross-country hiking trail that'll take us most of the way there. One of the guys from work hiked part of it."

"Mark Ryan, have you lost your mind?" Nancy stammered. "That's got to be… hundreds of miles!" George frowned, but remained studiously silent.

"Almost a thousand," Mark confirmed, leaning forward on his chair. Nancy gasped. "I checked the atlas last night. Look, I've thought this through. My friend Tim made about twenty miles a day. I figure we can do fifteen. That's just over sixty days. We'll be away from the major cities, and from the worst of the chaos. There are a lot of forests—plenty of water and game." He looked at George then, his earnest man-to-man gaze leaving no doubt as to his determination. "I can't let Lauren face this alone."

I had to admit—he did sound as though he'd given this serious consideration. Maybe he wasn't as crazy as I thought. Sixty days. That wasn't so bad, was it?

George still wore that severe frown, but he inclined his head in a tiny nod. "You won't make fifteen miles a day. Your friend didn't have to stop to forage and hunt along the way. There won't be any way to resupply. Plan for ten."

"George!" Nancy gaped at her husband. "You can't seriously be encouraging him. He can't take a seven-year-old girl into the woods for months alone! What if something happens to him?" Desperate tears sprang to her eyes.

Mark glanced my way. "I'm hoping we won't have to go alone. I've asked Anna to come with us."

So much for staying out of it. "I said I'd think about it." But I could already feel my resolve wavering.

Nancy's eyes narrowed at me. I suppose she was angry that I hadn't turned him down flat. "Then neither of you has a lick of sense in you. George, tell them."

George stared at us, not saying a word, and I found myself shifting under his uncomfortable scrutiny. Then he seemed to reach a decision. His gaze shifted to Mark. "You go find our girl."

Mark nodded in a solemn promise. "I will."

"I can't believe I'm hearing this!" Nancy hissed, shaking her head. She looked between the two men, but realized she was up against a pair of brick walls. "At least leave Lily with us. She'll be safe. You can't expect a seven-year-old to walk all that way. Ten miles a day!"

"Nancy…"

"I mean it. You go, get Lauren, and come back." She fixed him with a stern stare. "Don't put her in danger like this, Mark. She's just a child, for God's sake. Lauren wouldn't want it, and you know that. We'll take care of her."

She did kind of have a point—what mother would want her child put in that position? I watched Mark's reaction.

"I know you would, Nancy," he said, letting out a soft sigh. "But I can't do that. I want my family together. You're worried about us traveling now. How much worse will things be in three months? Six months? I believe we can get there. I don't know if we'll be able to get back. Not any time soon." He met her gaze, imploring her to see the truth in what he was saying. Then, as gently as he could manage, he put his foot down. "I'm her father, and she's coming with me."

Nancy's chair scraped against the floor as she stood up, her entire body stiff with rage. "You selfish son of a bitch. You're going to get our granddaughter killed." Jerking her arm away from George's attempt at a conciliatory pat, she glared at each of us and then stormed out of the room.

"Nancy," George called, but she kept going. A moment later, I heard the downstairs bedroom door slam shut. Sighing, he also got up from the table. "I'll talk to her." He clapped Mark on the shoulder once and followed after his wife.

That left Mark and I alone at the table. "Well. That went well." He frowned.

I couldn't resist the temptation any longer, and started on my breakfast. Between bites, I pointed out mildly, "She's right you know—it's going to be a huge risk."

"Anna, if we're right about this EMP being global, *everything's* going to be a huge risk. I have to do what's best for my family." He stabbed at a sausage with his fork.

We both fell silent then, and I watched him with a contemplative gaze. I had to admire his resolve. Seeing Nancy's fear, recalling the same worry that had kept me awake last night, I knew at that moment that I couldn't let them go alone.

"I'll go," I said. He looked up, confused. "I'll go with you. To Maine."

Mark's expression changed, relief and joy banishing the sullen frown. "Thank you. Really. Thanks."

I smiled back, even as I pointed out, "For the record, I still think this is a terrible idea."

"Then why are you doing it?" He squinted at me, his grin barely flickering.

I didn't want to insult him by saying I didn't think they'd make it alone. Didn't want to admit that I cared about them, or that facing this disaster on my own frightened me. So instead I just shrugged. "Because apparently I'm just as crazy as you are."

CHAPTER 12

GEORGE EVENTUALLY TALKED NANCY DOWN from Defcon 1, but she gave us both the silent treatment on her way upstairs to continue packing. In the meantime, Mark and I got the dusty old atlas open on the coffee table, looking over the terrain between here and Maine. "We'll need a better map; I don't know exactly where the route is. But from what I remember Tim telling me, it cut across upstate New York, then up through Vermont and New Hampshire." He traced his finger along way too much of the map.

"God, that's far," I murmured.

Mark offered an encouraging smile. "We can do it. My biggest concern is these mountains here." He gestured toward the stretch from eastern New York to New Hampshire. The shading indicated extensive mountain ranges. Adirondack Mountains. Green Mountain National Forest. White Mountain National Forest. I felt a growing dread as I read the names. "Best as I can figure, we'll be crossing through there in September, so the weather shouldn't be too bad. But it'll still be hard going."

George plopped down in his easy chair with a notebook and pencil in hand. "You'll want to travel light. I'll start making a list. Carry just what you need and not draw attention to yourselves. Live off the land as much as you can and stay off the roads."

"Thanks," Mark shot him a grateful look. As a hunter and former soldier, George had more field experience than both of us put together.

Lily wandered downstairs with a yawn. She stole Mark's seat on the couch next to me when Mark got up to get her some breakfast. Frowning at the atlas, she wondered, "Why are you looking at maps?"

I glanced toward the kitchen. "Your dad was just showing me something."

Mark saved me from further interrogation by returning with a Pop-Tart. "Daddy, is the power still out?"

"Yeah. It looks like it's going to be out for a long time."

A pout settled on her lips. She tore open the wrapping, and then asked, "Are the planes still broken too? When's Mommy gonna get here?"

Mark and I exchanged glances, his eyes crinkling at the edges. He perched on the corner of the couch beside Lily. "The planes are going to be broken for a long time too, princess. And the cars."

"Because of the invisible lightning?" Lily asked in a hushed whisper, her hazel eyes growing wide.

"That's right. But here's what we're going to do." Mark glanced at me, burying the sadness and anxiety behind a hopeful smile. "You, me, and Doctor Anna are going to walk to our cabin and wait for Mommy to come there."

"Walk?" Lily echoed, her voice pitching upward in surprise.

"That's right. See—we're here right now. And we're going to go up here." He traced his finger across the map, showing her the route.

"That's really, really far." Lily chewed her lip with a frown, echoing my own sentiments.

"Yeah, it'll take a while to get there, but we'll be camping out, and fishing. It'll be a big adventure. And you'll have a lot of neat stories to tell Mommy once we find her."

He certainly had a knack for spinning it. Lily took her cue from him and gave an eager nod. "We'll be like explorers! Are Grammy and Pappy going to come too?"

Mark hesitated, but George saved him from the awkward pause. "We're going to go to Aunt Ruth's farm and wait for you. You can come to us when the planes and cars are working again." He spoke in his usual gruff monotone, giving nothing away, but a grim glance at Mark hinted at how unlikely that was to happen any time soon. I had only known these people a day, but it broke my heart to think of them being separated indefinitely.

"Oh, okay." Lily's ready acceptance showed her blissful ignorance. She looked between the two of us. "When are we gonna leave?"

If only I could borrow some of her enthusiasm.

CHAPTER 13

GEORGE'S FRIEND FRANK MILLER CAME by later that morning to report that his wife needed some more time, and that the Jankowski's were considering coming along too. Nancy and George readily agreed to pushing back the departure to later that afternoon. After learning about Mark's plan, they weren't going to leave their beloved granddaughter one second before they had to.

George had some of the supplies we needed in his hunting gear, but Mark suggested heading over to the mall to get the rest of the things on his list.

"Oooh, can I go too?" Lily asked, only to flounce off in a pout when Mark told her she had to stay here with Nancy. Besides the fact that we could make faster time on our own, I thought he probably meant it as a peace offering for his mother-in-law.

Before we left, George asked us to come down to the basement with him. At first I thought he had heard something else on the radio, but instead of heading for the radio table, he went to the opposite end of the room. There stood a sturdy wooden gun cabinet that would have been quite stylish, had it not been for the gaudy deer heads stenciled on the glass windows.

"George," Mark protested as his father-in-law unlocked the cabinet. "We're just going to get some supplies."

George squinted over his shoulder. "Folks are gonna get desperate. May have already started—you heard what those guys said about Paris. They won't hesitate to kill you and take what you've got. Are you willing to kill to stop them? If not, you've got no business taking those girls out there."

I bristled at the implication that 'we girls' needed big, strong Mark to look after us, but I bit my tongue. I needed to see how Mark reacted.

"I'll do what I have to, to protect my family," Mark replied, setting his jaw in a determined frown.

George stared him down for a long moment, gauging his sincerity. "Then shut up and take the guns." He handed Mark the rifle and a handgun that looked like a police-issue automatic.

Seeing other handguns in the cabinet, I asked, "Can I have one?"

Mark checked the pistol, arching an eyebrow at me. "Whatever happened to 'do no harm', Doc?"

I rolled my eyes. "That doesn't stop me from shooting some asshole who's trying to kill us. I'm a doctor, not a saint."

Grinning at my response, George took a Glock semi-auto pistol from the cabinet and handed it to me. "You know how to use it?"

"Yeah." I shrugged to Mark's surprised look. "What? I used to go with my dad and sister to the range." It had always been more their thing than mine, but I tagged along. At least for a while.

"Well, if you're any good, you can probably get squirrels or rabbits with that thing. Maybe a deer if we're lucky," Mark mused.

Working the action on the weapon, I mumbled, "Let's hope that's all we need it for."

CHAPTER 14

ARMED AND NOT-SO-DANGEROUS, we set off for the shopping mall we'd passed on the way to Nancy and George's house. Winding our way through the neighborhood, we saw more signs of activity than the day before. The rain had stopped, and the neighbors gathered in small groups to talk about the blackout. Several had the hoods up on their cars, trying to get them started. Nobody panicked, but an undercurrent of anxiety hung like a dark cloud over everyone.

The people thinned out when their road met up with a larger four-lane highway. A bar, an exercise facility, a car dealership—one small business after another was closed and empty. Most of the cars were abandoned by now, and here and there we saw people walking with bags. We passed a McDonalds, open and packed with people. At least they had food—what hadn't already spoiled in this heat, anyway.

My feet and legs ached by the time we reached the mall parking lot, and we'd both worked up a good sweat even in the milder mid-morning sun. I sipped a bottle of water as we surveyed the area. The term "mall" didn't quite do justice to the giant collection of big box stores and retailers sprawled over several square miles. We could've spent hours searching the place, but fortunately Mark knew where we were going—an outdoors store in one of the satellite wings of the shopping complex.

Soon enough, we stood in front of the store. The three-story building sported floor-to-ceiling windows on each level, and we pressed our noses against the glass to see if anyone was inside. The parking lot held only a few cars, perhaps belonging to employees who were getting things ready to open before the blackout hit.

Mark tried the door and pounded on the window, but still nobody came. He sighed, and we exchanged glances.

"You sure about this?" Mark asked.

"We don't have much choice, do we?" I chewed my lip, but saw my own doubts mirrored on his face. It was a line I'd never even considered crossing.

George had given us a window punch tool he kept in the car for emergencies. Mark held up a hand to cover his eyes and then swung the tool like a hammer at the bottom corner of the glass panel. It created a spiderweb up the entire length of the door, and Mark pushed in the rest to clear a path.

The store featured a wide-open floor plan. Light poured in from the windows, giving the place an airy look even without artificial lighting. I stood in the entry threshold for a moment, half-expecting someone to come running out from the back to challenge us. When no one did, I let out the breath I'd been holding and surveyed the store.

"You know, most people would take months to plan a hike like this. Research the gear, get familiar with using it, get conditioned," I thought aloud. "We've only got a couple of hours."

"Better get started then," Mark said, undaunted. Slipping the window tool back in his pocket, he set off into the store.

What followed was the most surreal, stressful shopping trip of my life. Our lives might depend on every decision we made now. Choosing a sleeping bag seemed like a pretty simple task, until I stood in front of a rack with several dozen different models. This one was the lightest. That one squished up to a smaller size. This other one was the warmest. The red one had a "zipper draft tube", whatever the hell that was. Naturally, there wasn't one that had everything—that would be too easy. I blew out a frustrated breath.

"Hell with it," I mumbled, and picked one of the expensive ones. For two hundred bucks, how bad could it be? I kept telling myself we had no choice, but looking at the price tag still made me feel like a thief.

Later, I joined Mark in front of the book and map section. While he sifted through the maps and guidebooks, I picked up a wilderness survival guide. I thumbed through a book dedicated to edible plants next, one plant looking very much like the next one.

Mark chuckled. "Your pack's going to weigh a ton if you keep adding books."

Arching my eyebrows in amused defiance, I tossed both into the backpack that was serving as my shopping cart. "I'd rather have a sore back than starve to death."

"Point taken." He had a plastic folding map of Pennsylvania in his hands, and tilted it so I could see. Tracing a finger along a stretch in the north part of the state, he said, "This is the trail my friend took. North Country Trail. It follows the Finger Lakes Trail here across upstate New York, and then eventually meets up with the Appalachian Trail. Least we know the way now."

"At least." My sarcasm did little to dampen his enthusiasm. A rack of bikes lined the far wall. "We should get some bikes."

"For the trail?"

"Well, maybe not over the mountains, but we've got to go through the city to get *to* the trail. And back to your in-laws."

"Yeaaaah…I don't think that's a good idea." Mark eyed the bikes and made a face. "George said we should keep a low profile. Bikes will draw attention. And I have a bad history with bicycles."

"How does somebody have a 'bad history' with bicycles?" He just scowled and turned his attention to a rack of fishing lures, ignoring the question. Amused, I prodded, "Come on, there's got to be a good story."

"It's a terrible story." But he smiled, then relented. "Okay, fine." He picked a couple lures and then shifted over to the other side of the aisle with the cooking equipment, talking while he browsed.

"My college buddy and I decided to check out Nantucket Island over summer break. We rented bikes since the car ferry cost an arm and a leg. So there we are, two out-of-shape geeks who hadn't been on bikes since we were kids, riding across the island. Couple of miles in, we hit this hill, and I swear—it felt like fricking Mount Everest." He made a gesture with his hand to illustrate a steep slope.

I arched my eyebrows at him. "You know, you're not inspiring a lot of confidence for this cross-country hike idea."

"This was a long time ago," he countered, flashing that little smile again. "Anyway, we're almost to the top, asses dragging, and zoom— here come two girls on bikes, passing us like we were standing still. They're barely breaking a sweat, and one of them gives us a smug little grin over her shoulder when she passes. I look over at Jay and it's like —oh, it's on."

I chuckled at the image, and Mark bent down to open the box of the cooking set he'd selected. It had two pots, a frying pan, and dinnerware for four people. Mark started taking everything out and ditching the packing materials. He seemed a lot less troubled by this whole looting thing than I was.

While we worked, Mark continued his story. "So we kick it into high gear, and start tearing down the hill after them to redeem ourselves. We catch up, pass them, and just as I'm smiling back at the girls… bam." He abandoned the cookware to punch his open palm with his fist for emphasis. "I hit something in the road and wipe out, hard. Ass over handlebars."

"Ouch," I said with a sympathetic wince. Once the cookware was out and unwrapped, we started repacking it for easy travel. All the pieces nested inside each other like Russian dolls, which was admittedly pretty cool. Even the frying pan handle came off so it would fit inside the big pot with the plates. Mark took that, and gave me the smaller one with the cups inside, splitting the load between us.

"Ended up with a concussion, a busted collarbone and an ambulance ride. Not to mention a seriously bruised ego."

"Okay, I guess that qualifies as a 'bad history'. I imagine the girls were less than impressed."

"Oh, no, everyone was laughing their asses off," Mark admitted with a dismissive chuckle. "Until they all realized I was hurt. One of the girls knew first aid, so she took care of me."

Seeing his wistful smile, I asked, "You get her number, at least?"

"Oh, you bet I did." His grin was smug. "And then I married her. Well. Eventually."

I chuckled. "That was Lauren? Hell of a way to meet your future wife."

"Yeah, well, once someone's seen you being a complete dumbass, it's all uphill from there. But I swore off bikes after that." Mark chuckled. Then he got back to the task at hand. "We need a stove."

I finally decided to remark on his nonchalance. "Doesn't it bother you at all? Becoming looters?"

"Of course it does," Mark replied, bristling. "But we're just taking what we need. It's not like we're going out and lifting iPads for the hell of it. If things get back to normal, I'll write them a big check. Right now I'm just worried about surviving."

We continued ticking things off George's shopping list. Mark said, "If you can get these last few things, I'm going to go check the back room. They might have some winter gear stored back there since it's off-season."

I took the list. "You don't think we should hold off on that?" Even knowing that we'd need it later, my mind balked at the idea of carting around winter coats in the middle of summer.

"I'd rather have them now. God knows when we'll have another chance to get supplies. I'll see what I can find." He headed for the back of the store.

I was just about finished 'shopping'—including a few hygiene items that understandably hadn't been on George's list—when I heard a clatter from further down the aisle. Thinking maybe Mark had knocked something over, I went down to the end of the aisle to look. A question died on my lips, the color draining from my face. Mark stood halfway across the store with a police officer leveling a gun at him.

"Hands up! Get down on the ground now."

CHAPTER 15

THE OFFICER HADN'T NOTICED ME. I ducked down, peeking out from behind the shelves. Mark raised his hands, letting his pack slump to the floor.

"Okay, listen. This isn't what it looks like…" He frowned. "Actually, it kinda is what it looks like. But there's an explanation…"

The stocky young officer ignored Mark's protest, casting a nervous look back and forth. He looked jumpy, sweat beading on his forehead. "Shut up and get on the ground. Who else is with you?" I crouched down a little further.

"Listen, officer, let me explain…"

"I said on the ground! You're under arrest." He pulled out a set of handcuffs, and a cold realization hit me.

If he arrests us, we're going to die.

Not right away, of course, but I imagined us languishing in a holding cell while the city fell apart around us. Slowly starving to death while the food ran out and the fools in charge tried to get their act together.

Before today, I'd never done anything worse than a traffic violation. But now? All bets were off. Well, maybe not *all*. I had a gun tucked in my belt, but I wasn't about to use it to shoot a police officer just doing his job.

While my mind raced, the officer continued to face off with Mark. "Last warning, buddy. Get on the ground, or I'll put fifty thousand volts through you."

Volts? I realized he wasn't holding a regular pistol, but a boxy weapon with a yellow tip. A taser. His service weapon remained holstered.

Mark got down on his knees. "The taser won't work for the same reason your radio won't work. Your cell phone, the lights, your car, all of it. The blackout is worse than you think."

Mark's words boosted my confidence. Without the taser, maybe we could subdue him. I let my backpack slip to the floor, quietly unzipping the front pouch where I'd stashed my "bear repellent" pepper spray. I removed the safety cap and stepped out into the aisle.

"Hey!" I yelled.

The officer swung his weapon towards me, and I depressed the button on the canister. Pepper spray shot across the gap between us, dousing the policeman's face. He let out an angry, pained howl, and then he pulled the trigger.

As a doctor, I knew a taser worked by overriding your central nervous system. I'd seen those videos on the Internet of people being tazed—stiffening like a board when every muscle contracted at once and then toppling. None of that prepared me for what it felt like first-hand. I think I screamed. I certainly tried to, right before I hit the ground and saw stars.

An eternity passed before the electricity cut off and I stopped convulsing on the floor. My muscles had turned to jello, tingling painfully. After some time, I felt Mark's hands on my shoulders, helping me to sit up. "Anna? Hey, are you all right?"

My voice was thick with pain and disbelief. "You said it wouldn't work."

Mark gave me a sheepish shrug. "It was a gamble. I was trying to get him to listen about the EMP. Simple things without microchips will still work. Like flashlights or—apparently—tasers."

I scowled. "That would've been useful to know *beforehand*." I rubbed my jaw, which ached where it had connected with the floor.

"Sorry. Are you okay?"

"More or less." I groaned, then I remembered the police officer. He lay on the ground a few feet away, his hands cuffed behind him. "What happened—did you knock him out?"

Mark scrubbed his face with a hand. "Yeah, I hit him with a lantern." He scooted over to the unconscious young man. "Is he going to be all right? What should we do?"

I crawled over, still wobbly after the taser blast. Pressing my fingers to his neck, I let out a breath of relief when I found a pulse. I went to check his pupils next, then saw that his face was still covered in pepper spray. "Could you get me some of those water bottles?"

Mark grabbed them, then removed the caps for me once we realized my tingling hands lacked the grip strength to do so. I flushed the man's face with several bottles of water, rinsing off the spray residue. On the third one, he stirred, then woke up sputtering.

"Take it easy," I told him, pushing against his shoulder to keep him down.

The officer's eyes flicked from me to Mark, who had picked up the taser and now covered him with it. Fear flashed across the young man's face.

"Relax, we're not going to hurt you," I assured him.

Unconvinced, the officer tried to assert control. "Listen, I called for backup before I came in here. They're gonna be here any minute. They see you with a weapon on me, things are going to get real messy, real fast. Put it down and uncuff me."

"Nice try," I said flatly. "Like he told you, we know the blackout took out your radio."

Mark chimed in, "Everything will break down fast. Riots, looting, people fighting over food. You should think about getting your family and getting out of town. That's what we're doing."

The cop's resolve wavered for a moment, but he seemed incapable of accepting Mark's words. "You're crazy. All you're doing is breaking a half-dozen laws. Let me go before you make it worse."

Mark met my eye, and I offered a helpless shrug. How much more could we do to convince the guy? I finished checking his pupils, finding no sign of serious head injury.

"You should be fine." I rose, using a shelf to steady myself until I could take a step on my own. "I'm sorry about all this."

"Save it for the judge," the cop sneered.

Mark held up the handcuff key for the officer to see, then chucked it across the room. "You can go find that after we're gone. I hope you think about what we said." He started backing away from the officer, pausing to grab our backpacks of stolen goods. The other man just glared.

Outside, Mark ditched the officer's weapons, and we hurried away. It wasn't until we had put a fair bit of distance between us, with no sign of pursuit, that I could breathe again.

Checking over my shoulder, I frowned, "So now we're felons, I guess. Breaking-and-entering, resisting arrest, assaulting a police officer..."

Mark saw the look on my face. "I don't like it any more than you do, but we did what we had to. The world we knew—its rules—it's gone. We're just realizing it sooner than everyone else."

I heaved a sigh. "I just didn't think it would happen so quickly. Or that we'd be the ones leading the charge into anarchy. I hope you're right about all of this EMP stuff."

"I don't." When I shot him a confused look, Mark's mouth pressed into a thin line. "Anna, if I am right, millions of people are going to die. And I don't know what the world is going to look like after. I hope to God I'm wrong."

He had a point. The only thing more unsettling than the thought of facing a judge for all of this was the thought of *not* facing a judge, ever, because the world as we knew it was over. "Yeah. Well. Compared to that, I guess sending postcards to each other from jail isn't such a bad alternative."

He snorted softly, but the mirth was short-lived.

Neither of us believed he was wrong.

CHAPTER 16

WE WALKED BACK TO NANCY and George's place in silence. Mark's in-laws read our faces and didn't press for details, but Lily welcomed us both back with a warm hug that cheered me up. She couldn't wait to see what we'd brought.

I flopped on the couch, still feeling achy and drained. I watched from there while George, Mark, and an inquisitive Lily sifted through our loot. George tossed aside a bunch of things he deemed 'useless' and added a few things from his own stock. What remained after the cull made for an intimidating pile, yet it still felt like not nearly enough for three people to survive for months.

While George, Lily and Mark went off to construct some kind of smaller, lighter replacement for the fancy stove we'd selected, I stayed on the couch to rest. To my surprise, Nancy stayed with me instead of going with Lily, sitting across from me on one of the easy chairs.

"That looks like a lot to carry," she mused, surveying the piles of gear.

"Yeah. I'm still worried we're going to get on the road and realize we've forgotten something important." A frown touched my lips. That was the least of my worries about this crazy-assed expedition.

Nancy continued to watch me with a quiet frown. Her staring made me self-conscious.

I sat up and leaned my elbows on my knees. "Something on your mind, Nancy?"

"Why are you doing this?"

The accusatory tone took me aback, and I arched my eyebrows at her. "You'd rather I let them go alone?"

"I'd rather they didn't go at all." Nancy frowned. "But that's not my question. Why are *you* doing this? Traveling hundreds of miles with a man you just met? What do you get out of it?"

I didn't answer. My flippant response to Mark about being crazy wouldn't cut it here, but I wasn't sure I could articulate my thoughts in a way that would satisfy her. I frowned, considering what I might say to ease her mind.

"Is it Mark?" she prodded, when my silence stretched on.

"What?"

"Please. I may be old, but I'm not an idiot. He's smart, he's good-looking, he's kind. Months alone on the trail with him so far from his wife…" She fixed me with a stare that reminded me of my mother calling me on the carpet.

I let out a bark of laughter. "You think I'm doing this so I can seduce your son-in-law? No. Hardly." I tried not to be offended by her suspicion. She was worried about her family, and I was a stranger to them. "You don't have to worry about me."

"Why? Are you a lesbian or something?"

I arched an eyebrow. "What? I won't go after a married man, so I must be a lesbian?" Her frown told me that she didn't find it as amusing as I did, so I answered more seriously. "No, I'm not. But I'm not a home-wrecker either. My step-mother has the corner on that in our family." That last bit came out more bitterly than I intended.

The corners of her eyes creased as she studied me, still dubious. "That still doesn't explain why you're doing this."

I turned my palms up in a helpless gesture. "It's the right thing to do. Maybe that sounds cheesy, but… I feel like I need to help them."

"You're a doctor, though. You can help a lot of people."

"I won't stop being a doctor just because I'm traveling with them," I pointed out. "Maybe if there are other families when we get to Maine, I can be of use there." The idea of putting out a shingle as a rural doctor struck me odd after my experiences in conflict-zone clinics and big-city hospitals, but the world was different now. Truth is, I wasn't sure what "being a doctor" looked like any more. I had practiced medicine in a war zone before. It wasn't pretty, but at least we had supplies. This was something different.

Nancy still didn't look convinced.

I watched her for a moment, then ventured, "Did Mark tell you I have a sister?"

"No, he didn't."

"She's got two girls. Maddie's just a little younger than Lily. Morgan's only ten. And I keep thinking… what if it was my sister's husband, separated from her when all this happened? She'd be out of her mind worrying about them. And if he was crazy enough to try walking cross-country to get back to her, I wouldn't want him to go alone. I'd want someone to help him keep the girls safe." I shrugged again. "Seems like I'm that someone."

Finally, the cloud of suspicion lifted, and she just gave me a quiet nod of understanding. "You look after them," she said—part command, part plea.

"I will." It might not be worth much, but it was all I could offer.

CHAPTER 17

MARK WANTED TO LEAVE AS soon as we had our gear ready, but Nancy talked him into waiting until the Millers arrived with their vintage truck.

"We can give you a ride down to the parkway, at least," George offered.

So we waited, a gloom coming over everyone as they counted down their last hours together. Feeling like an interloper, I camped out on the couch with my survival book and gave them their space. Familiar butterflies danced in my stomach, reminding me of the nights before I set out on MSF missions. Eager to get going, but nervous about what we'd face. After reading the same page three times without a word of it sinking in, I gave the book up as a lost cause and just closed my eyes.

Some time later, Mark nudged me awake. "The Millers are here."

I rubbed the sleep from my face and rolled off the couch. Everyone else was already up and moving. With all the enthusiasm of a funeral procession, we all filed out of the house. The expression on Nancy's face as she cast one last look back at her beloved home tore at my heart. Who knew when—or if—they'd see it again? I couldn't help but think of all the refugees I had worked with at MSF.

Mark had loaded all our stuff before he woke me up, a sweet gesture I appreciated. It seemed the Jankowskis had decided not to come after all—maybe a good thing since I doubted there would've been room. Frank Miller's "old truck" wasn't a truck at all, but a vintage 1950s ambulance that looked more like a station wagon. Frank and his wife sat up front and the rest of us crammed into the back. Lily sat on Nancy's lap. I tried to give George the second seat, but he insisted I take it. He settled next to Mark onto the floor, where the stretcher would've been. The suitcases and backpacks filled up the rear.

And then we were on our way. It was surreal being the only car on the road. People stared as we drove through the quiet neighborhood, and Nancy waved goodbye to a few of their neighbors. It took only a few minutes to reach the highway, compared to the slog Mark and I had done earlier. We saw people walking, but fewer than I expected. Were the rest still holed up at school, or at work, or wherever they'd been, waiting for things to return to normal? How many were willing to make a long journey, like Mark?

A few walkers tried to flag us down, but Frank kept driving. I gritted my teeth, knowing we had nothing to offer them. But when we approached a young woman and two little kids walking down the side of the road up ahead, I couldn't let it go. The mother (I presumed) carried a toddler, his little head slumped over her shoulder, while the older child trudged along holding her hand.

"Mark…" I said softly.

"I see them. Frank, we should see if they need a ride."

"What are we going to do, put them on the roof?" Frank sounded incredulous, but he slowed down.

"There'll be room if we get out," Mark suggested. He looked at me for confirmation, and I nodded. Nancy's throat bobbed, and she clung to Lily a little tighter.

The young mother turned around when the car pulled off the road behind her. Facing a vintage ambulance packed with strangers, alarm and confusion mingled on her face. Nancy and Mary Miller got out and approached her, the two older women giving off a reassuring vibe.

After a brief discussion, Nancy announced, "They're going to come with us. They've got no place safe to go." The young mother hung back a little, looking overwhelmed. It was quite a leap—heading out of town with strangers based on a five-minute conversation. But then I suppose I wasn't one to throw stones there.

Mark, Lily and I got out to make room in the ambulance, and Mark started grabbing our gear from the back.

"I don't want to push yinz out," the young mother protested when she realized what we were doing.

"It's all right," I assured her. "We're getting out anyway and heading in the other direction."

Nancy strode up to him, a stricken look on her face. "Mark, please reconsider..." I couldn't hear all of her soft pleading, but I knew she was asking again for him to leave Lily with them.

"I can't do that, Nancy." Mark's jaw was set in determination. "But I swear, I'll take good care of her. And Lauren when we find her."

George came up to them then. "We'll say a prayer for you every night." A weathered hand came to rest on Nancy's back, rubbing it comfortingly. He handed Mark a folded piece of paper. "That's Ruth's address. You bring our girls back to us when it's safe."

I strode a few steps away from the ambulance, distancing myself from the hugs and the tears held back for Lily's sake. I hated goodbyes. I'd had to say too many in my day, and it never got easier. I remembered saying goodbye to Jess and her girls, and it was a kick in the gut. Hard to believe it was less than forty-eight hours ago.

As the others got back into the ambulance, Mark came over to me with my backpack and rifle. I slung both onto my back, wincing at the weight. "God, that's heavy."

"Not too late to back out," Mark pointed out. "You sure about this?"

Nancy watched us from the ambulance. I caught her eye and gave her a little nod, a silent affirmation of the promise I'd made. "I'm sure. Let's go."

The ambulance's engine roared back to life, and we waved to it as they drove off. "Come on, princess," Mark said, guiding Lily along with a gentle hand on her back. I fell into step behind them.

My God, we were actually doing this.

PART TWO

CHAPTER 18

THE SUN WAS HIGH OVERHEAD when the highway brought us to a tunnel that Mark said led downtown. "I don't want to go in there, Daddy. It's too dark." Lily clung to his leg, looking at the dark maw with terrified eyes.

"Don't worry, baby. There's nothing scary in there. Just a bunch of broken cars." Moving through the pitch-black tunnel, the only light coming from our paltry flashlights, we wove through the stalled vehicles, breathing hot, oppressive air that smelled of diesel fumes.

Emerging from the darkness, I blinked at the view. Mark had a sad smile on his face. "I remember the first time Lauren brought me this way."

I could see how it made an impression. Before the tunnel, we'd been on a bleak, almost rural interstate highway. I would've guessed we were miles and miles from the city. Yet here it was, a breathtaking panorama of the rivers and the downtown skyline.

The tunnel led straight onto a yellow bridge, and Lily moved over to the railing. "Aww, the fountain isn't on," she lamented. While reading about the city, I'd seen pictures of the majestic fountain that marked the point where the city's three rivers came together.

"It needs power to run," Mark pointed out.

Lily nodded, those hazel eyes sweeping up and down the water. I didn't mind her taking a moment to appreciate the view. It gave me a chance to lean against a support pillar and catch my breath. I sipped from my water bottle to replenish some of the sweat dampening my hair and clothes.

"Does the invisible lightning hurt boats too?" Lily wondered, chewing on her lip.

"I'd imagine so," I ventured between sips. "I mean, they've got engines the same as cars."

"Not necessarily," Mark said, enthusiasm creeping into his voice. "An outboard motor wouldn't have a lot of fancy electronics. It would be like the old ambulance." He stood behind Lily, clapping his hands gently on her shoulders. "Great idea, princess." She beamed proudly up at him. Mark scanned the river. "I don't see any marinas, but we'll keep our eyes peeled. There's got to be one somewhere."

"Hey, if it means less walking, I'm all for it." I took one last drink and tucked it back in its pouch, and then we got on our way once more.

We avoided the skyscrapers by following a couple bridges around the downtown peninsula. I could see where the 'city of bridges' nickname came from; it seemed like you couldn't throw a rock without hitting one.

The downtown area looked pretty deserted. I imagined most people would have left work and gone home by now. We saw others walking on roads and bridges, but none that were near enough for conversation. I didn't mind the solitude, even if it underscored the eeriness of our situation. I worried about running into another cop, especially with the rifle slung over Mark's shoulder.

"We can follow the bike path down along the riverfront," Mark pointed out as we reached the opposite bank and passed in front of an empty baseball stadium.

"Shame we don't have any bikes." I chuckled when he rolled his eyes at me. I was never going to let that go.

Flat and paved, the bike path would've been a pleasant walk if not for feeling like a sweltering pack mule. Lily weathered it better than I expected her to, only occasionally asking how much farther until we stopped. After a brief rest in a shaded area for lunch, we continued on until we came upon a marina.

"Hello?" Mark tried to get someone's attention, but the dock was deserted. We saw a rowing club with some kayaks outside, but after realizing that neither of us had any rowing experience, we nixed that idea. After a bit more searching, we found several smaller motorboats. Mark checked one of them out. "This one needs a key."

"This one too," I said after trying another. "Can't you hot-wire it or something? You're an engineer, right?"

Mark scoffed. "I write computer software; I'm not a car thief."

After breaking a window and searching the nearby building, Mark found some keys. It took a few tries to sort out the right one, but then the outboard motor roared to life. "We're in business now," he called triumphantly.

Zipping up the river in our stolen little boat, a warm breeze on my face, it was almost possible to forget what we were doing. To just pretend like I was out with a couple of friends.

Almost.

Nothing could completely dissipate that undercurrent of anxiety, especially with more dark smoke rising toward the clouds in the distance. A fire, somewhere, probably unchecked like the one at the airport.

As abruptly as the scenery had changed from rural to urban when we emerged from the tunnel, it changed back. Wooded hills and foliage lined the riverbanks on both sides. Buildings poked up over the tree line or became visible on the hillside—the only signs of civilization. At one point, there was even an old-school paddle steamer docked along a deserted stretch of shore.

After about half an hour, I'd guess—not having a watch was driving me insane—we saw a dam stretching across the river. White water churned at the base, and red warning buoys marked a big danger zone in front of it. "Did you know that was here?" I asked Mark.

"No. I mean, I've seen it before, but it didn't occur to me."

I scanned the shore through the binoculars. "Maybe we could carry the boat around?" I pointed. "There's some brush there, but we could probably make it through."

He frowned thoughtfully. "Let's try the lock. I think small boats can get through."

"Don't they need power for that?"

"Yeah, probably," Mark admitted with a grimace. "Guess we will have to go around."

Mark motored the boat up to the wooded shore. He offered a hand to Lily and me as we climbed out, and then we began unloading the gear. Pulling the boat up onto the shore wasn't so bad. Picking it up and carrying it, though, required an intricate dance of leverage, strength, and a lot of mumbled curses. It took a while, but we got around.

I flopped against the side of the boat, breathless and drenched from the exertion in the pounding afternoon sun. "Maybe we should've just left it and looked for another boat on the other side."

Mark chuckled, handing me my water bottle from the pile of gear and then guzzling from his own. "Just think how fast we'll be cruising once we're back on the river." I shrugged, still not convinced it was worth it.

After loading up the gear and getting settled, Mark steered us away from the shore. But instead of heading upstream as we expected, the boat started slipping backwards.

"Uh… Mark?" I prompted, alarm creeping into my voice.

"Yeah, I see it. Hang on." Frowning, he opened up the throttle on the motor all the way, trying to break free from the current. The engine roared for a second, then sputtered and died. Mark pulled the cord again to restart it, but nothing happened.

The boat continued to slide towards the dam.

CHAPTER 19

THE BOAT PICKED UP SPEED, coasting toward the white water where the river coursed around the broken barge.

"Now would be a good time, Mark," I hissed, clutching the edge of the boat. If we went over that wall, the undertow would smash our boat to bits—and us with it.

"I'm trying!" Mark growled back. He pulled the cord again ineffectually. "Damn thing won't start."

I grabbed the oar we'd tucked under the bench and started paddling. It slowed us down some, but we were still slipping backwards.

"Daddy, what's happening?"

Mark didn't answer Lily's frightened query. His brow sported a deep furrow as he concentrated on the engine. He fiddled with something on the engine. Still nothing.

I pulled the paddle through the water as fast as I could. "Mark, the current's too strong."

"Come on, come on," Mark mumbled. He gave the motor a rest for ten nail-biting seconds, then tried it again. Finally the engine roared to life. "Yes!"

Mark eased the throttle forward, careful not to flood the engine. I continued my frantic paddling until our backwards slide shifted to forward momentum and we started chugging upstream. Setting the oar back down on the deck, I leaned forward and tried to catch my breath.

"Let's not do that again," Mark deadpanned, and I could only offer a snort in return. It took quite awhile for my heart rate to return to normal.

Some time later, we came to another dam. After a collective *oh hell no*, we decided to call it quits for the day. Not wanting to piss someone off by camping in their backyard, Mark steered the boat toward a small island in the middle of the river.

The island was a strange oasis in the middle of suburbia, wooded and apparently deserted. A big highway bridge, eerily silent, stretched over the downstream half of the island. We pulled the boat up onto a flat, silty beach on the upstream tip, where we had a great view of the rushing dam. I didn't realize how uncomfortable the dull thrum of the motor had been until it stopped. Shielding my eyes, I studied the riverbank. I could see a few people on porches or in yards, going about their lives. I wondered how many of them had realized what was happening.

Mark took Lily to catch some fish on the other shore while I set up camp. I was just pounding the final tent stake into the ground when Mark and Lily returned carrying a couple of fish on a line. Mark gave an approving nod toward the tent. "That didn't take long."

Lily oohed and immediately went to climb inside. "This is so cool. Look—it's even got a window."

Mark and I smiled, then he said, "Got these for dinner. The fishing was pretty good over on that side—I think the dam currents help." He held the line out like he expected me to take the fish. When I just stared at them, eyebrows arched, he squinted. "I, uh—I figured you'd cook them up."

I crossed my arms. "And why would you assume that? Because I'm a woman?"

The deer-in-headlights look on his face showed that was exactly why. "Uhh… no. Of course not. I mean, I just figured… I caught them, you'd cook them. Isn't that fair?"

Lily chimed in from within the tent, "That does seem fair."

Well, if even a seven-year-old thought it was fair, I couldn't very well disagree. I sighed. "Fine." Resigned to the deal, I got out my knife and my survival book, flipping to the page on food preparation. I'd never skinned a fish before, but I'd dissected animals and performed surgery. How hard could it be?

Ten minutes into my task, I thought I was doing pretty well until I heard giggling behind me. "Oh my gosh. What are you doing to that fish?" Lily was poking her head out of the tent window, watching me with a skeptical look on her face.

My brows shot up. "What? You've never seen a fish cleaned before?"

"Not like that!" She giggled again, covering her mouth while her eyes danced with amusement. "You have to cut its head off first. And the scales."

Mark, trying to hide a smile, said, "Why don't you show her how, Lil. I'm going to filter some water."

I gaped at her. "You know how to do this?"

"Oh yeah. I'm pretty good at it. I can show you." Lily crawled out of the tent and plopped down next to me. I handed her the knife, and she expertly started gutting and filleting the fish, never batting an eye at the slimy fish bits. I was used to blood and guts, but I didn't expect that from a little girl. Guess Mark wasn't the only one who needed a kick to his expectations. "Your mom teach you all this?"

Lily chuckled again. "Oh, no. Mommy doesn't really cook. Well, I mean, she cooks some stuff. Like, sometimes she cooks a grain of rice."

I smothered a laugh. "A whole grain?"

"Yeah, in the microwave. But she doesn't cook fish. Me and Grandma did. Whenever Daddy caught the fish, me and Grandma would cook them. Grandma Ryan, I mean. She's in heaven now though, so now I only have one Grammy and Pappy." Sadness crept into her face, and I regretted asking. I glanced over at Mark, remembering how he'd said he didn't have any family besides Lauren and Lily.

Throughout dinner, I found myself thinking about my family. After twenty years in the Navy, my dad could take care of himself. For my mom, I couldn't decide if Hawaii would be better or worse off because of its isolation. I tried to sell myself on 'better' to ease my mind. My sister and her family were the ones I fretted about the most. Were the girls taking things as well as Lily, or were they freaking out? Did Jess find safety on her Air Force base? Not knowing was its own form of torture, but I said an extra prayer for all of them and tried not to dwell on it.

After supper, we cleaned up the dishes and sat around the fire pit chatting about what we'd seen on the river and what fishing and boating adventures they'd had at their cabin in Maine. We speculated about how many more dams we'd have to cross, and how long the fuel would last. As the conversation died down, I stood up and walked over to where the water lapped on the shore. "What are you doing?" Mark asked.

"Swimming," I replied with a smile, stripping down to just my tank top and underwear. They were both dark, so they served as decent swimwear. "Get clean; cool off a bit."

Mark averted his gaze, his expression caught between embarrassment and concern. "In there?"

"Don't worry, I'm a good swimmer."

"Have you seen that water?"

"I'm not planning on drinking it." Ignoring his disapproving frown, I waded out into the shallows and then splashed in. In the background, I heard Mark's resounding 'absolutely not' when Lily asked if she could swim too.

The cool water was a welcome respite from the oppressive humidity, and I emerged some time later unscathed and refreshed. Lily had on clean clothes and damp hair, having rinsed off with what was left of our boiled cooking water. As I fetched some fresh clothes from my pack, a shirtless Mark emerged from the tent. I almost did a double-take before snapping my eyes away. Damn, Lauren was a lucky lady. As I'd told Nancy, a married man held no attraction for me. But like an untouchable celebrity, that didn't keep me from admiring his well-defined abs and strong shoulders from a safe emotional distance.

When the sun went down, I expected the little island to plunge into darkness. Instead, a greenish-purple glow splashed across the lower part of the sky. Dim at first, then becoming more visible as the rest of the sky darkened.

"Daddy, are those the Northern Lights?"

"Looks like." Mark stared up at the colors. "But I've never seen them this far south before."

"Maybe it has something to do with the EMP?" I reasoned. I watched the lights dance across the sky. They were beautiful, in an eerie and unsettling way.

"Could be. Charged particles in the air. Who knows. Sure is pretty, though."

Lily scooted over, clinging to his side while watching the sky with wide eyes. "I wish Mommy could see them."

Mark shifted his arm around to hug her. "I bet she can. Probably even has a better view, since she's further north."

"Yeah, but I wish she was here."

"I know, princess," Mark murmured, and the sadness in their voices was palpable. "Me, too."

CHAPTER 20

TAKING ADVANTAGE OF THE CLEAR weather, I left the tent to Mark and Lily and rolled out my sleeping bag beside it. I lay awake for a while, watching the strange lights in the sky. The occasional sound of a gunshot in the distance punctuated the night air like fireworks, interrupting the constant drone of cicadas. Even once I dozed off, between the hard ground and the summer heat, I didn't get much sleep. The next morning, Mark rolled out of the tent looking about as tired as I felt. Lily, on the other hand, apparently could sleep anywhere. Her bright-eyed energy made me feel old.

After a quick breakfast, we tackled the second dam. It turned out there was a clear path from the shore up into some industrial building's parking lot. We emptied the boat and lugged it until we were well clear of the safety buoys marking the dam danger zone on the other side. We weren't going to make that mistake again. This process soon became old hat, as we'd end up crossing several more dams before the day was done.

With the Northern Lights banished by the sun, the world looked almost normal again. The thing I still couldn't get used to was the quiet. It had struck me in some of the remote villages in Africa too—no cars, no lawnmowers running in the distance, no radios or TVs playing. A hush had fallen over the world. We saw some people in the little riverside suburbs we passed, and even some other small boats. For the most part, they kept a wide berth. Only two days into the disaster, and already people were looking at each other with a pronounced wariness.

The neighborhoods dotting the riverbanks became fewer and further between as we continued north. The banks sported high hills and lush forests, making it feel as though we were traveling through the middle of nowhere. We stopped to siphon gas from cars a few times when our fuel ran low. Between that and the dams, it ate up a fair amount of time, but we still travelled over a hundred miles by Mark's reckoning. Just as the sun was dipping down behind the mountains and Lily began to doze off against my side, we came across an odd sight.

"Who the hell builds a lighthouse in the middle of a river?" Mark wondered aloud as we all stared at it. The lighthouse stood on a tiny island, watching over the river channel. As far as we could tell, it served no useful navigation purpose. A fork in the river headed east, towards where the creek intersected the North Country Trail.

Or so we thought.

Instead, we found that the east fork ended abruptly. A swirl of white water in front of a concrete face marked what I presumed was a spillway from a dam. The dam itself wasn't concrete, but a berm of earth rising a good hundred feet from the river. Signs warned us to stay back from the spillway.

"That's not on the map," Mark groused, frowning at his laminated map. "It looks like the river should connect."

"Well, obviously it doesn't," I pointed out dryly.

"Please tell me we don't have to carry the boat around *that*," Lily whined. It had been a long, boring day for her, stuck in the boat, and she wasn't in the best of moods. I suppose none of us were.

Mark continued to frown. "No, we're not getting the boat over that hill." He folded the map back up. "Damn it."

We exchanged glances. "Well… now what?" I wondered aloud.

We headed back to where the river forked. There had been some buildings there—maybe even a town. Mark figured we could find somewhere to stay and maybe some news about the blackout. After last night, and with months of camping lying ahead of us, I relished the prospect of sleeping in a real bed one more time.

We parked the boat on a deserted stretch of land, then hoisted our packs and started walking into town. The wooded road took us past a couple empty houses, then across a bridge into the town proper. We passed a gas station with a sign saying "pumps not working", and a mom-and-pop grocery store announcing it was "closed until next delivery". The absence of cars and people talking on phones struck me as strange, but things were pretty calm. A few people were carrying jugs of water up from the river. Several sported hunting rifles, making me worry less about the one poking up over Mark's shoulder. They gave us a sharp, suspicious look when they saw us. I tried to offer a friendly smile, but they looked more wary than welcoming.

We didn't have to go far before we saw a sign for the Riverside Inn, a big, old-fashioned Victorian house. A bell on the door rang when we entered, and a plump, elderly woman came out of another room to greet us with a warm smile. She introduced herself as Sharon, the owner, and asked if we needed a room. While she and Mark haggled over the cost, I took in some of the landscape paintings adorning the wood-paneled walls of the foyer. Lush forests and streams—that's what we'd be venturing into soon enough. The last time I'd felt this anxious and unprepared was on a plane to Haiti after the earthquake for my first mission abroad.

I refocused on the conversation when I heard Mark ask, "Has there been any news on the blackout?"

Sharon frowned. "You heard about the government's emergency message?"

I said, "We heard something yesterday. Widespread outages, don't panic, that sort of thing."

"That's the one," Sharon agreed, snorting. "About as helpful as the government ever is. Other than that, though, no word yet. It's hard to get news all the way out here with the phones and TVs down. We'll be all right, though. Folks around here take care of each other. Follow me; I'll show you up to your room." Flashing another smile, Sharon started leading the way up the stairs. She'd only made it about three steps up before she seemed to stumble and caught herself on the bannister.

"Whoa, easy there," Mark exclaimed. He was closest, and held his hands out tentatively to catch her if she fell.

"Are you all right?" I asked, peering around him in concern to study the older woman. I'd noticed her damp skin when we'd arrived, but chocked it up to the summer heat. Now I wasn't so sure. She did seem pale.

Waving off Mark's hand, Sharon forced a smile. "I'm fine. Just lost my balance there for a second. This way." Mark and I exchanged concerned glances, but then followed. I kept an eye on Sharon as we ascended the steps. She seemed steady enough—a little out of breath, but that wasn't uncommon at her age. She unlocked the door at the end of the upstairs hallway and led us into a small room. "My room's just downstairs if you need anything," she offered before leaving us to get settled.

Lily flopped down on a daybed tucked up against the far wall. There was also a double bed in the center of the room. I set down my backpack and stretched out my sore shoulders and back. Hauling the boat over so many dams had taken its toll, but I wasn't ready to settle down. Consumed by an inner restlessness, I told Mark, "I'm going to see if there's a pharmacy in town. Pick up some things for the trip they didn't have at the sports store."

Mark nodded. "You have your gun?"

Arching my eyebrows at him, I said, "I'm not planning to knock over the place."

Mark snorted softly. "I know. But you heard what George said. Things could get bad and we need to be careful."

Crouching by my backpack, I rolled my eyes. I grabbed a drawstring bag to hold the gear and some of our cash from the inner pouch, but pointedly left my pistol tucked away in the main pack. "I'll be careful."

On my way downstairs, I found Sharon in the kitchen, hunched over the countertop like she was using it to hold herself up. When she heard my footsteps, she pulled herself up and busied herself pouring water from a pitcher into a kettle. "Oh, hello. I was just about to make some tea. Would you like some?"

"No, thank you. Coffee's always been my weakness." Closing the distance, I studied the older woman. "Are you feeling okay?"

Sharon gave an embarrassed chuckle, the self-effacing 'I don't want to be a bother' reaction that I was all-too-familiar with. "Oh, I'm fine, dear."

I smiled, leaning against the now-defunct dishwasher casually to put her at ease. "Are you sure? Because you look a little pale. I'm a doctor, so—if there's anything I can do…"

"Thank you, but really, I'm fine."

"Okay." I didn't believe her, but I didn't want to push it with a stranger. She wasn't my patient; she hadn't sought me out for help. I'd check on her later, and try again before we left.

I turned to go, but then realized she could probably save me some aimless walking. "Is there a drug store in town?"

She gave me directions, and I set off. Even though the sunset had begun to paint the sky, the downtown area still buzzed with activity. Families gathered on the library lawn for a read-aloud. A few people haggled over bait outside a tackle shop. Neighbors barbecued in the parking lot of a small apartment building. It was a reassuring picture of normalcy at odds with the lack of cars and deserted businesses.

I found the pharmacy, noting the "EXACT CHANGE ONLY" signs plastered prominently on the door and all around the checkout area. Grabbing a shopping basket from the tray by the door, I offered a slight smile to the bored-looking girl behind the counter and beelined for the aisle with the first aid supplies. After the chaos at the airport and the strange journey to get here, shopping like a normal person felt surreal. Exam gloves, OTC painkillers, blister pads, and antibiotic ointment all went into the basket, all better than the junk from the pre-packaged first aid kit I'd picked up at the outdoors store. I paid the cashier and then headed back out.

On the way back to the inn, the sound of conversation and laughter drew my attention down a side-street. I wandered that way, curious, and saw people filtering in and out of a bar. The neon sign over the door was dark, and the porch lit only by lanterns, but that didn't seem to bother the patrons. I stood there and just stared for a minute; the images of people drinking and having fun were completely at odds with the doom and gloom that Mark and I had been preparing for these last two days.

I glanced back down the street towards the inn, then back to the bar, pulled by temptation. This was going to be our last night in a town for a while. Mark and Lily weren't going anywhere. Why not relax a little? I headed inside.

CHAPTER 21

WITH THE NASCAR SCHEDULE POSTED proudly on the front of the bar and Steelers memorabilia adorning the walls, Ike's bar was a far cry from some of the upscale places I'd frequented in California. The sun hadn't quite gone down, but they'd already lit some candles to brighten up the interior. The scent of candle smoke mixed with citronella to keep the summer mosquitos at bay.

I found a seat at the crowded bar, scanning the room while I waited for the barkeeper. Friends and couples gathered at tables, laughing and chatting—all completely oblivious to the looming disaster. How could something so normal feel so unnatural?

"Everything all right?" The man on the stool next to me was peering at me with concern through wire-rimmed glasses. Mid-thirties, with short brown hair and dark eyes, he gave off a friendly vibe.

Snapped out of my thoughts, I forced a smile. "Oh. Yeah. Just been a long day."

"Well, maybe I can buy you a drink and lighten it up?" He offered a hopeful grin. "I'm Owen."

"Anna. And that would be nice, thanks."

Owen was pleasant enough company, if a bit bland. He described his job with the local government as "mostly petitions and assessments," and the blackout was the most interesting thing to happen to him in years. When he asked what brought me to town, I answered vaguely that we were "hiking the North Country trail." I didn't want to sound like a loon by saying we were going all the way to Maine.

"Good time for it, I guess," Owen reasoned. "What with the power out anyway."

"Yeah," I said weakly, going along with him like it was just a weekend camping diversion.

Two beers and a game of pool later, I found myself increasingly distracted by thoughts of the blackout. Every story became a reminder of a world that we may never see again. Every drink and snack felt one step closer to the day when all the supplies ran out. Above it all—the fact that I knew what was coming and the rest of them didn't. Would it change things for them if they did? It was a familiar rock in the pit of my stomach; the same sense of foreboding I felt right when I had to deliver bad news to a patient or their family.

"Another round?" Owen asked after fishing the last of the billiard balls out of the table pockets.

I helped him corral them into the rack and offered an apologetic smile. "I should be getting back. We're heading out early tomorrow."

Trying to hide his disappointment, he nodded. "Sure, I understand. I should call it a night too. Council's having a meeting tomorrow about the blackout, so… guess we'll both be up bright and early."

I finished off the last of my beer and tucked my cue back into the rack. "Thanks for tonight. I had a nice time." He smiled at that. I was poised to go when my conscience tugged at me. I couldn't leave without saying something. Smothering a grimace, I turned back to him. "Owen? You should make sure the council has plans for a prolonged blackout."

He peered at me. "What? Why? They figured everything'd settle down in a few days."

"I hope they do. But my friend's an engineer. He thinks the blackout might've been caused by something called an EMP, and the power grid could be down for longer than that. Best to be prepared, right?"

Owen's brow creased, taking that in. I expected him to have a bunch of questions, as I had, but he just nodded. "Okay. I'll look into that. Thanks for the heads up."

I didn't know if it would make a difference, but at least I'd planted the seed. "Take care." I flashed him a subdued smile and then headed back out into the warm summer air. The sun had gone down a while ago, and the unusual Northern Lights once again danced across the sky.

When I arrived at the inn, something in the shadows of the front porch caught my eye. It wasn't until I got closer that I recognized the shape—an EMS stretcher. There was no ambulance to go with it, thanks to the blackout, but its presence could mean only one thing: someone was ill or injured.

My stomach dropped through the floor. Fearing the worst, I rushed inside.

CHAPTER 22

THE SCENE INSIDE THE INN shook me. A cluster of people surrounded the base of the stairs. Sharon lay sprawled on the floor, unmoving. Mark and a young black woman looked on worriedly as two paramedics worked on the innkeeper. One of the medics did chest compressions while the other rummaged in their bag. IV supplies and discarded medication packages showed that they had already tried a round or two of resuscitation. Lily sat on the stairs, peering through the bannister with wide, scared eyes. A battery-powered lantern on the floor cast eerie shadows all across them all.

Mumbling a curse under my breath, I hurried over.

"Anna!" Mark sounded at once relieved and annoyed to see me. "Where have you been?"

"In town." Brushing him off with that vague answer, I focused my attention on the medics. "How long has she been down?"

The one doing compressions peered up at me, sweat pouring off him. "Who are you?" he asked, terse but professional.

"Dr. Hastings—I'm an ER doc, I talked to her earlier. How long?"

His partner replied, "About twenty minutes. No response to epi or amiodarone. Our monitor and AED have been dead since the blackout, so we don't know the rhythm."

Seeing my frown, Mark asked urgently, "What's he saying?"

"Her heart's stopped, and she's not responding to the medicine," I translated grimly. "What happened?" I scanned Sharon for any obvious sign of injury, but saw only a minor laceration on her forehead, oozing blood.

Mark dragged a sleeve across his own sweaty face. "I don't know. Lil and I heard a crash and found her here. She was breathing for a minute but then she stopped. I did CPR and she ran to get help." He gestured towards the young woman standing nearby, who I presumed was one of the other guests at the inn. She hugged herself, a dull, shocked look in her eyes.

I nodded, fists clenching in helpless frustration as I watched the medic push some more medication into the IV and then shift over to put in a breathing tube into her mouth. I wanted to jump in, but they had things well in-hand. "Did you check for prescriptions?" I asked, searching for a way to help. They shook their heads. "I'll do it."

Mark moved with me as I carefully edged around the medics and started up the stairs. "What can I do?" he asked with eagerness bordering on desperation.

"Check the bedroom for pill bottles. I'll check the bathroom." We split up to head into the back rooms. Lily was a silent shadow behind her father.

I was rummaging through the medicine cabinet when I heard Mark call, "I found something!" We met up in the hallway, and he presented a handful of prescription bottles.

Scanning the labels, I mumbled the meds aloud, "Thyroid. Anti-depressant. Acid reducer." The fourth bottle lacked the distinctive rattle of pills, and I realized it was empty. "Shit. She went off her beta blockers."

"What's that mean?" Mark asked. "What's a beta blocker?"

"It's a heart medication. Stopping suddenly can be bad." I grimaced. "She probably ran out and couldn't get to the pharmacy because of the blackout." Gripping the empty bottle with white-knuckled frustration, I headed back down the stairs. The medics had traded positions, but were still at it. "Anything?"

The lead medic shook his head bleakly. "Another round of meds in; still no response. About time for more epi."

I listened to the rhythmic puffing of the bag mask for a long moment, pushing oxygen into Sharon's lungs, then let out a slow sigh. "You should stop," I told them softly. "She had a heart condition and she's been down too long."

Technically I had no jurisdiction here, but the leader tilted his head up, considering my words. After a moment, he stopped doing chest compressions and rocked back on his heels. "She's right. We're not going to get her back." His partner disconnected the bag from the breathing tube, halting life support.

Mark stared at us. "Wait, that's it? You're giving up? He said it was time for more medicine—you have to give it a chance to work!" His face contorted in agony.

Even though he'd only just met Sharon, doing CPR had invested him in the outcome. "Mark, she's been unresponsive for almost half an hour." I kept my voice calm and patient—the well-practiced, gentle tone I used on grieving family members. "She hasn't responded to the CPR or the medication, and it's unlikely that more meds will help. Her brain's been deprived of oxygen for too long. At this point she has no chance for a meaningful recovery. I'm sorry, but she's gone." I looked up at the old-fashioned cuckoo clock hanging in the lobby, reciting the time out of habit even though the records didn't really matter any more. "Time of death—zero-thirty-four."

Mark shook his head, lips twisting angrily. "This is bullshit." He stalked up the stairs. "Come on, Lily."

"Mark…" I started, but he wasn't listening. He'd already crested the landing. I blew out a frustrated breath, but gave him a minute to cool off while I returned my sad gaze to Sharon.

"What should we do with her?" one of the medics asked the other. "Can't exactly call the coroner."

The lead medic said, "We'll take her to the funeral home. Find Doc Cohen. He'll know what to do. Go get the stretcher."

His partner moved off, and I crouched down to help clean up the trash and pack away the gear. When the second medic returned with the stretcher, they wrapped Sharon in a sheet and lifted her onto it. I held open the door as they pushed the stretcher out.

The other guest wandered off before I could talk to her. I was left alone in the lobby, feeling like there was something more I should be doing. I'd never watched a cardiac arrest and then just walked away before. There was always some sort of aftermath: a family to talk to; paperwork to write; an exam room to tidy up. Now there was just silence and a vague sense of loss.

What a damn waste.

CHAPTER 23

I OPENED THE DOOR TO our room, and saw Lily curled up in Mark's arms on the little daybed, tears lining her face. Mark held her gently, but I could see the line of tension in his neck and the frown he wore.

I sat down on the edge of the double bed, facing them. "The medics took Sharon to the funeral home." Mark nodded.

"Why didn't the medicine work?" Lily asked plaintively.

"Her heart was very sick," I explained gently, leaning forward. "Too sick for the medicine to help. Your dad and the paramedics worked really hard to try to help her, though." I'd meant it as a compliment, but it only made Mark's frown deepen. Lily bobbed her head.

A strained silence settled. Mark was still pissed, but he neither wanted to unload in front of Lily nor leave her side. I tried to give them space by keeping busy. Taking off my boots and socks, I frowned at the raw spots where the cuff had rubbed against my ankle. I cleaned them up, wincing at the sting of antiseptic, and applied some moleskin so they wouldn't turn into full-fledged blisters tomorrow.

Lily eventually dozed off, and Mark carefully shifted her off his lap onto the daybed. He draped a light quilt over her to stave off the cool breeze blowing through the room's sole window, then planted a gentle kiss on her temple. I couldn't help but mentally contrast his tenderness with memories of my own father, the stoic navy man.

"You all right?" I asked.

"Better than Sharon."

"Yeah." My lips thinned. "Mark, you did everything you could."

Mark's face contorted in a scowl. "I didn't know what to do. Hell, I haven't taken a first aid class since before Lily was born." He turned towards me, anger flashing in his eyes. "Where the hell were you?"

I blinked, taken aback by his vehemence. "Hey, take it easy."

'Easy' apparently wasn't on his agenda. "It's been hours, Anna. I was worried sick. You said you were just going to the pharmacy!"

"I did go to the pharmacy. I just stopped on the way back."

"Stopped for a drink, you mean. I can smell the alcohol," Mark accused.

Guilt tugged at me, but I deflected it with an indignant anger. "Yes, for a drink. What's your problem? Where I go and what I do is none of your damn business."

His scowl deepened. "It's my business when you go off partying and we're left here dealing with a fucking medical emergency on our own. You think Lily needed to see that, after everything she went through at the airport?"

Bristling, I stood up from the bed and paced over to the dresser. I wheeled back to face him. "Seriously? You're going to blame me for that? It's not my fault she died."

"It's your fault you weren't here!" Mark started to raise his voice, then caught himself and hissed, "You're the doctor. You could've done something."

"No, I couldn't have," I snapped back, crossing my arms. "She was an old lady with a heart condition who went off her medication. I asked if she was okay before I left. She knew I was going to the pharmacy, for God's sake. She could've asked for help. It's tragic, but I couldn't have done any more than you did."

"Except you're the one that should've been doing it!" Mark insisted. "We're supposed to be a team, remember? How can I depend on you if I don't even know where you are?"

"This is what you call being a team?" My voice pitched up incredulously. "You're treating me like I'm a teenager who broke curfew."

"It's not about curfew, damn it, it's about responsibility."

"Really?" I made an effort to lower my voice when I caught Lily moving her arm out of the corner of my eye. "Who exactly am I supposed to be responsible to here? Sharon? I'm not her doctor. I'm not on call. You? I left you in a nice, safe hotel for a few hours and you're acting like I ditched you on the side of the road or something."

"Anna, don't you get it? There is no safety net any more. Our whole society is teetering on the razor's edge of collapse, and it's only going to get worse. If we're going to be traveling together, our lives are going to be in each others' hands. My *daughter's* life is going to be in your hands." Mark jerked a finger at me. "I need to know I can trust you!"

I wanted to argue with him, but his words had knocked the wind out of my anger. I paced for another few seconds, guilt surfacing. What if something had happened to one of them? What if there had been something different wrong with Sharon—something I could have treated? It didn't matter this time, but it could have. Beneath his bluster, Mark was just a worried dad under more pressure than anyone deserved.

"You're right," I said. Mark's brow creased at the unexpected reversal. Heaving a sigh, I sat down on the edge of the bed. "I'm sorry I wasn't here when you needed me."

Mark plopped down beside me, resting his arms on his knees. After a long moment, he said, "I suppose I can't really blame you for wanting a night to relax after the last few days. I just wish you'd told me first."

I appreciated the peace offering. "I've been on my own for a long time," I admitted reluctantly. "I'm not used to having anyone waiting up on me."

He slanted me a look that seemed somewhere between sympathy and pity. "You have fun, at least?"

I grimaced. "Kind of? It was weird. Going shopping. Seeing everyone just hanging out at the bar. Made me just want to jump up on the table and warn them."

"Now you know how I felt at the airport."

We lapsed into silence for a minute, but then Mark broke it by softly venturing, "I've never had someone die on me like that before."

I tilted my head to look at him. He had a pinched look around his eyes, blaming himself. I had to remind myself that Mark wasn't used to the emotional roller coaster of emergency medicine. "Mark, you started CPR; sent for help. You gave her a chance. Sometimes that's all we can do."

He met my gaze, wanting to believe, and finally gave a grateful little nod.

I clapped him on the shoulder. Weariness had crept up on me, and I stifled a yawn. "I'm going to turn in. You should try to get some sleep too."

"Yeah." He stood up. "You can have the bed; I'll roll out my sleeping bag."

I eyed the narrow gap between the bed and Lily's daybed, frowning. "Don't be silly. There's plenty of room."

"On the bed?"

The look of consternation on his face made me smile. "Yes, on the bed. Mark, we're going to be sharing a tent for the next few months. You can at least trust me to keep my hands to myself, can't you?"

That got a chuckle out of him. "Yeah. Okay. I guess I can do that."

We exchanged a smile, and I knew we'd be all right.

CHAPTER 24

WE DIDN'T LINGER AT THE inn the next morning. It felt wrong somehow, like we were no longer welcome without Sharon. It seemed surreal to think that a woman had died here last night. After a quick breakfast and checking in with the guest who had helped Mark the night before, we bid the place goodbye.

On the porch, Mark consulted his map. "So it looks like if we head further up main street, there's a road that'll take us to Route 666. We can follow it right to one of the campgrounds on the trail."

"Route 666?" I echoed incredulously, shifting the straps on my backpack. "You're kidding."

"Afraid not." Mark grinned. "Hope you aren't superstitious."

"What, with our amazing luck so far?" I deadpanned.

We set off, the morning sun still low in the horizon. Two hours later, we had still seen no sign of Route 666. We had barely seen a single soul, in fact, on the sleepy country road.

"Maybe we went the wrong way," groused a tired Lily.

Mark, like every man ever, was confident in his sense of direction. "No, this is the right road, princess. We'll hit the intersection eventually."

"But you said it wasn't far."

"We're heading in the right direction," Mark insisted. "We've got a map. We'll find it."

An hour later, though, I was starting to have my doubts that we were on the right path. Just when I was about to say something, we came to the promised intersection.

"See? I told you we'd find it," Mark gestured triumphantly toward the route sign. Lily just let out a put-upon sigh, unimpressed. Chuckling, Mark ruffled her hair. He hitched up his backpack straps before striding off down the road, oblivious to the little girl rolling her eyes at his back.

Route 666, a lonely two-lane highway with an unfortunate name, wound its way through woods and farmland. Lily had been an amazing trooper for the past two days, but by lunch time she'd hit a wall.

"Daddy, I'm tired."

Every twenty minutes or so it was something else.

"I'm hungry."

"I'm hot."

"It feels like my feet are going to *fall off*."

Mark tried to distract her as best he could with silly road-trip games like 'I spy', but Lily was having none of it. She nixed each of Mark's suggestions with increasing frustration.

"We could sing," I suggested, and immediately wondered what I was thinking. I hated to sing. Mark gave me an odd look and I just shrugged helplessly.

Lily didn't seem too keen on that idea either, though. "You don't even know any kid songs."

My eyebrows shot up in amusement. Now it was a challenge. "Hey! I was a kid once too."

"Yeah but I don't want *old* songs."

"Ouch," I said with a laugh, clapping a hand over my heart in mock-offense. "Come on, sing me one of your favorites."

Lily heaved a sigh. "Fine." She started singing, *"The snow glows white on the mountain tonight…"*

I figured *Frozen* would be a safe bet given her backpack, and she did a double take when I joined her on the second verse. I had to mumble through a few bits, not knowing all the words, but apparently I remembered enough to impress a seven-year-old. When the song was over, Lily eyed me suspiciously. "How do you know Frozen songs?"

"My nieces." My smile faltered, but I tried not to get too maudlin worrying about them. "I think they had the soundtrack on endless repeat when I visited them last time."

Lily perked up. "What are their names?" Thus began Lily's interrogation about my nieces. How old they were, what TV shows they watched, did they play with princesses or Barbies, and so on. After several 'me too's from Lily, I was starting to get the impression that she and my youngest niece would've been kindred spirits.

Lily must have gotten the same idea, for she asked, "Daddy, maybe when the airplanes are working again, Anna and her nieces can come and visit us?"

Mark shot me a somber look. "We'll see, princess. How about another song?"

"Oooh, yeah we can do the one where Anna and Elsa sing together," Lily suggested. "I'll be Elsa, of course…"

We got another half-hour or so out of the *Frozen* sing-a-long, but then it was clear to everyone that Lily had run out of gas. Lucky for us, it was about then that we spotted a sign for the campground. "We made it!" Mark tried to get Lily enthused about it, but the weary girl wasn't having any of it. She trudged along theatrically, as if her legs were weighed down by concrete boots. I paused to stare at the sign. *North Country Trail.* We were really here.

The campground sat right along a creek, and each little camping area had its own ready-made fire pit complete with an iron grill. As Mark got Lily situated and started setting up the camp, I said, "I'm going to try and set up a few traps and see if I can catch anything tonight."

Mark looked to the creek and back to me with a puzzled expression. "Why? I'm sure we can get some fish."

"All the more reason to practice now, since we're not going to starve if I screw it up." I transferred my survival book and a few other odds and ends into my daypack.

Mark frowned, but didn't argue with me. "Take the rifle, at least. In case you run into anything bigger than a squirrel."

My eyebrow raised at his concern, but it wasn't a bad idea. I picked up the rifle and Mark fished out a handful of bullets from the box in his backpack. "I won't go far," I promised.

I headed out of earshot just as Lily started peppering Mark with questions about what sorts of bigger animals he was worried about. "Are there bears in these woods? Maybe I should have gotten a bow. Oooh, then I could be like Merida."

Smiling to myself, I followed the creek away from the campground. The forest grew thicker, not a building in sight on either side of the creek. I tried to look for game trails like the guide book suggested, but either there weren't any around here or I wasn't looking in the right places. Eventually I gave up and just decided to put some traps in random spots near the creek. Even rabbits needed to drink, right?

The first trap I tried was a disaster. I couldn't get the sticks to balance right, and one of my attempts ended with the deadfall rock falling on my hand. "Shit!" Shaking out my stinging fingers, I sighed and tried again. It still fell, but at least this time I kept my hand out of the way. After a few more failures, I switched to one of the other styles of traps. That one had fewer sticks involved, and after a bit of fiddling I managed to get the rock balanced properly over the bait stick.

Grinning at my success, I got up to find another spot and try it again. As I moved, though, the sticks gave way and the rock fell. I sighed again and crouched back down to examine the trap, trying to work out where I'd gone wrong.

This was going to be a long trip.

CHAPTER 25

THE RAIN STARTED BEFORE DAWN, and by breakfast the ground around the tent was a swamp. Mark and I both ended up mud-splattered and soaked as we disassembled the tent and put away the equipment. "We should have stolen better rain gear," I snarked as a gust of wind blew my hood down for the fourth time in as many minutes. The thin piece-of-junk poncho—contrary to the picture on the package—lacked drawstrings to pull the hood tight. I pushed a wet strand of hair out of my soaked face and tugged the hood up once more.

Once everything was packed up, I sloshed my way along the trail while listening to Mark and Lily debate the practicalities of umbrellas in the forest.

"I thought you liked playing in the rain," I pointed out, smiling at her persistent problem-solving.

"Yeah, but not, like, for the *whole day*," Lily countered.

I had to give her that one.

The clouds finally broke after a few hours, but the persistent humidity just made it feel like we were in a sauna instead of a shower. A creek—swollen by the recent rains—paralleled the muddy trail. Blue stripes of paint on the tree trunks assured us we were on the right path.

The trail wound its way up a ridge, and we soon found ourselves navigating through a maze of rock formations. Giant boulders littered the ground between rock walls two-stories tall. "Careful, it's slippery," Mark warned from his position in the lead as he climbed over one of the boulders.

The path opened to a clearing, and we decided to camp there for the night. Exhausted after our second almost-full day of walking, we settled down for a quiet supper of the fish Mark had caught. *Only three more months to go!*

With storm clouds still threatening, we all decided to sleep in the tent. Though it was advertised as a "3-person tent", apparently that meant "three people who really like each other and don't mind sleeping shoulder to shoulder." At least none of us were claustrophobic.

The clouds opened up again just after it got dark, and I got soaked venturing out to re-tie one of the rain flaps that blew loose in the howling winds. Lightning lit up the dark sky. With the thick clouds, there was no sign of the Northern Lights we'd seen for the past couple evenings. Lily gave a yelp at a nearby clap of thunder. "It's all right, princess," I heard Mark consoling her as I ducked back into the tent.

We sat in the tent, a small solar lantern providing scant illumination, and listened to the storm rage outside. Even in the dim light, I could see Lily's white face as she clung to Mark's side, his arm around her protectively. We had arranged the sleeping bags so that she was in the middle, bracketed by the two of us. The sides of the tent buckled in and out under the force of the winds. "Will our tent blow away?" Lily asked plaintively.

"No, no, we're safe here," I assured her. "I put the stakes in really well." Or so I hoped, glancing up at the tent roof. The winds increased, buffeting the tent enough that I started worrying about the tent stakes, remembering a safety alert a year or so back about one of those giant bounce houses being blown away in a gust. Sleep did not come easily for any of us.

The next day at lunch, Lily plopped down on a tree stump and complained, "I don't want to camp any more. Can't we go back to Grammy and Pappy's?" When Mark reminded her that they'd left as well, she gave a put-upon harrumph. "Well then we can go to Aunt Ruth's."

"We can't, princess. We need to go find Mommy."

"I don't care! We should just go to the farm and wait for her."

"Lily…" Mark sighed, sparing me a brief glance before heading over to crouch down by the girl. "We have to go."

"No! I don't want to! Camping is stupid!"

"I'm going to go get some water," I said awkwardly. Mark gave me an absent nod. I collected the water jug and rifle and walked off, hearing the argument recede as I moved away.

I took my time down at the stream, intent on giving them some privacy. Poor Lily had been through a lot in a short amount of time. I wished for something I could do to make it easier for her.

I heard a crackling in the underbrush across the stream. I tensed and scanned the woods. It was just a doe grazing on some bushes, maybe thirty yards away. The deer, probably accustomed to hikers, seemed untroubled by my presence. Moving slowly so as not to spook it, I unslung the rifle and worked the bolt to load a bullet. The deer looked my way at the strange sound, and I felt a pang of guilt. I'd fired a rifle at the target range more times than I could count, but I'd never shot a living creature before.

Sorry, but we need to eat. I pulled the trigger, and the deer dropped.

Getting it back to camp was a challenge. That thing was heavier than it looked, and I slipped a dozen times trying to get traction on the muddy ground. With shins and ego bruised, I made it about halfway back to the camp before Mark and Lily found me.

"You all right?" Mark called as he approached, concern written all over his face. "We heard the shot."

"Yeah, just a deer."

Mark came over and held out his hand to take the rope. "Nice."

Lily immediately came over to see, and her face crumpled. "Nooooo. Why did you have to kill a mommy deer? She maybe had baby deers."

"It's kind of late in the season for fawns," I assured her.

Mark chimed in, "We're going to need the meat, Lil."

That didn't seem to help. "Why couldn't we just eat fish?"

Mark scoffed. "You were just complaining about the fish yesterday."

Lily frowned, her lips turning down in an impressive pout. "Well I like it more than I like eating a deer." She crossed her arms and started stomping back to camp.

I fell into step beside Mark as he followed, deer in tow. "That went over well."

"It's rough when your heroine kills Bambi's mom," Mark replied with a teasing grin.

I elbowed him in the arm gently, then said more seriously, "She's having a rough day, huh."

"She's just rattled. Doesn't like thunderstorms. She'll be all right."

It wasn't clear who he was trying to convince more—me or him, but I chimed in supportively, "Yeah, I'm sure she will." We got back to camp and Mark left the deer a good distance from the tent. I watched him untie the rope and said, "Hope you know how to clean one of those. I haven't gotten that far in the guide book yet."

The surprised look on his face was priceless. "Me?"

I offered him a sunny smile. "Well that was the deal, right? You catch something, I cook it, and vice versa?"

He started to open his mouth, trying to find some way out of it, when Lily chimed in grumpily. "That was the deal, Daddy. And I am *not* helping."

He looked between the two of us, realized he was trapped, and then raised his hands in a gesture of surrender. "That was the deal," he admitted with a resigned grin. "Guess I'd better get started." I grinned too and left him to it.

CHAPTER 26

A FEW DAYS LATER, WE came to a clearing near a stream. The water babbled peacefully along and provided a pleasant counterpoint to the occasional rustle of leaves or bird chirping. "Why don't we camp here?"

"Finally," Lily grumped with a sigh more befitting a teenager than a second-grader.

Smirking, I unbuckled my backpack and dumped it on the ground. "No complaints from me." I plopped down on the scrubby grass and then—after a moment's consideration—flopped onto my back with a soft 'oof'. "Man, if I wasn't starving, I could just fall asleep right here."

Even limited to Lily's pace, the first couple days of solid hiking had been brutal. We climbed over fallen trees where the storm had blown through, then up and down huge hills. My whole body ached, hell-bent on reminding me just how many muscle groups were involved in cross-country walking. And then there were the blisters. No amount of moleskin padding or even alternating between hiking boots and tennis shoes seemed to stop them. Every step tortured the raw spots like sandpaper on an open wound. Now that we'd stopped for the day, I couldn't wait to take my boots off and just let my feet breathe.

"I'll see if I can catch some fish tonight," Mark said, nodding towards the creek. We'd been fortunate that the trail crossed or paralleled so many small streams.

"Don't we still have deer meat left?" Lily asked. We'd spent the better part of a day drying the meat like my guidebook described and turning it into jerky so it would last longer.

Mark gave her a puzzled look. "I thought you didn't like the venison?"

She shrugged. "It tastes weird. But I like it better than fish." At least she'd stopped holding a grudge over me shooting the deer. Hunger over principles, I guess. Distracted by a bush, she called over, "Hey Anna—look. Are these blackberries?"

Holding in a sigh, I dragged myself back to my feet and came over to the bush she was peering at. "Yeah, looks like. Let's check the book to be sure—and you can tick it off as well."

It was a game we'd started—a sort of scavenger hunt to practice our plant identification skills. Once Lily had resigned herself to the idea that Mark wasn't going to give in to her demands to turn back to her grandparents, her attitude shifted. Every animal we saw, every cool-looking flower or misshapen tree was a new discovery on her epic camping adventure. Mark bore the brunt of her occasional bad moods, while I got to be the "fun aunt"—all the joys of interacting with a kid without needing to be the one nagging at them to brush their teeth or mind their manners.

Lily took the edible plants book from her backpack and flipped through the pages. "Here it is—blackberries!" she announced triumphantly once she'd found the right page. She started reading through the entry, carefully sounding out the words with a novice reader's diligent focus. "Blackberries are an agg… agger… what's that say?"

Mark limped across the clearing in my peripheral vision. He found a log to sit on and winced.

"Aggregate," I answered Lily, distracted. "Because it's a group of all those little bumpy things." I pointed to the little bumps on the berries, forgetting the technical term. "Why don't you pick some, and we'll give them a try. Watch out for the thorns."

Leaving her to the berries, I came over to where Mark was sitting. "You okay?"

"Yeah. This damn blister's killing me, though." He perched the offending foot onto his knee and started unlacing his boot.

"Let me see." Once he'd gotten the boot and sock off, I crouched, turning the foot to get a better view. At the base of his heel was an ugly blister. The skin was tearing off half of it, while the other half still sported a painful, fluid-filled sac. "Looks like it's getting infected. I should drain it before it gets worse." I dragged over my backpack and got out my medical kit.

"Greaaaat," Mark mumbled. I cleaned gently around the injured site with soap and water. He sucked in a wince but didn't complain.

Lily looked over from the berries, squinting as I held a sewing needle in the flame from my lighter. "Are you going to poke him with that? Like a shot?" When I nodded, her nose wrinkled and she suddenly lost interest. "I don't like shots."

I slanted a smile her way. "Nobody likes shots, but they're still important. This'll pinch a bit," I warned Mark, and then I lanced the blister.

Mark grimaced at the yellowish pus draining out. "Ugh. That's nasty."

I pressed on the edge to get as much of the gunk out as possible. "This? This is nothing."

He snorted. "I suppose it's all relative."

"What's the ickiest thing you've ever seen?" Lily asked, guardedly curious.

I looked between the two of them, arching my eyebrows. I really didn't think a seven-year-old needed to hear about gangrene or mangled limbs from shrapnel injuries, so I settled for a more kid-friendly answer. "Parasites." Off her blank look, I clarified. "Worms that live inside people. They creep me out."

"Worms? In people? Eeew." She made a face and waved a hand emphatically. "I don't even want to know."

"No, you really don't." Letting out a soft chuckle, I put some antibiotic cream and a fresh dressing on the blister. As I taped it down, I told Mark, "That'll help. Try to keep it clean so the infection doesn't get worse."

"Sure. Thanks. It feels better already." As I put the supplies away, he ventured, "Can I ask you something? How'd you end up in Africa? What—did you just wake up one day and decide to go work in a refugee camp?"

"No... not quite," I said, smiling. "My sister went to Afghanistan after 9/11, and I got kind of obsessed with the news over there. That's when I first read about MSF, and I don't know—it just grabbed me. Traveling around the world, making a difference... I guess it seemed like a grand adventure." I snorted softly at my idealism back then.

"So you went to Afghanistan?"

"Actually, no. I mean, I tried, but I didn't have enough experience to make the cut. But a couple years later, there was that big earthquake in Haiti and they were pretty desperate for docs. I guess my name was still in their system and they called me. That ended up being my first mission."

He nodded, listening with interest. "So Haiti. Sudan. That other place in Africa... I forget its name."

"CAR. Central African Republic."

"CAR, right. That's a lot of time away from home. Did you have to get a new job every time you came back?"

"Sometimes. This last time my boss got pissed when I asked for another leave of absence." My mouth twisted in a scowl, remembering the bitter argument that had burned bridges at my old hospital.

"I don't give a damn about what's going on in Africa. We hired you to work here, Doctor Hastings, and I'm tired of having this department short-staffed while you're off playing hero in some third-world shithole."

"Well then you can find someone else who doesn't give a damn. I quit."

Or something like that. I may also have called him an arrogant, racist son of a bitch on my way out. Omitting those minor details, I shrugged and told Mark, "Anyway, my contract with MSF was up and I didn't want to go right back into another mission so… here I am."

"Makes sense." He watched me with open curiosity. "What was it like over there?"

I shifted uncomfortably, slanting a glance to Lily. It was a question I got asked a lot, but not one I had a good answer for. What could I say about the atrocities I had seen? The displaced persons camp where thirty thousand refugees lived in squalor? Watching scores of children die from measles and malaria despite our best efforts? The brutal ethnic violence—massacres, mutilations, entire villages burned to the ground? Our mobile clinics being stopped and threatened by armed gunmen? The mortar shell that hit right outside our hospital doors?

I finally offered him a strained smile, and focused on the positive instead. "Hard, but worth it. The people there are wonderful. And I mean… I can save lives in a hospital here. But over there…" Lacking words to sum it up, I fell back to stories instead. "One time, we saved a whole village from a cholera outbreak. Another time we did this vaccination campaign—gave shots to hundreds of kids to protect them from diseases we don't even hear about in the States."

"Must have been pretty intense, though," Mark said, reading between the lines of what I hadn't said. He watched my face with a quiet sympathy.

"Yeah. I was maybe getting a little burned out," I admitted with a self-conscious chuckle, rubbing my eyebrow. *A lot burned out,* more like it. Even the head of mission had seen it, and encouraged me to take a break. "So I figured I'd work in the States for a bit. Come back to someplace where life was normal for a while."

"Little did you know, huh?" He offered a sad smile at the irony.

"Yeah. Little did I know."

CHAPTER 27

AS THE SECOND WEEK WORE on, things got easier. The blisters began to heal, and my muscles no longer protested quite as much. Even Lily built up an impressive tolerance to hiking for the better part of the day—the boundless energy of youth went a long way, I guess.

We made our way through groves of majestic, centuries-old trees; past mountain laurels and rhododendrons in full bloom. The light filtered down through the tall trees, while exotic-sounding bird calls echoed through the canopy. We were very much in the wilderness here, and I could see why the place had been registered as a national landmark. After the hectic pressure of life in a conflict zone, maybe this was just what I needed. I could let my mind wander and focus on nothing more than putting one foot in front of the other. Sometimes it felt like we were the only people in the world. It was relaxing—just as long as I didn't spend too much time thinking about why we were out here in the first place, or what kind of world we'd return to on the other side of the forest.

Mark and I fell into a routine of sharing camp chores—cooking, cleaning up, gathering water, putting up and taking down the tent—and spent a good portion of every day just chatting. It didn't take us long to discover some shared interests, and we talked at length about random things like history and movies. Mark chuckled at me when I admitted to my vice of medical TV dramas. "I can't believe you watch those. I've seen a few and they seem pretty over-the-top."

"Well the medicine is ridiculous, of course, but it's still kind of fun. Guilty pleasure, I guess." I stepped over a log and thought about just what it was I liked about them. "It is interesting to see how Hollywood sees doctors. The glamorized version of what we do."

That afternoon, we had to slog up a particularly brutal hill, crawling on hands and knees in a few places over huge rocks that were placed like stairs. The reward at the top, though, was a breathtaking view of a forested valley. The tops of lush green trees stretched out before us, like a carpet running all the way to another bank of hills in the distance. I stood there while we took a brief breather, drinking in the beauty and chugging some water.

"Hard to believe there's still so much unspoiled land here," I said.

Lily wasn't as impressed. "I bet there are a lot of wild animals living down there. Probably even some bears." She chewed her lip.

Mark assured her, "Bears won't bother us unless we bother them."

Or unless they smelled the meat in our packs. I bit my tongue, not seeing any reason to fuel the poor girl's nightmares.

Mark frowned at the clouds in the distance to the west, dotted with flashes of lightning. Shielding his eyes with one hand, he stared at it. "Looks like there's a storm brewing."

Chewing her lip, Lily followed his gaze. "Do you think it'll be a big storm like the last one?"

"Nah, I don't think so, princess. It might even miss us completely. It's still pretty far away." Mark began ushering her back to the trail, musing aloud, "Times like these I miss my weather app."

"Well, this past week it would've been a broken record," I said dryly. "Hot. Hot. Oppressively hot."

"Hot and raining," Mark added.

Not to be outdone, Lily chimed in, "Stupid hot." We all laughed.

Despite Mark's prediction, the storm came straight for us. We felt the shift in the air—the dropping pressure and temperature accompanied by the winds picking up—well before the rain started. There was a blissful reprieve from "stupid hot" for about an hour, but then the clouds opened up and we soon found ourselves wading through a muddy swamp.

The rain came down in sheets, a brisk wind making it almost horizontal at times. Our raincoats barely put up a fight; soon we were all soaked through. We came upon one particularly steep descent where the runoff traced down like a waterfall. Not far from the bottom of the slope, a swollen stream wound its way through the trees. My foot slipped in the mud and sent me sliding inelegantly down the slope on my back, just narrowly avoiding crashing into Mark. "You all right?" he called. He carefully picked his way down, holding onto Lily's hand to keep her from wiping out as I had.

I groaned and got to my feet, shaking mud off my hands. It caked the back of my legs as well. "Yeah, I'm fine." I tried to wipe my hands on my pants, but only succeeded in smearing the mud around.

Lily came over, chuckling. "You look like a mud monster."

I made a mock-roaring sound, waving my muddy hands at her like Frankenstein's mud-monster.

"Eeew! Stay away!" Lily made a face, squealing, and then giggled.

Mark stepped closer to the stream. "I think we were supposed to ford here." He studied the other side, then pointed. "Yeah. I see the blazes on the other side." If I squinted through the rain hard enough, I also could see a blue marker painted on a tree on the other side, indicating the trail route. One look at the stream, though, told me that fording it was out of the question.

"No way are we getting across that until the rain stops." The churning water broke over rocks, leaving white tips in its wake.

"Yeah," Mark agreed glumly. "Guess we're camping here for the night. We should…"

Whatever he was about to suggest died on his lips as we heard a dull rumbling sound. Mark titled his head, perplexed. "What the hell is that? An earthquake?"

Lily's eyes boggled wide and she stepped close to me, clinging to my arm. The mud was forgotten. I patted her arm, shaking my head. "No, not an earthquake." I'd been in one of those before.

Mark looked from left to right along the stream, and his eyes locked on the upstream side. A slight slope and some trees in the way kept me from seeing what he was seeing, but I did see the shift in his bearing. His whole body tensed, and his mouth grew slack for an instant. He roared, "Get back up the hill!"

I didn't know what had spooked him, but my stomach lurched at the look on his face. I didn't hesitate. Pulling Lily by the hand, I started running for the slope. I'd barely made it five steps, though, before a wall of water rolled through the tree line, heading right for us.

CHAPTER 28

LILY SCREAMED. I HAD JUST enough time to scoop her up and pull her to my chest before the wall of water hit us. I'd been knocked flat by ocean waves countless times before, but this was different. The wave hit low, sweeping my legs out from under me and then carrying us downstream. The shoreline zoomed by, branches and debris swirling all around us.

"Daddy!" Lily cried, squirming in search of Mark. I tightened my grip, fearful of seeing her swept away by the churning torrent of water. I couldn't see him either. Hopefully he was just upstream from us, in my blind spot.

The creek didn't seem that deep; I felt my leg smack against the rocky creek bed a few times. I tried to stand up, but I couldn't get my feet planted. The fast-moving current just bowled me right over every time. Once, we went under and came up sputtering. I worried that our backpacks would sink us, but Lily's was small and mine surprisingly buoyant.

Over the roaring of the creek, I heard Lily cry out in terror. It was a heart-wrenching sound, but at least it told me she wasn't drowning. I scanned the shore for something that we might be able to grab onto, but nothing came within reach.

"Anna!" Lily's shrill cry caused me to snap my eyes forward. A tree had fallen across the stream, and we hurtled towards it.

"Hold on!" Her arms wrapped around my neck so tightly it almost choked me.

When we were nearly upon the tree, I twisted my body sideways, trying to shield Lily from the impact. We struck the trunk with a bone-rattling crash that robbed my lungs of breath. The stream immediately tried to yank us under the tree, but I flailed out with one arm and managed to loop it around a thick branch. For a minute I just hung there—one arm on the branch and the other around Lily, catching my breath while being pelted by loose branches and God-knew-what-else going past us in the water. Lily clung to me, whimpering quietly in a safe little bubble between me and the tree trunk.

I didn't fool myself into thinking we'd be okay here for long. My arm was already shaking under the strain of holding us back against the current. And at any moment the water could rise further and swamp the tree, or something bigger could come downstream and hit us. I tried to pull us up, but we barely budged an inch. Between Lily and my backpack, it was like trying to do a one-handed pull-up with twice my body weight. Not happening. I couldn't even unbuckle and shrug out of the pack without risking Lily.

"Lily, listen—look at me." Wide hazel eyes found mine. "I need you to hold on tight, okay?" She bobbed her head frantically. "I'm going to get us out, but I need both hands."

"No!" She tightened her grip in panic. "Don't let go! I'll fall."

I grimaced at the pressure on my neck. "I won't let you fall. I promise. Just hold on." Tentatively I stretched out my arm, ready to jerk it back to her if I had to. My fingers touched another branch, but just when I got a solid grip it snapped off in my hand, sending me flailing backward against the log. Lily cried out and her grip loosened. My heart skipped a beat, but I grabbed her before she slipped. She wailed in my ear, full-on crying now.

"It's okay. It's okay. I've got you," I assured her breathlessly.

I swung my leg up out of the water, trying to get a foot on the splintered remnants of the branch that had broken off. Once, twice, three times I tried, but my boot kept slipping off the narrow elbow whenever I tried to put weight on it. I wanted to scream in frustration.

"Lily! Lily! Anna!" We both heard Mark's frantic searching. It came from behind us, upstream on the shore.

"DADDY!" Lily screamed back. "Daddy help!"

"Over here!" I chimed in for good measure. I'd never been so glad to hear someone's voice.

Mark's eyes widened when he saw us. "Hang on, I'm coming!"

Dumping his pack and rifle, Mark bounded over the tree roots and then crawled across the log on hands and knees. The rain continued to pour down, stinging my face as I tried to look up at him. Bracing himself with a leg on either side of the log, he reached down for Lily. "Give me your hands, Lil." The stranglehold on my neck loosened as Lily stretched her arms up toward her father. He pulled her up as if she weighed nothing, cradling her protectively against his chest. "I'll be right back," he promised me as he twisted around. With Lily clinging under him like a baby monkey, he crawled back to the edge of the log and lowered her carefully to solid ground. He pointed to a rise farther back from the pull of the raging stream, his words lost to the rush of the water in my ears. Still white-faced, Lily nodded and retreated.

Mark hurried back to the middle of the log. "I'll pull you up!" he called. I might have been able to do it myself without Lily's added weight, but my hand had started cramping and my arms felt like jello. I didn't dare risk it. I just clung to the fallen tree for dear life until Mark's strong hand clamped around my wrist and yanked me half out of the water. From there, I was able to get a foothold and help him. I didn't even care that his hands ended up in a few awkward places as he hauled me up onto the slippery log. "Keep going—I'm right behind you." Mark's calm confidence spurred me on, and I made my way across the log on hands and knees.

There I collapsed, sinking down to my knees in the mud while struggling to catch my breath. "Little further," he urged, glancing back at the stream. "We'll be safe up on the rise there. Come on, lean on me." He quickly slung his own gear back over one shoulder and then pulled me to my feet.

Once he'd made sure I reached the top of the slope safely, he rushed over to Lily and engulfed her in a fierce hug. I fumbled with the chest strap of my backpack, which felt like it had added an extra twenty pounds of water weight. I leaned forward, hands on knees, and tried to calm my ragged breathing.

Mark pulled back and looked Lily up and down. "Are you okay, baby? Are you hurt anywhere?" He gently smoothed the wet hair back away from her face. Lily gave a barely-perceptible shake of her head. Letting out a breath, Mark's face flooded with relief.

He glanced my way, then shuffled over with one arm outstretched. The gesture surprised me, but not in a bad way. He pulled me into a friendly, comfortable embrace, and I felt some of the tension melt away as I joined in the three-way hug. Mark didn't say anything, but he didn't have to. I'd seen the gratitude written all over his face.

We'd made it. We were really okay.

But a nagging voice in the back of my head couldn't help but wonder: *for how long*.

CHAPTER 29

IT WASN'T UNTIL LATER, WHILE helping Mark set up the tent, that I realized I was hurt. A nagging twinge in my knee developed into a full-blown throbbing. My ribs ached where I'd hit the log, and I could feel the sting from a dozen scrapes and bruises from being dragged along the creek bed. I hobbled around as we set up camp.

Later, when Mark was out getting water, I slipped into some dry shorts and took stock of my injured knee. Lily scooted over to me with her stuffed cat in tow. "Does it hurt a lot?" she asked.

"Nah, it's not too bad," I assured her. "Just bruised." Tilting my head, I studied her somber face. I know Mark had already checked her over, but still I said, "What about you? Are you okay?" She bobbed her head silently, but I wasn't convinced. In a gentler tone, I asked, "I don't know about you, but I was pretty scared out there."

Wide hazel eyes tilted up at me, both relieved and surprised. "You were?"

"Totally. Grown-ups get scared too, you know. We just usually don't like to admit it. Especially the boys." I smiled and jerked my head in the direction Mark had gone. That got a conspiratorial little grin from her. "I think you've been really brave." Her smile widened the tiniest bit, and that brought a smile to my lips as well. "You think you could help me clean up the rest of these scrapes?"

Lily proved to be an able medic, dabbing peroxide on the small cuts and affixing Band-Aids on a couple of the larger ones. As she worked, I said, "Nice job. I'll have to get you to be my assistant more often."

Lily puffed up proudly. "I want to be a vet when I grow up." She got the last bandage into place and declared, "There. All better." I smiled, but I could see her expression turning serious once more. "Anna?"

"Hmm?"

"I'm glad you came with us." She hugged me tightly.

I patted the back of her head, smiling even as sore ribs protested the squeeze. "I am, too."

That evening, Lily slept in her spot in the middle of the tent and Mark shuffled around her feet to crouch next to me. "You doing all right?"

I smiled faintly. "Yeah, thanks. Wish we had some ice -" The lone chemical ice pack from my first aid kit had worn off hours ago. "But I'll manage. How about you?"

He nodded, but his eyes had a worried cast when they drifted over to Lily. "Yeah, I'm fine. Listen, I, uh… I wanted to thank you. If you hadn't been there to grab Lily…" He wrung his hands together, his face growing haunted at the thought of what might have been.

"Sure. Though I should be thanking you, too, for pulling us out."

"Yeah, no problem." Mark shrugged off the thanks, a preoccupied frown lingering. "She's been through a lot."

"She's all right. Kids are resilient." He flashed a weak smile. A few seconds ticked by in silence, and then I ventured, "You know, it's not too late to turn back."

"Back?" He pulled his gaze off Lily, brows knitted.

"To the last town. Or to your in-laws. Ruth's farm?"

Mark shook his head, his lips drawing together in a stubborn frown. "No. I'm not giving up. Lauren's waiting for us."

I started to rub my face in frustration, but stopped when a twinge in my arm reminded me of the stitches there. "Mark," I said as gently as I could. "She might not be." He scowled, but I pressed on. "Look, I know that you want to have hope, and that's great, but the truth is that you don't know where she is. We could go all that way and never find her."

Working his jaw, he bit back whatever his initial retort was going to be. After a pause, he said, "She's out there *somewhere*. You want me to pretend that she isn't?"

"No, I want you to be realistic. We all almost died today, Mark. Could you just consider for one second that maybe this wasn't such a great idea?"

He shook his head, his expression darkening. There was a long pause before he spoke again. "Anna, I'm sorry you got hurt, and I'm grateful to you for saving Lily. But I'm not going to let a blackout, or a storm, or a flood, or *anything* stop me from getting my family back together." He waved his hand with a gesture of finality, utter conviction in his tone. "If you want to turn back, nobody's stopping you."

He started crawling back around to the opposite side of the tent, the discussion over in his mind. My eyes tracked him, stewing in silent irritation.

We both knew I wasn't going to turn back and leave them.

CHAPTER 30

IT TOOK TWO DAYS FOR the waters to recede enough for us to tackle the stream, and then we were on our way once more. Further along the trail, an overlook showed us how a sharp horseshoe-shaped bend in the stream had put us in the worst possible position when the banks overflowed. Counting our blessings, we left the old-growth forest behind and entered a rockier part of the trail that had more elevation changes than a roller coaster.

Though the 'up' parts were grueling in their own way, the downward slopes took a toll on my still-healing knee. I muddled through with an elastic bandage and some ibuprofen, but neither could keep the constant ache at bay. Mark seemed pretty understanding, slowing his stride and picking up more than his share of chores—gathering water, collecting firewood, and the like. Even so, I had the nagging suspicion that he was frustrated by our slow pace.

During a respite from the sweltering heat of the afternoon, Mark ventured out hunting while Lily and I set up camp. We both jerked in surprise when we heard the gunshot some time later.

"I hope he didn't shoot anything cute," Lily mumbled, still not entirely sold on the whole hunting thing.

I smiled at her over the fire pit we were constructing, laying another rock into place. "I hope he got a big buck. We'll have jerky for days."

Mark didn't have a buck, or a deer at all. He returned to camp grim-faced, with a bushy-tailed lump hanging from a string. He tied the squirrel—or what was left of it—to a branch. I peered at the thing, chuckling. "Damn. What did you use on it—a cannon?" Lily wrinkled her nose at the mess and walked away.

Mark just scowled at our reaction. "You try hitting that tiny little head at thirty yards." He sat down near the fire pit, scrubbing a hand through his short hair. "Hope you can get at least a little meat off of it." My brows lifted in a dubious look. He frowned and said, "Fish still aren't biting."

I frowned, too. Fish had been a staple of our meals, but the flood had disrupted that supply. We could still see fish in the streams, but they didn't take Mark's bait. The jerky from our first deer had almost run out. We still had some store-bought (well, store-pillaged) trail mix and meal bars, but we were burning through those faster than expected. Our plan to live off the land wasn't working out so great.

"I'll try setting some traps again," I said, dragging myself to my feet. I'd slacked off on the so-far-fruitless endeavor when I hurt my knee.

"Don't think that's going to get you out of skinning that squirrel." The levity didn't quite reach his eyes, and I realized he was more worried than he let on.

I didn't catch anything with the traps that first night, or the second, or the third. Each morning I felt a jolt of anticipation as I looped around the forest, only to be disappointed that the little critters had once again eluded me. I was beginning to despair of it ever working.

As the third week of our journey wore on, our food reserves dwindled almost as fast as my stock of painkillers. Mark had spotted a deer once but missed the shot. Lily and I spotted a second buck while foraging for blueberries, but I didn't get the rifle ready before something spooked it and sent it bounding off through the woods.

"It's maddening," I complained to Mark later that night. "We're surrounded by a whole damn forest full of wildlife, and we can't get enough to eat."

Mark nodded in sympathy. "At least you found some berries," he observed, dumping a few from his cupped hand into his mouth.

"Yeah," I scoffed. "Eat up."

It wasn't that we were starving, exactly. We did have some food. But nuts, berries, wild greens salad and a few squirrels just didn't provide enough calories for a full day of hiking over hills and manual labor. Mark didn't have an abundance of fat to burn in the first place, but I could see him getting leaner as the days wore on. I had to tighten the belt on my own jeans, losing weight that I didn't really have to spare. I imagined the familiar echo of my mother's voice telling me I was too skinny. Lily fared the best; we both made sure of that. She remained blissfully ignorant of our food situation, while Mark and I went to bed with stomachs rumbling in protest. "What did you find?" became a loaded question when one of us came back from foraging, tinged with hope and inevitably disappointment.

One evening, while laying traps, I spotted a cluster of little claw prints in the mud. A swath of grass nearby that had been worn down like a tiny path. Realizing that this must be one of the game trails my guidebook talked about, I crouched down and set up a couple traps along its length.

I whooped in triumph when I found two traps triggered the next morning. The first one was empty, but under the second rock I found a pancaked chipmunk.

Mark didn't seem quite as thrilled with my success, holding up the chipmunk with a dubious squint when I brought it back to camp.

"What is this supposed to be—hors d'oeuvres? You'd get more meat off a chicken wing."

I shoved his arm lightly. "I don't get to pick what animals go into my trap any more than you do your fishing hook."

He chuckled. "Speaking of which…"

Lily emerged from the tent, cutting him off. "Anna, guess what. I caught a fish! It was really big. Come see!" Her exuberance was adorable. Mark and I exchanged a smile, and then I let Lily lead me off by the hand to show me her catch.

We continued on the next day, following the blue blazes toward a reservoir that had loomed large on our map for weeks. It marked the last leg of our journey in Pennsylvania. "The fishing should be better there," Mark reasoned. "If we're lucky, maybe we can find a boat and zip across; cut twenty, thirty miles off the trip." It didn't sound like much—thirty miles. Before the blackout, we could've hopped in a car and made that in half an hour. Now, though, that distance represented several days of slogging through the forest.

The trail brought us to a ridge overlooking the vast man-made lake. It should have been a picturesque view: the morning sun glistening off the sea of blue, with lush hills as a backdrop. Instead we stared, dumbfounded.

Lily was the first to speak. "I thought you said there would be a big lake there, Daddy?"

"There was." Mark shook his head, unable to comprehend what we were looking at. The lake was just a giant mud flat, as if someone had drained a bathtub. A stream through the center and puddles here and there were all that remained.

"My God. What happened here?" Freakish weather and a lack of electricity were one thing, but what could have caused an entire lake to vanish?

"The dam," Mark breathed in horrified realization. I shook my head, not following. He pointed west. "The reservoir formed when they dammed up the river. With all the rain we had, and no power to operate the dam's flood controls…the dam must have failed." I sucked in a breath, thinking of all the dams we'd crossed on the way up here and what that meant for the people downstream.

"Is that what caused the big flood we saw?" Lily wondered in a hushed voice.

Mark shook his head. "No, princess. The flood would've gone that way. Down towards the city."

"The city?" Lily looked up at him, suddenly wide-eyed. "Do you think Grammy and Pappy are okay?"

Mark patted her shoulders. "I'm sure they're fine. Aunt Ruth's farm is nowhere near the river."

If only we could say the same for everyone else in the flood's path.

The trail paralleled the reservoir for several days, casting a pall over the journey with its constant reminder of a tragedy unseen. For almost a month it had just been the three of us, safe in our little bubble in the forest. We'd faced our share of hardships, but now I was preoccupied thinking about those who hadn't been so fortunate.

One afternoon, Lily and I ventured out to see if we could find some fruit and set the traps. We paused to refill our water bottles at a small stream paralleling the reservoir. Kneeling by the stream, I scooped up some water with cupped hands and splashed it on my face and neck. The cool water proved a welcome respite from the sticky heat.

"Awww, hi there," cooed Lily happily.

Who the hell was she talking to? With a jolt, I realized that she was no longer right beside me. My head snapped around. Lily had wandered twenty feet or so upstream, crouching to say hello to a Golden Retriever. The dog looked like it had been through a war, its tan fur matted and muddy.

"Lily, no!" Visions of dog maulings and rabies set off warning bells in my head. She jumped at the tone in my voice, jerking her hand back. The dog's ears pulled back as well, his head dipping as if I'd scolded him.

"What's the matter?" Lily asked.

"Get back here. Slowly so you don't spook him. Stray dogs can be dangerous."

To my dismay, Lily didn't immediately move. "He's not dangerous. Look, his tail's wagging. He's friendly, see?" Before I could reach her to stop her, she stretched her hand out and petted the dog's scraggly head. His ears perked back up, his tail kicking up a notch with its wagging. By the time I came up beside her, he'd thrown himself on the ground and exposed his belly for her to pet.

Okay, so maybe he wasn't a vicious beast. That didn't do much to temper my irritation. "He could have bitten you, Lil," I admonished her. "You can't just go up to strange animals like that."

"Sorry," she said, but the contrition in her voice was at odds with the fact that she was still rubbing his tummy. His ribs were visible, and there was a scabbed-over gash on his left flank. "I think he's lost. See— he has a collar."

I twisted the collar to see his identification, relieved to find a current rabies tag attached. "Bear," I read the name tag aloud. That was an ironic name if ever I heard one. On the back side was his owner's address—somewhere in Bradford, Pennsylvania—and a now-useless phone number. The dog twisted his head, looking up at me with mournful brown eyes, and I knew what was coming next.

"Can we keep him?"

I scratched under his chin, resolve weakening. He'd obviously been on his own for a while, and our chances of finding his owner were slim to none. Rummaging in my belt pouch, I dug out a strip of jerky. Bear gobbled it out of my hand, his tail thumping fiercely against the ground. "We'll have to talk to your dad about it. Let's get him cleaned up a bit first, though." I figured it would be a good test of his temperament to see if he'd let me give him a bath in the stream.

"Okay!" Lily beamed, recognizing that for the victory it was. "Come on, Bear!" She got up, clapping her hands on her knees to get the dog's attention as she stepped out into the calf-deep water. Bear bounded up happily, splashing in after her.

I sighed and chuckled. Mark didn't have a chance.

CHAPTER 31

"YOU TOLD HER SHE COULD keep it?" Mark stared at me in incredulous irritation. Apparently he wasn't much of a dog person.

"No, I told her she had to talk to you. Telling a kid they can't have a dog is definitely a 'Dad Job'." I looked over to the porch, where Lily was crouched and chattering at a still-damp Bear. "Good luck with that."

Mark gave the sigh of a man who knew he'd already lost. "Maybe we can teach him to hunt," he reasoned as he wandered over to Lily and our new dog.

It turned out we didn't have to teach him anything. Maybe his prior owner had been a hunter, or he'd been on his own in the forest long enough to figure it out for himself. Either way, he swiftly displayed a talent for running down rodents and pheasants and depositing them at my feet with a proud, sappy, doggy smile. It was a nice—if gruesome—

supplement to our fishing and hunting. Lily and Bear became inseparable, and I loved to see her smiling more. Even Mark seemed to warm up to the dog. Truth be told, the gentle animal was good for all of us.

With the reservoir behind us, we followed the trail northeast through the forest. After a few more days' travel, Lily noticed one of the signs at a campsite. "Daddy, why is 'Allegheny' spelled wrong?"

"We're in New York now, Lil. They spell it 'Allegany' here."

Lily's eyes widened. "Wow. We walked to a whole other *state*?"

I smiled at her wonderment, while a voice in the back of my head said, *Only three more to go.*

We'd just passed the five-week mark after the blackout when we ran into the first people we'd seen in weeks, a young couple in hiking boots and small backpacks. Bear smelled them first, and barked to warn us before they'd even come into view. His tail started going a mile a minute as they approached.

Mark greeted the newcomers with a raised hand. "Hi there."

"Hi," the young man responded. He had the sunken eyes and sallow skin of malnourishment. "Hey, you don't have any food you could spare, do you?"

Mark glanced my way and I nodded. He said, "Yeah, why don't you guys join us for lunch?" He extended a hand. "I'm Mark. This is Anna and Lily."

"Peter," the young man replied as he shook Mark's hand.

His companion chimed in with a shy little wave from behind him, "Kerry."

The boys went off to catch some fish from a nearby stream, while Kerry helped Lily and I by the campsite. "We haven't seen too many other travelers," I remarked. "Where are you guys headed?"

"West," she replied vaguely. "Just anywhere away from the coast, really." With hooded eyes, she murmured, "Things are bad in the cities." Sparing a glance to Lily, I didn't ask her to elaborate. I could imagine the breakdown of social services well enough.

I got the fire started, and we chatted for a bit. A rustling of grass drew my attention to Peter returning. Alone. "Where's Mark?" I wondered, brow creased.

"He'll be along," Peter replied. Something was different about his voice, and the deliberately-expressionless look on his face set off warning bells. "Kerry, get the packs. We're leaving."

"What?" The surprised look on Kerry's face told me she hadn't known about this.

I got to my feet. "What's going on?"

"I said get the packs," Peter repeated, more sharply. Kerry jumped and started getting up, then Peter leveled a cold stare at me. "Theirs too."

"Like hell," I growled. "Lily, get over here. Get behind me. Now." With a bewildered look on her face, Lily scooted behind me.

Peter drew a long survival knife from a scabbard on the back of his belt. "You don't want this to get messy. Just give us the gear and nobody gets hurt."

Fear flooded through me. "What did you do to Mark?" Bear picked up on the tension and started barking, his hackles rising. He didn't do anything beyond cause a racket, though. Some guard dog.

"He's alive. You do what you're told, you will be too."

My pistol was tucked away in my backpack's side pouch. It had seemed like the safest way to carry it, but I was kicking myself for that now. I'd never get it out in time. Our rifle leaned against a tree, just out of reach. I edged slowly toward it, talking to keep them busy. "You take our gear and we're going to die out there." I fixed my gaze on Kerry, who was looking between me and Peter uncertainly. "You want to be a murderer now?"

"Peter, can't we just..."

"Shut up and just do what I say! Get the rifle."

Kerry flinched. Her eyes flicked to the rifle, then to me, and we both lunged for it at the same time. My hand grasped it first, but she crashed into me and we both went sprawling. We rolled around on the ground, struggling for an advantage. Kerry's eyes were filled with desperation. She popped me in the nose and then looked shocked by what she'd done. Ignoring the pain that made my eyes water, I wedged a foot against her hip and pushed. Kerry rocked back enough that I could wrest the rifle away from her. I came up into a crouch, cracking her hard in the jaw with the rifle butt. She went down like a sack of potatoes.

"Anna!" Lily's terrified screech made me spin towards her, raising the rifle.

Peter jerked Lily close to him, holding his knife in front of her face. "Drop the gun, bitch." Lilly stood ramrod-still, fists clenched and eyes wide.

"Let her go!"

"I'll cut her!"

I held up a staying hand, letting the rifle dip aside so it wasn't pointed at him. Edging closer, I pleaded breathlessly, "Look, you don't have to do this. Just let her go, and I'll give you all the food we have. Come on. You don't want to hurt a little girl." My heart thudded in my chest. I was almost within arm's reach now. To do what, I wasn't sure, but my words didn't seem to be having an impact.

Motion behind Peter caught my eye. Maybe he heard something, or just saw me looking that way, but he half-turned in that direction. As he did, the knife wavered away from Lily. I lunged forward. Grabbing Lily's arm, I pulled her to me just as Mark stepped up and walloped Peter in the face with a heavy piece of driftwood. Peter staggered sideways, and Mark hit him a second and third time until he finally went down. As Mark lowered his makeshift club, looking stunned, I crouched down to snag Peter's knife from his limp fingers.

Lily rushed into Mark's arms. "Are you okay, baby?" She nodded, crying against his shoulder. "Anna?"

I dabbed at my nose, wiping away a trickle of blood with the back of my hand. It was tender, but didn't seem to be broken. "I'm fine, yeah. How about you?"

"Just a headache. Bastard sucker-punched me," he snarled, straightening up. "Let's get our stuff and get out of here."

"Are they dead?" Lily asked, her voice shaky when she looked at Kerry and Peter's fallen forms. Bear came over and nudged his face against her side. She hugged him too.

"No," I assured her. Peter's face was a bloody mess, but I could still see his chest rising, and I hadn't hit Kerry *that* hard. I glanced to Mark. "What should we do with them?"

He hugged Lily once more and then scooped up his backpack. "Leave them." I looked back at the couple, at war with my own conscience. Seeing my hesitation, Mark snarled, "He had a knife on my daughter. He's lucky I don't put a fucking bullet in his head right now."

The uncharacteristic anger took me aback, but I didn't really have a better idea for what to do with them. Leaving them felt wrong, but anything harsher would be a death sentence, which I wasn't prepared to pass. I gathered my things in silence, anxious to get out of there before they woke up.

We walked in silence for the rest of the day, and Lily barely let go of her father's hand all afternoon. The bumps and bruises we'd suffered were minor, but we'd all been shaken. For the first time since the blackout, I felt like we had as much to fear from our fellow survivors as the EMP itself.

CHAPTER 32

WE GOT A GLIMPSE OF how bad things had become when we reached a town for the first time since entering the forest. Several bodies had been left to decay in the parking lot of a burned-out superstore. I pressed my hand to my nose to ward away the smell, and Mark ushered Lily away before she could get much of a look at the gruesome sight. Beyond the store, the houses on this side of town were all deserted. Broken windows and smashed-in doors showed the handiwork of looters.

Further in, we did see some signs of life. The sign outside the town had read "Population: 1588", but there couldn't be more than half that many remaining. What we found reminded me more of a refugee camp than rural America—hollow-eyed, malnourished people wandering the streets, scrounging for scraps.

"Good Lord," I breathed. "I hadn't expected things to get this bad so fast."

Mark looked around with a grim frown. "Me either. But Lauren told me once that the average city has only three days of food storage. With no shipments coming in…"

Lily edged closer to Mark, taking his hand. Her lip turned down in an empathetic pout when she did the mental math. "But it's been a whole month, Daddy. They must be really hungry." Mark squeezed her hand and nodded, lost for words at the pervasive poverty.

People watched us warily as we walked by, giving us a wide berth. We passed a house where a couple of boys were throwing a football around in the front yard. They weren't starving-Ethiopian skinny, but clearly they were suffering. I met Mark's eye, and we shared a somber look.

"Can we give them some of our food?" Lily asked.

Mark shook his head, looking pained. "I wish we could, baby, but we're almost out of food ourselves." Catching fish and trapping rodents didn't leave us much of a buffer.

In the next block, Mark's gaze lingered on a sickly old man on a porch swing. A few streets further on, we heard the crack of nearby gunshots. We quickened our pace, driven by the threat bubbling just beneath the surface.

The skies opened up in a heavy downpour before we'd made it back to the trail. We decided to take shelter in a deserted-looking house off a wooded drive on the outskirts of town. Mark peered into the front windows. "Hello?" Pounding on the door, he called again, "Anyone here?" We waited a minute for any potential occupant to show themselves, then he said, "Doesn't look like anyone's been here for a while. Should be safe enough."

He used the butt of his rifle to knock in a window pane next to the door, then reached around to unlock it. Soon we were dripping in the foyer, stripping off our drenched ponchos before moving into the living room. Blocky Swedish furniture and metallic shelving units accentuated the place's modern decor. A collage of photos in the main hallway showed a couple in their thirties, smiling and carefree. I wondered what had happened to them.

In the kitchen, we discovered that we weren't the first people to have been here since the blackout. The back door had been kicked in and the cabinets methodically ransacked.

"Looks like whoever beat us here cleared the place out," I observed after a quick search of the kitchen. I held up a lone can of soup that had escaped notice in the back of a lazy susan. "Just this."

Lily bounded over excitedly. "Can we have this for dinner?" she asked, practically drooling at the prospect of having something normal for a change. Mark and I shared a muted smile at her enthusiasm.

She conked out on the couch soon after dinner, stretched out with her feet on Mark's legs. Bear curled up at my feet. "You want to carry her upstairs?" I asked.

Mark shook his head. "Nah, I figured we'd just camp out down here."

"And pass up a chance to sleep in a real bed?"

He shook his head, looking around at some of the artwork on the walls. "It feels weird, being in someone else's home like this. It's one thing to take things from a big-box outdoors store. But this? This is more personal." He returned his gaze to me. "Wouldn't it bother you? Strangers breaking into your home—looting your stuff."

Frowning, I considered his words. "Well, I don't have a home. But hypothetically? I like to think I'd be okay with it. I mean, if I wasn't there, and someone was in need? It's just stuff."

Mark gave a grudging nod acknowledging my point, then he squinted at me. "Wait, what do you mean—you don't have a home? You don't have an apartment somewhere?"

"I've been in Africa for two years, remember? Before that, I moved around a lot. My sister keeps a few boxes for me, but other than that? A suitcase, a backpack and a laptop—that's pretty much my life."

"A regular nomad." He tilted his head, studying my face with a sympathetic crease around his eyes. "Must get lonely."

"Sometimes," I admitted. "But you get to know the team; the villagers."

"I'm surprised you didn't stay out west," Mark observed. "You seem to get along well with your sister."

I shrugged, a frown taking hold. "She wanted me to. That's actually what we were talking about when the blackout hit." I wondered dismally if it would end up being the last thing we ever said to each other.

"Don't like Seattle?" Mark guessed, distracting me from those grim thoughts.

"No, it's fine I guess. It's just my dad lives there too." Seeing Mark's puzzled expression, I clarified, "When I was a kid, he ran out on us. Jess forgave him; I didn't." I could rant for days about how his selfishness had shattered our family; how I would listen to my mom crying when she thought Jess and I were asleep; how hard it was for her to support us both on her own. But I didn't elaborate, and Mark didn't press for more. He probably sensed the landmine buried there. "Anyway, they hang out all the time. I try to be civil for her sake, but there's only so much of the doting grandpa schtick I can stomach."

"Well, it can't be worse than the war zones," he reasoned.

"You'd be surprised."

Mark flashed a brief smile at my deadpan response, then grew more serious. "I don't think I could handle it." For a moment, I thought he meant my family, but then he elaborated, "What we saw today? Bodies in the street, people starving, gunshots… it was horrible. And I know it was nothing compared to what it was like over there. How did you stand it?"

I shifted uncomfortably, rubbing my temple. Usually when people asked about my missions, I glossed over the hardships. It wasn't the sort of thing befitting polite dinner conversations. This time, I felt like I owed him an honest answer. "It isn't easy. It usually hits you worst when you're alone, when you don't have the work to distract you." My voice grew more distant as I let the memories in. "Everybody has their own way of coping. Some people blogged or visited the chaplain. My friend was into yoga. I'd jog around the basecamp with my earbuds in. This one Aussie surgeon must have slept his way through half the female staff." Mark's brows arched in a silent but amused 'oh really'. I tried to hide a smile as I waved a hand vaguely. "What can I say? He was cute and I was a sucker for that accent."

I shook my head, the smile fading to a more somber expression. "Anyway. You do what you can during the down-time to escape for a little while. Focus on the ones you can help and pray for the rest."

He gave a solemn nod. "Doesn't feel like enough."

I smiled sadly. "Welcome to my world."

CHAPTER 33

WE SKIRTED AROUND THE TOWNS after that, sticking to the forests that stretched between the little towns dotting upstate New York. I got better at trapping, and the five Finger Lakes provided an abundance of streams for Mark to fish in. Occasionally we'd find an abandoned house or cabin with some dry or canned goods left behind. We couldn't carry a lot with us, given all our other gear, but it was a nice cushion. After the incident with Peter and Kerry, we kept our guard up, and the few travelers we saw were just as likely to pass with a suspicious look as they were to stop and swap news with us. Our days became a comfortable routine of hiking, foraging, preparing the food, and other mundane camp chores.

We'd been trekking through a heavily-forested area one afternoon, the shade from the tall oak trees giving us some reprieve from the summer temperatures. A debate about which game to play next paused when we saw the sun glistening off a large pond up ahead. "Oooh, can we go swimming, Daddy?"

Mark looked my way and I shrugged to say I didn't mind. "Sure," he said. "It'll be nice to cool off for a bit."

Lily let out a whoop and jogged ahead of us. Bear, picking up on her enthusiasm, barked happily and started trailing after her. As soon as he reached the edge, the dog charged into the water, kicking up a spray. Lily dumped her backpack in the grass, took off her shoes and socks, and followed after him. Mark and I strolled up to the pond at a more leisurely pace as Lily and Bear splashed around with each other.

"This is day forty-five, you know," I pointed out mildly as I released the straps on my pack and shrugged it off. Mark gave me a curious look. "When we first planned this whole thing, you thought we'd make it in two months. But we're not even halfway there, are we?"

"We got off to a slow start, sure, but we're moving faster now. George thought it would be closer to three months anyway. I think we've got the hang of things now. Don't you?"

"Fast enough to make it there before winter?"

"We'll get there." He left his gear in the grass and started toward the lake, taking off his shirt as he went. "Have a little faith, Anna," he called back to me. Then he smiled. "Last one in's cleaning the fish tonight."

"Oh, sure, when you're already almost there." I chuckled at the unfair advantage as I stripped off my outer layer of clothes and shoes and waded into the cool water.

A game of 'Marco Polo' was followed by Mark digging out a foam football he'd scavenged along the way. We tossed it to each other—and to Bear. He couldn't catch to save his life, but he seemed to enjoy paddling around and chasing after the ball after it bounced off his nose.

At one point Lily forgot who she was supposed to be throwing it to, wailing the ball at an unsuspecting Mark's head. It bounced off in a random direction, and Mark let out a theatrical 'oof', putting his hand to his head as if wounded. Lily giggled, and Mark leveled a look of mock indignation at her. That only served to make her giggle more. "It's on now," he warned with a grin. "Sea monster attack!"

Lily squealed in a mix of delight and playful fear as Mark dove under the chest-deep water. When he surfaced right beside her, Lily splashed water at him ineffectually. Mark heaved her up into the air for a few seconds, making monster noises while she shrieked with glee. Then he let go, letting her cannonball back in. She came back up, laughing and wiping her hair out of her eyes. Lily mumbled something to Mark, and he looked at me with a mischievous gleam in his eye.

"Oh no," I protested. "Don't even think…" Before I could finish my sentence, Mark was going under again.

I tried to backpedal, but Mark closed the distance quickly. I let out a surprised yelp as he scooped me out of the water. With arms behind my legs and back, he just held me there.

Seeing the look on my face, his smile flickered for an instant before settling on an unapologetic grin. "You're not going to hit me, are you?"

"I should." But his amusement and Lily's cackling muted my irritation. I smiled in spite of myself. Rolling my eyes, I waved a hand to give him permission. "Fiiine."

His grin widened, and he tossed me back into the water. Once I got my footing, Lily and I teamed up against him for an epic splash battle. It was probably the most fun I'd had in… longer than was probably healthy.

It was a beautiful afternoon, until suddenly it wasn't.

Bear had decided to turn 'fetch' into 'tug-of-war', and I was trying to wrest the football away from him when I heard Lily cry out behind me. By the time I had turned around, she was already full-on wailing. Her face contorted in pain, tears streaming down her cheeks.

Mark was at her side in an instant. "Lil, baby, what happened?" He looked around to find the source of her distress. "Did something sting you?" Lily was too hysterical to answer. Mark picked her up, standing up straight so she came out of the water. Blood streamed from her foot. I was on my way over even before his frantic cry. "Anna!"

The bottom of her foot had a deep gouge in the middle. "I'll take her. See if you can figure out what cut her."

Mark hesitated only briefly before shifting the crying girl into my arms. I carried her out while Mark ducked under the water to scan the bottom of the pond. Bear trailed behind us, dropping the ball in the grass to see what was wrong with his little packmate. He shook the water off his coat, sending droplets spraying all over us.

My first instinct was to put Lily down and go fetch my medical kit, but she clung to me tightly and her cries tore at my heart. I sat down with her in the grass with her in my lap, holding her close with one hand while I put pressure on her foot with the other. She buried her head against my wet tank top, sobbing. "Sssh, you're okay." I murmured nonsensical reassurances to her.

Mark sloshed out of the pond. "It was this." He held up the bottom section of a glass bottle, its jagged edges jutting upward and smeared with blood. "Damn it, I should have made her keep her shoes on."

"It was an accident, Mark. Don't beat yourself up."

He crouched down beside us. "How are you doing, princess?"

"It hurts," she wailed.

"I know," I said gently. "I'll get you some medicine for it." I gave her back to Mark and scooted over to get my medical kit.

"You're going to be fine, baby," Mark assured her. His brow furled worriedly and he looked to me. "Is it going to need stitches?"

"Yeah, a few." I smiled, and met Lily's frightened gaze. "Don't worry. I'll take good care of you."

An injection of lidocaine took the sting away, and I irrigated the wound as much as I could with some clean water. Seven neat stitches and a dressing later, I patted her leg. "There we go. All done." I made her drink some of the children's ibuprofen. "We'll need to keep it clean, so that means no more pool parties—at least until the stitches come out."

Lily made a face, then. "How am I going to walk with a hurt foot?"

I looked at Mark questioningly. "We'll rest here a few days and then see how you're doing," he said.

"Maybe you can make me crutches, like when Mommy hurt her ankle."

"Maybe," Mark said, his smile turning sad. "We'll figure it out."

Mentioning Lauren had brought a distant look to Lily's eyes. Mark seemed to pick up on it, and gave her a comforting squeeze. Feeling a pang of awkwardness, I excused myself with a mumble about getting changed. Mark called after me, "Thanks."

Smiling weakly, I nodded. After washing my hands and grabbing some dry clothes, I ducked behind a tree. Instead of getting dressed right away, though, I leaned against the tree and sighed. Looking back through a 'V' in the branches, I watched Mark and Lily for a long moment. Out here, alone in our little bubble, it was sometimes easy to forget why we were doing this. To imagine that it would always be just the three of us. But inevitably the truth would rear its uncomfortable head. Once we found Lauren, it would be time for me to move on. Whatever promises Mark had made, I couldn't imagine them welcoming me as some sort of live-in nanny forever. I knew I shouldn't let myself get too attached.

Who was I kidding? It was way too late for that.

CHAPTER 34

WE CAMPED AT THE POND the next day so Lily could rest her foot, getting caught up on some gear repair and foraging. That evening, Bear and I returned to camp with a duck that I'd shot and he'd fished out of the stream. "You know how to prep one of these?" I asked, holding it at arm's length toward Mark.

He surveyed it with a wrinkled nose. "I'll see what I can do." He took it from me and eyed the neat bullet hole in the bird's neck and watched me lay the rifle against a notch in a tree. "How'd you learn to shoot so well? Kind of an odd past-time for a doctor, isn't it?"

I shrugged, smiling faintly. "It was more my sister's thing than mine, but my dad taught us both."

"He took you hunting?"

"No, just to the range. And then after medical school, my boyfriend and some of our friends from the naval hospital liked to go shooting sometimes." I shrugged again. "I had a knack for it, I guess."

Lily looked up from greeting Bear to squint at me. "You had a boyfriend?"

I laughed. "Yes, I had a boyfriend. Is that so hard to believe?" She lifted her arms in an exaggerated shrug. Snickering, I knelt down beside her. "Let me see that foot, smart aleck."

"Can you give me more purple medicine?" she asked, grimacing as I lifted her foot to get a better look. "It's hurting more."

I frowned. "More than this morning?" She nodded. I removed the bandage and examined the stitches. The skin around them was red and angry-looking, with ugly pus seeping from the bottom edge.

Mark must have seen my expression change. "What is it?" Lily heard his tone and chewed her lip worriedly.

"It's okay," I assured her, flashing a brief smile. "Just a little infection. I'm going to need to take a couple of the stitches out, and clean it some more to get the germs out. And I'll give you a shot of antibiotics to help it get better."

"Another shot?" Lily complained.

"I know. Sorry, sweetheart. Mark, could you boil some water for me please?"

I cleaned out the wound thoroughly before supper, and again later that night. I left the wound open to drain, and expected that and the antibiotic booster would be enough to get the infection under control.

When I awoke the next morning, I was surprised to find Lily still sleeping. Usually she got up at the crack of dawn. "She seemed tired, so I figured I'd let her get some extra rest," Mark explained when he saw me looking that way. The weather had been clear and hot, so we'd slept in the open instead of pitching the tent.

I rubbed the sleep from my face, nodding absently to him. "Yeah, she probably needed it."

When Lily did wake up, her plaintive cry of, "Daddy?" had Mark and I immediately moving to her side. It only took one look at her face to see that something was wrong.

I forced a smile to greet her, trying to hide my concern. "Hey, sweetheart. How are you feeling?" I checked her temperature; her forehead was hot to the touch. Mark sat beside her, his brows knitted in concern.

"My head hurts," she admitted in a small voice. "Can I have some more medicine?"

"Sure, I'll get you some." Mark lifted her up so she could drink it. "Here, drink some water too." I brought the bottle to her lips and she drank greedily. While Mark patted her hair and chattered softly to her, I removed the bandage to check on her foot. Only a well-practiced medical poker face kept me from gasping out loud when I saw the red streaks on her leg, moving away from the wound. Feeling the swollen lymph nodes in her neck only made my heart sink further.

"What is it?" Mark asked warily. I guess my poker face needed some work. I stood up without answering, taking a few steps away. Mark took the hint and joined me, his expression showing a growing alarm.

"The infection's gotten worse, and it's entered her lymphatic system."

"What?" He looked back at his girl, incredulous. "I thought you said the antibiotics would fix her up?"

"I thought they would." I waved a helpless hand in the air. "It's unusual for it to get so bad, so fast."

"So what does that mean? How do we fix it?" Mark fired off the questions with increasing alarm. "Can you give her another shot of antibiotics?"

"No, that won't help with this."

"What, then?" My throat bobbed. When I didn't answer right away, he prompted more sharply, "Anna? What do we do?"

My eyes locked on Lily, my brain spinning through the possibilities. None of them were good. Mark called my name again, and I swallowed hard and met his gaze. "Where's the nearest city?"

"What? Why?" I gave him a pointed look. Despite his frustration, he answered me, "The one we passed through day before yesterday, I guess?"

I shook my head. "That was just a little town. I mean a real city. Somewhere with a proper hospital."

Mark's expression turned grave. "Northeast. Probably…two days' walk. Why? You're starting to scare me."

Two days? That was too long. I shook my head. "We need to leave now."

I turned to start getting my gear, but Mark caught my shoulder and forced me to face him. "Anna. Tell me what's going on."

I didn't want to tell him, because I didn't want to hear it myself. Finally I let out a sharp breath. "She needs stronger antibiotics than I have. Hopefully we can find some in a city."

"And if we don't?"

The words caught painfully in my throat. "As the infection gets worse, it'll spread throughout her body. She'll go into septic shock, and then her organs will start to shut down and she'll die." Mark rocked back as if he'd been hit, his eyes widening in disbelief. I clasped his arm and squeezed it. "We need to hurry."

Mark nodded, his face ashen. Tossing a pot of water on the campfire, he started stuffing things back in his pack. Bear perked up. Oblivious to the danger, the dog was just excited to get back on the trail.

I returned to Lily's side to gather up my medical supplies. "What's Daddy doing?" she wondered, her voice sounding heartbreakingly weak.

"He's getting everything ready to go. We're going to head into the city and get you some new medicine to make you feel better." I tried to make it sound like a trip to the drug store, instead of the desperate race that it was. Hoping that she couldn't read the worry in my face, I smoothed back her hair and smiled down at her. "You're going to be fine, sweetheart. I promise." Her head bobbed, a little smile showing her faith in us.

We broke camp in record time and used the rain tarp from the tent as a makeshift stretcher for Lily. Back-tracking along the trail took us to a highway that Mark said we could follow north to the city. It felt strange to be out of the forest, weaving our way between stalled cars instead of trees and rocks.

The sun beat down on us, the asphalt reflecting the heat and reminding me of our journey away from the airport back when this all started. This time I didn't have the distraction of Lily's constant chatter. She slept most of the way, and Mark and I marched on in stony-faced silence.

Lily didn't weigh much, but even half her weight on top of my backpack caused the muscles in my arms and back to burn. I gritted my teeth and soldiered on, but by lunchtime my hands cried uncle. I veered off to the side of the road and gently set down my side of the tarp in the grass.

"Why are you stopping?" Mark asked roughly. "We need to keep going."

I rubbed my right palm. "My hand's cramped up. I just need a minute." When the cramp had subsided, I gulped down a healthy portion of my water bottle. "We're going to need to find a stream soon and filter some more water."

"Later." Mark moved to the side of the makeshift stretcher. "I'll carry her. Grab the tarp."

I snagged his arm. "Mark, stop. We can't run the entire way there. It won't do Lily any good if you collapse from heat exhaustion or dehydration." He scowled off into the distance, chomping at the bit, but I didn't back down. "Take five minutes and drink some water. Doctor's orders."

Finally he gave in, sitting down cross-legged by Lily. Her features were pale but peaceful in her sleep. Mark wrapped one hand around hers, grudgingly sipping from his water bottle with the other. I left my pack in the grass and joined him. Watching him sidelong, I tried to think of something to say. I'd comforted worried parents before, but this was different. 'We're doing everything we can' platitudes weren't going to cut it. Lost for words, I just slipped an arm around his shoulders. He glanced my way briefly in surprise, but didn't seem to mind the gesture. I said a silent prayer for Lily.

We sat that way in silence for a few minutes before finally he spoke. "I can't lose her, Anna." His voice was scratchy; raw with barely-contained anguish.

"I know." I squeezed his shoulder. "We'll get to the city; get her the medicine. Whatever it takes, right?"

His jaw tightened into a resolute line. "Whatever it takes."

CHAPTER 35

THE TRIP SHOULD HAVE TAKEN us two days according to Mark's map and our usual pace. We made it in just over twenty-four hours, marching through the night and carrying on well past the point of exhaustion to arrive the next afternoon. My hands had blisters from carrying the tarp, and the knots in my shoulders caused a dull ache to radiate up my neck and into my skull. Lily had slipped into unconsciousness, teetering on the edge of shock. Kids could compensate for a while before crashing, but we didn't have much time left before she fell off that cliff and began to suffer irreparable damage.

The little villages we'd passed through since entering New York didn't prepare me for what to expect in the city. I anticipated something out of Mad Max, but instead we found a ghost town. We passed abandoned houses, abandoned shops, and then a deserted school bus depot that gave me the creeps.

"Where is everybody?" Mark asked, as unnerved by this as I was. Giving my hands a break, he cradled Lily in his arms.

I shook my head. I thought a curtain moved in one of the houses we passed, but I looked again and saw nothing. It was eerie. I cast frequent glances over at Lily, fighting the illogical fear that she would die if I took my eyes off of her. I caught Bear looking up at her several times as he walked along between us.

We had the streets to ourselves for several blocks before seeing another human soul. The trio of young men sitting on the stairs of someone's front porch watched us suspiciously as we passed by. I kept looking over my shoulder, but they had quickly returned their attention to each other.

"Hang in there, baby," Mark murmured to Lily, quickening his pace.

Working our way north along long-abandoned residential streets, we eventually came to the highway. Just when we were beginning to wonder if we were on the right track, the blue "H" of a hospital sign had us both breathing a sigh of relief and picking up our pace. The signs directed us down a tree-lined drive that was probably very picturesque before the grass and weeds had been allowed to grow wild. The hospital sat in a wooded suburban area along the shore of a big lake.

Mark suddenly paused, then veered off the path into the woods adjacent to the hospital's parking lot. "Hang on. Something doesn't look right." Laying Lily carefully down in the grass, he knelt behind a tree and scanned the hospital with binoculars. I petted Bear's head anxiously while I waited, the pair of us keeping watch over Lily. After a few minutes of frowning, Mark handed me the binoculars. "Damn it."

Every entrance I could see had been barricaded with junk, or vehicles pushed in the way and flipped over. Armed men stood watch at the corners of the building, with at least one roving patrol. "It's like an army camp," I mumbled.

"They're not soldiers, though. Some kind of gang, maybe?" Mark speculated. "I guess the hospital would've been a valuable place to control."

Movement near the far corner of the building caught my eye. I zoomed in with the field glasses, and saw a Hispanic youth being shoved by a white guy carrying a hunting rifle. The youth staggered a few steps, then turned and held his hands outstretched. His lips moved, his panic-stricken features suggesting he was pleading with the gunman. The other man said nothing; he just lifted his rifle and blew the kid's brains out. The echo of the gunshot reached us an instant later.

"Holy shit!" I breathed, recoiling from the sight.

"What is it?" Mark asked. I let him take the binoculars, silently pointing in the direction of the incident. Even without the binocs, I could see the gunman dragging the youth's body unceremoniously across the asphalt, towards the forest beyond. I looked away, queasy. "Son of a bitch," Mark mumbled under his breath. He flopped down, rubbing his face in dismay.

"What are the odds they'll want to trade for some food?" Even warlords had to eat, right?

Ignoring my semi-rhetorical question, Mark scooped up Lily. "Let's go."

Rather than heading straight for the hospital, though, Mark headed in the opposite direction, through the sparse woods. "Where are you going?" I wondered aloud.

"There were some buildings back here." Sure enough, we soon came to another parking lot, and a row of buildings. After peering in a window briefly, Mark handed me Lily and used his rifle to smash in the glass on the front door of an abandoned dermatology office. We were inside in seconds, though I still didn't understand why. "Mark, what are we doing here? They're not going to have the kind of medicine we need."

Mark slipped his arms under Lily's shoulders and knees to take her back from me, setting her down gingerly on one of the plush couches in the waiting area. Bear trotted around, checking the place out. "I'm going over to the hospital. I'll leave my pack here," Mark finally explained. "Be more mobile without it."

His pointed use of the singular didn't escape my notice. *"You're going to head over,"* I echoed, brows lifting.

Mark kissed Lily's temple, murmured something softly to her, then slanted me a glance. "That's right. You're staying here with Lily."

I folded my arms, frowning at him. "Like hell."

"Anna, I'm not going to debate this with you."

"That's right. Because it's not a debate. I'm going with you." I blew out a breath, nostrils flaring. He thought he could just cut me out of this? Just like that?

Mark sighed. "Anna…"

I cut him off. "No! This isn't up to you, Mark. You think I'm just going to sit here and twiddle my thumbs while you go off to try and trade with some crazy gang?"

He touched Lily's arm for a moment then got up and moved over to his backpack. "This is my family—my responsibility," he said, an uncommon sharpness in his voice. He removed his spare pistol clips from the front pouch of his pack and pocketed them.

"That's bullshit and you know it. And anyway, you don't even know what medication we need."

"So make a list."

"It doesn't work that way! It's not like I can just write you a prescription." I watched him pick up the rifle and work the bolt, taking note of the odd hunch to his shoulders and the way he wouldn't look me in the eye. A sinking dread churned in my stomach as I realized what he was planning. "You're not going there to make a deal with them."

Mark froze for a second. *Busted.* He shook his head. "I don't know what you're talking about."

I closed the distance between us and tugged on his shoulder, forcing him to face me. "Don't lie to me, Mark."

With a sigh, he dropped the act. "You think those guys are going to trade with us? And even if they did, what have we got to offer them? A hunting rifle?" He lifted the rifle, snorting derisively. "Some goddamn venison jerky?"

"So—what? You're just going to charge in there and take them all on? All by yourself?" Mark didn't answer, turning back to his battle preparations. My voice pitched up in frustrated disbelief. "Have you lost your mind?"

"I have to do *something*."

"And getting yourself killed—that's your master plan?"

"Give me another option!" Mark roared, wheeling back at me. "I mean it, Anna. Show me another way." He jerked a hand toward Lily, his desperation palpable. His face scrunched up, pained creases around his eyes. "My little girl is *dying*. This is her only chance!"

I wanted to shout back at him, to knock some sense into him, but the truth was I didn't have another answer. I couldn't argue with his logic. Lily didn't have time for us to comb the city hoping to stumble upon hospital-grade antibiotics. This was her best chance.

It was her *only* chance.

When I said nothing, Mark crouched back down by his pack and fished around for our half-empty box of rifle bullets. I ran through an inventory in my head, trying to think of something we could trade, or something that would help us help Lily. But Mark was right—we didn't have anything. Even if they wanted our guns, that would leave us defenseless and they'd probably just turn around and kill us. The only other thing even remotely valuable we had was my medical kit.

No, I realized with a sudden jolt. Not the kit itself. I swallowed past the sudden lump in my throat. "There's something else we have to trade." Mark gave me a skeptical frown. "A doctor."

Shock, then anger swept across his face. "No."

"You know I'm right."

He stood back up again, facing me. "I know you're crazy. No, Anna. Absolutely not. I'm not sending you off to be raped and murdered by a bunch of psychopaths."

The raw description made me flinch, but again I couldn't refute his point. Though some part of me was touched by his concern, the double standard sparked my temper. "So it's okay for you to risk your neck, but not me?" He just frowned, and I shook my head stubbornly. "This isn't your decision."

"It's my daughter!"

"Stop throwing that in my face! I know she's not my kid! That doesn't mean you're the only one who gets to care about her!" All the worry and tension of the past couple days came spilling out, my voice raw with anguish. "You know what, Mark? You have Lily. You have Lauren out there somewhere, probably waiting for you in Maine. I don't know where my family is. I'll probably never see them again." Saying that out loud, even though I'd known it all along, was more heart-wrenching than I thought it would be. "You and Lily are all I've got. So I'll be damned if I'm going to sit on my ass watching her die while you go off and get yourself killed playing Jason Bourne. I'm going to help. Whatever it takes, remember? I don't need your approval, and I sure as hell don't need your permission!"

Mark paced back and forth, scrubbing a hand through his hair. He looked at me as though seeing me for the first time. Bit by bit, his expression softened. He stepped forward, extending an arm towards my shoulder. I was confused at first, but then realized he was drawing me into a hug. I leaned into his embrace, my anger melting away, and clung to him for a minute. "We'll do this together, Mark. Whatever happens, at least we'll have each others' backs."

His chin touched my forehead, moving slightly in a nod.

"So, do you have an actual plan?" I mumbled, some of my bluster eaten away by the fear of what faced us.

He had no answer at first, but then he sighed. "I have an idea."

CHAPTER 36

WAITING UNTIL DARK WOULD HAVE been prudent, but neither of us thought Lily had that kind of time. Mark kissed her forehead and murmured something quiet by her ear. It was the closest I'd ever seen him to tears. I scratched Bear behind the ears. "You keep a good watch on her, bud," I murmured, voice tight. Leaving them there was one of the hardest things I'd done.

Moving across the hospital parking lot, we dashed from the cover of one abandoned car to another. The gang only seemed to have a single patrol circling the grounds, but that didn't stop my heart from leaping into my throat every time we moved. A derelict ambulance stood in front of the door to the ER, its compartments left hanging open after being stripped clean. We hoped there'd be room to squeeze in the doors behind it, but instead found a mountain of toppled furniture and boxes heaped in the doorway.

"Shit," Mark mumbled. "We're not getting in that way."

"We'll have to try one of the other doors." I glanced back and forth, looking for the patrol.

Frowning at the obstacle, Mark hopped over a decorative planter and peered in one of the tall windows lining the ER waiting area. "It looks clear." He smashed the butt of his hunting rifle against the window. It didn't break, so he hit it again.

I winced as the dull thuds carried through the parking lot. "Someone's going to hear that," I hissed. "We'll find another way in."

"Lily doesn't have time for us to screw around," Mark insisted. He kept pounding, and a spider-webbed pattern spread through the entire pane of safety glass. My head swung back and forth, expecting gang members to descend on us. Eventually Mark punched through, then he cleared out the rest so we could climb through. However I felt about Mark's methods, we were committed now.

Climbing inside, we hurried through the registration area and into the ER proper. Open drawers and ransacked cupboards showed that looters had beaten us here, but they'd left a lot behind. An untouched crash cart tucked away in a back room proved to be a gold mine—IV supplies, needles, saline, and valuable medications like epinephrine and dopamine. The gray computerized supply system near the admin area yielded a few more odds and ends.

But no antibiotics.

"Anything?" Mark asked, his desperation palpable as he watched the entrance. So far nobody from the gang had come to investigate, but it was only a matter of time.

I shook my head, slamming one of the cabinet doors shut in frustration. "We need to find the pharmacy." I spotted a hallway leading deeper into the hospital. "This way."

The hallway grew darker the further we got from the ER's abundant natural lighting, and my flashlight cast a meager pool of light in front of us. In my mind, hospitals were a hive of activity: bright lights; the hum of the ventilation system; the beeping of medical equipment; the drone of a hundred conversations. Here, though, the only sound came from our shoes tapping on the linoleum floor. Without air conditioning, it was probably close to ninety degrees and stale as a tomb. I had never been particularly claustrophobic, but being utterly surrounded in pitch-black silence was an unsettling and oppressive kind of sensory deprivation. We saw no bodies, and I tried not to think about what had happened to all the patients.

We came to a door with a blue sign labeled "Pharmacy" beside it, and my heart quickened. "Here it is."

"Damn, it looks like a bomb went off in here," Mark whistled, swinging his flashlight across the room. Many of the shelves were bare, and one of the shelving units now lay on its side across the aisle. Bottles, boxes, and little blue plastic shelf organizers littered the floor. "How can I help?"

I thought for a second, then motioned toward one of the aisles. "Start here. Grab anything you recognize. If you've heard of it, it's probably useful. Read off the names of the rest. I'll start in the next row."

As fast as we could, we searched through the mess. Under other circumstances, it would've been like Christmas—so many things that might save a life someday. I wanted to take it all. I found some Benadryl for the next bout of poison ivy, a lone bottle of Demerol pain pills that had rolled under the shelf, some lidocaine for sutures, and a few other odds and ends that went into my daypack.

Despite the bounty, we still didn't turn up any antibiotics.

I grew more and more frantic as I checked the final shelf. When it, too, yielded nothing, I rubbed both hands over my sweat-soaked face and hair. "Damn it, they can't all be gone." Helpless frustration boiled over, overwhelming me. "Fuck!" I slammed my fists down on the shelf and hurled a handful of useless bottles and boxes of meds down the aisle in a clatter.

Coming up behind me, Mark laid a hand on my shoulder. "It's got to be here somewhere. We'll turn the whole damn hospital upside-down if we have to."

I took a breath to steady myself. "There are a few other places we can try." As we passed the pharmacist's desk area, I noticed another annex beyond the pneumatic delivery tube system. We'd missed it in the darkness on our way in. "Wait. Over here." I led the way with my flashlight.

We split up, Mark reading names while I methodically scanned the shelves. "Car-ba-maz-e-pine?" Mark puzzled over the syllables on a drug label. "Where do they even come up with these names?" I didn't answer, figuring he didn't really want a lecture on Latin and drug name origins. He kept reading, "Cef-tri-"

My heart skipped a beat. "Ceftriaxone?" I darted over and grabbed the bottle, looking at the label for myself. "This is it! Thank God." I threw my arms around his neck, clinging to him while letting out an overjoyed chuckle.

I almost kissed him, and the impulse had me doing a double-take. *Where the hell did that come from?*

Mark's grin turned to a confused squint at my expression. "What is it?"

"Nothing. Just relieved." Chocking the feeling up to stress and sleep deprivation, I shook it off and released him. "Let's get the hell out of here."

Slipping the pack over my shoulder, I headed out of the alcove and opened the door.

And came face-to-face with a man carrying a shotgun.

CHAPTER 37

"WELL, NOW. YOU'RE A DAMN sight prettier than the vultures we usually get," the gang member drawled. A fireplug of a guy, he had a bald head and biceps as thick as my legs. His creepy smile set my teeth on edge as I backpedaled away from the doorway.

Baldie advanced on me, just as Mark emerged from the alcove to my right. Baldie's head turned, and I grabbed the barrel of his shotgun and pushed it upwards. The gun went off while we were wrestling over it, sending plaster raining down on our heads from the new hole in the ceiling. The blast sounded like a thunderclap close to my head, feeling as though someone had punched me in the ear. One hand went instinctively to the side of my head, and Baldie wrenched the gun from my grasp.

Before he could bring it to bear on us, Mark lunged forward and clubbed Baldie in the chin with the butt of his own hunting rifle. Baldie staggered sideways, dropping his shotgun. Amazingly, though, he didn't go down. Was he on drugs? That hit should have shattered his jaw. Mark gaped at him for a moment.

I dove for the loose weapon, but my fingers had barely touched metal when Baldie's powerful knee connected with the side of my face. My vision exploded in stars, and I was only dimly aware of his meaty fists clamping down on my shoulder and hip so he could hurl me head-first into the shelves. Everything got pretty hazy after that, just a distant cacophony of grunts and crashing.

That blackness encroaching on my vision would have been a sweet release from pain and exhaustion. Clinging to the thought of Lily and how much she was depending on me, I managed to resist its pull until my head cleared. When I opened my eyes, another gang member had joined the fray. This guy was taller than the first—taller even than Mark—with short, dark hair and a day's stubble on his jaw. Even in the dim light cast by a lantern on the floor, I could see tattoos spiraling up his arm.

Mark tackled Baldie. The pair of them careened into the next set of shelves, which toppled over with a tremendous clatter. Baldie took the brunt of it. While he was stunned, Mark smacked him square in the head with a broken piece of shelf. This time Baldie stayed down.

"Behind you!" I yelled as the tall guy bore down on Mark. The second ganger seemed to notice me for the first time, surprise registering on his face. His hesitation gave Mark the opportunity to come up swinging, landing a few strong blows. I tried to get up to help Mark, but had to catch myself on the shelves as a wave of dizziness swept over me. Pressing a hand to my aching head, I winced at a sticky wetness dripping from my temple down my face.

While I was steadying myself, the ganger had gotten Mark in a choke-hold, unfazed by Mark frantically elbowing him in the side and kicking at his shins.

Without thinking, I pulled the pistol from the holster clipped to the back of my jeans and leveled it at the taller man. "Let him go." I held the gun with both hands to try to keep it from shaking.

"So you will shoot me?" He had an accent—Russian, maybe, or Eastern European. "I don't think so." Mark's struggles slowed, and then he went completely limp. Holding Mark upright like a human shield, Tattoos kept me from getting a clear shot as he drew his own pistol and leveled it at me. Now we were locked in a stand-off. "Drop the gun," he said in a clipped tone. "I won't hurt you."

With the ganger between me and the door and Mark unconscious, I didn't have a lot of options. Licking dry lips, I took a shaky breath and ventured, "Look, I don't want to hurt anybody either. We just needed some medicine."

Tattoos scoffed. "Everyone needs medicine."

"It's not for us. It's for a little girl. His daughter." I nodded towards Mark. I thought of Lily—all alone—and tears sprang to my eyes. "She's dying. Please. This medicine is her only chance."

He frowned, and something flickered across his face. Suspicion—but also, perhaps, a hint of sympathy. Or maybe that was wishful thinking. I met his gaze, pleading for all I was worth. "Her name's Lily. She's seven years old. Let us go, and you'll never see us again—I swear. You guys have a whole fucking hospital worth of stuff. This little bag? It's nothing to you, and everything to her. Just walk away. *Please.*"

Tattoos seemed to waver, but then his eyes narrowed. "How do I know it isn't some trick? You will say anything."

He was right. I would have said anything. Done almost anything.

Almost.

I lowered my pistol slowly, holding my arms slightly outstretched. "I'm not going to shoot you." My voice wavered, standing defenseless before him. This probably ranked pretty high among the stupidest things I'd ever done. I stepped closer. His pistol was now just inches from my heart. I held his gaze, swallowing past the lump in my throat.

"If you're going to shoot, then shoot. But if you kill me, you're killing Lily too. Please, just let us go."

Those intense brown eyes scrutinized my face, his brow creased in puzzlement. I held my breath, half-expecting a gunshot. Then his expression shifted, and his pistol dipped. A giddy relief swept over me. Maybe we could actually get out of this.

Voices in the hall doused my hope. "Nikolai? Carl?"

In the heap of ruined shelves, Baldie groaned and stirred. I started to raise my pistol, but Tattoos—Nikolai, I presumed—caught my hand in a gentle grasp. He shook his head, lips drawn in a grim line. "They'll kill you if you try it. Trust me."

Trust him? That was a hell of a leap of faith, but what was the alternative? Take on God-only-knew how many gangers single-handed and go out in a blaze of glory? That was hardly a choice at all. I let him take the pistol.

The voices got closer, still yelling, and Nikolai shouted back, "In here!" He resumed training his pistol on me, putting up a show (I hoped) for his buddies, who turned up a few moments later. There were two of them: a black guy in his thirties with an Iron Man T-shirt, and an older man with salt-and-pepper hair and a well-worn dress shirt. Baldie picked himself up off the floor with a groan, pressed a hand to his bleeding skull. I flinched as he gave the still-unconscious Mark a kick to the ribs.

I crouched down to check on him, only to have Baldie shove me backwards and into a table. Fists clenched and heart pounding, I pulled myself up and stood rigidly. Whatever Nikolai's intentions, he was only one guy. Fear flooded my veins, not knowing what they were going to do to us. To me.

"What the hell happened? We heard a shot," the older guy demanded. He hardly looked intimidating at a glance, but his gravelly voice and the way he carried himself exuded authority. He had a pistol in a police-style shoulder holster, making me wonder if he'd been a cop before all this.

"Caught a couple looters," Baldie grunted. He yanked the bag off my back, nearly pulling me over in the process. He tossed it to the older guy, who I presumed was their leader.

I rubbed my shoulder where the bag strap had dug into it. "We just needed some medicine."

The boss aimed his flashlight into the bag, rummaging for a second, then he turned the light on me. I winced and held up a hand to block the piercing LED until it receded. He held up a bottle of medicine from my pack, the pills within rattling as he shook it. "Medicine, huh? Needed a fix, more like."

I was confused, until I remembered the bottle of Demerol we'd found. "We're not junkies," I snapped back in irritation. "The medicine is for his daughter. She's very sick."

The boss ran some of the IV tubing from my pack through his fingers, frowning in consideration. He stepped closer to me, and his head tilted. "You a nurse or something?"

I hesitated. What answer was most likely to get us out of this alive? My head hurt, and I had a hard time thinking straight. I decided to just go with the truth. "I'm a doctor."

"What kind?"

What kind? I peered at him. *What was this—a job interview?* "Emergency room doc. Why?"

"Well ain't that something." He shoved the IV supplies back into the bag, and tossed it to Nikolai. "Bring her." Nikolai took my arm and gave a gentle tug to follow.

Baldie nudged Mark again with his foot, his face twisted in a snarl. "Shaw, what about him? You want me to take him out and put a bullet in his head?"

"No!" The desperate cry escaped my lips without conscious thought. I tried to tug free of Nikolai's grasp, but he held fast and kept me from doing anything rash. "You can't do that."

The boss—Shaw, apparently—wheeled back on me and grabbed my jaw. He forced my head up, squeezing hard enough to bring tears to my eyes. His eyes held a dangerous menace that shook me. "You're in my house now, Doc, and I'll do whatever the fuck I want. You cooperate, he gets to keep breathing. We clear?" I bobbed my head in a tiny nod, unable to find my voice. He released me and started marching toward the door, waving a hand to his men. "Bring 'em both."

CHAPTER 38

THEY SHOVED ME INTO ONE of the ER trauma rooms and dumped Mark in an inelegant heap by the door. As soon as they'd gone—leaving a man on guard outside the sliding glass doors—I crouched down beside Mark. He was still out cold, but didn't seem to have any other serious injuries. Lifting up the hem of his shirt, I dabbed away a trickle of blood from his nose. His head moved, consciousness slowly returning.

I shook his shoulder. "Mark. Mark, wake up."

He awoke with a jolt and came up flailing, some part of his brain still stuck in fight-or-flight mode. I caught his arm and leaned my full weight on his chest to hold him down. "Mark! Take it easy!"

Recognition flashed in his eyes, and he stopped struggling. "Anna. What?" Confused eyes scanned the unfamiliar surroundings. I relaxed my grip and helped him sit up. "What happened?" He touched his jaw gingerly, wincing.

Sighing, I flopped down beside him. We sat shoulder-to-shoulder with our backs against the cabinets. "We got our asses kicked," I reported flatly. "They locked us up in here for now."

He jerked up straighter, alarm registering on his face. "The medicine?"

"I don't know. The boss guy took it." Despair sapped my energy. We'd been so damn close, and now we were back to square one. No, worse than square one. I ran a hand over my face, fighting back tears of frustration. The hand came away wet with blood, and I frowned at it. I felt a cut on my forehead, and the sting of a bruise forming where Baldie's knee had connected.

Mark smacked a hand against the cabinet and huffed at the door like a caged animal, desperation oozing from his pores. He looked at me, and concern creased his brow. "They hurt you?"

"I just hit my head on the shelves," I assured him, trying not to think about how long we'd remain unharmed. I dabbed gingerly at the swollen cut above my brow. "Is it still bleeding?"

He tilted his head to look and then nodded. "Here, let me…" Mark rose and rummaged in the top cabinets for a moment before returning to my side with supplies. A few dabs of peroxide and some winces later, he was pulling the skin tight with some butterfly strips.

"Not up to your standards, I'm sure, but…"

"It's fine. Thanks." I clapped his arm lightly.

He caught my hand and covered it with his own, his lips pulling together in a grim line. "We're going to get out of here. I promise. We'll get the medicine. Get back to Lily." He stood up, talking to himself as much as me. "Just need to find something to fight with."

Much as I admired his determination, fighting these guys head-on hadn't worked out so great for us the last time. We needed a better way. I tried to think of something, but this headache was killing me. Maybe if I just closed my eyes for a minute…

I barely had time for my eyelids to touch before the exam room door slid open roughly, startling me. Shaw came in first. Following him were Nikolai and Iron Man, carrying another guy on a padded stretcher. "On your feet, Doc," the boss ordered. "Got a patient."

I dragged myself up, frowning at the man on the stretcher. He couldn't have been much past twenty, and his youthful face was pale and bathed in sweat. In the hospital, we called that look 'circling the drain'.

They set him down on the exam table and stepped back. "You didn't tell me the doc was a babe, Dad," the young man said, smirking despite his condition.

My eyes flicked to Shaw, noticing the resemblance and the worried cast to his eyes. I'd seen that look on parents' faces a million times before, too, most recently on Mark's. I asked, automatically, "What happened?"

"Ran into another gang scouting for food. One of them got lucky with a knife." Junior pulled up the hem of his gray T-shirt to reveal bloody bandages wrapped around his midsection. Even in pain, he puffed himself up with forced bravado and tried to downplay the injury. "Ain't nothing."

Reflexes took over, pushing past the headache and exhaustion. I tugged on a pair of exam gloves and went to work. After cutting away the bandages, I found a narrow stab wound, almost surgical in its precision, just under his left rib cage. The edges were red and inflamed, still oozing blood. "When was this?"

"Couple hours ago. Ow—hey, take it easy, Doc," the young man complained when I palpated around the wound.

Shaw watched me check his son's blood pressure and other vital signs. "So what's the verdict? You going to stitch him up or what?"

I drummed my fingers lightly on the bed rail, frowning thoughtfully. I glanced over at Mark, who tilted his head in an unspoken question, then back to the father. "He doesn't need stitches; he needs surgery."

"You're gonna cut me open?" the young man echoed in wide-eyed alarm.

"You're bleeding internally, probably from a laceration of your spleen," I told him, my tone grave. "I need to stop the bleeding. You're in the early stages of shock already, and it's only going to get worse."

His father ran a hand over his face, shock and worry taking over. He might be a ruthless gang leader, but beneath that he was still just a frightened father. "You can do it, though, right? You've got the stuff here you need?"

I watched the younger Shaw for a moment. Even in disaster zones, we would think twice about operating under these conditions, but he would die without surgery. This was his only chance—and Lily's. I took a breath, steeling myself, and turned to face the boss. "There are always risks in any surgery. Doubly so now. We don't have a ventilator, blood bank, a surgical te…"

Shaw cut me off, stepping closer to get in my face. "I don't want to hear excuses," he snapped. "Can you do it or not?"

The older man wasn't physically imposing, but there was something in his eyes that unsettled me. "I need a few things from the OR, but yeah—I can do it," I told him. "I'll get him stable, and then you're going to let us walk out of here."

Shaw stared at me incredulously for a second, and then he laughed. "Can you believe the stones on this bitch?" he asked his guys. Iron Man chuckled, too, but Nikolai just looked worried. "You ain't in a position to negotiate, Doc."

I swallowed hard, my throat tight. "I sure as hell am. You need me. I save your son, you let us go—with the medicine to save his daughter. That's a fair trade."

He moved so fast I never saw the punch coming. It plowed into my stomach and dropped me to my knees, gasping for the air that had been knocked out of me. I was vaguely aware of Mark shouting angrily behind me, then a scuffle. Shaw grabbed the back of my hair and jerked me roughly around to face Mark. Iron Man had him on his knees, a pistol jammed up against his temple. Terror washed over me, convinced we were both about to die. The thought at the front of my mind wasn't some memory from my own life, but the image of Lily in that office, all alone.

"You listen close, Doc," Shaw's voice was low, practically spitting with venom. "I don't trade for what I can take. You're gonna help my boy, or I'll start taking pieces off your old man there."

I caught Mark's eye. Far from the breath-stealing fear I felt, his eyes showed a steely determination. He gave an almost-imperceptible nod of approval. I was gambling with his life—and Lily's—but his faith bolstered my confidence. "I told you my terms," I rasped breathlessly, arms cradling my sore stomach. "And while you're screwing around showing how tough you are, your son's bleeding to death."

Shaw jerked my hair, making me gasp. "Shoot his foot. We'll work our way up."

"Shaw." Nikolai spoke up, stepping forward as Iron Man shifted his pistol to Mark's leg. Iron Man paused, his questioning look swinging between Nikolai and the boss. "You think she will be any help to Jason if you shoot up her husband? Beat her senseless?" I didn't correct his mistake about Mark, not daring to speak. "We should let them help him and go. They are not worth the headaches."

I felt the tension spike as Shaw stared at Nikolai. Finally Shaw tugged my hair to pull my ear closer to his mouth. "You'd better be as good as you think you are, Doc," he hissed, then released me.

"Yeah," I mumbled with a shaky scoff. "No pressure."

CHAPTER 39

NIKOLAI VOLUNTEERED TO ESCORT ME up to the OR to get the surgical supplies I needed. Standing in front of an instrument tray, surrounded by the dead machines of a modern operating suite, the doubts hit me full-force. I'd performed surgery under austere conditions before, but never like this. And never on my own. I hadn't been lying to Shaw about the risks. What if something went wrong? I sagged against the counter, fear coming to a boil.

Nikolai studied my face in the dim light from the lantern. "There is a door at the end of the hall. It goes to the upper lot. No guard."

"What?" I peered at him. He was letting me go? I shook my head. "I can't leave. Not without the medicine. Without Mark. Lily's counting on us."

He stepped closer, standing by my elbow. "It is terrible, but that is the world now. People dying every day. Your husband would want you to live."

"He's not my husband. They're my friends. We're just traveling together."

His eyebrows lifted in surprise, then his lips thinned. "More reason for you to save yourself. Even if you save Jason, Shaw is not going to let you go. It is not his way. That is why he agreed so easy."

"I know." There was a slim chance that Shaw's better nature would prevail, but I wasn't going to bet on it.

Once again he looked surprised. "You know—and you are doing this still?"

"I'm still a doctor." And I thought it might get Shaw to lower his guard and give us a chance to escape, though I kept that part to myself. I added a few other things to the tray and covered them in a sterile sheet. Tilting my head to look up at him, I asked, "Why are you trying to help me? You're one of them."

He frowned. "Not by choice. It is the same with you. Shaw thinks I am useful to him because I was a soldier. I can fight."

"Why not leave?"

"To go where?" Nikolai snorted, waving a hand vaguely. "You have seen the cities. People starving everywhere. The roads are death. Live with the wolves or die with the sheep—that is how it is."

I eyed him shrewdly as I stuffed some gauze pads and packs of sterile gloves into the bag. "You don't really believe that, or you wouldn't be trying to help a couple of sheep."

"You are no sheep," he asserted with an amused snort.

I supposed that was a compliment. "And you're no wolf, much as you pretend to be." He didn't disagree, a tiny smile tugging at his lips. I grabbed a few more things off the shelf, marveling that this place hadn't been hit worse by looters. I supposed that the average scavenger didn't have much use for specialized surgical gear. I turned back to face him. "You know, I've seen disasters—hurricanes, genocide, famine… it brings out the worst in some people." I paused and corrected myself. "In a lot of people. But it can bring out the best in people, too."

"Ah, I see," Nikolai said, as if solving a great mystery. He had a nice smile when he wasn't being so serious. He leaned against the counter next to me. "You are optimist. Dangerous thing to be, these days."

I almost denied it. Mark was the real optimist, not me. But I supposed it was all relative. "Everybody needs a little optimism in their life. Otherwise what the hell do you have to live for?" That caught him off-guard, and his expression turned contemplative. I watched him in the lantern's glow, instinct warring with reason. Instinct won. "Prove me right."

His brow creased. "What?"

"Help us get out of here. Get away from these assholes—this ghost town. Come with us to the next town, or the one after. I know there has to be something better out there."

"You want me to come with you?" Nikolai lifted his brows incredulously. "Are you being serious?" When I bobbed my head, he made a face. "I don't think your friend will be very happy with this."

I hitched a shoulder. He had a point there, but we'd cross that bridge when we came to it. "Leave that to me. You help save Lily, and he'll owe you one."

He seemed to chew it over for a moment, then said, "Are you going to even tell me your name?"

I supposed I owed him that much. "Anna."

"Anna." It sounded more exotic with his accent. "So. What can I do?"

He smiled. Despite the peril we were still in, I allowed myself a little smile as well.

CHAPTER 40

I HADN'T BEEN THIS NERVOUS about a surgery since my first solo appendectomy in Haiti. ER docs were trained in a number of surgical techniques, from cracking a chest to doing a crash C-section, but I wasn't a proper surgeon. Much as I hated to admit it, I was out of my league. Even that time in Haiti, I'd had a whole team with me. Here I only had a very green-around-the-gills Mark for a surgical assistant, and Nikolai squeezing the bag-mask that was breathing for the unconscious Jason. A nervous Shaw paced at the foot of the bed, while Iron Man stood guard by the door.

"Please don't let me screw this up," I mumbled under my breath, and made the first incision.

It was indeed a splenic laceration, as I'd suspected. As soon as I opened the abdomen, blood gushed from the incision and spilled onto the floor. My surgical gown caught most of it, but some splashed on my boots.

I thought I was going to lose Mark right there. "Jesus," he gasped. His face turned white as a sheet and he swayed for a moment.

"Mark, hey, I need you. Take a breath. You've got this."

"Uhh…." He sounded sick. "Anna, I don't know. God, that's a lot of blood."

"You can do it. Just pull back on this retractor here." I tapped his gloved hand with mine, focusing his attention on what he needed to do. "Little more. There, that's perfect. Just hold it."

With the abdomen exposed, I isolated the injured spleen and set to work trying to suture it. I found myself missing the frigid temperature of a real OR, as sweat stung the cut over my eye and soaked my shirt under the stifling gown.

Everything seemed to be going well, until suddenly things went off the rails.

"No pulse," Nikolai reported flatly. In addition to squeezing the bag, his job was to make sure Jason's heart stayed beating. It was a paltry substitute for a suite of vital sign monitors.

"What? Shit." My eyes flicked to the blood bag hanging from an IV stand. We'd managed to get three units of donated blood before the operation—two from Shaw's guys and one from Mark—but we'd already burned through two. "Hang the last unit. He needs volume." I abandoned my suturing to grab a bag of saline fluid, and hurriedly hooked up the IV tubing.

"What the hell is going on?" Shaw growled, his face ashen.

"He's lost a lot of blood. His heart stopped beating."

Shaw backed up a step, rubbing a hand over his mouth. He grabbed my shoulder, and I felt the cold steel of his pistol jab against my temple. "You get him back, you hear me?"

I froze and lifted my hands, ragged breathing making my surgical mask puff in and out at a rapid-fire pace.

Mark looked ready to leap across the operating table. "What do you think she's doing? Back the hell up and let her work!"

The fabric of the surgical gown crinkled under Shaw's clenched fist, then he abruptly released me and backed up a step. "Just help him. Don't let him die."

"I'm trying!" I snapped at him. "I don't work well with a goddamn gun pointed at my head." He didn't put the gun away, but he did move back to the foot of the operating table. He started pacing from one cabinet-lined wall to the other.

Concentration wrecked, I took a shuddering breath to steady myself and picked up the IV tubing once more. In short order, Jason had two bags of fluid going and a shot of adrenaline to kick-start his heart. I started chest compressions, but it was swiftly becoming clear that we were fighting a losing battle. The minutes blurred. Mark and I traded off on compressions.

We passed the point where I would have asked my hospital team if anybody had any last-ditch ideas. We passed the point where I would have called the code. Every time I looked to Nikolai to see if Jason's pulse had returned, he just gave a grim shake of his head. Jason was gone, and we were just going through the motions at this point.

A sinking dread flooded through me. Finally I straightened, pulling off bloody gloves and then my surgical cap and mask. I used the motion to hide my hand closing around a scalpel on the instrument tray, braced to defend myself against the inevitable explosion once Shaw learned his son was gone.

"What are you doing?" Shaw demanded. "Why are you stopping?" His face wore the expression of every parent who'd lost a child in my trauma room, trying to deny what they already knew was happening.

"We've done all we can," I said, my voice guarded but gentle. "I'm sorry. Jason's dead."

He didn't explode. His only outward reaction was a clenched jaw, and his eyes were cold and blank. "You bitch," he said quite calmly, and he started to raise his gun at me.

A lot of things happened at once. Mark shouted something and lunged across the table, but couldn't quite reach Shaw. I grabbed Shaw's wrist and leaned in, keeping him from raising it fully. The gun went off, ricocheting off the floor. I tried to strike with the scalpel, but Shaw grabbed me in turn. As we wrestled, there was another gunshot from behind me. Shaw's head jerked, and blood splattered over my face. I stood frozen in shock as his body fell sideways, landing in a limp heap at my feet. Nikolai turned his gun on Iron Man next, firing again just as the other ganger slipped out the trauma room door. The bullet shattered the glass, raining shards down in the hallway. Iron Man scrambled away.

"Holy shit," Mark breathed, wide eyes staring at Shaw's body.

Nikolai chucked aside his surgical garb. "We have to hurry, before he brings back help."

"We?" Mark looked at Nikolai, then at me. "Anna, what's going on?"

His urgent question snapped me out of my stunned daze. "He's with us." Seeing Mark open his mouth in shocked outrage, I held up a hand to cut him off. "I'll explain later. Let's get the hell out of here first."

I didn't have to ask him twice. He headed for the door, trailing discarded surgical garments in his wake and pausing only long enough to scoop up Shaw's pistol and ammunition. Nikolai was right behind him. I dragged a sleeve across my blood-splattered face as I followed.

"We have to find the bag with the medicine," Mark said.

"Here." Nikolai pointed to the admin desk in the central area outside the trauma rooms. "Your weapons, too." Sure enough, our stuff was sitting on the desk.

"Thanks," I told him. I checked the supplies, confirming that the precious antibiotics were inside, and breathed a sigh of relief.

Mark picked up our hunting rifle and handed my pistol back to me, the whole time watching Nikolai as if he suspected it were all a trick. "We can go out the way we came in. This way."

We made it back out the broken window and onto the sidewalk before the gang caught up with us. "Get down!" Mark yelled, pulling me down behind a planter as gunfire rang out. Bullets chipped away at the planter's base, sending chips of concrete and puffs of dirt flying everywhere. Nikolai had ducked behind a support pillar, and leaned out occasionally to fire back at the guys creeping across the lobby. More of the lobby's window panes splintered under the cross-fire, and I heard a cry as one of Nikolai's bullets found its target.

"Go for the cars!" Nikolai shouted. "I will cover you!"

He'll cover us? It sounded like something out of an action movie, but I gulped and nodded. "Go!" At Nikolai's signal, Mark and I dashed away from the building. Nikolai followed. We hopped over the stone wall and into the cover of the parked cars. One of the gang members tried to come out, but scrambled back inside when Nikolai or Mark winged him. That was apparently enough for them to decide "to hell with this" and retreat back into the building. Abruptly, the parking lot fell quiet. All I could hear was our heavy breathing and the ringing in my ears.

"Let's get out of here before they change their minds."

CHAPTER 41

WE RAN FOR OUR LIVES, but the gang wasn't inclined to follow. When we got back to the doctor's office, Mark beelined to Lily's side. "Lily, baby, I'm here." He smiled through tears, holding her hand. "We're back. We got the medicine."

Bear tried to wrap himself around my legs until I crouched down to rub his ears and tell him what a good guard dog he'd been. Then he went over to investigate Nikolai, who kept a grim watch by the door.

As I rubbed some hand sanitizer over my grimy fingers, I realized how badly my hands were shaking. Trying to ignore it, I started laying out supplies. Lily breathed shallowly, her skin so pale. *Please don't let it be too late.*

"What happened to her?" Nikolai wondered, a preoccupied frown on his face as he watched me work.

"She cut her foot; got an infection. She's in shock," I explained. Mark watched the exchange with a frown. He was itching to get answers about Nikolai, but first things first.

I managed to get the alcohol prep package open on the third try, but getting the needle tip onto the syringe proved to be impossible. After a few close calls of almost dropping it, I stopped with a frustrated sigh and sat back on my heels. I brought a trembling hand up to rub my face, but feeling the sticky blood there did nothing for my nerves. Damn it, now I had to sterilize my hands again.

Mark watched my fumbling with a growing concern. "Are you all right?"

He meant well, but the inane question was the final straw that caused my frustration and stress to boil over. "Do I fucking look all right?" He backed off, raising his hands in surrender.

A strained silence followed. "I can do it. Just give me a minute." I rubbed my right hand with my left, trying not to think about the maelstrom of terror we'd just been through. Mark wordlessly handed over his half-empty canteen. I gulped down some water, the lid clanking against the side as I held it.

"You need something stronger than water," Nikolai observed dryly.

I snorted. After taking a few deep breaths, I picked up the syringe again. I let my brain run on auto-pilot, going through the tasks so familiar I could do them in my sleep. It took longer than it should have, but eventually Lily had an IV in her arm with a bag of life-saving medications and fluid flowing into it.

Finally able to let out the breath I'd been holding, I brushed the hair off her hot forehead. "You be strong, sweetheart."

Mark gave an approving nod, still holding her other hand. "When will we know?"

"Next twelve hours are critical." I shoved the remaining supplies back into the bag and stood up, wobbling until I caught my balance on the wall. "We shouldn't stay here. It's too close to the hospital. Can you help Mark carry her?" I asked Nikolai, who nodded.

Mark stayed by Lily's side, but glared up at the other man. "Hang on. You still haven't told me what the hell he's doing here."

"I will check that no one is following," Nikolai offered, ducking through the door so we could talk.

I leaned against the wall, arms crossed. The rush of adrenaline I'd felt at the hospital was starting to fade, exhaustion lurking just beneath the surface. "We made a deal. He helps us get away, he can come with us to the next town. Somewhere better than here."

"Oh, hell no," Mark stood up, his face turning red with outrage. "No way is that guy coming with us. He's one of them, Anna. Have you forgotten the fight in the pharmacy?"

"He's not any more. Or have *you* forgotten how he saved our lives back there?"

"He's a thug!" Mark insisted. "Who knows how many people he hurt before we came along. Now, what, we're supposed to believe he's suddenly grown a conscience? For all we know he's just going to turn on us the way he turned on the gang. We can't trust him."

"He's the reason we got the medicine back. We owe it to him to hold up our end of the deal."

Mark jabbed a finger in my direction. "*Your* deal. Not my deal. I didn't agree to any of this."

I stiffened, glaring right back at him. "That's right, because you *weren't there*. You weren't exactly available for consultation."

"I didn't even want you to go in there in the first place." Mark scowled.

"Oh my God, are you still hung up on that?" I asked, incredulous. "We agreed! We both thought that was the least-shitty plan we had. You still think 'guns blazing' would've worked out better? You saw how many of them there were."

His jaw jutted out stubbornly. "I would've figured something out."

"Oh really? What were you going to do, huh? Tell me. I'd really love to know what your grand plan was."

He paced across the room, fists clenched. "I should've found another way!" The roar took me aback, and I set aside my righteous indignation long enough to recognize the shift in his expression. It wasn't just anger, but something else. Guilt. Shame. He turned back on me with anguished eyes, waving a hand towards my bloody face. "My God, Anna, you got beat up. You've got a man's blood all over you. You could've been killed. I never should have let you go with me."

I'd been so wrapped up in my own feelings, I hadn't stopped to think about how he was processing all of this. He still blamed himself for Lily getting sick in the first place, and now this.

The edge in my voice softened. "Mark, this whole overprotective thing is sweet, but you keep acting like it was your choice. It was mine." He scowled. "I mean it. We both knew the risks. If we had to go back and do it again for Lily? Neither one of us would hesitate. So let's just be thankful for how things turned out, okay?"

Still not entirely convinced, he at least gave me a reluctant nod. I steered the conversation back where we started. "I'm not asking you to trust Nikolai. I'm asking you to trust me. He just wants to come with us for a few weeks. I don't think that's too much to ask for the guy who risked his neck to help your daughter."

A long stretch of silence made me dread more argument, but finally he nodded. "All right. For you. But if he steps out of line, I'm going to have to kick his ass."

Remembering the fight in the hospital, I didn't have the heart to tell him that the ass-kicking would probably be the other way around. "Fair enough."

"I'll go tell him." At least he was gracious enough to do that much. "If you get the gear together, we can put some more distance between us and the hospital before nightfall." He stopped by the door. "And Anna? Thanks."

I glanced over at Lily and the IV hanging beside her, and allowed myself a smile.

CHAPTER 42

WE MADE OUR WAY THROUGH the woods down to the lake, figuring that if the gang came after us they'd look toward the city. After a mile or two, we eventually found a cluster of houses on the lakefront. Mark checked to make sure it was abandoned, then kicked in the door. The house was small but homey, and a thin layer of dust suggested nobody had been here in awhile. A big bay window had an impressive view of the lake, allowing light to flow into the front room.

Mark laid Lily down on the couch. Bear camped out at her feet, resting his head on his paws. His dark eyes betrayed his canine concern, but he had nothing on Mark's gaunt and worried features. After changing out the empty bag of saline for a fresh one and making sure the IV was situated, I grabbed my pack.

"I'm going to go get cleaned up." Fretting over Lily, Mark didn't respond. Nikolai nodded. I headed down to the lakeshore.

Nikolai found me there some time later. The trees had started to cast long shadows, the last remnants of daylight ebbing away. There was just enough light to see by, the sunset painting the sky over the lake with a beautiful mix of pinks and purples. I had washed off the sweat and blood, changed my clothes, and now sat cross-legged on the edge of the shore, watching the water lap at the rocks. It helped to calm me. So did a few sips from the medicinal whiskey I'd been saving.

"I see you took my advice," Nikolai said, smiling when he saw the bottle in my hand.

"If ever there was a day that called for it…" I held out the bottle to him in a silent offer. He came closer, taking it, then sat down in front of the rock where I'd laid my clothes out to dry. I couldn't get all the bloodstains out; I suppose they'd always be there as a reminder.

"You were gone for a while. Mark wanted me to see if you are all right." He took a sip of the whiskey. "Though I think he is afraid to use the word."

I snorted. "Well, I suppose I can't blame him." He watched me, eyebrows raised silently, and I couldn't duck the question any longer. "I'll be fine." Emphasis on the future tense, because right now I was anything but.

Nikolai handed the bottle back. I drank a little more and then stoppered it. Just a few sips had given me a buzz that made me feel warm and took the edge off my nerves. Too much more on an empty stomach and I'd be drunk off my ass and useless. Tempting as that was, Lily still needed me. I rolled the bottle back up in my sweatshirt and slipped it back into my pack. Hugging my knees to my chest, I sighed and looked back out at the lake. Nikolai seemed content to just sit and enjoy the view.

"How long were you in the army?" I wondered suddenly, breaking the silence.

"Two years. In Ukraine, before I come to America."

"You're Ukrainian?" He nodded, and I had to adjust my mental assessment of him being Russian. I watched him for a moment, marveling again at how calm he was after everything that had happened. "Did you see any combat?"

"A little. Fighting the—how do you say…" He waved a hand, fumbling for a second before coming up with the word. "Separatists."

I nodded again, falling quiet for a moment. "I've seen wars. People dying. Too many people." A quiet shudder ran through me, thinking about the mass graves in Sudan and the carnage at the airport after the blackout. "One time mortar shells fell in our courtyard, broke a bunch of windows. But I've never been in the thick of it. Being shot at, shooting at people…" I trailed off with a grim shake of my head.

"The world is different now. We do what we must, to survive."

"Yeah," I agreed softly.

"You did well, though. I have seen soldiers not keep their head so well."

"I don't know about that," I demurred. "I was scared out of my mind."

He shrugged. "In the army, my sergeant says anyone not scared in battle is a fool. Brave is doing it anyway."

I shifted uncomfortably at the praise, rubbing a knuckle along my eyebrow. "Well. I suppose that's one thing the ER teaches you, is how to stay calm in a crisis." Steering the conversation away from myself, I said, "Thank you, for what you did back there. You gave Lily a chance." I shot him a grateful smile, but it faded as worry took hold. "I just hope we got it to her in time."

He dipped his head in acknowledgement. "She is very important to you. You have known them a long time?"

"Not really. We met the day the blackout started, actually. But we've been through a lot together." Skipping a rock across the lake, I smiled faintly. "I suppose she wormed her way into my heart."

"And Mark?" Thick black eyebrows lifted questioningly.

"I told you, we're just friends. I'm helping them get to Maine. Mark thinks that his wife will be there. Their family has a cabin."

"Maine? That is very far, yes? In the north?" When I nodded, he said, "Long way to go for someone else's family."

I shrugged. "Well, you should be able to relate to that. Going out on a limb for strangers." Nikolai waved a hand to grant my point, a corner of his mouth quirking upward.

"Anna!" Mark's shout from the porch caused me to jolt upright, and it took me a second to realize how happy he sounded. "She's awake!"

I was on my feet in an instant and hurrying inside. Sleepy eyes looked up at me from the couch, and my heart leapt. Smiling so wide it hurt, I crouched down next to the couch. "Hey, sweetheart. How are you feeling?" I brushed some hair out of her face. Her fever hadn't broken yet, so she still wasn't out of the woods. But the fact that she had woken up was a good sign indeed.

"Sleepy." She moved the arm with the IV in it, a makeshift splint keeping it secure. "I don't like this thing. It feels funny."

I patted her shoulder. "I know, but you need it. It's for the medicine that's helping you to get better. You're going to be just fine. You just need some rest so you can fight off the germs." Bear's tail thumped against the ground, and he inched forward to put his paw on her leg and get in on some of the loving reunion action.

"I knew you'd get it." Her tiny smile and the faith in me made every bit of awfulness pale in comparison. Then she frowned, registering my swollen cheek and the butterfly strips over my eyebrow. "You got hurt."

"I'm fine," I assured her, smiling at her concern. "Don't worry."

She nodded, taking me at my word. Her brow creased as she looked behind me. "Who's that?"

Looking up, I realized that Nikolai had followed me in. "That's Nikolai. He's uh…" Wow, how to explain that one to a seven-year-old. "He's a new friend. He helped us get the medicine for you."

"Hi," Lily said, offering a timid little wave.

"Hello," the big Ukrainian replied, sounding a little awkward. "I am glad you are feeling better."

"You get some rest, okay?" I told Lily. Patting her arm, I stood up and let Mark take the space I'd vacated. Nikolai clapped me on the back of the shoulder, offering a nod of celebration.

Lily drifted back off soon after that, and then it was just the three of us for a tense candle-lit supper in the dining room. I found some rice and canned corn in the pantry, which was a nice supplement to our left-over venison jerky. After the meals we'd skimped on the way here, it felt like a feast. Yet Mark ate with a sullen expression, equal parts worried about Lily and annoyed about Nikolai's presence.

I couldn't stand the silence any longer. "What did you do before all this, Nikolai?"

"I worked on the gas pipeline. Installing meters, doing inspections."

"Really." Mark sounded surprised. I don't know what he had expected—gangster? Or maybe the idea that anyone had a mundane life before all this was amazing enough in its own right.

"I know you were a doctor." Nikolai's gaze shifted to Mark with polite interest. "What about you?"

"Software engineer. I worked for a company in Boston that made manufacturing equipment."

Nikolai took a sip of water before remarking, "I came to America to study engineering. Mechanical. But I never finished."

"What happened?" I wondered between spoonfuls of corn.

Nikolai smiled wistfully. "A beautiful woman. We married, and I switched part-time so I can work and support us." Then the smile thinned. "Then, you know. Life happens. There are always things we mean to do, that we never get back to."

Mark nodded sympathetically, the corners of his mouth dipping downward. "Yeah. It's easy to fool ourselves into thinking we've got all the time in the world." He let out a mournful sigh. "You're married?"

"I was." The grim emphasis on the past tense became clear. "She died."

"I'm sorry," I said softly, which Mark affirmed with a quiet agreement. "The blackout?"

Shaking his head, Nikolai sipped at his coffee—another luxury we'd found in the kitchen cupboards. "No, it was a few years before. Car crash." It may have been years ago, but the sadness in his voice was still fresh. "Sometimes I think it is good that she did not have to see the world this way."

"You mean the way that gangs like yours are making it?" Mark challenged mildly.

I frowned. "Mark."

Nikolai held up his hand to stave off my reproach, meeting Mark's disapproving gaze head-on. "You are an engineer. Do the maths. There are more people in the cities than food for them to eat. We fight to survive. What choice is there?"

"That's bullshit." Mark gestured with his spoon. "The world is what we make of it. What's the point of surviving if we lose our humanity in the process?"

Nikolai scowled. "You Americans always like things to be black and white."

"Some things are black and white; right and wrong."

"Right and wrong," Nikolai echoed sardonically. "Like how you break into someone's house and steal their food and things?" I felt a pang of guilt about the jeans and T-shirt I'd appropriated from the upstairs closet.

Mark couldn't deny it, but shook his head. "We don't *hurt* people."

"No? Tell that to Carl, or Shaw."

"That was self-defense!"

"It isn't self-defense if you are stealing from someone."

"It wasn't even your stuff! You guys took over a goddamn hospital. Think of all the people who could've been helped by the supplies in there."

"You think someone will come along and set up a charity hospital? That is not the world any more."

"Why'd you help us?" My sudden interjection caused both the guys to stop hammering at each other and look at me. "If survival's the only thing that matters, why go out on a limb for us?" It didn't jive with the rationalizations he was offering, but maybe they were just that—rationalizations of a guilty conscience.

Nikolai's expression softened, though he still frowned in Mark's direction. "I am not a monster who would watch a child die." Then he gave me the tiniest of smiles. "And maybe I am missing some optimism." I smiled back at the reference to our conversation in the OR.

Mark wasn't amused. "Lucky us," he said dourly. "I'm going to go sit with Lily." He picked up his tray and sulked his way back to the living room.

"He is not a fan," Nikolai observed with a wry expression.

After eating another forkful of rice, I shrugged. "He'll come around."

I hoped so, anyway. Otherwise it was going to be a long trip.

CHAPTER 43

THE NEXT DAY, WE HEADED out of the city and back onto the trail. Nikolai and Mark fashioned a makeshift litter for Lily out of a blanket, some duct tape, and a couple old broomsticks. It was certainly better than the tarp we'd brought her here on. The guys carried her, both chivalrously refusing to let me take a turn. Setting aside the affront to my inner feminist, I didn't mind. I ached from an array of bruises, and I hadn't gotten much rest the night before. I think I was asleep before my head hit the pillow, but I didn't stay that way for long before I woke, the tendrils of some hazy nightmare clinging to me and robbing me of breath. I couldn't remember anything specific from the dream, but it had left me shaken in a way I couldn't describe. I'd spent the rest of the night keeping watch over Lily, with Bear resting his head on my leg.

We didn't make very good time, but it was a relief to be out in the forest again. I wouldn't feel safe until we were in another zip code.

Lily napped off and on, but in-between she gave Nikolai the third degree. "How come you talk like that?"

"I was born in Ukraine."

"Where's Ukraine?"

"Across the ocean."

"My friend Oliver at school is British. Britain is across the ocean too. He talks with an accent, like you. Well, not actually exactly like you. His accent is British so it's different. Is Ukraine near Britain?"

"Ukraine is on the other side of Europe. It is very far."

"Did you come on an airplane? We came on an airplane from Boston."

Chuckling to myself, I gave Nikolai a clap on the shoulder. "Good luck with that," I stage-whispered to him. I picked up a stick and tossed it for Bear to fetch. He bounded off down the trail to retrieve it.

"It's such a relief to see her chattering away again," I said to Mark as I came up beside him.

Mark nodded heartily. "You can say that again. How are you feeling?"

"I'm all right." Not really, but I was on the mend at least. Bear pressed the stick into my hand, and I tossed it for him again.

"Mark, I think your daughter missed her calling as interrogator for the KGB," Nikolai observed good-naturedly. I chuckled, and even Mark had to smile at that one.

"What's the Kaygeebee?" Lily wondered, slurring the letters together. And so the game continued.

Over the next few days, we slowly increased our pace and fell into new routines as a quartet instead of a trio. We avoided traveling during the hottest parts of the day, since summer was slow to give up its hold on the northeast. The shorter days gave Lily and I extra time to recover, and Nikolai a chance to ease into the rigors of long-distance hiking. He was in great shape, but he said he hadn't walked this much since boot camp. Each afternoon I carefully tended to his blisters, but he never complained.

Mark still hadn't warmed up to him, but Nikolai got along well with Lily and me. He was eager to learn trapping and foraging, and tolerated Lily's constant curiosity like a champ.

Poor Lily was in that awkward state of healing where she was better enough to be awake most of the day, but bored out of her mind just laying there on the cot. Mark and I took turns trying to amuse her. Mark would play silly travel games like 'I Spy' and spotting things that started with each letter of the alphabet. With me she liked to act out scenes in her imagination. The stretcher was, by turns, a carriage, a fire truck and a spaceship, depending on which story struck Lily's fancy.

"Mister Nikolai—do you want to play?" she asked the quiet Ukrainian one afternoon when we were putting together a game.

"Erm. I will, only I am not sure how to play."

"Oh it's easy," Lily said brightly.

Mark chimed in dryly, "Yeah, maybe you can be the bad guy."

I rolled my eyes, but Lily did one better. "No, Daddy, you can be the robber trying to steal our treasure. Mister Nikolai can be my knight." The scowl on Mark's face was priceless.

When we stopped later that day for lunch, I sat next to Nikolai under an ash tree. "You were a good sport playing with Lily. I think even Mark has to give you props for that."

Nikolai let out a 'hmmf' that suggested he wasn't holding his breath on kudos from Mark. "I try. I am not very good with children."

"You do all right." I watched him for a moment, then asked tentatively, "So you and your wife—you never had kids?" I worried that it would be a sore subject, but I found myself curious about our new traveling companion.

"No." A sad smile touched his lips. "But she would have been very good. Daniella was a schoolteacher. She always had so much love for her students." He looked off into the forest, consumed by memory, but then shifted his gaze back to me. "What about you? You have never married?"

"No. Came close once."

"Close?"

"I was engaged to a guy in medical school, but it didn't work out." I shrugged.

When I didn't elaborate, Nikolai prompted, "What happened?"

I started twisting the granola bar wrapper from lunch into foil origami, frowning and debating how much I wanted to say. "We had dated off and on all through school, then fourth year he proposed. I thought he was the one, you know?" My mouth twisted at how wrong I'd been. "After graduation, Charlie and I tried to get assigned to the same hospital for residency, or at least the same city, but with our rankings and specialties—" I waved a hand, glossing over the byzantine complexities of the national match system. "Long story short, we ended up in different states. We said we'd make it work; try to transfer next year. But then six months later, he broke things off. Said the whole long-distance thing wasn't working for him; his life was 'going in another direction', whatever the hell that means." I shrugged. The wound still ached after all these years.

Nikolai's mouth twitched downward, but he stayed quiet and let me ramble.

"After that, I guess work got in the way. Residency. Missions overseas. I dated some, mostly guys from the hospital, but it's hard to get serious when you never stay in one place for long." That was only half true. Charlie calling off the engagement had pulled the rug out from under me. Work became my refuge. My escape. It was easier to focus on putting broken bodies back together than to deal with my own problems. Over the years, escape gave way to habit, and here I was.

Nikolai squinted in a way that made me suspect he knew I was holding back, but he didn't call me on it. He just smiled. "Their loss, then." He held my gaze with those intense brown eyes, and I found myself mustering up a faint smile back.

Then Mark doused the campfire with a pot of water, and the moment was broken. "You guys ready to go?"

I cleared my throat, breaking off the gaze. "Uh, yeah. Let's get going." Nikolai offered me a hand up, and I held onto it a second or two more than necessary. This day was looking better already.

CHAPTER 44

AFTER A WEEK OF TRAVELING, we decided to take some time off to do some camp chores and make some more jerky. Nikolai and I headed off to put out snares. As we followed a game trail through the woods, we heard the rushing of water and discovered a large pool being fed by a waterfall. The water cascaded down the rocks in a three-tiered waterfall, the last leg just over head height. It left the pool in a stream, winding its way back towards the direction we'd camped.

We approached the water cautiously, checking the area for any signs of people or animals before letting our guard down. "It's beautiful," I remarked. Nikolai gave a soft grunt of agreement.

It wasn't until he started stripping off clothes that I realized he was intending to go for a swim. "You coming?"

I was too busy gawking to answer. Ripped chest, six pack, and boxer briefs—it was enough to make my breath catch in my throat for a second. Nikolai smirked when he saw my face, and it widened into a grin when I blushed. Damn pale skin.

I cleared my throat, trying to regain some semblance of dignity. "Yeah, okay. Guess it's not every day you get to swim under a waterfall." I started taking off my outer layer as well.

He sloshed out into the pool. It didn't take long before he was in water up to his waist. I stripped down to my underthings, all too aware of him watching me as I waded out to join him in the water. "You are going to swim in your boots?" he asked, perplexed.

I suppose it was an odd sight. "Lily cut her foot in the water—that's how she got sick. Call me paranoid."

He gave a soft aah and shrugged. "These days I think it is good to be a little bit paranoid."

I dove in, gliding across the pool. Swimming with my hiking boots was a pain in the ass, but such was the price of paranoia. The water was cool and clear, and I did spy some fish under the surface. We swam and chatted for a while, enjoying the pleasant quiet of the valley and each others' company. I tried not to stare too much at his muscles. At one point, though, though, my curiosity got the better of me. "Your tattoos—are they like those Russian mafia ones?"

Before today, I'd seen only glimpses of the tattoos adorning his arms and torso, but now I could see the elaborate ink in all its glory. A spiderweb stretched across his right shoulder, and I could pick out a rose, an eagle and some kind of cathedral in the array of images drawn on his chest. It reminded me of a guy I'd seen in a movie about the Russian mob once. I wondered idly if Ukraine had the same thing.

Nikolai chuckled. "You think I'm mafia?"

"I never know with you," I pointed out good-naturedly.

"There are many things you don't tell me about you either," he said. "But no, I am not mafia. The gang—they make the same mistake as you. They think I am some kind of crime boss. It came in handy." He let his gaze drift across the pool for a moment, a distant look on his face, then looked back at me. "I saw you have one too." He must have noticed the tattoo on my abdomen when I took my shirt off—a leaping dolphin. "You did not strike me as woman with tattoos."

I wasn't sure how to take that and arched an eyebrow. "What kind of woman do I strike you as?"

"That is easy," he said, amusement twinkling in his eyes. "Smart. Beautiful. Little bit crazy." He held his fingers up an inch apart to illustrate, and laughed when I splashed water at him. "You have big heart." I wanted to be irritated by his smug assessment, but it was hard to do when he was being so damn flattering. That pesky blush reared its head again. "Your tattoo—what is the story?"

"That guy I told you about—the one I was engaged to—he had a bunch of tattoos. I went with him once when he was getting a new one, and this caught my eye. Reminds me of home." Thinking of Charlie now made me conscious of how long it had been since I'd been in a serious relationship.

"It is very nice." Then he looked thoughtful. "So… you like men with tattoos."

My eyebrows lifted. "Depends on the man."

"Does he have ink?" A little jerk of his head in the direction of the camp indicated Mark.

"Not that I know of." Though I had seen enough of him to be pretty sure he didn't.

"Then I have advantage."

I snorted. "It's not a contest."

"Then definitely I have the advantage." His grin widened.

"Maybe," I finally admitted, with a little smile. That was enough encouragement for him to take a step closer, into my personal space bubble. When I didn't back away, he touched my side under the water, his fingers brushing lightly over the dolphin. His touch sent a pleasant tingle through me. Something had changed between us, and I could tell from the look in his eyes that Nikolai could sense it, too.

I stared at him for a long moment, then closed the distance between us to seek out his lips with mine. He drew me in against that well-toned chest, strong hands settling on my back. We stood like that for several minutes, making out like the world had ended and we might not get another chance. Which wasn't far from the truth, really.

I murmured between kisses, "Mark and Lily are going to wonder what happened to us."

Nikolai gave a non-committal grunt, "Let them wonder little longer." He dotted kisses down my neck to my shoulder, eradicating any trace of willpower. "I am not in a hurry to go back."

Ah, what the hell. I wasn't in any hurry to go back either.

CHAPTER 45

MARK WAS ALL FROWNS WHEN we finally made it back to camp. "You could've told me you were going to go swimming. I thought something had happened to you guys." Despite my apology, and genuine guilt, he continued to be in a grumpy mood all afternoon.

"I think he is jealous," Nikolai mumbled at one point, jerking his head toward Mark.

I dismissed the idea with a snort. "He's just pissed at me for making him worry. Again." Nikolai shrugged, unconvinced.

That night, I lay awake for a longtime, trying to pick out the stars through the canopy of trees. The northern lights continued to stretch across the sky, a familiar sight by now. I thought of Nikolai— everything we'd been through together, from the calm confidence at the hospital to the easy smile when playing with Lily. While it still paled next to the strong connection I felt with Mark, there was something there. A potential for something more. And anyway, Mark was off limits. Untouchable. Nikolai was anything but.

I padded over to where he slept, a blanket draped over my shoulders. He jerked awake, muscles tensing as if ready to face some threat, then relaxed when he saw it was just me. His expression shifted with a dawning realization, and he smiled. "You woke me up from a good dream," he teased as he pulled me closer for a kiss.

Smiling back, I promised, "I'll make it up to you."

Seeing our blankets next to each other the next morning did nothing for Mark's mood, and he continued his cold shoulder routine until lunchtime. Eventually I'd had enough of the awkward silence. While Nikolai was off collecting water from the stream, I sat down beside Mark. A brief flick of his eyes in my direction was the only acknowledgment of my presence, and he went back to getting out the meal kit.

Arching my eyebrows at him, I said dryly, "You going to give me the silent treatment all the way to Maine?"

When only a frown answered me, I thought the answer might be yes. Then he said, "Is this really a smart idea? Having some fling with a guy like that?" He spoke in a low tone, pitched only for me. Not that Lily was paying us any mind; she and Bear were playing fetch on the other side of the campfire.

I don't know why it pushed a button, but it did. I snapped back, "I'm sorry he doesn't meet with your approval. Next time I'll try to find someone who's as perfect as your perfect wife."

The hurt, angry look that flashed in his eyes made me regret my words. "Leave Lauren out of this," he growled. "You hardly know this guy."

"You hardly knew me when you asked me to walk across the country with you," I pointed out.

"That was different, Anna, and you know it." Mark jabbed a finger toward the stream. "You didn't give me any reason to distrust you. He has."

I frowned, following his gesture for a moment before turning my irritated glare back on Mark. "You know what, Mark? This isn't about you. The world has gone to hell; we've nearly been killed so many times I've lost count, and…" I stopped shy of enumerating how trekking through the woods with him and Lily had resulted in a jumble of mixed-up feelings. "It doesn't matter. I'm a grown woman and I'm entitled to have a fling with whomever I damn well please. I don't need to justify it to you."

Mark sighed and held up his hands in surrender. "You're right. I just worry about you, you know? I don't want you to get hurt." It was sweet of him, in a frustrating big-brother sort of way. But then he had to go and ruin it. "I hope you're being… you know… careful with him."

I rolled my eyes and then shot him a narrowed look. "Wow, I'm so glad you warned me. I totally missed the day they taught safe sex in medical school."

"Anna…I didn't mean it like that," he protested, but I wasn't listening. I stood up and stomped away, back to the other side of the camp. Mercifully, he let it drop.

A more surprising concern came from Lily about a week later. I was brushing her hair one evening when she asked out of the blue, "Are you and Mister Nikolai going to get married?" Mark and Nikolai were down by the creek, out of earshot.

"What?" I drew back in surprise, the brush pausing in mid-stroke. She'd seen me hold his hand and give him a kiss goodnight, but her question was a hell of a leap. "No, sweetheart. We just met."

"Oh. Yeah, like how Anna should've waited longer before she said she'd marry Hans," Lily said thoughtfully. It took me a second to realize she was talking about *Frozen* again. "Then she would've known he was actually a bad guy."

I chuckled softly. Important life lessons from Disney movies: don't marry people you just met at a party. "Something like that. But we know Nikolai's not a bad guy. He helped us fight the bad guys to save you."

"Yeah. But you like him."

"Sure." I resumed my brushing, smiling at the thought. "But it takes more than just liking somebody to marry them. And anyway, I don't know how long he's going to keep traveling with us." The deal had been to the next town. We had passed through a nearly-deserted hamlet yesterday, but I presumed he was holding out for something better. I was in no hurry for him to leave, and Mark at least had not tried to run him off at the first sign of civilization.

"Good."

"Good?" Her matter-of-fact response took me aback. "I thought you liked Nikolai?"

"He's nice."

I'd known her long enough to recognize that slight dip of her head. There was something she was holding back. "What's the matter?"

Her little shoulders shrugged beneath the waves of golden hair. Finally she spat it out, in a very small voice. "I don't want you to marry Mister Nikolai because I want you to marry Daddy."

I froze. What the hell does one say to *that*? "Oh, Lily…" My mouth opened and closed a couple of times, fumbling for the words. "That's really sweet, but… your dad's already married to your mom."

"But you don't think we're going to find her," Lily said, and I could hear the tears in her voice. "I heard you tell Daddy."

Shit. How long has she been carrying that around? It had been ages since Mark and I had argued about finding Lauren. I didn't think she'd heard us. Setting the hairbrush aside, I shifted her on my lap so I could see her face. I brushed away the tears on her cheeks with the back of my hand, feeling like an absolute ass.

"Oh, sweetheart, sometimes grownups say things we don't mean." I looked into those watery hazel eyes. Whether I believed we'd find Lauren or not was irrelevant; I needed *her* to believe it. "We're going to make it to Maine, and I bet your mom's going to be there waiting for us. You know, it's a lot closer from Boston to Maine. She doesn't have as far to walk as we do."

"But what if she isn't?"

"Do you really think your dad's going to stop looking for her?" I arched my eyebrows at her, challenging gently. She considered that for a moment, then shook her head. "That's right. He loves her very much, Lily. Wherever she is, I know she won't stop trying to find you. And I promise, I won't stop looking either. Okay?"

She nodded tearfully, and then threw herself against me in a fierce hug. I held her close, patting her back gently, until she relaxed and pulled back to peer at me. "If Daddy wasn't married, would you want to marry him?"

Those earnest eyes were watching me expectantly. I should have answered 'no, of course not' for a number of reasons, but I just froze with a stupid look on my face. Eventually I stammered, "I... I don't know. It's kind of hard to imagine."

"Okay." Lily smiled, seeming satisfied by that answer. But it had unlocked a train of thought that left me more unsettled than I cared to admit.

CHAPTER 46

THE DAYS AND MILES PASSED in a blur as we continued our trek across central New York. One afternoon, we came to an overlook that took my breath away. Forested hills, stretching out as far as the eye could see, were separated by lush green clearings. The leaves had just started to turn, yellows and oranges sprinkled here and there like highlights. Off to the west, the sunlight reflected off a small lake. We all stood there for a few minutes, catching our breath after the arduous climb up.

We had walked for days without even seeing a town, or even another person, and from our vantage point there was nothing but wilderness. Having seen how things were in the last town, I could only imagine what it was like now in the bigger cities, with no power and transportation: rampant starvation, anarchy, people murdering each other over scraps. How many dead? Millions? Tens of millions? Even after seeing atrocities in Sudan and C.A.R. and the destruction in Haiti, my mind balked at the thought of death on that scale. It was hard to reconcile that with the peaceful isolation on the trail.

Lily's voice snapped me back from my grisly daydreams. "I wish Mommy could see this."

"Me too, princess," Mark murmured. His voice was off, and when I looked at him I could see that a sad pall had crept across his face. Nonetheless, he gave Lily's shoulders a comforting squeeze.

A few days later, Nikolai and I ventured out to see if we could shoot some game for supper. "Stay safe," Mark warned me with a pointed look before we left.

"Yes, Dad," I teased him, rolling my eyes.

It was a pleasant afternoon; a nice breeze kept it from being too muggy. Nikolai wondered idly, "Did you go hunting before the blackout?" When I shook my head, he asked, "How do you learn all these things?"

"We got a couple 'how not to get completely screwed and die in the wilderness' books back when this all started." I stepped over a fallen log and mused, "You know, if things ever get back to normal, I'll have to write a big thank you note to those authors."

Slanting me a perplexed look, Nikolai asked, "You really think things will be 'normal' after all of this?"

The question erased my brief bit of levity. "No. Not in our lifetimes." I slanted a rueful look his way. "But I hope things will be better for Lily."

"You care for her very much," Nikolai observed, ducking to avoid a low-hanging branch.

"Of course I do." He just nodded and kept walking. There was a distance in his eyes that gave me pause. "What's the matter?"

"Nothing."

"Hey," I said gently, reaching for his hand and tugging to get him to stop walking and face me. Bear trotted ahead a few steps then turned back and canted his head at us as if to say, *Come on, humans, let's get a move on. We've got birds to hunt.* Ignoring him, I fixed my attention on Nikolai. "What is it?"

He looked like he might say something, but then the crack of a gunshot echoed through the forest.

I jumped, but the shot wasn't aimed at us. Fear clutched my heart at the immediate thought that Mark and Lily might be in danger, but the direction and distance were all wrong. The shot was ahead of us, and much too close to be them. We hadn't seen another person since leaving the last town. What was going on?

Exchanging concerned glances, Nikolai and I moved cautiously forward. Bear, sensing our reactions, perked up in alert. We crested a small rise, which gave us a better vantage point to a valley bisected by a stream. The foliage cut down visibility, but a splash of blue against the greens and browns down below helped us pick out a small group of people, maybe a hundred yards away, along the edge of the water. Muted cries filtered up to us, frantic but unintelligible.

Pulling my binoculars from their pouch, I focused on the group. There were three of them, dressed for hiking. Large backpacks like ours sat around the remains of a fire. One man was lying motionless on the ground, a panicked woman grabbing his bloody shirt and trying to pull him up.

"Oh my God." I stared slack-jawed at the people. They all appeared to be unarmed, making it clear that—whatever was happening—it was anything but a fair fight.

I heard another gunshot, and the binoculars gave me a close-up view as blood and gore sprayed from the woman's head. I jerked back and almost dropped the binoculars. The woman slumped lifelessly over the man she'd been tending.

Nikolai took the binoculars from my limp fingers, scanning the area beyond the family—at least, I presumed they were a family. "I see him —on that rise there." He pointed to a hill directly opposite us, the besieged family directly between us and the shooter's position. I squinted but couldn't see anything until another shot rang out. Then I spotted the muzzle flash in the area Nikolai indicated.

I forced my eyes back to the family. The third person—a kid who couldn't have been far out of his teens—was clutching his arm and scrambling behind a tree for cover. "We have to do something."

"Too dangerous," Nikolai said immediately, lowering the binoculars with a grim shake of his head.

I took the binoculars back from Nikolai and looked down at the boy again. His eyes were wide with terror, head swinging back and forth looking for some avenue of escape. "He's just a kid, for God's sake. We can't just leave him there." A bullet chipped harmlessly off the thick tree he was cowering behind, making him flinch. My fingers clenched tightly around the field glasses, helpless frustration washing over me.

"We show ourselves, we get a bullet in our heads next."

"So what—we just sit here and watch him die?"

Nikolai frowned at me. "What else do we do? You want us to go charge in there like your cowboys?"

I cursed under my breath. What the hell was I thinking? We weren't cops. We weren't soldiers. While I watched, the sniper rose to his feet. Oblivious to me studying him from afar, he began moving cautiously along the ridge. He wore a hunter's camouflage, hunched over with his rifle at the ready.

"He's moving in to finish him off," I said, heart racing with newfound urgency. I gave Nikolai another turn with the binoculars.

"I only see one man," he mumbled.

"Look—this ridge curves over that way. We can follow it around and cut him off before he makes it to the kid. As long as we stick to the far side of the crest, he won't be able to see us."

Nikolai squinted in the direction I indicated, frowning. "This is not a good idea. That boy is nothing to us. What will Mark and Lily think if you are killed doing stupid heroics?"

Bringing up Lily was a low blow, and I glowered at him. "He's a boy who doesn't deserve to be murdered by some psycho. Mark would understand, and we're wasting time arguing about it."

Without another word, I scurried back down the ridge, hopefully out of sight if the sniper happened to be looking our way. Bear followed, and I heard Nikolai's feet skid on the dry leaves behind me. I was reassured that he would stick by me even though he thought I was being irrational.

"You know we must kill him, yes?" Nikolai challenged matter-of-factly. He checked that his shotgun was ready.

I swallowed hard but nodded, the rifle feeling heavy in my hands. I wasn't that naive. We'd given Peter and Kerry a pass, but this guy was *killing* people. We couldn't call the cops, or drag a prisoner with us all the way to Maine. It made me uneasy, but there was no other way. "I know."

"And you are okay with that?" He sounded surprised.

"Who knows how many people he's killed in cold blood, Nikolai," I said, catching my balance on a tree as some loose rocks threatened to send me into a tumble down the slope. "If we don't do anything to stop him, and he hurts someone else—then that's on us too."

Nikolai gave a soft grunt to that, probably unconvinced by my logic but at least no longer doubting my resolve. We fell quiet after that, not wanting to draw attention to ourselves. After several minutes, we had come far enough to have a chance of intercepting the guy. Since we were below the crest of the ridge, there was no way for us to know his exact position. Motioning for me to stay put, Nikolai whispered, "Stay here. I will go look." He borrowed my binoculars, and crept up to the top of the hill to locate the sniper.

I watched him crest the top of the hill, anxiously awaiting his return. I felt, more than heard, Bear give a very soft growl by my knee. "Quiet, boy," I whispered, squinting in the direction he was looking. All I saw were trees.

The seconds ticked by, but I couldn't stand the waiting. Quietly as I could, I moved up the hill. My eyes scanned the forest, every muscle coiled and on alert as I reached the top of the ridge.

The crack of a rifle, close and straight ahead, made me jump out of my skin. Nikolai's shotgun boomed from somewhere off to my left, followed by another rifle shot. I took cover behind a sturdy oak tree, worried about being caught in the cross-fire, and motioned for Bear to get down.

I didn't see Nikolai, but movement caught my eye and I drew in a sharp breath. It was the sniper, moving in a low crouch across the slope barely ten feet away. I lifted the rifle to my shoulder and leaned against the tree to steady myself. The barrel wavered in my trembling hands. His back was to me, completely oblivious to the gun trained on him. The parallel with his victims was not lost on me.

My heart hammered in my chest, the blood rushing in my ears like a freight train. I thought of the people he'd attacked, but no amount of righteous anger could overcome what felt like a ten-ton weight holding my trigger finger in place. *Nothing stops me from shooting some asshole who's trying to kill us*, I'd said blithely to Lily's grandfather, but the reality of it wasn't so simple.

I don't know what made him look my way. Maybe I rustled a branch, or Bear's paw disturbed some leaves. Whatever the reason, he spotted us and his eyes went wide. Now that I could see him clearly, I realized how ordinary he looked—mid-twenties, with short brown hair beneath his camouflaged cap, and a day's stubble on his cheeks.

"Drop the rifle." I hoped I didn't look as terrified as I felt. I could see him weighing his options, deciding whether he could shoot me before I shot him. I jerked the rifle for emphasis. "Drop it now." What the hell was I going to do with him if he did? One problem at a time.

Glaring daggers at me the whole time, he let the rifle thud into the tall grass. "Step away from it." He lifted his hands to just above waist level, palms out, and took two steps back. I left the shelter of my tree and slowly moved closer, keeping the rifle trained on him the entire way. Bear stayed obediently behind.

"Nikolai! I got him!"

He didn't answer.

"Nikolai?" Dread pooled in my stomach as the silence stretched on. "Nikolai!"

I didn't mean to take my eyes off of the sniper. It was only for a split second—an instinctive glance up toward Nikolai's position—but the sniper saw it, and he launched himself at me.

I fired, but he was moving too fast and I only grazed his shoulder. Bear started barking as the sniper crashed into my stomach like a football player coming in for a tackle. The momentum carried us down the slope, rolling head-over-heels a couple times before we went off a grassy shelf and were briefly airborne through a six-foot fall. I stretched my arms out to protect my head, and felt a white-hot pain explode in my right forearm when it took the brunt of my weight coming down. The rest of me hit the dirt an instant later, a bone-jarring thud that drove the air from my lungs and left me seeing stars. The lower slope wasn't as steep. We only rolled a few times before coming to a stop.

Dazed and winded, I tried to get up. I only made it as far as my knees before a blinding pain in my arm stopped me cold.

Groaning, I tried to get my bearings.

Where was the sniper?

Where was my rifle?

The sniper had lurched to his feet nearby, his shoulder bloody. More blood dribbled down his face from a cut on his scalp. I spotted my rifle laying on the slope a few feet away and started scrambling for it— awkwardly crawling with just one hand for balance. He stopped me short with a sharp kick to the side that sent me sprawling and wheezing. Another kick followed, then another and another, the steel toe of his boot driving into my chest like a jackhammer. I cried out and curled into a ball in a vain attempt to ward off the blows.

The man let out a surprised shout. I glanced up just in time to see Bear barreling down the hill towards him. The charge was enough to send the sniper stumbling away from me. I could only stare, slack-jawed, as the gentle dog barked and growled at the guy. Bear didn't bite him, more's the pity, but I counted myself lucky he had any protective instincts at all.

I struggled up into a crouch and remembered my pistol. My right arm was useless, but with my left I fumbled with the catch on my pistol holster and managed to get the weapon out. The gun wavered unsteadily as I leveled it at the hunter.

Bear yelped when the other man kicked him away, and I fired. Even left-handed, after months of shooting squirrels and rabbits there was no way I could miss a man-sized target at this range. The bullet hit him on the right side of his chest. He fell back on his rear end.

I lurched to my feet just as Bear lunged forward again. "Bear, come. Come." The command was more of a whimper, but Bear obeyed and moved to my side. Cradling my right arm against my chest, I took a few halting steps toward the downed sniper, keeping my gun on him.

"Wait! Please," the other man blurted, looking frightened now for the first time. He got to his knees and held his hand out in front of him, as if that could ward off the bullet. His other hung limply by his side, blood already staining the shoulder of his jacket. "Please, I have a family. They'll die without me."

My resolve wavered, but then I thought of the family he'd attacked. That could've been Mark and Lily and I. It could be another family tomorrow if I let him go. My voice was clipped, anger warring with anguish. "Those people you killed were a family too. Were they even the first?"

He scowled, pumping his hand in a staying gesture. "Come on. We're all just trying to survive, lady."

His face showed no sign of remorse. I knew, in my heart, that if I spared him he'd do it again.

He opened his mouth to say something else, but I didn't let him finish. The gun jerked in my hand, splitting the silence of the forest, and the sniper slumped lifelessly into the tangle of underbrush.

My knees buckled. I sank down on them, choking out a horrified sob. *My God, what have I done?* Bear nudged my shoulder with his head, and I buried my face in his fur for a minute. "Good boy," I whispered tearfully.

I didn't want to move. Everything hurt too much, and I felt sick. But a desperate worry drove me to my feet once more. I grabbed a spindly birch tree for balance. Once the world stopped spinning, I plodded uphill. Bear followed close behind me, ears pinned back with worry. "Nikolai!"

Making my way back up the slope was torture. Once, I slipped. A consuming agony washed over me and I vomited on the hillside. It took considerable willpower to force myself to keep going, but Nikolai still hadn't answered. Something was terribly wrong.

I found the spot where the sniper had tackled me. Remembering that Nikolai's shot had come from the left, I staggered in that general direction, calling his name.

It was Bear who found him, leaving my side to dart up the slope. He barked a couple times, and that's when I spotted the blue denim of Nikolai's jeans sticking out from behind a tree. "Nikolai!"

CHAPTER 47

I WANTED TO RUN TO Nikolai, but all I could manage was an unsteady shamble. Using my rifle as a crutch, I lowered myself to my knees beside him. His face was covered in blood, flowing freely from an ugly rip near his left ear.

"Nikolai? Can you hear me?" I felt for a pulse, and found one strong and steady. "Thank God." Stifling a pained cry as I leaned over him, I rubbed the knuckles of my good hand hard against his breastbone. He groaned and tried to shift away. "Nikolai! Come on, open your eyes."

His eyes fluttered open, and slowly focused on me. "Anechka." He had taken to calling me that, explaining it was a more intimate nickname for 'Anna' in Ukrainian.

"I'm here, Nikolai." I gently gripped his chin and turned his head so I could see the wound better. Despite the copious amount of blood, it seemed shallow. "You're going to be okay. The bullet only grazed you."

He grimaced and tried to reach a hand up to his head, but I gently pushed it aside. Alarm flashed in his eyes as he remembered what had happened. "The hunter?"

I swallowed hard, reliving the moment in my head. The smell of cordite; the way his head snapped back; the spray of blood. "He, uh…" My voice sounded distant and shaky to my ears. "I got him."

Nikolai understood without me saying more. "Good." He groaned as I pressed my neckerchief against the wound.

"Just lie still. Hold that to stop the bleeding." Biting back a wince, I sat back against the tree and closed my eyes. Bear laid down beside me, watching me worriedly.

"You are hurt," Nikolai said in sudden realization. There was an edge of concern in his voice I hadn't heard before. Grunting, he sat up and scooted over. "Your arm? Tell me what to do."

"And my ribs. God, it hurts," I gasped out breathlessly. I hadn't examined the arm before, but Nikolai gingerly peeled back the sleeve and muttered something unpleasant in his native language. The arm bent inward at a sickening angle, as if there were an extra, unnatural joint in the middle of the forearm. The bloody white edge of my ulna jutted out through the skin. Nikolai's fingers gently probed my ribcage, but stopped when I yelped and tried to pull away.

"I am sorry," he murmured. "What do I do? Do you want me to set it straight?"

I shook my head. "No, not here. Better with Mark to help. Just…" I winced, licking dry lips. "Just rinse it out and try to find something to splint it with." Nikolai nodded and rose. After an unsteady moment, he headed off to find some suitable sticks.

Having calmed down from my initial adrenaline-fueled panic, I was able to take better stock of the injuries with a clinical detachment. Compound fracture of the right forearm. Maybe a wrist fracture too— or at least a bad sprain. No pins-and-needles sensation or pale skin that would indicate nerve or blood vessel damage. A couple cracked ribs, but no labored breathing or other signs of a lung injury. It could have been a lot worse, though right now that was a paltry consolation.

When Nikolai returned a few minutes later, he had the sniper's rifle slung over his shoulder, and some strips of cloth and sticks in his hand. He crouched beside me. "This will hurt. I am sorry," he warned in advance before using the sticks and cloth to form a makeshift splint around my forearm. I jammed my other fist into my mouth to stifle the screams, tears streaming down my cheeks.

Nikolai murmured soft, soothing words in Ukrainian, his face scrunched up in concentration as he worked. Finally, he used the sniper's T-shirt as a sling to pin the tortured limb across my chest. Touching my cheek lightly, he said, "You rest. I will go find the boy."

In all the madness, I'd almost lost sight of why we were doing all this. There was still a hurt kid out there. I shook my head, though. "No, I want to go with you."

Nikolai cast a dubious look at my arm, but bit his tongue. "Come, then." He scooped up the weapons and then offered me a hand up. Bear followed close to my heels as we made our way back up the ridge.

Each agonizing step challenged my will to keep going, but eventually we made it back to where we'd seen the family. I spotted the mother and father first, both lying in the grass near the stream. Nikolai crouched down and checked for a pulse, looking back at me with a grim shake of his head. We saw no sign of the son.

"Hello? We know you're out there. It's safe now." I winced at the strain that raising my voice put on my ribs, and had to pause for a second for the stabbing pain to subside. "The guy who shot at you..." I tripped over the words, and the truth I didn't want to think about.

Nikolai chimed in, "He is dead. We will not hurt you."

"Just get the hell out of here!" The angry, tearful voice came from somewhere to my right. Squinting in that direction, I saw the boy hiding in the 'V' formed by a misshapen tree, looking nervously between Nikolai and I.

I held up my hand so he could see I wasn't holding a weapon, and took a tentative step closer. "Take it easy. We just want to help."

I could see that the boy seemed to be about fourteen or fifteen, with short, curly black hair. Blood had splattered across his face, and he was struggling to rein in his fear. He didn't seem to be badly hurt, at least. "Why should I believe you? For all I know, you're the ones who were shooting at us."

"You heard the shots." Nikolai rose slowly from his crouch, arms outstretched. "You think we would shoot at ourselves?" I could see the seeds of doubt beginning to show on the boy's face. Nikolai inched the sniper's rifle down off his shoulder and held it by the strap so the kid could see it. Then he tossed it into the dirt halfway between us and the tree. "That is his rifle. His body is back there."

The kid must have read something into my sickened reaction, for he scrutinized my face for a few seconds and concluded, "You killed him."

I swallowed past the lump in my throat and bobbed my head. "But not before he shot Nikolai and kicked my ass." I could see his expression shift, picking up on a shared grief and anger. "What's your name?"

"Joshua."

"I'm Anna. This is Nikolai. And Bear." The dog was wagging his tail in a friendly greeting, and seemed to catch the boy's attention. "Look, Joshua—our camp's a couple miles that way. Our other friends are there. We've got food, shelter, medical supplies. I can see you're hurt." He glanced toward his arm, where the sniper's bullet had left a bloody rip. "Well, so are we. We can all help each other. Okay? What do you say?"

I could see him weighing the choice. Deciding whether he could trust us. Finally he nodded. "What about my parents?" Joshua's voice cracked at the question. "I can't just leave them like that."

"We will bury them," Nikolai answered without hesitation, and I slanted him a grateful look.

That seemed to be the deciding vote, and Joshua nodded tearfully. "Okay."

Nikolai looked at me, and we exchanged a satisfied nod. "You have a shovel?" he asked Joshua.

Sitting down hurt like a bitch, but I found a rock to lean against and watched while Nikolai helped Joshua take care of his parents. Staring down the length of the stream, I had to remind myself that at least what we did wasn't all for nothing.

CHAPTER 48

IT HAD TAKEN SEVERAL HOURS for Nikolai and Joshua to dig a pair of graves for his parents, whose names, I learned, were John and Amanda. I'd recited the 23rd Psalm while a tearful Joshua looked on. By the time we got back, the reds and oranges of sunset were streaking across the sky.

"My God, what happened?" Mark exclaimed as we entered the camp.

"We had trouble," Nikolai said, half-carrying me as I leaned against him. "A hunter shooting people on the trail."

Mark's eyes went wide. "She was shot?" He looked me up and down, eyes lingering on the splint.

"No, but she fought with him. Broke her arm. Put her bedroll out please?"

"*She* fought with him? Where the hell were you?" Mark's accusing glare landed on Nikolai.

"Not his fault," I mumbled through a clenched jaw.

Nikolai ignored the insult. "The bedroll?" he prompted testily.

Gritting his teeth, Mark let it go. "Right, yeah." Once Mark had done so, Nikolai took a knee and helped me down onto it. I let out a cry of pain through gritted teeth.

"Are you okay, Anna?" Lily asked, scooting over beside me with wide, worried eyes. Bear came near and she clung to his neck.

"I'll be all right," I told her, though my tremulous voice probably couldn't fool even a seven-year-old. I said to Mark, then, "This is Joshua. The hunter killed his parents. I told him he'd be safe with us."

Mark looked back to the teen, who was standing uncertainly on the edge of camp. "Yeah—of course. Josh? I'm Mark. Sit down. Have some water." He poured us each a cup, handing one to Joshua and bringing the other over to me. He helped steady my hand as I lifted it to my lips. "What can I do?" he asked, hazel eyes searching mine with worry as obvious as his daughter's.

I shook my head, dreading my own answer. Licking my lips, I gritted out, "Need you and Nikolai to set my arm."

"Set it?" Mark echoed, eyes widening in alarm.

Giving the barest of nods, I said, "Straighten it and clean it. Lots of water. Can't let it get infected like Lily's foot." I started undoing the knotted strips of cloth holding the makeshift splint in place.

Mark took over for me, making short work of them since he could use both hands. "Jesus," he breathed once he saw the damage, his face going white.

"There's a better splint in my pack," I mumbled. "The orange plastic thing. And some painkillers."

He rummaged around in my backpack until he found the splint and the medicine. "Just one?" he asked, tipping pills out into his palm.

I desperately wanted to say two, but I needed my wits to talk him through the splinting. "One now, one after." He helped me take the pill, tipping the water bottle up to my lips.

While we did that, Nikolai molded the bendable plastic splint into the proper shape for a forearm. He looked to Mark, a grave expression on the half of his face not covered by the makeshift bandage. "I will hold her and do—how you say?"

"Counter-traction," I supplied, licking my lips nervously. "Mark, just pull slowly and firmly until the bone lines back up straight."

Mark rubbed his chin again and balked, "Anna... I've never done anything like that before. It's... I can't."

"You have to. Nikolai can't do it on his own. If you don't—it won't heal right. I won't be able to use it." My stomach clenched with that sobering thought. There were no fancy orthopedic surgeons any more —no reconstruction or rehab. That desperate realization made me look Mark squarely in the eyes and plead, "Please. You can do this."

Mark gulped but nodded. "Okay." He rubbed his face and repeated, "Okay."

"Just clean it first. Lots of water. Use that syringe thing." He'd seen me use my makeshift wound irrigator before. "And you'll need to do the same thing for Nikolai's head and Joshua's arm after."

While they got everything ready, Lily scooted closer to my side, clearly concerned but eyeing my arm with a child's innocent curiosity. "Is that what a broken arm looks like?" Her eyes widened. "Is that the bone sticking out?" Far from being horrified or squeamish, she peered at it with a scientist's fascination. "My friend Sarah from school fell off the monkey bars and broke her arm but I didn't get to see it very much. Only after it got a cast put on it. She got a pink cast and we all got to draw on it."

Desperate for a distraction, I asked through a clenched jaw, "What did you draw?"

"A puppy, 'cause she loves puppies. And they're cute." Gravely, she observed, "I bet it hurts a lot."

Understatement of the century. I could only nod, not trusting myself to answer.

Mark glanced over at her. "We're going to take care of it. It's going to hurt a lot for a minute but then it'll be better afterwards."

"Like a shot. There's a big pinch, but then it doesn't hurt much after that," Lily reasoned.

I winced. Mark squeezed my uninjured hand reassuringly. He nodded to Lily, "Kinda, yeah."

Lily mumbled something about being right back. She dashed over to her backpack, rummaged in it for a moment, and came back with her stuffed cat. "Here, you can borrow Beauty. Mommy always says if I hug her when I have to get a shot, it won't hurt as much."

My attempt at a smile looked more like a grimace, but I was nonetheless touched by her concern. "Thanks, sweetheart." I tucked the cat under my good arm.

Mark then looked at me with raised eyebrows, his anxiety written all over his face. "Are you ready?"

My lips drew into a thin line. "No. But let's get it over with."

CHAPTER 49

I COULDN'T REMEMBER MUCH OF the actual bone-setting, which was probably a blessing. Lily told me later that I yelled and cried a lot and said some bad words (sorry, Lauren). Then I passed out.

The painkillers started to wear off late that night, and I awoke to a darkness so complete it made me wonder if my eyes were actually open. Groaning, I tried to orient myself, but the tree canopy was thicker here and there was no moon. Usually I went to sleep with my backpack near the head of my bedroll, my trusty flashlight clipped to it. I reached for it, only to be stopped by a sharp jab in my ribs when I tried to lift my arm over my head. Smothered by darkness, I felt a rising panic.

I must have made a sound, for a flashlight clicked on to my left. "Anna?" Mark called, his sleepy voice soft with concern.

The sudden light was blinding at first, but I blinked a few times and could see enough to quell the fear. Instead of Nikolai sleeping beside me, as I'd grown accustomed to, the much smaller lump of Lily had curled up within arm's reach—or what would've been arm's reach if my arm wasn't splinted and secured across my chest in a makeshift sling. Bear was curled up at her feet as always, and Mark just beyond them. I couldn't see Nikolai or Joshua, but I assumed they were both around somewhere.

Mark moved over to my other side and knelt beside me. Seeing me looking at Lily, he smiled. In low tones, to avoid waking her, he explained, "Lil wanted to keep an eye on you and share Beauty." The stuffed cat was positioned strategically between us on the bedding.

"That's sweet," I whispered, my voice scratchy. Without me having to ask, Mark picked up a water bottle that had been left nearby and unscrewed the cap. He helped me sit up enough that I could sip from it a few times. "Thanks." I lowered my head back onto the bedroll.

"How're you feeling?"

I shook my head to say 'don't ask'. My arm felt like someone had jabbed a hot poker lengthwise from my wrist up to my elbow. It was a deep, abiding pain that kept my jaw clenched tight. The ribs were more of a dull ache, except when I moved.

"Do you need some more medicine?" He tilted his watch to see the face in the glow from the flashlight. "It's been long enough."

"In a minute. Have to get up." I started trying to lever myself up on my good elbow—which was also the side with my injured ribs. All I accomplished was doubling myself over in pain.

"Hey, hey, take it easy," Mark chided in an urgent whisper. "What do you need? I'll get it for you. Just lie still."

Still hunched over, I gritted my teeth and winced. "I need to pee." My frustration made me snap more than I meant to. It was ridiculous to be embarrassed. I was a doctor, for God's sake. But it was different being on the receiving end. And this was *Mark*.

"Oh," said Mark, with a deer-in-the-headlights look on his face that would've been comical under different circumstances. "OK, let me… umm…" He hedged, trying to figure out how to help me up and away from camp without hurting me worse. We managed, but it was awkward as hell, with Mark averting his eyes and generally acting like he'd rather be *Anywhere But Here*. Honestly I couldn't blame him.

"True test of friendship, huh?" he quipped as he helped me back to camp afterwards.

I couldn't help it—I chuckled. That was a mistake; the laugh stabbed into my side, and I gasped. "Ow. God, don't make me laugh."

"Sorry." He eyed me with concern before easing me back down onto my bedroll. He put a few more logs on the smoldering embers of the fire, stoking it until it came to life again, and then brought me a water bottle and another pill. Seeing the way my hand shook while drinking, he asked softly, "Are you okay?"

I hesitated for an instant before giving an evasive, "I'll live."

"That's not what I meant." In the flickering glow of the firelight, I could see a tender concern. "Are you okay?"

"No," I whispered, and with that admission the tenuous thread holding my self-control together came undone. Everything that had happened washed over me in a crushing wave of emotion. I covered my face to hide the way my expression crumpled.

Mark shifted to sit beside me, drawing me in against his chest with one arm and patting my back lightly. "Hey, it's all right. We'll get through this," he murmured in my ear. "It's going to be okay." I sniffled, cheek against his shirt. One of his hands drifted up to stroke my hair. "Do you want to talk about it? You know I'll do anything I can to help, right?" His tentative voice suggested he really didn't know what that might be.

"I know," I murmured. I wasn't normally a touchy-feely share-your-feelings sort of girl, but I felt adrift, overwhelmed. He was throwing me a life preserver.

I told him everything. The words came spilling out in a rush. Seeing Joshua's family gunned down, convincing Nikolai to help, fighting the sniper. "I executed him, Mark." I voiced the confession in a soft whisper. I didn't want it to be real. "He begged for his life, and I looked him in the eye and shot him." The thought made me feel sick again, and I started trembling. Mark felt me shaking and dragged a blanket up over my shoulders. I appreciated the gesture, but the wool did nothing to quell the cold that gripped me from within.

"You did what you had to."

I tilted my head to look at his face, seeing his earnest expression. "What if what he said was true? What if he had a family, and they die because of me?"

"You can't know that," Mark said gently. "He was probably just lying to save his own ass. And even if he wasn't, you don't know what will happen to them. Maybe they'll be all right. Either way, he made his choice. You gave him a chance to surrender and he attacked you. Look at you. God knows what he would've done if he'd gotten the upper hand a second time."

I played with a loose thread hanging from the bandage holding my splint in place, considering his words with a quiet frown. "Maybe he was just a guy trying to provide for his family. How far would you go to protect Lily?"

He didn't hesitate. "Not that far." I looked up in surprise, eyebrows arched, and he shook his head. "It's one thing to defend yourself, but to just start picking off innocent people? There are lines that shouldn't be crossed. You know that, too. That's why you couldn't shoot that guy in the back."

"Yeah. I guess."

"Listen, I know it didn't work out like you wanted, but you did the right thing. Joshua's alive because of you. I'm just glad you're all right...-ish." He added the last 'ish' as a clumsy afterthought, probably remembering my last explosion over the word.

"Ish," I echoed softly, my lips quirking upward briefly in spite of myself. The humor was short-lived. "It hurts so much, Mark," I whined, tears threatening once more.

The arm around my shoulders gave a gentle squeeze. "I know," he murmured, his voice soft with sympathy. "The medicine will kick in soon. It'll get better."

"Always the optimist." I couldn't stop thinking about how soon it would be before we ran out of painkillers.

"Someone around here needs to be," Mark countered with a good-natured smile. Then more seriously, he added, "It'll be okay, Anna. I'll take care of you." He eased me down so I was laying across his lap, my head supported by his opposite arm.

I prided myself on my independence, but right now? I needed his optimism, his confidence, his strength.

I needed him.

CHAPTER 50

THE NEXT DAY WE WERE on the road again. Even popping Ibuprofen like candy barely touched the pain, but I had to face the harsh reality that it might be weeks before I would walk comfortably. Weeks we couldn't afford to spend lounging around here if we wanted to make it to Maine before winter. The guys split my gear between them and I trudged along as best I could. Simple tasks like changing clothes and going to the bathroom became elaborate productions, and I hated feeling so helpless. I saved the stronger painkillers for night, when they helped me overcome the pain to get some measure of rest. If only they could stop the dreams. Every time I closed my eyes, I remembered that day and saw the face of the man I killed.

Nikolai and I hadn't spoken about what happened with the sniper. We'd barely spoken at all, other than the daily necessities of camp chores and traveling. I wondered if he blamed me. It had been my idea to go after the sniper—my fault he got shot. At one point I tried to talk to him about it, but in typical guy fashion he denied anything was wrong. His evasion only compounded my foul mood.

When we stopped to camp that night, I figured I'd try to talk to him again. "Nikolai, could you give me a hand changing this dressing please?"

"I think Mark can do it," Nikolai said matter-of-factly. "I am going to set the traps."

Mark and I exchanged baffled looks as Nikolai headed off into the woods without another word. Mark came over and crouched beside me, frowning. "What was that about?" he asked. "Everything okay with you two?"

I stared in the direction Nikolai had gone, stung by his abrupt departure. "I don't know." I chewed my lip.

"You guys have a fight or something?" he wondered. While we talked, he began carefully unwrapping the cloth that covered the open wound on my arm. "Should I take these other ones off?" he wondered, pointing to the elastic bandages holding the splint in place.

"No, just the dressing. And no, we didn't. Unless he's still pissed I went after the hunter and got us both hurt."

"Maybe he feels guilty," Mark ventured.

"Guilty? It wasn't his fault. I was the one who insisted on going."

"Yeah, but he couldn't protect you. You know how guys are." Mark's lips quirked up.

"Maybe." I sucked in a breath when he moved the arm too much.

"Sorry. I'm not very good at this." Mark's smile turned sad. "Lauren was always the family nurse."

"It's okay," I assured him through gritted teeth. "You're doing fine." Much as he tried to be gentle, some jostling was inevitable. The splint wrapped around my forearm in a 'C' shape, open at the top. Once the bandage was off, the opening revealed the gash left where the bone had poked through. It was still jagged and raw, red at the edges from a minor infection.

Mark stared, concerned, at the injured limb. "How will we know if we set it right?"

I shrugged, chewing my lip. "Wait and see." I didn't want to burden him with the knowledge that a break this bad should be stabilized in the operating room with pins and plates, not a cheap-ass padded splint. "You need to clean it again."

Then it was Mark's turn to wince. "This is going to hurt me as much as it hurts you," he joked.

"I doubt it," I grumbled, and braced myself for another agonizing wound cleaning.

Over the next few days, our path finally took us out of the wilderness and into a more civilized stretch. It had Mark and I on edge after our last experience in a city. We skirted around the forested suburbs of a small town, camped for the night, and then followed a footpath along a large stream. Across the stream was more forest, but on our side the trees were interrupted by roads and small buildings. A light breeze made the humidity more bearable than usual.

"What river is that, Daddy?" Lily wondered aloud. She was peering at the map, trying to pinpoint our location.

"That's not a river, princess—that's the Erie Canal." Thus began a game of twenty questions, starting with 'what's a canal' and then veering off into the history of the Erie Canal and the early settlers and trading posts in the area. Mark was happy to be off in history professor mode again. I tuned out, focusing on just putting one foot in front of the other.

Nikolai had been walking ahead of us, keeping watch. After scanning the path and tree line with binoculars, he said suddenly, "There are people up ahead. We should get off the path." My head snapped up, anxiety jolting through me.

"What?" asked Mark, staring at Nikolai with a perplexed squint. "Why? We should talk to them. They might know something about the towns ahead."

"Or they might try to kill us," Nikolai pointed out dryly. Mark gave an exasperated sigh.

Joshua shifted nervously, looking as frazzled as I felt. "Nikolai's right—we shouldn't take a chance."

Lily carefully folded her map, peering up the path. "I don't see anybody."

"They are coming around the bend up there, still pretty far. Hard to see them without these -" Nikolai held up the binoculars. "- so I think they have not seen us yet." Handing the binoculars to Lily when she gestured for them, he said, "We move now they will never know we were here."

"And we'll never know what information they have," Mark countered. "Hell, it would be nice just to *talk* to someone else. We haven't seen anyone for weeks."

"Except the hunter who attacked us," Nikolai said.

Mark looked to me. His annoyed expression seemed to be silently pleading for me to talk some sense into Nikolai. Chewing my lip, I surprised him by saying, "Maybe he's right." I cradled my injured arm, ignoring his incredulous look. "We don't know their intentions."

"We can't just assume everyone we meet is a bandit," Mark protested. He looked from one face to another. Logically he had a point, but I couldn't shake the intense, visceral dread I felt at the prospect of approaching strangers on the trail. Mark looked from one of us to the next. Seeing varying degrees of fear and wariness reflected back at him, he realized he was out-voted. "Okay. Fine. We can go around this time."

We veered off the path, taking the long way around. When we returned to the trail, we saw no sign of the other people. I found myself wondering who they were. Wayward travelers, like us? Or a roaming band of thugs, like Shaw's gang? I suppose we'd never know.

Dark clouds rolled in late that afternoon and the wind kicked up. "Going to be a nasty one," Mark speculated, squinting up at the sky. In the absence of constant weather updates on our smartphones, we'd gotten accustomed to picking up on the more old-fashioned signs of bad weather, like the kinds of clouds and the way the wind was picking up. "Why don't we stop for the night at that building up there?" He got no argument from the rest of us.

The empty house he spotted had been abandoned long before the blackout, with a knocked-over realtor signpost in the front yard. We were all disappointed that there wouldn't be anything to scavenge and nothing to sit or sleep on. Mark set up my bedroll as soon as we got inside, and I sank down gingerly onto it with my back propped up against the wall.

I let my gaze drift around the room. Lily had gotten out her coloring book and was cheerfully scribbling away. Nikolai checked over the fireplace, then said to Joshua, "This should work. Come—we will get some firewood." He grabbed his shotgun, and then he and Joshua headed out, Bear trotting along behind them.

Mark came over to sit beside me. "How are you doing?"

Grimacing, I leaned my head back against the wall. "Ask me again after the painkillers kick in."

He quirked a sympathetic smile, then his expression turned serious again. Lowering his voice, he said, "Anna, about this afternoon…" Even as I grimaced, he went on, his voice gentle, "Listen, I know you're hurt and upset; you've got every right to be. But I don't want Lily being afraid of everyone we meet."

I watched Lily as she colored. She glanced up, caught my eye, and smiled. I forced a smile back, thinking how much I adored that carefree innocence she had. Maybe she'd be safer if she lost it. How much could we really shield her from the dark shadow that had fallen over the world? I didn't know, but I didn't want to be the one to take it from her.

I sighed. "I know. I don't either. I just got spooked, I guess, seeing those people." I shook my head. "I just wasn't expecting it to hit me so hard." I heard the boom of a shotgun in the near distance and jerked. Logic told me it was probably just the boys hunting, but it still made my heart race with anxiety.

Mark slipped an arm around my shoulders for a companionable half-hug. "You'll be all right." I offered a weak smile, appreciating his faith in me. Lily came over with her coloring book then, distracting me by showing off the princess she'd finished. We sat like that for a while —Mark on one side, Lily on the other—and I felt my pounding heart slowly return to normal.

Nikolai and Joshua returned safe and sound, Joshua triumphantly bearing a wild turkey he'd bagged. He was so proud, and it was the first time I'd seen him smile since his parents were killed. Nikolai's smile faded when he saw me sitting with Mark and Lily, though. His eyes met mine for a moment, and I felt a stab of guilt. For what, I didn't know. Accepting the comfort of a dear friend when I was hurt and miserable?

We feasted on the turkey for supper, happy to have something other than deer and small game for a change, and then everyone settled around the fireplace as the storm rolled in. I listened to Joshua and Lily babbling about some video game they both loved. Their enthusiasm provided a much-needed distraction.

The scene was at once comforting in its normalcy and jarring in how our world had changed so much and so fast.

CHAPTER 51

ALTHOUGH IT STARTED RAINING SOON after we arrived at the abandoned house, the storm didn't really kick up until after dark. When the lightning started, the flashes through the curtain-less windows lit up the entire room, illuminating the slumbering forms of my companions. Joshua shuffled restlessly in his sleep, his dreams troubled like mine. Poor kid. Every now and then Bear would get up to investigate the sound of the rain and wind pounding the house. Eventually he settled down beside me and I started petting his head.

At one point, a vicious thunderclap jolted Lily awake. She looked around, frightened and disoriented. "Lil, sweetheart, it's okay," I called softly. "It's just a storm. Go back to sleep." She picked up her blanket, pillow and Beauty and came over to where I was sitting. Bear scooted aside as she forced her way in-between me and the dog, draping one hand across his back and resting her head on my thigh. Nestled between me and Bear, she eventually fell back asleep.

I found myself wishing I could do the same, but I was only able to doze for short stretches at a time. The storm lasted most of the night, with the restless Bear and I keeping each other company. Mark was the first one up in the morning, and he smiled seeing Lily asleep on me and the dog. "Morning. The storm wake Lil up?"

"Yeah," I said, my voice scratchy. "Just for a bit; she went right back to sleep."

Mark stretched and came closer, his smile fading into a concerned peer. "You get any sleep?"

Lips tightening, I shook my head. "Not really."

He crouched down beside me. "You look flushed." He touched the back of his hand to my forehead then my cheek. "You've got a fever." There was suddenly an edge of alarm in his voice. "Is it your arm?"

I had been in denial, wanting to pawn off my malaise and weakness to fatigue. "I didn't look," I said evasively. Of course, I didn't need to look. We both knew what it had to be.

"Let me see," Mark demanded, dropping to a knee and unwrapping the ACE bandage holding the dressing in place. The light in here wasn't great, so he borrowed my flashlight for a better look. My eyes saw the arm and then looked away, dismayed. The edges of the wound had become inflamed, yellow pus visible in the center.

"Shit," he mumbled. "What do we do?"

"Just keep cleaning it. We can use the saltwater solution again. Hopefully it won't get any worse."

"Anna…" he protested, unsatisfied with my answer.

I could see the worry written all over his face, and knew that it was mirrored in mine. "That's all we can do, Mark. We used all the antibiotics on Lily. Don't tell her, okay? I don't want her to worry."

He reached for my good hand and gave it a comforting squeeze. "Okay. We're coming up on another town. Maybe there'll be a clinic or a drug store or something that hasn't been completely cleaned out.

We'll look for some antibiotics for you, and some pain meds too." I nodded, but—as usual—I didn't share his optimism.

The town Mark staked his hopes on was another ghost town. The canal path led through the heart of downtown, where it looked as though a fire had raged unchecked. Dozens upon dozens of buildings were burned to the ground, ashes still drifting in the wind. We just stared, mouths tensing in a grim line at the sobering sight.

Eventually we found an urgent-care in the intact part of town, but it looked as though a plague of locusts had come through and taken everything that wasn't nailed down. A nearby Walmart with a pharmacy wasn't much better. Soon we were on our way, still empty-handed. I tried not to be too disappointed, but fear followed me like a shadow.

That afternoon, we kept heading northeast, into a rural area dotted with small farms.

"You know, I think the corn's probably in season," Mark mused as we skirted the edge of a cornfield.

"Okay, Farmer Mark, if you say so." My teasing was strained, my jaw aching from being clenched so much. Pained, weak and feverish, I felt like shit. But there was nothing to do but keep walking.

"We used to go to the harvest fair around this time, smartass," Mark shot back, amusement tempering the words.

"This isn't the kind of corn you eat," Joshua observed. "It's field corn, for the cows." Seeing us all looking at him curiously, he shrugged. "I went to my uncle's farm sometimes in the summers."

Mark looked to Joshua, "Where's your uncle's farm?"

"Kansas. That's where we were going when…" Joshua's voice trailed off, his face souring. Though he was holding up as well as could be expected, the tragedy still weighed heavily on him.

Mark balanced his map carefully on his hands, examining it while we walked. He pointed at some trees bordering the cornfield. "If we cut through those woods there, we should be able to link up with the road on the other side. Save ourselves a couple miles going all the way around."

We made our way through the sparse trees, skirting the edge of the farm. As the rows of corn came to an end, we could see the rest of the farm stretched out across the plain—a modest white house, a barn, and a couple red-paneled buildings. "Look, Daddy! Cows!" Lily cried excitedly on seeing a dozen of the beasts milling around in a fenced-in paddock. She stepped up to the edge of the fence. "Ooooh and there's a llama!" I thought it was probably an alpaca, its puffy head looking quite comical in contrast to its shaved body.

When Bear started barking, I thought he was yapping at the cows. Then I heard the neigh of a horse across the field, and saw two riders trotting our way. Both sported rifles. One of them pointed his gun into the air and fired.

I froze at the gunshot, my stomach doing a flip-flop. Beside me, Joshua went white, a panicked look in his eyes. He swung the dead sniper's rifle down from his shoulder—he'd been carrying it for me— and raised the weapon to his shoulder.

"Josh, no!" I lunged sideways, knocking the weapon off-center an instant before he pulled the trigger. The blast went off harmlessly into the air. He tried to yank the barrel away, causing a stabbing pain to ripple up my arm and across my ribs, but I didn't let go.

"What the hell, Anna?" Joshua snapped, at once gaping and glaring at me.

"It was a warning shot," I said through gritted teeth. "Take it easy." I let go of the barrel, but kept a wary eye on him to be sure he didn't do anything stupid.

The riders came closer. One was a white man in his forties and the other a black teenager. Both wore weathered work clothes, stained with sweat, and muddy boots. The younger one sported an angry frown. They both held rifles ready but not pointed at anyone in particular.

As the riders closed the distance, Mark told Lily to go over to me. I guided her behind me, standing between the riders and the kids. Mark stepped forward with his arms held up in a placating gesture. He left his rifle on his shoulder, but Nikolai and Joshua both had their guns out. "Everyone just relax. We don't want any trouble."

The elder rider spoke as he reined in his horse near the animal pen. "This is our land. You'd better be moving on and not getting any ideas about our stock."

Mark and I exchanged glances, and then his expression showed a dawning realization. "Oh. Look, we weren't after your animals. We were passing through the woods there to the road."

Peering around me, Lily piped up, "I saw your llama. It's soooooo cute." That got a look from the farmer, and I thought a corner of his mouth quirked up for a split second.

Mark nodded, then gestured towards the riders. "So how about everyone puts their guns away, and then we'll get the hell out of here and not bother you or your nice cows here any more. Okay?" He looked between the farmer, Nikolai and Josh in turn. "Okay?"

The older rider's eyes traveled across us, sizing us up. He glanced back to the younger one and mumbled something I couldn't hear. The boy grumbled a bit, but flipped the safety on his rifle and slid it into a makeshift scabbard on his saddle. The elder farmer then looked to Joshua. "Your turn."

Joshua balked, gripping the rifle tightly. He glared at the farmer. "You just want us to put down our weapons so you can kill us."

"Josh, they're not going to hurt us," I told him. "Sling your rifle."

"You don't know that! It could be a trick!"

The elder rider frowned at the exchange. "Son, if I wanted to do you harm I'd have done it already."

"I'm not your son!"

"Josh," I said gently, putting my hand on the barrel of his rifle again. I lowered my voice again, trying to get him to look at me. "Josh, I need you to trust me. Give me the rifle." I tried to tuck my own anxiety away as I held his gaze squarely. "It'll be all right."

Joshua's face twisted as if he was physically wrestling with himself. I continued to stare him down, and finally he released his grip on the weapon and stepped back with an angry huff. I handed the weapon to Mark, who flipped on the safety and slung it over his shoulder. Josh stared up at the farmer with a defiant anger, fists clenched as if he were ready to leap up onto the horse and tear the guy apart if he proved me wrong.

Mark looked to Nikolai, then, with an expectant lift of his brows. Nikolai sighed, realizing he was out-voted, and slung his shotgun. An instant later the farmer did the same, and I let out a breath I didn't realize I'd been holding.

"There," Mark said, continuing to play peacemaker. "Everyone's cool." He looked around for a moment, then awkwardly said, "So I guess we'll go. Lil, come on."

As he motioned Lily over, I started to realize how much my side hurt after that little wrestling match with Joshua. I leaned against the fence for a moment, trying to find a more comfortable position, but that only made it worse. Mark caught sight of the pained grimace on my face. "You okay?"

Suddenly I didn't feel well at all. My face felt flushed, and beads of sweat broke out on my forehead. "I don't…" I didn't get a chance to finish the sentence before a wave of dizziness overtook me. The last thing I remembered was Mark reaching for me as I fell forward, darkness carrying me off into oblivion.

CHAPTER 52

I AWOKE TO THE FEELING of something tugging at my injured arm. I swatted at it, only to have my hand caught in a gentle grasp and laid on my chest. Eyes blinking open, I squinted at the unfamiliar surroundings. I was lying in bed, my boots off and a light quilt pulled up to my chest, with no memory of how I'd ended up there. A plump, brown-skinned woman stood next to the bed, spraying something onto my arm from a nondescript bottle. She looked to be in her mid-forties. Long curls swept over her shoulders as she bent over me, intent on her work. Alarm jolted me wide awake, and I looked around for my companions.

"Easy, lovey," the woman shushed me when I started to sit up, placing a gentle hand on my shoulder. "You're safe."

"Where am I?" My voice sounded weak and scratchy. "Where are Mark and Lily?" I'm sure I didn't mean to leave off the other boys, but I was still out of it.

"They're downstairs. Don't worry, everyone's fine. I'm Kayla Williams—you're in my home. How are you feeling?"

"The farm," I realized. I sank back down onto the pillows, letting out a soft sigh. "Like I got run over by a truck. How long was I out?"

Kayla gave a soft mmm hmm. "Two days. You were burning up when Stephen brought you in. You gave everyone quite a scare—especially your Lily."

I blinked, gaping at her. "Two *days*?" My stomach flip-flopped as I took it all in. I glanced at my arm. "What's that stuff you were spraying?"

"Herbal remedy—mostly oregano oil. It's a natural antibiotic. The infection's clearing up, your fever's down—I'd say you're on the mend. Your guardian angel was looking out for you." She flashed a bright smile, then asked, "Feel up to eating something?"

Truthfully, I felt like going back to sleep, but I needed to build my strength back up. I gave her a weak nod. She secured the straps on my splint and straightened. "All right, I'll go downstairs and see what we've got. And I'll tell Lily you're awake." She smiled once more before disappearing into the hallway. Left alone, I stared up at the ceiling and tried not to think about how close I'd come to dying.

I heard Lily's little footsteps racing up the stairs just a few minutes after Kayla left. "Anna!" she cried with glee as she bounded into the room. She threw herself onto the bed, mumbling a soft apology when the tackle-hug caused me to suck in a pained gasp. "Are you feeling better? Daddy said your arm made you sick, like my foot did."

"Yeah. I'm a lot better now. Mrs. Williams took good care of me."

"She's really nice," Lily agreed.

"Where's your Dad? And Nikolai and Josh?"

"They're out helping Mr. Williams and Anthony with the animals." Then she was babbling at a mile a minute, telling me all about the "awesome" farm. In addition to the livestock we'd seen before, they had pigs, chickens and a goat named Amber that provided fresh milk every morning. "I actually never had goat's milk before. I didn't really like it at first but now I think it's kind of yummy," she explained. "And the chickens make lots of eggs. And I got to ride one of the horses. His name was Star and he was brown with a white mark on his nose that looked like a star—that's how come they call him 'Star'. Usually he's for my new friend Jaden to ride, but he let me have a turn and Daddy said I could, and it was so cool!"

She was still at it when Kayla came in with a tray of food. "Lily, Jaden was calling for you when you're done visiting."

Lily beamed at me. "We're going to finish building our castle. Maybe you can come see it when you're all done eating. I'm glad you're feeling better, Anna." She gave me another hug and then bounded off to play. I watched her go, a faint smile settling on my face.

"Jaden's my youngest," Kayla explained. "He's eight, so they've been fast friends. He's thrilled to have someone to play with." She set the tray down on the nightstand and then helped me sit up.

"I'm sure Lily is too," I said, stifling a groan when I moved. "We haven't seen another kid for ages." I shifted my arm to a marginally-more-comfortable position while she fussed with the tray. The smell of some kind of broth wafted over to me, making my mouth water. "You just have the two?"

Kayla moved the tray to my lap, resting it carefully and making sure it was steady before she sat down in a chair next to the bed. "Anthony is the one you met in the field. He's fifteen, my little man. He's really stepped up since all this started. Gabbie's my oldest—she's a sophomore at Columbia." A worried pall came over her face when she mentioned her daughter.

"You haven't heard from her, then?" I asked softly, my spoon pausing halfway to my lips. She shook her head. "I'm sorry."

A corner of her mouth quirked up in a sad smile. "Gabbie's a smart girl. Tough, too. She'll be all right. We'll just keep praying for her to make it home." She was far calmer about it than I think I would have been.

I tasted the first spoonful of broth and said, "This is delicious, thank you." I ate some more, then smiled. "Lily's really taken with your farm —she was going on and on about all the animals."

"She's a sweet one. Can't stop singing your praises either." I smiled at that, embarrassed, and Kayla went on, "Think you'll feel up to getting cleaned up after you eat?"

"Oh, God yes," I said, desperately enough that it made her chuckle. The only thing better than a bath right now would've been some painkillers.

"All right. I'll go get the bath ready. Just shout if you need anything."

I finished my lunch half-heartedly, finding myself without much of an appetite despite having not eaten for two days. Kayla returned some time later. She helped me downstairs to what was once a playroom, judging by the toy shelves shoved into one corner, but now held an old-fashioned cast-iron tub filled with water. "Do you need some help?" Kayla asked, probably noticing that I could barely stand.

"Yeah, sorry," I admitted, blowing out a frustrated breath.

"Don't be sorry. You've had a 103 fever for two days." Though she couldn't have had many years on me, she gave off a motherly vibe that put me at ease. "Here, let's get these clothes off."

"Probably would be a service to mankind to burn them, but I don't have many others." The lame joke was accompanied by a sharp wince as my T-shirt got stuck on the splint, requiring some finesse to navigate it around the stiff plastic. I leaned against the edge of the tub, gritting my teeth for a moment until the pain receded.

"We'll find you something." Kayla clucked her teeth and made a disapproving noise upon seeing the swath of bruises painting the entire left side of my torso an ugly bluish-purple. "My goodness, lovey."

I frowned down at the ribs. "Wish I could say it looked worse than it was, but…"

Kayla gave a soft mmm to that. "I'm sure. We'll get you something for the pain when we're finished here. What happened?"

I tensed, the unpleasant memories flooding back again. "We fought with this guy—a hunter—shooting at Josh's family on the trail."

"Lord have mercy," Kayla breathed.

"We were too late to save his parents, but we stopped him before he got Josh."

Kayla gave a soft mmm to that. "At least you were there for him. A lot of people would have looked the other way." She helped me get the rest of my clothes off and climb gingerly into the tub. The water was cool, a welcome respite from the heat that stubbornly refused to give way to autumn.

The conversation lapsed while I got cleaned up. Kayla spared some real shampoo— a rare luxury—and the faint scent of strawberry was a welcome change from the usual eau de wilderness. Cleaning the wound on my arm brought a fresh wave of agony, but after such a close brush with death from infection, I clamped my jaw down and didn't complain. Seeing the expert way she flushed the wound out, I said, "You seem like you've done this before."

Kayla smiled. "Three kids and farm—I get a lot of practice." I closed my eyes and relaxed in the cool water while she tugged gently with a comb to get the tangles out of my hair. "My mother was big on herbal remedies, so I picked up a lot from her. With Dr. Sloane gone, I've been the closest thing to a doctor around here."

"What happened to Dr. Sloane?"

"Cancer," Kayla reported grimly. "He'd been getting chemo treatments over in Syracuse before the blackout, but then everything collapsed. Shame, too. He was a good man; a good doctor."

I pressed my lips together solemnly. "I'm sorry to hear that."

"Mark tells me you're a doctor too?"

"Yeah. Emergency medicine. But I did a lot of field work overseas, so I've done a little bit of everything."

She peppered me with questions about my time overseas, and we chatted for a bit before Kayla helped me out of the filthy water and into some clean clothes borrowed from her son's closet. The button-down shirt slid easily over my splint, but after watching me fumble unsuccessfully with the buttons left-handed, Kayla took pity and did them for me. "There you are. Let's get you back to bed. You look like you're about to fall over."

She was right, but I managed to make it back to the bedroom without collapsing. As she tucked me back into bed, I said, "'Thank you' doesn't seem like enough. You saved my life."

She smiled. "You just get yourself well. That's thanks enough. Get some rest." She opened the door and then was gone, and I was asleep in no time.

CHAPTER 53

I AWOKE LATER THAT NIGHT to find Mark reading some mystery thriller by candlelight in the chair next to my bed. "Sleeping beauty finally awakens," he teased with a broad smile when he saw me stirring.

"More or less." Stifling a yawn, I smiled back. "All done with your chores, Farmer Mark?"

He closed the book, leaning forward. "I'm not convinced the chores are ever actually 'done' around here. But we knocked off for the day. How're you feeling?"

"Better. Kayla's garden has the good stuff." I was still pretty wiped out, but it was a far cry from being at death's door. I noticed his damp hair and borrowed clothes. He was clean-shaven, too, missing the usual two-day scruff I'd grown accustomed to seeing. "You clean up nice."

He just smiled. "I'd almost forgotten what it was like to take a shower every day—even if it is from a barrel outside."

"Tell me about it. Kayla seems pretty awesome, though. Lily really likes her too. What's her husband like?" I hadn't seen him since our first meeting.

"Quiet. Hard-working. He and Nikolai have really hit it off, if you can believe it. They spent most of the evening tinkering with the water pump." He saw the pall come over my face at the mention of Nikolai and said, "He stopped by earlier while you were sleeping. Nikolai, I mean."

But you're the one who stayed. Keeping that thought to myself, I just nodded, and the conversation lapsed into an awkward silence. After a stretch of quiet, Mark's fingers brushed lightly against my splinted hand, pulling my attention back to him. "You scared the shit out of us, you know." His face was etched with worry.

"Some doctor I turned out to be," I mumbled. "Two of us nearly dying from simple infections." The thought sent a shudder through me.

Mark must have seen it, for his hand wrapped around mine. "It's not your fault. No hospital; no medicine; you did the best you could. I'm just glad you're all right. Kayla and Stephen said we can stay until you're well enough to travel. So you just rest up and get better, okay?" I nodded, giving him a wan smile, and he patted my hand. "I'll let you get back to sleep." Releasing my hand, he closed his book and rose.

I stopped him before he took a step, asking tentatively, "Could you stay for a little bit?"

Fortunately Mark didn't seem to think less of me for it. He just smiled and sat back down. "Sure." Seeing the book in his hands seemed to remind him of something, and he held it up so I could see the cover. "Oh, I think you'd like this one. Borrowed it from Kayla. It's about some kind of drug company coverup." And then he was chattering on about the book, and Kayla's collection, keeping me company until I drifted off again.

CHAPTER 54

I SLEPT OFF AND ON for another two days, thanks to some kind of herbal tea concoction Kayla cooked up. She told me what was in it—a mixture of sedative, painkiller and anti-inflammatory—but the names of the herbs just went in one ear and out the other. As a doctor, I was naturally curious and made her promise to explain it to me once I was feeling better. As a patient, I didn't care what the hell was in it, as long as it took the pain away. It also kept the nightmares at bay, and I felt more rested than I had in a long while.

Lily spent most of her time around the house, so she was always popping in to visit. She introduced me to her new friend Jaden, and we played countless board and card games together. Kayla nursed me back to health with her diligent care. Nikolai came by a few times, but it was Mark who reliably found me in the evenings to share the day's events and chat about the book he was reading. Although I could tell the farm work was exhausting, our time here seemed to be a welcome respite for him as well. Relaxed was a good look on him.

By the fifth day after our arrival, I was finally feeling strong enough—or stir-crazy enough—to brave going for a stroll around the yard. It was the first I'd seen the area around the house. A traditional red barn and silo towered over the property, with the white farmhouse set back in their shadow. From the porch, I could see a pond, fed by a small creek, with the edge of the forest just beyond it. The cornfield stretched out to the west, and a pair of horses roamed in a fenced-in corral near the barn.

Kayla had given me a proper sling and splint—both relics from one of her boys breaking his arm years ago—and I fiddled the straps into a more comfortable position as I walked down the porch steps into the yard. Bear came running over from the barn, barking happily when he saw me. "Easy, boy," I chided when he started bounding around my legs like a dog on crack.

"He has missed you." I heard Nikolai's call from the barn and held up a hand to shield my eyes. Nikolai leaned over a tractor parked just inside the large double doors.

"Nice to know someone did," I mumbled, still grumpy about him being scarce the past few days. I started walking towards the barn. Bear had thrown himself at my feet, but scrambled after me without any trace of disappointment when I stepped around him. Nikolai came out from behind the tractor, wiping his greasy hands on a blackened rag. Shirt off, tattooed chest glistening with sweat, he looked like something out of a blue jean commercial. Damn, but that man was gorgeous. I could still see the groove the bullet had left by his ear, but it was healing nicely.

Nikolai either didn't hear or chose to ignore my muttered remark. "It is good you are feeling better." He sounded sincere enough on that point, at least, the words accompanied by a soft smile.

"Amazing what four days of bed rest can do." The injuries still hurt, and would for weeks, but at least I could stand up straight without wanting to cry. Bending over was still a challenge, though, so Bear had to make do with head scratches rather than the belly rubs he so desperately wanted.

Nikolai gestured toward the tractor. "The transmission is having problems, but there are no electronics. Joshua and I, we think we can fix it. Help them with the harvest."

"That's great."

Hearing his name, Josh poked his head around the side of the tractor. "Hey, Anna," he called in greeting. "Glad you're feeling better."

"Thanks," I called back, then looked to Nikolai. "You want to walk with me?" Nodding, he tossed the grease-stained rag back toward the tractor and—tragically—pulled his T-shirt back on. He motioned for me to lead the way.

We left the barn and followed a gravel path down to the corral. Even that short jaunt was enough to tire me out, so I leaned against the fence for a breather. Nikolai hadn't said anything, so finally I slanted him a look. "You've been avoiding me." His jaw tensed, but he didn't deny it. After enduring the silence for several seconds, I prompted, "Is it about the hunter? Are you pissed because I didn't listen to you?"

A surprised look played across his face, and he shook his head. "No. You were right to help them. Joshua would be dead now."

Hearing him say that was a relief, but also puzzling. "What is it then?"

He sighed. "You know."

"No, I really don't." I thought back to what Mark had said about him feeling guilty, but I didn't think that was it. "Come on, Nikolai, talk to me."

His jaw set in an unhappy expression, and for a minute there I thought he was going to blow me off again. Finally he said, "You and Mark."

"Me and Mark?" I blinked at him, eyebrows lifting incredulously. "What—you're jealous because he's been taking care of me?" His scowl was answer enough. The fact that he cared enough to even be jealous was sweet, in a maddening kind of way. "You could have stepped in, you know. It would've been nice to know you cared if I lived or died." I meant it to be a sarcastic jab, but it came out harshly. I suppose I was more stung about that than I wanted to admit.

"You know that I do," he grumbled. "But sometimes I think you are happier when he takes care of you."

There was a ring of truth to that. I stepped closer to him, resting my hand on his side. "Maybe I was. Mark and I have been a team for a while now. I guess maybe it's easier to let down my guard with him. I'm sorry I didn't think about how that'd make you feel."

Nikolai put his hands on my shoulders, but there was a distance in the way he held me, and in his disappointed tone, "I think it is more than a team, Anechka."

"What are you talking about?" I asked, squinting up at him.

"The way you act with him. He is blind, but I see it. You are in love with him."

I let out a bark of incredulous laughter. "You're kidding." Then I realized he was serious, and shook my head. "Nikolai, it's not like that."

"No?" Those intense brown eyes searched mine, and I couldn't help but shift uncomfortably.

"No! Look, I care about him, okay? You know that. He's my friend." My tone sharpened, irritated that I should have to defend my friendship. At the same time, guilt nagged at me. Was there something to what he was saying? "He and Lily are a part of my life. I'm not going to apologize for being close to them."

He had no answer, only a grim-faced silence. I went on, "I care about you, too, Nikolai. When I found you in the forest, and I thought you were dead…" I shuddered at the memory.

His expression changed, and I thought that maybe finally he believed me. "You were worried for me."

"Of course I was. But if you can't get past being threatened by Mark, then this isn't going to work. You have to trust me."

Nikolai considered my words with a thin-lipped frown for several seconds, then exhaled slowly. "I trust you, Anechka." He cupped my cheek with his hand, his thumb caressing my face. "I am sorry I did not protect you."

So maybe Mark hadn't been that far off after all. I offered him a tentative smile and leaned into his hand. "I'm sorry my crazy plan got you shot. I think that makes us even." I watched his face. "Are we okay?"

His hand shifted behind my neck and gently pulled me closer for a gentle kiss. He was sweaty and dirty from working on the tractor, but I didn't care. His other hand rested with a feather-light touch on my lower back, careful not to hurt me. I had missed the soft warmth of his mouth on mine, and let the kiss linger until he broke it off.

"That's a start, at least," I said, smiling up at him. I gave him another quick kiss before releasing him. "I suppose I should let you get back to earning our keep."

He stepped back. This time, though, he hooked my arm in his as we walked back to the barn, where Joshua was still hard at work on the tractor. "You want I should walk you back to the house?" Nikolai asked.

"I think I'll hang here for a while." I found a spot atop some hay bales where I could stay out of their way. "I'll just sit here and supervise."

"You mean sit there and watch my ass," Nikolai said, with a chuckle, picking up a wrench and bending over the engine once more. Joshua groaned theatrically from underneath the thing.

I grinned, eyebrows lifting. "Well, now that you mention it... you could take your shirt off again."

He snickered and shook his head, but he obliged me before going back to work.

CHAPTER 55

AS THE DAYS AT THE farm wore on, I finally felt human again for the first time since I'd been hurt. Still in pain, but well enough, at least, to start trying to pull my weight. Kayla worked like an old-time prairie woman. Making bread by hand, carrying water, scrubbing clothes over a washing board—her to-do list each day had a million things on it, and yet she constantly rebuffed my offers to help. After the fourth or fifth time, she just chuckled and said, "It really is true what they say, about doctors being the worst patients. Go. Rest. Sit your butt down and play with the kids."

Later that morning, I kept Kayla company in the garden while she painstakingly pulled out weeds that, to me, were indistinguishable from the herbs and vegetables next to them. "It's like our own little pharmacy here," Kayla observed, pausing to tip her hat back. The weather had finally started to cool off, making it pleasant to work outside.

"You guys are lucky. You've got just about everything you need here." I let my eyes drift across the farm, past the barn where Nikolai was working on the tractor again. A peal of laughter came from the kids as they ran around near the barn, playing tag in front of the silo.

"We've been blessed," she agreed. "It's a lot of work, though, now that the power's gone. Hopefully Nikolai and Josh will get the tractor working again. You know, if…"

She stopped when the crack of a gunshot echoed through the air. Her face froze in alarm, and we were both on our feet in an instant, scanning the horizon. We couldn't see anything, but several more shots rang out from down over the hill, past the cornfield. Mark, Stephen, and Anthony had ridden out early this morning to deal with the cows. The creek wound down that way, and my first thought was that they'd taken the cattle down there and run into some kind of trouble. The thought made my heart skip a beat.

"Kids, go inside now," Kayla said, her voice calm but firm. Sober little faces didn't argue with her. They ran inside, taking Bear with them.

Nikolai crossed the courtyard from the barn, rubbing his grease-stained hands on a rag. His jaw was set, his face wearing that stony, intense expression I'd seen when I first met him. Joshua trailed close behind him. "Kayla, you have our weapons?"

"Everything's locked up in the basement. Come, I'll get them."

"You go. I will keep watch," Nikolai said. I caught his eye for a moment, mouthing a silent 'be careful' to him as he stood by the door armed with nothing but a wrench.

Kayla ushered the kids and dog down to the basement, and used her keys to unlock the gun cabinet there. Joshua took the rifle and shotgun and bounded up the stairs.

My pistol was there as well, the belt wrapped neatly around the holster. Kayla pressed the small bundle into my hand and said in a low voice, "You should stay down here with the kids."

I almost protested, thinking she was trying to shield me, but her serious manner made me realize she was trusting me to protect them. I nodded. "All right. But shout if you need me up there."

She went over to Jaden and gave him a warm hug and a kiss on the forehead. "You listen to Anna, little man." She murmured something else, probably an 'I love you', and then she was heading back upstairs with our rifles and a shotgun. The door closed behind her, leaving us with just a lone kerosene lantern for light. Jaden plopped down on a ratty old couch that they kept down here, and after a moment, so did Lily. They began chattering softly to each other.

"Do you think it's bad guys?" Lily wondered.

"If it is, my Dad will kick 'em off our land," Jaden said, puffing himself up with false bravado.

"And my Daddy will help too."

I wished I had as much faith as they did, but my insides were tied up with knots of dread. I paced at the bottom of the stairs and strained my ears for any sign of trouble up above.

The minutes stretched on, but then Bear perked up, his ears picking up something mine couldn't hear. I glanced back at the stairs, tensing, and almost jumped out of my skin when he started barking. "Hush, Bear," I snapped. He plopped down at Lily's feet, chagrined.

I heard the slam of a door upstairs, then mumbled voices and the clonk of booted footsteps on the wooden floor above. No gunshots, though. That was a good sign, right? I let out the breath I'd been holding when I heard Mark's voice. "Anna! We need you up here now."

Something about his voice caused the tension to return in full force. "Stay here with Bear," I told the kids before taking the stairs two at a time, adrenaline smothering the lingering soreness in my ribs. Mark was waiting for me in the kitchen. Overcome with relief, I almost hugged him, but then I took stock of his pale features and the blood on his hands.

I gasped, looking him up and down for signs of injury. "Are you hurt?"

"I'm fine. Nikolai too—he's standing guard outside. But Anthony's been shot. He's bleeding really bad. Come on."

I followed Mark into the living room, where a barely-conscious Anthony was cradled in his mother's arms on the couch. Tears streaked her anguished face, her hand clutching a bloody rag against his shoulder.

"What happened?" I asked.

Stephen's face bore new lines of worry, making him look haggard. "Three men by the creek. They wanted our horses. I killed one, Mark winged another. They ran off, but Anthony was hit. There's so much blood," he gasped brokenly, drawing a sleeve across his face.

"It's okay, baby," Kayla said to Anthony, unsuccessfully trying to keep her voice steady.

"Mama, it hurts," he moaned, fear and pain making him sound far younger than his fifteen years.

"I know, baby. I know." Kayla looked to me, then, wide-eyed. "It won't stop."

"Let me see." She lifted the rag, which was now soaked clean through with blood. Blood pulsed from a tiny bullet hole in Anthony's shoulder, and when I rolled him onto his side, there was no sign of it exiting. "Damn it," I mumbled. "It got the artery. Okay, hold pressure on it." I looked around the guys, who hovered worriedly nearby. "Stephen, let's get him over to the table. Mark, you know where I keep my medical kit in my pack, right? I'll need that. Kayla, get me some boiled water and linens."

Joshua caught my arm as the others split up to their respective tasks. "He's going to be okay, right?" The crisis, so soon after his own trauma, had left his features ashen.

I patted his arm. "I'll do everything I can, I promise. Can you go downstairs with the kids and keep them distracted? They're pretty scared."

"Yeah, okay," he said immediately. Having a job gave him an anchor to cling to, and he disappeared down to the basement.

I hurried into the dining room. Stephen had laid out Anthony on their large oak dining room table, and Kayla was putting a pot of water on the fireplace.

"I have your kit." Mark's voice came from behind me as he came down the stairs with the bag in his arms. I motioned for him to bring it over to the kitchen counter, and started dousing my hands and my meager assortment of instruments with rubbing alcohol. It was the best I could do for sterilization in the time we had.

Mark must have seen the dread and doubt I was trying to hide from Kayla. He touched my elbow and murmured, "You can do this."

I looked up at him, grateful for the support. All I could think about was how the last surgery with the gang at the hospital had ended. I tried to shake it off. "Clean your hands too. I'll need your help." Then I turned back to the wounded boy on my "operating table". "Hang in there. This shot is going to make you sleepy and dull the pain." I gave him a mild sedative and a nerve block for his shoulder, wishing I had proper anesthesia. Taking a deep breath, I went to work.

CHAPTER 56

THE SURGERY TOOK THREE MISERABLE hours. The bullet had nicked Anthony's subclavian artery and damaged some tendons. Sewing everything back together was a pain in the ass, since I didn't have much grip strength in my right hand and even the slightest motion of my wrist sent a jolt of pain up and down my arm. I worked as fast as I could, but I still worried that blood flow to the arm had been disrupted for too long.

Mark had proved an able surgical assistant, handing me instruments and holding things when I needed. The whole thing left him looking green around the gills, and he went to get some air as soon we were done. He found me in the kitchen afterwards, washing the blood off my hands with water from a pitcher. Kayla and Stephen had taken their son upstairs to rest. In a quiet, concerned voice, Mark asked, "You think he's going to make it?"

"He lost a lot of blood, but he's young and strong, so… he's got a good chance. The bigger question is whether he'll use the arm again. I did my best, but… he deserves a real hospital, not a one-armed doctor doing surgery on a dining table."

Mark squeezed my shoulder. "You did everything you could. He's damn lucky you were here."

"Thanks. I just wish I could do more, you know?" I sighed as I dried off my hands on a floral-patterned towel. "How are the kids?" I asked, changing the subject.

"Scared, but they're okay. Josh is keeping them busy brushing the horses. Once we get things cleaned up here, I think it's safe for them to come in. How's your arm?"

He could see me cradling it, jaw clenched, so there was no point in lying. "It hurts. I kept hoping my wrist was just sprained, but I'm thinking it's probably fractured too. I need to learn how to work left-handed." My lame joke was tempered by a wince.

Squeezing my shoulder again, Mark moved over to the medical kit. "Here, take some Motrin and go lie down for a while." He got the bottle out and even opened the one-armed-doctor-proof lid for me. "I'll clean up here and get the kids."

"Thanks." Without thinking, I leaned in and planted a light kiss on his cheek.

He smiled, but gave me a confused squint. "What was that for?"

Honestly, I was as surprised as he was. I had no idea what had come over me. I tried to rationalize it as being grateful for these little acts of kindness after another insanely stressful situation, but in the back of my mind I couldn't help but think about what Nikolai had said. Flustered, cheeks flushing, I played it off lamely, "Just for everything." Leaving him befuddled by my odd behavior, I took the pills and fled.

CHAPTER 57

AFTER SOME REST, I PUT on a brave face and helped Joshua distract the kids until it was time to put them to bed. Kayla emerged from Anthony's room long enough to kiss Jaden goodnight, then returned to her vigil.

I tossed and turned in my bed for a few hours before giving it up as a lost cause. Flashlight in hand, I padded down the hallway to check on Anthony. I knocked very softly on the door before entering, but I needn't have worried about waking them. Anthony was still in a deep slumber after the surgery, and Kayla was wide awake in the same chair I'd left her in earlier. The strain on her normally-happy face was evident in the soft glow from a kerosene lamp.

"Hey," I greeted softly. "I just came by to check on you guys."

Kayla rose to greet me, ignoring my hand-wave urging her to keep sitting. She stepped close with her arms outstretched, engulfing me in a gentle hug. Awkwardly, I patted her back with my good hand. "I didn't get a chance to thank you earlier," she murmured. "For saving my baby."

I didn't have the heart to point out that he wasn't out of the woods yet, so instead I demurred by pointing out, "Well, I was only here to help because you saved me first."

Kayla held me for another minute then released me. "God works in all things," she said with a faint smile, which became strained when she looked at her boy. "Even when we don't understand it."

I nodded quietly, watching the unconscious teen. "I don't think I could do what I do without believing things happen for a reason. After everything I've seen." Dark images came unbidden into my thoughts. I shook them off with effort and said, "Why don't you go get some rest? I can sit up with him for a while."

"Thanks, lovey, but I'm going to stay. He woke up for a few minutes earlier, and I want to be here when he wakes up again."

"You want some company? I can't sleep anyway."

"You still need your rest too, you know." It was a mild reproach, but she perched herself on the corner of Anthony's bed and motioned for me to take the chair. I did so, stifling a wince. Kayla covered her son's hand with her own, then turned her gaze to me. "When we were in the garden earlier, I was going to tell you—Stephen and I would like it if you'd all stay here."

I canted my head at her, brow creasing. "Stay? You mean… indefinitely?"

Kayla nodded. "These are bad times, lovey. Good people need to stick together. You said it yourself—we have everything we need here. With all of us, we can protect each other, manage the farm work. The kids are already inseparable." She slanted a glance to Anthony briefly. "There's a lot of good you could do around here, as a doctor. Not just for our family, but for the neighbors too."

"Wow. Kayla, that's…I don't know what to say." I fumbled with my gratitude, overwhelmed. After a few moments, I shook my head.

"Thank you. If it were just me, I'd take you up on that in a heartbeat. But Mark's not going to stop. Not after coming this far."

"You know there's nothing but mountains between here and Maine?" Kayla frowned. "The weather's just starting to turn here, but up there? It might already be snowing."

"I know. Believe me, I've tried to talk him out of it. Maybe he'll change his mind this time, but I'm not holding my breath." I shrugged, offering a weak smile. "I go where they go."

Kayla made a soft sound of acknowledgement to that, then peered at me. "Girl, I have tried my very best not to be nosy, but I just can't stand it any more. What is the story with you and those boys?"

The question caught me off guard. "What?"

"When you all first got here, I would've sworn that you and Mark were an item. The way he spent every free moment by your side while you were sick." Color rose to my cheeks. She couldn't possibly have seen it in the dim lantern light, but I must have a crappy poker face. She smirked and pointed at me. "See, that's what I'm talking about. And anyone with eyes can see how much that little girl adores you." She lifted her hands, miming weighted scales. "But then there's Nikolai. I saw you kiss him by the barn the other day, and the couch hasn't been slept on the last few days." Again my face betrayed me, and she gave a knowing, "Mmm hmm. So come on—dish."

I tried to rub an embarrassed smile off my face, then cleared my throat. "Uh… okay. Well. It's complicated, I guess. Mark and Lily and I have been traveling together since this thing started. I mean… you've seen them." I waved my good hand in a vague direction to indicate them. "They're awesome. Then Nikolai joined us, and, well… we kinda hooked up.

"Oh?" Her voice went through three octaves on one syllable. "So you have a thing for both of them?"

My nose wrinkled. "It sounds horrible when you say it like that."

"I just call it like I see it, lovey." Kayla's eyebrows lifted in amusement.

"Thanks a lot." I mock-scowled at her, and then sighed. "Anyway, now Nikolai's jealous. He thinks I'm in love with Mark."

"Are you?"

It would have been so easy to voice an indignant denial, but I wasn't so sure any more. Seconds ticked by in silence while I wrestled with my feelings, then finally I admitted, "I don't know? I mean, I love him as a friend. Maybe there's a spark there, but it doesn't matter. I'm not going to have an affair with a married man."

"That wouldn't stop a lot of people," she pointed out mildly.

"It stops me." The firm response was more for my benefit than hers. I'd gone too far by kissing him on the cheek today. I couldn't entertain the possibility of anything more. I shook my head, my voice growing softer. "I'm sure it'd stop him, too. I can't even hope for it, you know? That would mean hoping we never found his wife, and I know how much she means to them. I would never wish for that."

Kayla watched me for a long moment before reaching over to pat my hand. "I know you wouldn't wish for that, lovey, but you have something special with him and Lily. Even Nikolai can see it—that's why he's jealous." She smiled. "I think you're exactly where you need to be."

"Even with Nikolai?"

Her chuckle was subdued, but it was still good to see her laugh—even a little—after the events of the day. "Well. I can't say I *approve*, exactly. But damn, girl, that is one fine-looking man."

That was one thing, at least, we could agree on.

CHAPTER 58

ANTHONY BOUNCED BACK FASTER THAN I would have imagined, the heartiness of youth coupled with Kayla's herb garden. By the next day he was awake, talking, and complaining about everything. I ordered him to bed rest for at least a week, not wanting to risk infection or pulling out his stitches, and he scowled. "What am I supposed to do for a week? No internet—no TV. Come on."

Kayla cut him off. "Better to be bored than dead. Now hush and be thankful." She pulled a book off his bookshelf and set it on the nightstand. "Plenty more where that came from. Drink your tea." Smirking, I left my patient in his mother's capable hands.

As I was feeding the chickens later that morning, I heard the roar of an engine from the barn, followed by a whoop of victory. Joshua sat on top of the tractor, a triumphant grin on his face. Nikolai stood beside him, clapping him on the shoulder. The engine rumbled steadily, and

Joshua drove it forward a few feet. He caught my eye and I smiled at the pride in his expression.

The next week saw all hands on deck for the harvest. Nikolai and Stephen attached some kind of harvester gizmo to the front of the tractor and a wagon to the back, allowing it to drive through a row of corn and fill the wagon with mulched-up corn for the animals.

Of course, the regular farm chores didn't stop just because it was harvest time. With Anthony out of commission, everyone else had to pick up the slack. Kayla finally gave in and allowed me to pick up some of her lighter housework and kid duties so she could pitch in with the manual labor. By the end of the week, the field was bare and the silo full.

A couple of the neighbors stopped by during the week as well. Someone from the closest farm had heard the engine running, and word about the tractor spread almost as fast as word about there being a doctor around. With Kayla as my medical assistant, we saw a baby with croup, stitched up a guy who'd gouged his hand pretty badly skinning a deer, splinted a broken leg, and consulted on managing a variety of chronic medical conditions without a functioning healthcare system.

The adults were all gathered in the living room one night after supper when Kayla ventured, "We're so blessed that you were here to help us."

Stephen chimed in, a worried edge to his tone. "We really wish you'd reconsider staying, We're worried about you, continuing on this time of year. Won't you at least stay until spring?"

Mark and I exchanged glances. I'd hoped he might at least consider it, but wasn't surprised when he said, "We're really grateful for the offer, but we need to be moving on. I don't want to leave Lauren alone there all winter."

Stephen nodded. "I understand." He reached over to squeeze Kayla's hand. Disappointment was written all over her face. "When do you think you'll head out?"

"I want to keep an eye on Anthony for a couple more days," I said. Much as I would have liked to monitor his progress until he was fully healed, that would take weeks. I tried to catch Nikolai's eye to gauge his reaction, but he was busy frowning down at his hands.

"That'll give us time to get the gear ready. And give the kids some warning," Mark added.

The discussion cast a somber pall on the celebration, but we pressed on, enjoying each other's company and drinking more wine than we should have. At one point, I met Kayla's sad gaze and found myself getting teary-eyed.

I didn't want to leave.

CHAPTER 59

KAYLA SPENT OUR LAST FEW days giving me a crash course in herbal medicine, drawing from her personal experience and a book she had. "You've got to know this stuff if you're going to be a doctor these days, lovey." She was right, of course. It wasn't like I would have access to a decent pharmacy any time soon.

Recognition was going to be the hardest part; I wouldn't know a "Spring Beauty" if it came up and bit me on the nose. Because of that, Kayla focused her instruction on the things she could show me from her own garden, ones that also happened to be pictured in our "edible plants" book, and the plants even a vegetation-dummy like me could recognize. (Fun fact I learned: pine tree needle tea was a good source of vitamin C, something that would be vitally important once our vitamin supplements ran out. It would suck to go all that way only to die of scurvy.)

I tried taking notes, but it hurt too much to write with my right hand, and my attempts to write left-handed ended up looking like something a kindergartener had scrawled. Kayla eventually just took the notebook from me and started doing it herself.

While we were working, Joshua came over to the garden. I smiled up at him in greeting.

He smiled back, but there was a nervous edge to it. "Anna, can I talk to you?"

"Sure." I excused myself from Kayla, thanking Joshua when he offered a hand to help me up. We walked away from the garden, our boots crunching on the gravel path. "Everything okay?"

Joshua hooked his thumbs into the pockets of his jeans. "Yeah. It's just…" I waited patiently for him to continue. "I don't want you to think I'm not grateful or anything, for what you've done for me… but… I was kinda thinking maybe I'd stay here." It surprised me more than it should have, and he read my speechless silence as disapproval. "The thing is.. I like it here. Stephen and Kayla have been really nice to me—they said I could stay. And with Anthony hurt, he won't be able to help out as much with the chores for a while, and the tractor…"

I cut off his nervous fumbling with a smile. "Josh, it's okay." I stopped walking and faced him.

"It is?"

"Of course it is. We'll miss you, but I'm glad you found somewhere you feel like you belong." Part of me envied him that.

"I just feel like I'm abandoning you guys."

I clapped his shoulder lightly. "Don't. We'll be fine. And you're right —Kayla and Stephen can use your help here. I'm sure your parents would be happy you ended up with good people like them."

"You're good people, too, Anna." He surprised me again by drawing me into a gentle hug. "Thank you."

I patted his back. "You're welcome." Joshua released me and backed away, his shoulders hunched bashfully. As I watched him go, my smile turned sad at the thought of leaving everything here behind.

That night, as we lay in bed, I voiced those doubts to Nikolai. "I get why Mark's doing this. Why he doesn't want to leave Lauren to fend for herself all winter. But still… part of me wishes we weren't leaving."

Nikolai was silent for a few moments, then ventured, "We could stay. Even if Mark and Lily go."

"And send them off into the mountains on their own?" I shook my head. "They need us, Nikolai."

He frowned, and I snuggled in against his chest. "But I wish we would all stay," I admitted softly. "Maybe that's selfish of me, but…" I sighed.

"You have told him this?" When I didn't reply, Nikolai knew the answer was 'no'. "Maybe you should."

"Maybe," I mumbled half-heartedly.

But I didn't.

CHAPTER 60

ALL TOO SOON, THE EVE of our departure arrived. We checked the gear, packed our bags (with a few extra supplies courtesy of the Williams family) and sat down to enjoy one last dinner together.

Stephen deviated from his usual grace that night. "Heavenly Father, we thank you for this food and for all our blessings, especially for the new friends you brought to us in these difficult times. We ask that you go with them, keep them safe on their journey, and lead them to Lauren. Amen." A soft chorus of 'amens' echoed around the table.

Kayla had prepared a special supper, pulling out all the stops for us with fresh meat, salad, and biscuits. I tried to enjoy the meal, but all I could think about was how much I'd miss watching Lily run around playing with Jaden like the carefree little girl she should be allowed to be. Or tending garden with Kayla and having another woman to talk to. Or even just the selfish little comforts, like having a warm bed to sleep in, and real food on the table.

I tried not to begrudge Mark his desire to have his family back together. But tonight? It was really, really hard to stamp down on that bud of resentment.

For dessert, Kayla brought out a special treat. "Cookies!" Lily exclaimed. "Daddy, look! Miss Kayla made cookies!" She practically bounced out of her seat.

"I made some extra for you to take with you. They should travel really well."

"Thank you, Kayla," Mark said with a sincere smile.

While Kayla passed around the cookies, I caught Nikolai's eye and saw that he looked about as glum as I felt. I tried to give him an encouraging smile, but he just looked away, his expression clouding with… guilt? And then Stephen gave him a pointed look that I didn't understand. As I puzzled over what that was about, I was distracted by Kayla putting a cookie on my plate. I muttered a soft thanks to her.

Then Nikolai cleared his throat. "Everyone. I have to say something." We all looked his way. I figured he was going to give some kind of 'goodbye, thank you' speech, although that seemed out of character for him. He wasn't the sentimental type. And he still wouldn't look at me.

"I am staying here," he said.

A stunned hush fell over the room. I was dimly aware of Mark staring at me in shocked concern, and Kayla leaning in to mutter, "Did you know about this?" to Stephen. But mostly I just stared at Nikolai with a slack-jawed tunnel vision.

"Anna?" Lily's plaintive voice called to me, her face white. "Are you gonna stay too?"

I jerked out of my surprise to look at her, meeting that wide-eyed frightened gaze. "No. I'm going with you." Nobody else said a word, and they were all looking at me. Even Nikolai finally did, his forehead creased in silent apology.

That wasn't enough. I pushed my chair back, the legs grinding against the hardwood floor and stood up stiffly. "Outside," I barked to Nikolai, jerking a thumb toward the door. Without waiting to see if he followed, I stormed out.

CHAPTER 61

I STOMPED DOWN THE PORCH steps and out into the courtyard, far enough from the house for some degree of privacy. Only then did I wheel on Nikolai, who had reluctantly trailed along behind me. His mouth was set in a guilty line, hands in his jean pockets. "You had this all worked out with Stephen, didn't you?"

"I talked to him before, yes." He sighed. "I am sorry. I should have told you first. It is only… I did not know how to say."

"So you decided blurting it out in the middle of dinner on the night before we're leaving was the way to go? What the hell is wrong with you?" I started pacing back and forth in front of him.

He watched me complete three full circuits in silence, glaring at him while I tried to channel my anger into rational words. Suddenly he said, "Stay with me."

I scowled. "You know I can't do that."

"You can." His voice was quiet but insistent. "You are free woman. It is safe here, and they need us. We can be happy here. I will take care of you."

"I don't need you to take care of me!" It was probably harsher than he deserved, but I didn't care. "But if you're so set on being my knight in shining armor, maybe you should—oh, I don't know—try sticking around instead of running out on me."

Then it was Nikolai's turn to snort. "Yes, I should trail after you to Maine like a dog so you can kick me to curb when Mark's wife isn't there."

I stiffened, stopping my pacing so I could face him. "No. We're going to find her." I didn't know if I actually believed that, but I *wanted* to—for Mark and Lily's sake, if not my own.

"Stop it, Anechka. You are not naive like Mark. You know you will probably never find her. You are chasing a ghost."

"You don't know that! But even if you're right—Mark's not going to stop looking for her. And I'm not going to string you along for months and then drop you like a hot potato first chance I get. That's not who I am." It stung that he would even think that about me, but it was a stark reminder that despite the intense situations we'd been through, we'd really only known each other for six weeks. "And when we do find her, what do you think is going to happen? You think Mark's going to want me just hanging around forever?"

"He said you could stay with them."

"Yeah, you think he really thought that through? Thought about what his wife might think about it? Once he gets his family back, all bets are off and you know it." Mark would keep his word at first, but eventually I feared obligation would give way to resentment.

Nikolai frowned. "It is not only that." He gestured towards the farm building. "Look at this place. You have seen the cities, the forests. This is good as it gets. You want me to leave it and risk my neck to go find someone else's wife?"

"No, I want you to leave it for *me*. If you want to stay, then stay. But don't put it on me because of something you think I *might* do months from now. That's bullshit."

He chewed over my words, pacing a few steps and scrubbing his close-cropped hair with a frustrated frown. Finally he turned back to me. "Maybe so. But that does not change things. I am staying; he is going. You must choose—me or him."

"It's not that simple, Nikolai! You're asking me to choose between you and Lily, too. My God, you saw how she reacted in there." I jerked my hand toward the house. "I promised her I'd help to find her mom. Whatever I feel about you, whatever I feel about Mark, I *promised* her. She's been through hell, and she needs me. Why can't you understand that?"

Nikolai scowled. "Take Lily out of it. Do not hide behind the child. What if you were choosing just for you?"

My eyes narrowed in indignation. "I'm not hiding. And what difference does it make? You're talking about a fantasyland. Without Lily, I never even would have met either one of you!"

"Who would you choose?" Nikolai insisted. That intense stare was boring into my eyes, demanding an answer. "Tell me the truth. You owe me that."

I knew the answer. He knew it too, but I refused to play his stupid hypothetical game. "You're trying to make it black and white, but it isn't. You want to play fantasy? We can do 'what ifs' all day long. What if he wasn't a father? What if he wasn't married? Hell, what if *your* wife was still here?" That was probably a low blow, and it earned me a deserved frown. "None of it matters. This is our reality. They're going, and I'm going with them."

His expression was resigned, a faint grimace on his lips. "And I am staying. I am sorry, Anechka." He turned without a word and walked off toward the barn.

CHAPTER 62

MARK FOUND ME SITTING ON the porch swing. Nikolai had gone back inside, but I wasn't ready to face everyone. Truth be told, I was feeling foolish.

Mark sat beside me, a worried look on his face. "You okay?"

"I'm a big girl, Mark," I said, sharper than I meant to. "I've been dumped before. It's not the end of the world." I gave a bitter snort at the unintended pun. "End of the world. Hah."

"Yeah. I know you'll be all right. But listen, Anna…" He paused as if he wasn't sure how to continue. "I know you and Kayla have gotten close. And with Nikolai…" He fumbled with the words, his voice soft and tentative. "I just want you to know—If you want to stay… I understand. You've done so much for us already. I can't ask you to leave your boyfriend and walk hundreds more miles with a broken arm." Despite the words, his hazel eyes showed a sadness that warmed my heart. He didn't want me to go.

"You don't have to ask. You'd have to break both my legs to keep me from going." His reaction to that wasn't what I expected, a pensive look that made me worry. "What's wrong?"

When he finally spoke, his words were soft and reserved. "I'm worried that you'll come all that way and end up regretting what you left behind."

I sighed. "Look, Mark, I won't lie—there's a part of me that wishes we were staying. And not just because of Nikolai. This is a good place. Good people. Probably about as good as it gets with the world falling down around our ears. You know that, right?"

His head bobbed. "I know. But I can't give up. She's the love of my life, the mother of my child. I have to try." The intense look in his eyes pleaded with me to understand.

I reached over and squeezed his hand. "I know. And I promised I'd help. I'm not quitting now." I frowned at my arm. "I'm just worried I'm going to slow you down."

This time Mark didn't hesitate. "We'll manage." He watched me for a moment, an odd look on his face, and then said, "Nikolai's a fool to let you go, Anna. You deserve better." Trying to cheer me up, he joked, "Will it help if I go kick his ass?"

It got a weak chuckle out of me, but the mirth was short-lived. "Not really, but thanks." Part of me wanted to tell him the real reason why Nikolai was leaving. Get everything out in the open. But that would only make things awkward. I wasn't that selfish.

Mark nodded, and gave my leg a comforting pat. "You should come inside. It's our last night here. We won't see them again for a long time."

"There's Mark the Optimist again. I would've said 'never'."

His lips quirked up in another sad smile, and it was telling that he didn't disagree. "All the more reason to come in and hang out. The kids want to play a game." He rose, heading for the door. "But it's up to you."

"Yeah, just a couple minutes." As he reached for the doorknob, I called out, "Mark? Thanks."

Mark smiled, more easily this time, and nodded before ducking back inside.

CHAPTER 63

LEAVING THE FARM WAS A heart-wrenching experience. Lily took it better than I'd expected, but as I watched her give Jaden a cheerful hug goodbye, I realized she was acting as though they were going to hook up again next week for a playdate. It hadn't really sunk in that we would never see them again. This was one of those times I envied her innocence.

I said goodbye to the boys, hugged Joshua once more, and thanked Stephen for his hospitality. When I reached Kayla, she held out her arms and enfolded me in a careful hug made awkward by my backpack and the rifle slung over my shoulder.

"Be careful out there, lovey," Kayla murmured by my ear, squeezing me gently.

"You too," I whispered back. "Thanks for everything." There was more I wanted to say, but I choked up. I patted her on the back with my good arm and then reluctantly released her.

She saw the look on my face and patted my cheek. "It's okay. I know," she said, rescuing me from my awkwardness. I wasn't sure she *did* know what her kindness had meant to me, but I also knew that I couldn't articulate it without breaking down into tears. And that I couldn't do in front of everyone. "You'll be all right." She smiled sadly. "Be blessed."

Nikolai was standing apart from the Williams family, brows knitted in a grim expression. Lily was chattering at him. "Maybe someday when the cars are working again, you can come up and visit us. And then you can meet my Mom. And we can play castle rescue some more."

Nikolai's mouth perked up briefly in a sad smile. "Maybe so." She flung herself against him in a fierce hug, little arms wrapping around his waist. He bent down to say something softly to her. I couldn't hear what he said, but she glanced at me with a conspiratorial smile on her face and then nodded. Nikolai gave her shoulder a light pat and rose.

To my surprise, Mark stepped over to them and extended his hand to Nikolai. "Thank you," he said, gruff but obviously sincere. "For saving Lil, for everything you did. Thanks." Surprised but gracious, Nikolai clasped his hand and shook it. Mark's mouth twisted, and he glanced my way for a moment. "I still think you're an idiot for leaving her," he said to Nikolai, a teasing fondness in his voice.

Nikolai took the insult in stride. He clapped Mark's arm good-naturedly and then released his hand. "Safe travels."

With a solemn nod, Mark looked at me once more. Guiding Lily with a hand on her shoulder, he steered her over to speak to the others, leaving Nikolai and I alone.

My anger with him had dimmed as the hour of our leaving grew closer, and I'd decided to part as friends. Truth be told, I still wished he was coming with us. "I hate goodbyes," I told him.

"It is not too late to change your mind."

"Funny, I was going to say the same thing."

He offered a sad smile. "You know where to find me."

"Yeah." For all the good that did me. I rested a hand on his chest, then impulsively leaned in to kiss him. I'd intended it to be a quick parting kiss goodbye, but Nikolai turned it into a kiss to remember, to remind me of what I was giving up. When our lips parted, I nuzzled the whiskers on his jaw and whispered. "Stay safe, Nikolai." It was easier to say than goodbye.

"Goodbye, Anechka." He kissed my forehead and then let me go.

I looked at him one last time, then turned and started walking. Away from the man who wanted me and the place I wanted to stay.

It made as much sense as anything else in this world gone mad.

PART THREE

CHAPTER 64

MARK STOOD ON THE CREST of a hill, frowning, with a compass in one hand and a map in the other.

"You really have no idea where we are, do you?" I grumbled.

"The lake should be there."

Lily sighed like a teenager. "There's no lake, Daddy." Her deadpan assertion was accompanied by a 'See?' gesture at the wooded terrain before us.

"I can see that, thanks," Mark shot back with a good-natured dose of sarcasm.

It had been a week since we left the rural area around the Williams' Farm and crossed into Adirondack National Park in northeastern New York. There the faithful blue trail blazes we'd followed from Pennsylvania abruptly came to an end. We'd reached the end of the marked portion of the North Country Trail, and now had to navigate across a string of unrelated trails and roads, some of which proved to be harder to follow than we'd hoped.

Mark stared at his map for another minute. "I think we must've been on this trail, instead of that one. So we should be here." He pointed to a spot on the map, then gestured with his hand in the air. "If we go that way about two miles, we should hit another trail that will take us to the lake."

He gave me a questioning look, and I just tugged on my backpack's straps and shrugged. "Whatever you say." Mark frowned at my subdued response.

I stifled a yawn as we moved on. Injuries and nightmares had conspired to wake me at odd intervals the last few nights, and I was running on fumes. To top it off, the restless nights had given me entirely too much time to think. About Nikolai, alternately pissed at him for ditching us and pining for the lost companionship. About Kayla and the others, missing them and worrying. And about Mark.

At the farm we'd spent a lot of time apart—him off doing farm work with Stephen while I recovered and helped Kayla. Now that we were back together 24/7 and playing quasi-family, it was harder to deny the attraction I felt. Yet every time I found myself admiring his smile or stealing a glance at those lean muscles when he had his shirt off, I felt a wave of guilt smack me upside my head. *He's married, dumbass. Knock it off.*

Throw in the constant ache of cracked ribs and a broken arm, and I was a sullen mess.

A few hours later, we'd still seen no sign of trail or lake. Instead we found ourselves treading into increasingly-soggy ground. The ground ahead looked even worse—little islands of high grass sprouting up around patches of water. Birdsong echoed all around us, several brightly-colored birds flitting through the air. It was as beautiful as it was impassable.

Mark took a step and ended up in knee-deep water. Cursing under his breath, he pulled his foot back out. His boot stayed lodged in the muck.

Lily found this hysterical, pointing at him and laughing. "It ate your boot!"

Mark's face scrunched up in a grimace as he crouched down and fished the boot back out. He upended it and a fountain of muddy water poured out. "I'm glad you find this so amusing."

I heaved an annoyed sigh. "Mark, we can't cross this. We should just backtrack and find the right trail."

He shook the last drips out and put the sodden boot back on. "We do that, and we'll lose a whole day. We can skirt around it."

"It could go for miles. We don't even know if the terrain will be passable there either. We'll just end up even more lost."

"We're not lost," Mark insisted. "I know where we are."

I snorted. "Yeah, me too. We're in the middle of a damn swamp!"

Mark huffed and took the map from his front pocket, jabbing a finger at various points. "Look, here was the trail we were following. Here's the lake. We're in this lowland part in-between. All we need to do is go around the bog and we'll be right where we need to be. If we go back, we'll have to backtrack all the way to the trail we missed and then follow it around. It'll be ten, fifteen miles out of our way." His finger traced a circuitous route around to the lake. "Trust me. I know where we are."

I rubbed a hand over my sweaty face, scowling at the map. I didn't have his confidence, but nor did I have the energy to argue about it. I gave in with a surly, "Fine," and started walking in the direction he'd indicated.

It took us several more hours to circle around the swamp, with Mark using a long branch to poke at some of the dicier-looking spots along the edge. Then we slogged our way overland. I considered us pretty adept at hiking by now, but bushwhacking off the beaten path required a whole new level of effort. We frequently had to divert around hills too steep to climb or areas blocked by dense undergrowth or fallen trees. Tree branches snagged on our clothes and left us scratched and frustrated. I pulled off more ticks than I cared to count during our rest breaks, adding tick-borne diseases to our never-ending list of worries.

The lack of a trail also meant no bridges or easy crossings on the streams. We waded across most without issue, but on one I lost my footing on a mossy rock and splashed down onto my side. The fall sent a jolt of pain through my chest and arm, and I knelt there in the water for a few seconds, wincing and catching my breath. Bear danced around me like he thought I'd started some kind of splashing game.

"Anna?" Mark's concerned voice called from the opposite bank, taking a step towards me.

I waved him off. "I'm fine." It came out less as an assurance and more like a grumble. Exhausted, annoyed, and grimacing in pain, I sloshed out of the stream.

Mark gave me a skeptical look. Probably picking up on my mood, he said, "Why don't we camp up on that hill. It's getting late anyway. I'll see if I can get us some fish."

I grunted in acknowledgement. We climbed the hill, away from the potential flood zone, and I started ridding myself of a sodden backpack and dripping gear. "So are you finally going to admit we're lost?"

He blew out a scoffing breath. "We're not *lost*. We're just a little off-track."

I sighed. "God, you are such a man."

"I'll take that as a compliment." He grinned at me.

"It wasn't meant as one," I mumbled, though I didn't think he heard.

Lily came over with a bright smile, carrying a small foam football. "Anna, you want to play ball with me and Bear?" Bear trailed after her with his tail wagging, watching the ball with keen interest.

"Not right now, sweetheart." I removed the outer shirt I wore over my tank-top and started wringing it dry.

"But it's no fun just with one person," Lily whined. "Just for a couple minutes till Daddy's done cooking dinner?"

"Maybe later, okay?"

"But I'm bored. And so's Bear. Please?"

"I said not now!" The stung look on her face made me regret the sharpness in my words. Lips curling down in an Oscar-worthy pout, Lily huffed off to go play with the dog before I could even apologize.

Mark watched the exchange with a worried furrow in his brow, but he said nothing. It wasn't until later, after he had a pair of trout roasting on a spit, that he sat down beside me. "What's going on with you today?"

"Nothing," I said in as even a tone as I could muster. "I'm fine."

"Nothing? Come on. You've barely said ten words to me today, and now you're snapping at Lily. You haven't been yourself all week." He nudged me with a gentle elbow, causing me to look up. "I know you're upset about Nikolai, but…"

"Nikolai?" I scoffed. "Right. Because I couldn't possibly have anything bigger on my mind than the guy who ditched me." Nikolai's abandonment had stung more than I wanted to admit, but it wasn't the thing keeping me up at night.

"What are you talking about?" The oblivious look Mark gave me only poured fuel on my irritation.

"I'm talking about our friends, Mark! We just abandoned them. What if those bandits come back again? Or Anthony takes a turn for the worse? Or someone else gets hurt or sick? Do you even care?"

"Of course I care!" Mark snapped back. "But guess what—I care about Lauren too. What if *she's* in danger, or sick, or…" Glancing over at Lily and Bear, Mark stopped himself. He rose to his feet and took a step away before turning back to face me, exasperated. "We discussed this."

I rose to my feet as well. It was awkward arguing with someone who loomed over you. "Discussed? No, Mark, a *discussion* implies two sides to a conversation. You had your mind made up before I even opened my mouth."

Scowling, Mark waved a hand in a vague westerly direction. "I made up my mind before we left Pittsburgh. I thought you understood that. What, now I'm supposed to give up on my wife just because you hooked up with some guy along the way?"

"That's not what I'm saying! And stop making this all about him!"

"Then what, Anna? Because I really don't get where this is coming from. You're the one who was adamant about coming with us. You could have stayed."

I let out a frustrated grunt. "God, you and Nikolai—you both think it's so easy, don't you? Stay or go. Him or you."

"What do you mean, him or me?"

I hadn't meant to let that slip out, and just waved a hand, hoping he didn't press the question. "You really think I could've just stayed behind while you and Lily went trekking off into the mountains alone? After everything we've been through? It wasn't a choice."

He lifted his hands in an exasperated shrug. "Then why are you so upset?"

"Because you didn't even ask, Mark!" The emotion spilled out without me consciously realizing what had been bothering me. "And neither did he. You both just went ahead and decided what you were going to do without talking to me—without even stopping to think what I wanted, or how I felt. You were both ready to just walk away without a second thought, and that *hurts*!"

Mark frowned. He opened his mouth to say something, but Lily called from across the camp, "Hey, Dad?"

He held up a 'one minute' finger to her, and then shook his head at me. "That's bullshit. I told you I'd understand if you wanted to stay with them. What more do you want from me?" I scowled, having no answer to that, and he pressed on. "You knew from the start that this was all about getting back to Lauren. Nothing's changed. You'd understand that if you..." He stopped, grimacing as if the words had left a sour taste in his mouth.

"If what?" I bristled, voice pitching up incredulously.

"Nothing."

"No, tell me. If I was married?"

He huffed a frustrated sigh. "No. If you weren't such a damn nomad! You've said it yourself, Anna. You have a family you hardly see; a new job in a new country every year; a guy in every port. I've been with Lauren for *fourteen years*. When was the last time you actually committed to anything or anyone?"

His words stung, especially since there was some truth to them. "What the hell do you call this?" I gestured to our little camp. "I committed to you and Lily. I risked my *life* for you!"

Lily cut in more insistently, "Dad!" When Mark looked her way with barely-contained annoyance, she pointed him at the campfire. "The fish is burning."

"Shit." Mark abandoned the argument to rescue the scorched trout.

I stalked a few steps away and leaned against a tree, fists still clenched. Even as I fumed, guilt tugged at me. He was right about one thing—he'd never wavered from his quest. His determination and devotion to his family were what I admired most about him. It was crazy to be pissed at him for putting his family first, wasn't it?

But I was.

CHAPTER 65

AFTER A TENSE SUPPER OF charred trout, we retreated to our respective chores. A strained silence fell over the camp. Even Lily picked up on the mood and curled up with Bear to color quietly in her notebook, out of the line of fire. We barely spoke to each other before turning in for the night.

I wanted to apologize. I'd been unfair, but so had he. It felt like we were at an emotional stalemate, and the silence dragged on.

A cold drizzle the next morning turned into a downpour by midday, chilling us to the bone and putting added pressure on already-frayed tempers. Lily was the first to break.

"I don't want to hike any more," she whined, kicking at puddles as she trudged beside the sodden dog.

"Just a little farther and we can stop for lunch," Mark offered.

"I don't want to stop for lunch. I want to stop forever." Her lower lip jutted out in a theatrical pout, water dripping from the brim of the baseball cap tucked under her raincoat hood. "I want to go back to Jaden's farm."

Mark sighed, slanting me a frown as if this were somehow my fault. "You know we can't do that. We need to keep going so we can find Mommy."

"I don't care!" Wet hands clenched into fists and she stopped walking. "Why can't she find us instead?"

"Because we know where she is, and she doesn't know where we are, silly." Mark made it a dozen steps before realizing that she wasn't following. "Lil, come on."

"No! I'm not going unless we go back to the farm."

Mark gritted his teeth. "This isn't open for discussion. Let's go." She crossed her arms and didn't budge an inch. "Lily Rose, I said let's go."

"I'm not going!"

I sighed, "Maybe we should just stop early for lunch."

"Maybe you should stay out of it," Mark snapped.

It caught me off-guard. I recoiled back in shock for a second before anger flared. "Seriously? What's wrong with you?"

He exhaled sharply, rubbing his face. "Just… let me deal with this, Anna."

"Yeah, you're doing a bang-up job so far," I fired back. "Bear, come on." The leaves on the branches were sparse enough now that I could give everyone some space while still keeping them in sight. I tilted my head up towards the sky, letting the water course over my face. Maybe that would chill the steam coming out of my ears. Rain dripped past the neckline of my jacket, but the shoulders of my shirt were already so soaked I barely noticed.

Bear seemed torn, looking back at Lily before falling into step behind me. His paws splashed in the mud and added more to the filth already caked on his belly. After a short walk, I glanced back and saw Mark sitting beside Lily on a log, speaking quietly to her. She flung herself against his chest, and he wrapped his arms around her. Seeing them like that deflated my anger.

I caved to Bear's unspoken plea to keep walking, doing a circuit through the woods while Mark and Lily hugged it out. I had stopped to pick some berries when Mark called over. "Anna, we're going to stop till after lunch."

I fixed my annoyed look on Bear. "Gee, why didn't I think of that." The dog stared back up at me with innocent brown eyes, and I ruffled the wet fur on top of his head.

The rain didn't let up, and lightning flashed in the distance. After a soggy lunch of stale chips and trail mix, I was putting away our baggies of food when Mark crouched beside me. "I'll do that," he offered. I shrugged and let him take over, settling down on a nearby log.

A long stretch of silence passed until finally Mark spoke, "Listen, Anna...I'm sorry about earlier."

The contrite furrow in his brow convinced me of his sincerity. I waved off the apology. "It's fine. Everyone's been stressed."

"It's hard, being back on the trail." He sighed. He worked for another minute in silence, then ventured, "You know, I didn't realize how much you guys wanted to stay with the Williamses. You and Lil— you really connected with them."

"I wanted us *all* to stay," I corrected mildly. "But I understand why you couldn't." Now it was my turn to sigh and admit, "I'm sorry I snapped at you about it. Nikolai had a choice to stay, but you didn't."

He slanted me a relieved smile. "I miss them too, you know."

"Really?" That surprised me. He hadn't seemed that close to Kayla and Steven.

"Sure. Well, maybe not Nikolai." His tone told me he was teasing— at least partially. There was probably a nugget of truth in there as well. "It was nice to see Lily hanging out with the boys. Doing regular kid stuff for a change." His eyes drifted over to her. "Gave me hope that maybe there could be something approaching 'normal' after all this."

"Yeah. It was nice to be around a family—a community," I agreed wistfully. "Having a roof over our heads and getting to sleep in a real bed."

"You got a bed. I had a couch," Mark pointed out with a smile. "Still, it was nice. I miss their shower-barrel contraption. Being clean for a change."

"I miss Kayla's cooking. No offense."

"Really," Mark deadpanned. He waved an index finger in the air between us. "Between the two of us, you think *I'm* the one who should be offended?"

"Have you forgotten the burned fish last night?"

"I was distracted," he complained, which was true. After a shared chuckle, he nudged my arm gently. "I know that leaving the farm isn't the only thing that's eating at you, though."

I tensed. "What?"

"I'm not blind, Anna." I frowned at the echo of Nikolai's words. "You're exhausted. You haven't been sleeping, and you're hurting more than you let on." He studied my reaction, and saw the confirmation written on my face. "Why didn't you say anything?"

Excuses popped into my head. Not wanting to slow them down. Not wanting to seem weak. Not wanting to let a seven-year-old outlast me. But I just shrugged. "I don't know. Stubborn pride, I guess. Kayla told me I was the poster child for how doctors make the worst patients."

He snorted. "Well that part's certainly true." Then more seriously, he said, "We'll go easy the next couple days. Let you catch your breath."

"Taking it easy isn't going to get us to Maine," I pointed out with a frown.

"We'll get there. I get that you're used to being independent, Anna, but you don't have to shoulder everything on your own. You've got us now. Just tell me what I can do."

Touched by his concern, I bobbed my head. "I know. Thanks, Mark."

Mark looped an arm lightly around my shoulders, squeezing me in the gentlest of hugs. After a long moment in the embrace, he said, "We should get moving." I nodded, and we both stood up.

As we gathered up the gear, I smirked. "You know, there is one thing you could do."

Mark heard my tone and squinted suspiciously. "What?"

"You could admit that we're lost."

He scowled at me, but his eyes twinkled.

I chuckled. "You can't bring yourself to do it, can you?"

"I *could*, if it were true."

"You're full of shit." We grinned at each other.

"Okay," he admitted with exaggerated reluctance. "We might be a *little* lost."

"Just a little, huh?"

He held up his fingers a fraction of an inch apart to illustrate, but I still counted it as a victory.

CHAPTER 66

AS IT TURNED OUT, WE were more than a little lost. After almost a week of bushwhacking through the untamed forest, we still hadn't found the road, the trail, or the lake. We were pretty sure we weren't going in circles, but the hilly terrain made it impossible to travel in a completely straight line. We did our best to just keep moving east. Mark spent a lot of time frowning at the map, rubbing his stubbled jaw, but hesitated to make further predictions about our progress.

Autumn had emerged in full force, and we moved through a sea of yellows and oranges, leaves raining down like snowflakes and crunching underfoot. As dusk approached, the air had a decided chill to it.

"It smells like winter," Lily observed out of the blue as we pushed our way through some brush.

I peered at her, smiling. "What exactly does winter smell like?"

She pondered it for a moment, then replied very seriously. "Like… cold and a little sparkly."

I chuckled. Before I could ask what 'sparkly' smelled like, we emerged from the brush and found ourselves on asphalt. "It's the highway," Mark declared with a triumphant whoop. "I told you we'd find it!"

"Yeah, like, three days ago," Lily teased dryly.

Mark glanced my way with a 'can you believe this?' look. "Did she turn thirteen when I wasn't looking?"

I chuckled and shook my head. "Don't look at me. She's got a point."

"Traitor." Though he was grinning when he said it.

We camped that night, and the next morning followed the highway back to the trail. It took us on a winding trek east through the mountains. The path often went up above the tree line, where we were met with biting winds and breathtaking views—a canvas of fall colors, backed by serene mountains with a dusting of snow at the peaks. We hadn't seen any snow ourselves, but I found myself donning my fleece sweater in the evenings and brushing frost off the tent in the mornings.

With the high peaks at our backs, we eventually descended from the Adirondacks into lake country. One day we crossed over a multi-lane highway. A few abandoned cars dotted the lanes, long ago picked clean of anything useful. In the distance, a cluster of figures moved south, some carrying packs or pulling wagons or wheelbarrows. They were too far away to hail, and moving in the opposite direction.

A stolen rowboat from an abandoned dock got us across Lake Champlain and over the border into Vermont. "Seven hundred miles," Mark said when we set foot on the opposite shore. "It's hard to believe."

"Do you think we'll be there by Christmas?" Lily wondered, adjusting the straps on her backpack. They were starting to look ragged after months on the trail. Bear bounded around us, happy to be out of the confines of the boat.

"We'll see," Mark replied, his mouth twitching in a blink-and-you'd-miss-it frown.

I knew what he was thinking. Based on the estimates when we left Pittsburgh, we should have been there a month ago. Instead we still had almost three hundred miles to go. Much of it through the mountains, with winter upon us.

The distance had never felt so far.

CHAPTER 67

VERMONT PASSED BY IN A blur, deserted highways and backcountry trails taking us on a winding tour through the famed Green Mountains. The rolling hills, covered in evergreens, seemed almost tame compared to the Adirondacks we'd so recently left behind. Occasionally we'd see a picturesque farm or hamlet, but we kept our distance. Not even Mark the Optimist was willing to take the chance of running into another gang. The forest was our refuge.

We saw few people along the way. I'd expected there to be more travelers, but Mark speculated that the main exodus of refugees would have come and gone months ago, headed for fairer climes in the south and west. I wondered how many had stayed in the cities, clinging to the hope that the government would come and rescue them, until finally it was too late to leave. How many had fallen to bandits and gangs? To diseases left untreated, simple ailments now turned deadly?

I clung to my faith for solace, but in the quiet stretches of the trail, alone with my thoughts, this new world seemed bleak and lonely. Mark and Lily were the one constant bright spot through it all.

The weather turned colder with each passing day, and several mornings we'd emerge from our tent to find snow clinging to the trees and covering the ground like a blanket. With the morning sun glistening off the branches, it looked like something out of a postcard. I imagined I'd enjoy it a lot more if we didn't have to spend the day slogging through it.

"We need some of those ice spike things for our shoes," Mark declared with a sigh after he climbed over a fallen log and skidded on an icy patch behind it. "Maybe some snowshoes or cross-country skis too. You ever been skiing?"

"Only if you count water-skiing," I said dryly. "Where the hell are we going to get snowshoes?"

"One of the towns, maybe, if we can find one that's not too picked over."

As I frowned at the prospect of venturing into town, Lily piped up, "What about one of those ski places? Like where we went with Grandpa?"

Mark pursed his lips thoughtfully. "That's actually a good idea." She grinned proudly. "There's got to be a resort here in the mountains somewhere. Might even find some food and stuff."

The nearest resort Mark could find on his map was a day's hike off the trail, so we pressed on for a while longer before making camp for the evening. The temperature dropped precipitously when the sun went down behind the hills, and a freezing wind cut through us as we got everything situated inside the tent for the night. I think Lily might have been asleep before her head even hit the ground. Bear had curled up next to her sleeping bag, and she had one arm slung across him.

"At least someone's warm," I remarked, jealousy creeping into my voice.

Mark draped the blanket across them both, and planted a kiss on her forehead. "Smart girl." His expression turned to concern as he shifted his attention to me. "How are you doing?"

"Oh, fine. Just freezing my ass off." I huddled in a ball, hands tucked under my armpits, but couldn't stop shivering.

"I know, I can hear your teeth chattering from here. Put some dry clothes on."

Logically he had a point, but my brain still balked. "That would mean taking these off."

"That's usually how it works, yeah," he deadpanned. "Trust me. If your base layers are wet, you'll never get warm."

I sighed. "Fine, fine. Just turn around." I tried to stay under my blanket as much as I could, but still hissed, "Shit, it's cold."

"Probably below zero with the wind chill, yeah." Even with his back turned, I could hear the smile in Mark's voice. "You'll get used to it."

Thinking of the miserable doctors I'd seen trying to adjust to the heat in Haiti, I remained skeptical. I changed clothes faster than I ever had, then gave him the all clear to turn around.

"Better?" he wondered.

"A little." I zipped up my fleece, frowning at the stiff redness of my hands. "My fingers are numb." Especially my right hand. The immobility and bulkiness of the splint had made it impossible to keep as warm as the other.

Mark frowned in concern. "Let me see." I might be the doctor, but Mark had the cold weather experience. I held out my hands for him to examine. "Frostnip. You need better gloves so it doesn't turn to frostbite."

"I need to not be in freezing temperatures all day," I mumbled. "What I'd give to be at the beach right now."

"I'd rather have the snow."

"You're insane."

He chuckled. "Slathered in sunscreen is no way to live. Snow makes me think holidays, ice fishing with my dad, sledding with Lil, cuddling with Lauren in front of the fire…"

"I suppose it has its upsides," I conceded, even if I wasn't feeling them right now.

Mark unzipped his own fleece. "Come here. Tuck your hands in. Don't want it to turn to frostbite."

I arched an eyebrow, but scooted over next to him. "Is that how guys hit on girls in Boston? 'Here, let me warm you up.'"

"Yeah, it's pretty much my go-to move when I'm not flying over handlebars," he deadpanned. We shared a chuckle, then he said more seriously. "You know I didn't mean it like that."

"I know." I smiled, never doubting his gentlemanly intentions. I slipped my hands inside the warm bubble of his sweater. He wrapped his free arm around me, settling the blanket over us both to corral our collective body heat. Much as I loved my winter sleeping bag, this was better.

Neither of us said anything for a good long while. Feeling slowly returned to my hands, and in time I stopped shivering. Head on his chest, his steady heartbeat threatened to lull me off to sleep right there. I wondered what he was thinking about.

As if he'd heard my thoughts, he ventured, "Today's the sixteenth."

He said that like it should mean something to me, but it didn't. "What's the sixteenth?"

"Last week was our anniversary. Fourteen years. I completely spaced." I couldn't see his face, but I could hear the guilt in his voice.

"You're hardly the first guy in history to forget your anniversary." Pointing out that Lauren would never even know seemed insensitive, so I said instead, "It's hard to even keep track of what day it is out here. Everything blurs together."

"It's not just that. The longer we're apart… I don't know, it feels like she's slipping away from me somehow." He paused. "I really thought we'd be there by now. I just keep thinking about what it must be like for her, after all this time. Wondering if she's ever going to see us again, maybe thinking we're dead. What if she's moved on?"

It felt weird, talking about Lauren while snuggled up with her husband, innocent as it may be. "Mark, I know I haven't met Lauren, but after everything that you and Lil have told me… there's no chance of that. She loves you. A few months apart isn't going to change that."

His glum tone made me think my reassurances had fallen on deaf ears. "People can change, though. Maybe she's met someone." When I didn't immediately agree, he insisted, "It happens."

"I know," I agreed softly. "It happened to my mom."

He shifted, trying to see my face. "What?"

I sighed. It wasn't my favorite topic. "I told you my dad was in the navy right? One time he came back from deployment, and I heard him and Mom fighting upstairs…" My brow creased at the memory, and I cleared my throat before pressing on, "He was leaving us for another woman. One of the other officers."

"Damn. How old were you?"

"Ten," I answered, remembering clearly the day that had shattered our family. "Thing is though, Mark, the cracks were there long before that. He had his foot halfway out of that marriage already. That's not going to happen to you. We're going to find Lauren. And you and Lil— you're going to have your family back."

"When did you get to be such an optimist?" I could hear the smile in his voice, and he gave my shoulders a squeeze. "I thought that was my job."

"What can I say? You've been a bad influence on me." I smiled too.

"Wonders never cease." Mark fell quiet after that, probably thinking about Lauren again.

Guilt tugged at me, knowing it should be her here in his arms, and not me. "Is Lauren the jealous type?"

"Jealous of what?" he asked flippantly. "Rescuing a friend from frostbite? I think she'd understand."

My smile was short-lived. "Not just this. Everything. All the shit we've been through. Months together 24/7. I'd be jealous if it were my husband."

He chewed on that for a moment before admitting, "Maybe a little, yeah." I snorted at what I presumed was a colossal understatement. "She'll come around. You saved our lives, Anna. That'll go a long way."

"I hope you're right." I paused. "Maybe we don't mention this though."

Mark let out a soft 'heh'. "Yeah. Maybe not."

CHAPTER 68

THE SKI RESORT SPRAWLED ACROSS the mountainside, a disjointed complex of villas, recreational activities, and shops, with a big lodge right near the parking lot. We reached the lot a few hours before supper, weary after a long day following a winding mountain road uphill.

"I don't see any smoke," Mark noted, his breath puffing in the frigid air. We had wondered if we'd find anyone camped out in the resort. With shelter and supplies, it seemed like a natural target for looters (like us, I supposed) or for people to hole up. But we saw no signs of habitation as we approached.

The front door of the ski shop was only an empty frame now, chips of broken glass scattered all around the entrance. Inside, display stands had been toppled, scattering gear all over the floor. The wind whistled through broken windows, and I started to worry that we'd wasted a trip.

Mark went in first, rifle in hand, and grinned back over his shoulder. "Jackpot."

Someone had beaten us here, to be sure, but they'd left a lot behind. Dropping our packs by the door, we started picking through the remnants. "This is my new favorite place," I said, almost giddy as I found a pair of waterproof gloves that fit.

"It's like an early Christmas," Mark agreed. Wool sweaters and socks, better hats and gloves, goggles, and even a pair of ice axes all went into a pile to be added to our packs. Lily even picked up a small, plush husky wearing a branded sweater.

"No snowshoes," Mark lamented.

"What about those skis?" The back wall, filled with boots and skis on display, had barely been touched by whoever got here before us.

"I think snowshoes will be better over rough terrain, especially with all these hills," Mark mused as he fished through a pile of gloves on the floor. "If we can find a map of the place, there might be somewhere else they keep rental equipment."

We only had a few more hours of daylight left, so we decided to stay the night in one of the guest houses. The hotel rooms in the lodge might be more luxurious than the quaint cabins, but a stone fireplace and wood stove appealed more than Egyptian cotton sheets and flatscreen TVs we couldn't watch. On the way over, we found a big resort map posted on a wooden kiosk. "This place here—outdoor center." Mark pointed to a spot on the map. "Sounds promising."

Lily gauged the distance from the 'You Are Here' marker and frowned. "Do we have to go all the way over there? I'm tired."

Mark rapped his knuckles on the map thoughtfully. "We should do it tonight, princess. That way we can get an early start tomorrow." Seeing the way Lily's shoulders deflated, he slanted me a glance. "How about you stay in the house with Anna and I'll go check it out." Lily brightened instantly.

"We can also head over to the lodge and see if there's any food left," I suggested.

"Do we have to?" Lily groaned.

"It's not far—it's that big building right there. And they might have snacks." I said, pitching my voice higher to entice her.

Lily weighed a short walk against the possibility of chocolate. Chocolate won. "Okay."

Mark and I exchanged smiles. We hid our packs in one of the guest houses and then split up, Mark offering a quiet, "Take care," to us before heading up the path with Bear. I watched him go for a long moment before turning to Lily. "You ready to go hunt for some chocolate?" She grinned back at me.

Inside the lodge's kitchen, we found a few canned veggies and beans, and a box of mac and cheese. A search of the ransacked back storeroom even turned up some snack-sized bags of cookies and pretzels. Lily led the way back to the cabin, clutching her loot with a new-found spring in her step.

I started a fire, and we settled in to wait for Mark. I always felt a low current of anxiety whenever we were separated, but Lily distracted me by prattling on as she munched on her cookies. "Do you remember when I brought you cookies at the airport?"

"Of course I do. Made my day." We both grinned. I motioned to the bag of cookies. "Save a few for your dad." I heard a thump outside, which sounded like a footstep on the cabin's wooden stairs. "That should be him now." Since we'd broken the lock getting into the place, I got up to unlock the door chain for him.

I was just reaching for the chain when the door suddenly exploded inward.

The door smacked me hard in the face, sending me flying back against the wall. I sank to the floor, stunned by the sudden, unexpected violence as much as the blow to the head.

Two men burst in. The one in the lead was about forty, wearing a puffy blue winter jacket and brandishing an old police revolver. Behind him was a younger guy carrying a tire iron. Or was it a crowbar? My brain remained strangely fixated on the distinction, as if that mattered right now. Their clothes were dirty and worn, scruffy beards adorning their chins. I thought I could see some resemblance between them. Father and son, maybe? Brothers?

Lily screamed, shrinking back into the couch cushions with a wide-eyed terror etched onto her face. Anger flared within me at these bastards for scaring her like that, briefly supplanting my own fear. With a hand on the wall for balance, I lurched to my feet. Blue Jacket grabbed my shoulder and shoved me back against the wall. I sucked in a breath as he jabbed the revolver against my cheek. I held up my hands. My heart tried to pound its way through my chest.

Tire Iron brushed past, heading for the back of the cabin without sparing me or Lily a second glance. He peered in the bedroom and bathroom and frowned. "Back's empty." He fixed me with a glare. "Where's the other guy?"

I blinked. They knew about Mark. How long had they been watching us?

Blue Jacket poked me harder with the gun. "Answer him."

I swallowed hard, my voice sounding shaky. "He went to the lodge." I lied about where, hoping to throw them off the trail if they went after him. "He'll be back any minute. Our stuff's over there. Just take what you want and go. Nobody needs to get hurt."

With a tug on my sweater, Blue Jacket pulled me away from the wall and over to the couch. "Sit down and shut up."

Lily crawled into my lap, burying her head in my shoulder while she sobbed quietly. I wrapped my arms around her. "Sssh. It's going to be okay."

If only I knew how.

CHAPTER 69

THE MEN CONFERRED QUIETLY, AND I watched them with wary eyes. My brain spun, looking for a way to escape. I could only hear the odd word, but then suddenly Blue Jacket moved over to the front door. He pushed it closed, the shattered latch leaving it partly ajar. He took up a position by the front window, where he peered through a tiny gap in the curtains. Watching for Mark, I presumed.

Everything about his bearing screamed violence, from the look in his eyes to the way he held his gun. There was no disguising the damage done to the front door, so they wouldn't let Mark get that far. He'd be dead before he even hit the porch. That thought filled me with a bigger chill than the frigid draft coming through the broken door.

Tire Iron dumped Mark's pack on the ground and started rooting through the gear, tossing things aside or placing them in a haphazard pile. With both of them focusing their attention elsewhere, I looked for a weapon. My pistol was with my jacket, too close to Tire Iron to be useful. The nearest thing I might use was the lamp on the end table. I scooted closer, shifting awkwardly with Lily on my lap.

"Here he comes," Blue Jacket hissed. He moved close to the door so he could see out onto the porch, and raised his revolver.

Tire Iron rose. "Not a sound out of either of you," he warned, waving the club for emphasis. My stomach lurched. I was in Tire Iron's field of view now. He was bound to notice if I kept creeping toward the lamp.

"Got a shot?"

"Not yet."

Seeing a murder plotted so cold-bloodedly right before my eyes sickened and enraged me. "Please, you don't have to do this."

"I said shut up!" Tire Iron hissed. He raised his club as if to strike, and it had the intended effect of making me flinch and shrink back. "One more word…" His ominous warning trailed off, and then he moved back to the window.

I wanted to scream—to vent my anger at them—but I knew they were immune to reason. I had to warn Mark.

I needed a diversion.

Leaning in close to Lily's ear, I spoke in barely a whisper, "Lil, I need you to scream as loud as you can and run into the bathroom. Lock the door and hide in the bathtub."

She shook her head vigorously. "They'll shoot me."

Her plaintive cry made me feel like the world's biggest asshole for asking that of her, but I didn't see any other way. "I won't let that happen, I promise." I shifted her a little on my lap so she could see my face, brushing aside her tears with the edge of my thumb. "I'll protect you. But we have to help your dad, too. Trust me."

For a moment, I was worried that she wouldn't be able to do it, but then she glanced over to the men at the door. Her resolve hardened, and she bobbed her head in a tiny nod. The faintest of smiles touched my lips. "That's my brave girl."

The fear rushed back almost instantly. If I screwed this up and she got hurt…

I cut off that thought. There was no time for second-guessing. "Okay. Go," I hissed.

Lily bolted for the bathroom, and was halfway across the room before the two bandits even realized what was happening. In her most ear-piercing voice she shrieked, "Daddy help!"

The two men stared at her in disbelief. In that moment of distraction, I grabbed the stem of the table lamp and jerked it hard enough to rip the plug out of the wall.

Outside, Mark shouted in panic, "Lily!" I imagined him rushing forward, slipping the rifle off his shoulder.

Tire Iron went after Lily, but she nimbly slipped away from his grip. I stepped between them, swinging the lamp like a baseball bat. My home run swing smashed his nose, poleaxing him to the ground. He rolled around there, clutching his face. Blood seeped through his fingers. The thin metal lamp post snapped in half from the impact, becoming useless.

Behind me, Lily slammed the bathroom door shut.

Blue Jacket nudged the front door open with his foot and took aim. The revolver boomed in his hand. Bear started barking, but I couldn't tell if Mark had been hit.

No, no, no. I sucked in a gasp. *He had to be all right.*

I stepped toward the door, trying to work out how to help Mark without getting shot. I didn't realize that Tire Iron had recovered until the heavy weight of his metal club thudded into my calf. My knee buckled, sending me tumbling to the floor. More blows rained down in rapid succession—back, arm, shoulder—each drawing a pained cry and leaving a brutal welt behind. My thick sweater was all that saved me from a few more broken bones.

A fresh exchange of gunfire from the door gave me the strength to fight through the pain and fear. When Tire Iron's next blow smacked my ribs, I managed to trap the metal bar under my arm. A twist and a pull wrenched the club from Tire Iron's grip, and it went skittering across the floor.

I tried to scramble towards it, aiming a kick at his head to create some distance. Tire Iron took the kick on the shoulder instead, and then he was on top of me. I fought with all I had, raking my nails across his face and popping him once in the jaw. None of it fazed him. He snarled, the blood dripping from his nose making him look even more fearsome, and started pummeling me with his fist. I raised my splinted arm in a futile attempt to ward off the hail of punches, but it was like trying to fight an enraged bull one-handed. One fist slipped past my guard. My cheek exploded in pain, stars dancing in my vision.

"Mark!" I shrieked, a desperate, sobbing plea. I didn't even know if he was alive, let alone in a position to help.

"Get the fuck off of her!"

Relief flooded through me at the sound of Mark's voice. Mark barreled at Tire Iron, tackling him. As they rolled to the side, Mark dropped his rifle.

The two men engaged in a vicious melee, slamming into furniture and breaking knick-knacks around the room. Tire Iron fought with a white-hot rage, but Mark held his own. He hammered a fist into the bandit's already-broken nose. I tried to will myself up to help him, but rubbery legs wouldn't cooperate.

I spared a glance to see what had happened to Blue Jacket. He was sprawled in the doorway, blood pooling on the floor beneath his head. One of Mark's bullets had shattered his skull, leaving behind a gruesome mess. I tore my gaze away from the sickening sight.

Mark and Tire Iron were both bleeding now from blows to the face. Mark slammed a splintered table leg into Tire Iron's shoulder, and I could hear the collarbone crack from across the room. Somehow, Tire Iron still didn't go down. He landed a kick that sent Mark flying backwards over an end table. The bandit then rushed toward the door.

At first I thought he was going to run. But as he slowed his pace, I realized his gaze was locked on Blue Jacket's revolver, lying inches from his lifeless fingers.

I can't let him get that gun.

Fueled by a fresh burst of adrenaline, I scrambled over to where Mark had dropped his rifle. I had it up on my shoulder an instant before Tire Iron's hand closed around the revolver. Without thinking, I fired. A splotch of red appeared on Tire Iron's chest. He staggered back against the wall, a shocked look on his face, and then slid to the floor.

An eerie quiet descended on the cabin once the echo of gunshot had faded. I knelt there frozen for a minute, breathing hard. My brain struggled to process what just happened.

Mark rose, staring at Tire Iron in slack-jawed surprise before snapping back to himself. He scooped up the revolver for safe-keeping, then rushed to my side. "Anna? Are you hurt? Where's Lily?" he demanded, panic in his eyes.

"She's fine. In there." I pointed toward the bathroom. He hesitated, looking at me in concern. "I'm okay. Go."

Mark nodded. "Keep an eye on that guy." He rose and headed off toward the bathroom where Lily was hiding.

Movement by the door nearly made me jump out of my skin, but it was only Bear coming in. I touched his snow-dusted fur with a trembling hand. Soon it wasn't just my hands shaking; a violent shivering wracked my whole body. I felt sick to my stomach, and sweat beaded on my face despite the cold air from the open door. I wanted nothing more than to curl up and collapse on the floor, but I had to watch Tire Iron.

He hadn't moved from where he'd fallen. His head had lolled to the side, eyes locked on his dead companion—father, brother, friend, I still didn't know. The pink-tinged spittle on his lips was a telltale sign of a lung injury.

Finally he looked at me. "Go on and kill me, then. Get it over with."

My finger twitched. It scared me how much I wanted to pull that trigger again. To get revenge for the terror on Lily's face, the pain they'd inflicted, and the helpless horror I'd felt while watching them plot Mark's death. I wanted to make sure he never hurt anybody else ever again.

Then I remembered the sniper who'd killed Joshua's family. The look on his face when I'd shot him. I felt sick all over again, and knew I didn't need another face haunting my dreams. My fingers relaxed their grip. "I'm not going to kill you."

"Why the hell not?" The accusation was undermined by a pained wheeze. "You shot me."

"Only to stop you from killing him," I retorted. "I'm a doctor, not a murderer."

And as a doctor, there was only one thing I could do.

I rose on shaky legs. Tire Iron watched me suspiciously as I set aside the rifle and retrieved my medical kit. I carried it across the room, but stopped a few feet short. A visceral reaction gripped me, making it hard to take another step. Just a few minutes ago, he'd been snarling and beating the shit out of me. But looking at him now, I saw only echoes of the monster within. Sweat beaded on his face, his skin pale. He was helpless. Dying.

I knelt down beside him. "Let me see." Opening his jacket and shirt, I found a neat bullet hole just left of his breastbone. A hole I'd put in him. I shoved that thought aside and focused on the wounds. It barely bled, but little air bubbles emerged with each exhalation.

The chances of saving him were slim. Maybe it would be better if I didn't even try. The thought was fleeting, banished by the oath I'd sworn. I took his right hand and guided the palm over the hole. "Your lung's collapsing. Press tight here."

He groaned as I applied pressure via his own hand. "You shouldn't waste your time on me. I don't deserve it."

"You sure as hell don't," I snapped. "Shut up and let me work." I donned my stethoscope and started listening to his breathing.

Tire Iron didn't shut up. "I should've stopped him." His voice grew weaker, talking to himself more than me. "I should've…" He stopped abruptly, eyes lolling back in his head.

I checked for a pulse. Nothing. He was gone.

With a defeated sigh, I tugged the stethoscope from my ears. I sank back onto the floor, tears stinging my eyes for reasons I couldn't explain.

As Mark emerged from the bathroom, a hysterical Lily in his arms, I met his eyes. Neither of us knew what to say. We could only exchange a shocked look at the destruction around us.

CHAPTER 70

WE MOVED TO A DIFFERENT cabin, but we couldn't leave behind the horror of what had happened. It hung like a cloud over our every word and action, leaving us all badly shaken. Mark had moved a dresser in front of the door and dragged the bed into the living room near the fireplace. Now we all sat on it, Lily huddled between me and Mark in a group hug. She clung to him, tears streaming down her face.

"I want Mommy," she wailed.

"I know, baby," Mark murmured, smoothing her hair back. He caught my eye, an anguished look on his face.

"I wanna go home."

"I know."

I patted Lily's back, my heart breaking to see her like this. She'd been through so much, been so strong through it all, but this was the straw that had finally proved too much. We had nothing to offer but hollow-sounding consolations.

We stayed that way for a while. Just being there for her—for each other. Staring at the flames dancing in the fireplace, my mind replayed the events of the evening like a twisted video stuck on autoplay. I heard the crash of the door splintering; the gunshots. I saw Tire Iron, dying from the bullet I'd put in him. I saw the crater left in Blue Jacket's skull. Refocusing my eyes on Lily, I used her face to anchor my racing thoughts and push back against a vague queasiness.

Eventually Lily cried herself into a fitful sleep. Careful not to wake her, Mark extricated his arm from under her, stood up, and walked over to the dining area. I watched him pace back and forth like a caged animal. Finally he stopped, leaning against the back of one of the chairs.

I stood up and joined him by the table. "She's going to be okay," I offered softly.

"Is she?" His vehement tone took me aback. "My seven-year-old was just held at fucking gunpoint. She knows we just killed two people."

The reminder sent a shudder through me. I crossed my arms defensively. "They didn't give us any choice. They were going to shoot you as soon as you got close to that door."

"I know. That doesn't make it better." Mark shook his head, scowling. "I didn't think it would be like this. I knew it would be the Wild West in the cities. But out here? It's just so goddamn senseless." His hands squeezed the back of the chair, twisting until finally the top strut of the backrest gave way under the stress of his white-knuckled anger. I imagined he would've picked the chair up and smashed it into little bits if he weren't worried about waking Lily. Instead he flung the splintered pieces onto the table. I flinched at the clatter, my nerves still frayed. Not knowing what to say, I just stood quietly and let him vent.

Mark rubbed his face. "I heard her scream, and my heart just stopped…" His voice trailed off. Jaw clenched, he struggled to keep his face from crumpling.

"I know." I didn't tell him I'd felt the same when they shot at him. "She'll be all right, Mark. She's a tough girl." I came up behind him. "Come here." I tugged on his shoulder. Mark let me turn him around and draw him into a hug. He wrapped his arms around me, squeezing gently. His cheek nestled against my hair. Truth be told, I needed the hug as much as he did.

We stood that way for some time, before finally Mark pulled back. He studied my face, then frowned and touched a thumb beneath the bruise on my cheek. Despite putting some ice on it earlier, it was already shaping up to be quite a shiner. His voice softened. "Are you okay?"

I shook my head, not knowing what to say. How could either of us be anywhere near "okay"? Tears sprung to my eyes. "No more than you are," I whispered. "But it would be pretty messed up if we were okay after that." My throat bobbed, thinking of the dead bandits. "I tried to save him. The one I shot. He was too far gone."

Mark considered that for a moment, conflicted feelings written all over his face. "At least you tried. I don't think I could have, after what they did."

I shook my head, my expression locked on a point in the distance past Mark's shoulder. "I almost didn't. I thought about it." Saying it aloud brought a rush of shame. "There's a part of me that's glad I couldn't save him." I frowned. "Maybe not glad. Relieved. At least I know he won't hurt anyone else."

It still felt surreal, after so many years thinking of myself as a healer, to know that I had ended two lives. What did that make me? A vigilante? A murderer? The lack of easy answers left me unsettled.

Rubbing my arm gently, Mark said, "Anna, it's okay. You're a doctor, but you're still human. I think you're entitled to a few reservations about helping the men who attacked us."

"Maybe," I conceded. I leaned my head back against his shoulder, just wanting to hold him. To be held. He obliged.

"I'm so sorry this happened to you," he whispered, a pain in his voice I hadn't heard before.

"It's not your fault."

"Sure it is. You wouldn't even be here if it weren't for me." His voice simmered with self-recrimination. "I shouldn't have left you guys alone."

I tilted my head up and saw the deep furrow across his brow. "Mark," I said gently, "You can't be with us every minute. And you didn't force me to come along. I'm glad I did. There's nowhere else I'd rather be."

He seemed perplexed by that. "Not even with your family?"

I pictured my sister and her family, feeling a pang of sadness. "I mean, if I could snap my fingers and have them here with us, I would. I miss them. I worry about them all the time." I sighed. "But Jess and I have always gone our own ways. We'd see each other a couple times a year. She had her career and her family; I was bouncing around on missions overseas. I pray they're all right, but...I know this is where I'm supposed to be." I paused, then ventured tentatively, "You and Lil are my family, too, now. You know that, right?"

"I know." His eyes flicked to the sleeping Lily, then back to me. "I don't know what we'd do without you."

Our eyes locked, and there was something unmistakably intimate in his expression. He reached one hand up to cup the side of my face, his hand warm and gentle against my cheek. I became hyper-conscious of just how close his head—his face—was to mine.

I kissed him. It was just an impulsive gesture—a light press of my lips to his.

Mark froze, his eyebrows arching halfway up his forehead. Instantly I jerked back, mortified.

"I...I'm sorry," I stammered, wondering what had come over me. "I shouldn't ha..."

Mark smothered my apology with his mouth, silencing me with a kiss that put mine to shame.

I should have stopped him; pushed him away. But in that moment, tasting those lips I had dreamed about for so long, rational thought checked the hell out. I pulled him closer and let myself kiss him back.

It went on for a while, months of pent-up desire finally given free reign. I wanted this moment to last forever. I wanted more. But then his hand touched the back of my neck, and the cool metal of his wedding band was like a bucket of ice water dousing my passion.

Lily.

Lauren.

What the hell am I doing?

"Wait," I mumbled breathlessly against his lips. He broke off the kiss. His expression was frozen in a sort of stunned uncertainty, as if he couldn't believe what we'd just done.

I guess that made two of us.

My lips still tingled, but shame sat like a lead weight in my stomach. I put a hand on his chest and whispered in a pained voice, "Mark, we can't do this."

His face hovered inches from mine. If he kissed me again, I didn't know that I had the willpower to deny him a second time. When he pulled back, I felt equal parts relief and disappointment.

"No," Mark murmured. "No, you're right." He let me go, taking a step back from our embrace. "But God help me, I want to." I could hear the self-loathing in his voice.

Regret snuffed out any joy I might have gleaned from such an admission. All I could do was watch as he turned and fled into the lodge's back bedroom. The sound of something being thrown across the room echoed back to me a few moments later. Sinking down onto the couch, I buried my face in my hands.

CHAPTER 71

SLEEP DIDN'T COME EASILY, BUT exhaustion eventually gave me no choice. When I jerked back awake again, it took me a minute to get my bearings. The first streaks of sun had begun lighting up the cabin, and neither Lily nor Mark were in sight.

A clatter from the kitchen jolted me, my nerves still frayed after the attack. Rising from the couch, I stifled a groan as a host of bruises made their presence known. I made my way over to the kitchen area, where I found Lily and Mark making breakfast.

"You guys have been busy," I observed. Lily came over to greet me with a subdued hug. I squeezed her back gently, kissing the top of her head. She looked tired, with no sign of her usual smile. The prior night had rattled us all.

Mark tensed when I came into the room, and I had a hard time looking him in the eye. None of us said much during breakfast, and

Mark wouldn't look at me either. I ate without relish, my mind spinning on how he and I were going to manage the rest of the trip with this Wall of Awkward between us.

I offered to clean up the dishes, but Mark waved me off. He started clearing the plates away, while Lily wandered off to sit with Bear over by the couch. Feeling a tug of guilt, I followed Mark over to the sink. A quick glance my way showed that he had taken note of my presence, but neither of us seemed to know what to say.

As he scrubbed the pan with some melted snow, he finally asked, "You feeling okay?"

I shrugged. "Sore, but I'll live."

"You're not wearing your splint," he observed. "How's your arm?"

"About as good as it's going to get, I think. I need to start exercising it." Wrestling with Tire Iron had convinced me of that. I figured if it hadn't re-broken then, it was probably healed enough to take the splint off. Tugging up my sleeve, I showed him the afflicted arm. It felt strangely naked and vulnerable without the weight of the brace on it. An ugly scar remained where the bone had protruded, and the muscles looked weak and atrophied from disuse. It still ached sometimes, and I'd probably never regain full mobility with it, but I counted my blessings that it hadn't been worse.

"It healed better than I would have expected, considering everything. You did a good job, Doctor Mark." I offered a tiny smile.

He returned it, his eyes locking with mine. Memories of last night flashed unbidden in my mind. His expression shifted, thinking the same thing.

Mark jerked his gaze back to the dishes. I crossed my arms, pulling my sleeve back down. We stood there, him scrubbing a plate with melted snow and me leaning against the counter nearby, an uncomfortable silence hanging between us.

He eventually slanted me another look. "This is harder than I thought it would be."

"Tell me about it," I mumbled.

Setting the plate aside, he grimaced. "Look, I'm sorry about last night."

A frown pulled at my lips. "No, this is my fault," I assured him, keeping my voice low so Lily wouldn't hear. "You're a married man; there's no excuse for what I did."

"There's no excuse for what I did either," he murmured. "Fourteen years Lauren and I have been married. *Fourteen years*, and I never once looked at another woman. Never even crossed my mind. I would never—" He slanted me a sidelong look, and the guilt radiated from him as clearly as the warmth from the fireplace.

"I know. You don't need to explain." Swallowing my pride, I did it for him. "She's your wife. That's all that matters. Last night was just a mistake."

Mark shook his head. "It's more than just last night, Anna. These last few weeks…something's changed between us. You know that as well as I do."

I didn't know what to say. All this time, I'd thought I was the only one who felt something. I suppose I'd been as blind as I'd assumed he was. My eyes drifted across the room to Lily. Much as his words tugged at my heart, I had to be strong for her. I couldn't do to their family what my stepmom had done to ours. It scared me to think just how close I'd come to doing what my father had done. To becoming what I hated.

"It doesn't matter what we feel," I told Mark flatly. "This isn't just about you and me. We can't hurt Lily and Lauren like that."

Mark nodded, following my gaze. "I know we can't, but what—we just pretend like nothing happened?"

I shrugged. "Do you have a better idea?" His silence told me he didn't. "I'm sure it'll be awkward for a while, but we'll just have to manage somehow. Like seeing your ex at work every day."

"Speaking from experience?" he asked with lifted brows.

I made a face. "Perils of dating other doctors, I guess."

"I suppose so. Anna..." There was something in his tone—a tentative uncertainty that made me peer at him. His jaw worked for a few seconds before he continued. "If things were different..." He stopped, brow creasing.

If things were different. There was a whole heap of heartache wrapped up in those words. "They aren't," I said firmly. "Better not to even think about it." I turned away before he could see the pained look that settled on my face.

Sometimes doing the right thing really hurt.

CHAPTER 72

WE COULDN'T GET AWAY FROM that resort fast enough, fleeing from everything that had happened there. Back on the trail the next day, we left the Green Mountains behind and linked up with the Appalachian Trail, which we'd be able to follow the rest of the way to Maine. It was a relief to be back on well-marked paths, the white blazes and markers leading us through great swaths of evergreens glistening with white.

While Mark and I tried to carry on as normal, for Lily's sake if not our own, what had happened still dragged behind us. It was like an anchor we couldn't escape, weighing us down with guilt and regret. Troubled dreams reliving the attack only made things worse, and I couldn't talk to Mark about them. New walls had gone up, enforcing an emotional distance that neither of us truly wanted. I worried about how I'd face Lauren if we found her; if she'd be able to see right through me to the feelings I had for her husband. How could I have been so stupid? All we could do was keep moving forward.

We crossed over the border into New Hampshire, the last state before Maine. Lily, who had been withdrawn since the ordeal at the cabin, could barely contain herself. She didn't seem to register Mark noting that we still had a ways to go. Relieved to see her back to her old self, we didn't try too hard to dampen her enthusiasm.

Mark kept trying to convince me we'd been lucky with the weather. The snow wasn't deep, and the temperatures hovered just below freezing. Even with the wind chill, it was bearable as long as we were moving or in our sleeping bags. But for a girl raised in Hawaii and California, waking up to find that my wet socks had frozen didn't exactly strike me as 'lucky'. I missed summer, humidity and all.

Soon we reached the White Mountain National Forest and started up into the Whites. There, everything changed.

The ground became rocky and treacherous. We found ourselves scrambling on hands and knees over boulders, following trails that looked more like rock slides than hiking routes. Steep ascents left our leg muscles burning. Some stretches had log staircases that were almost like ladders, with precarious drops on either side. At one point, we dead-ended in a rocky gorge, only to realize that the trail continued up some metal rungs hammered into the side of a twenty-foot cliff face.

"What the hell?" Mark scowled up at it in exasperation.

"How're we going to get up there?" Lily asked, holding up a gloved hand to shield her eyes.

Mark used his ice axe to scrape the ice off one of the rungs, then tested his weight on them. "Seems sturdy," he concluded. "I'll go up first with the gear."

He made three trips up and back, carrying our packs, and then a fourth time to guide Lily up. We had figured on making some kind of pulley harness for Bear, but it turned out to be unnecessary. When Lily started climbing, he just ventured into the scrub beside the trail and made his own way up, planting his paws on ledges so narrow my heart skipped a beat.

I followed up the ladder as soon as they'd cleared it. Upon reaching the ledge, I looked ahead of us and saw another rocky path ascending. My breath fogged in a sigh.

Even Lily huffed in frustration. "I'm tired of mountains."

You and me both, kid.

CHAPTER 73

STOP.
THE AREA AHEAD HAS THE
WORST WEATHER IN AMERICA.
MANY HAVE DIED THERE FROM EXPOSURE
EVEN IN THE SUMMER.
TURN BACK NOW IF THE WEATHER IS BAD.

We stared at the big yellow warning sign, bone-weary from days of roller-coaster rock paths through the mountains. A biting wind assaulted us, stinging our cheeks. Did that count as bad weather?

"You've got to be kidding me." I slanted a disbelieving glance at Mark, dread pooling in my stomach. He frowned at it for a long minute, a furrow etched into his brow.

Lily, meanwhile, was perplexed. "Does that mean there are tornadoes and stuff?"

Mark shook his head. "No, princess, it just means it can get really cold."

"Like a blizzard." Lily surmised.

"Maybe. But we've got good weather now." There were some clouds in the sky, but nothing that would suggest an imminent storm. "We're used to the cold."

"Speak for yourself," I mumbled.

Mark ignored me. "We'll be fine," he insisted.

Lily seemed untroubled by the prospect of a snowstorm; I supposed growing up in the northeast had its benefits. Mark's confidence did little to ease my misgivings, but I knew exactly what he'd say to any objections I raised. We couldn't just bushwhack around the mountain; we'd need to backtrack all the way to a road and go clear around the entire range. Probably through towns that posed their own set of hazards. It would add weeks onto our journey, pushing us further into winter.

Mark met my gaze, waiting for me to state the obvious: *We could turn back.*

Instead I offered a faint smile. "Well, we should get going before the weather changes."

Mark smiled back, surprised but not about to wait for me to reconsider. Lily took our decision in stride and fell into step behind Mark as we made our way past the ominous marker.

The trail wound its way upward, a grueling slope punctuated by heaps of boulders and fallen trees. Eventually we left the trees behind, venturing up above the timberline. Without the buffer of the forest, the winds bit into us even more fiercely. I tugged my scarf tighter around my face, balling my hands up inside my gloves and repeatedly squeezing the handles of my trekking poles to keep the blood flowing.

The terrain turned desolate, rocky fields surrounding us and looking like the surface of the moon. It was impossible to see an actual trail on the ground; hip-high cairns of rocks marked the way. When we finally reached the summit, our legs rubbery and our ragged breaths making little puffs of fog, we didn't quite get the vista I'd expected. Low clouds hung over the area, making it feel like the summit was suspended in the clouds. We stared at the sight, beautiful yet eerie, as we caught our breath. "It's like Cloud City," Lily mused. She wasn't wrong.

The path down the opposite slope wasn't much easier, the icy, rocky terrain making each step precarious. Our poles and traction cleats helped, but not enough. Slipping and sliding, we abused our knees and shins. It was a miracle none of us broke an ankle. The trail took us across a line of ridges, the clouds still blocking most of what might have been a majestic view on a clear day.

The first sign of trouble came when the winds started picking up. The temperature dropped sharply, and more clouds blew in from the west. Then the snow began. Mark and I exchanged worried glances. He stepped in closer to speak quietly to me, his tone somber. "I don't think the tent can take the winds if we set up here—we're too exposed."

"You think we can make it to the hut?" Our map and the trail signs had promised shelter at a small lodge, but there was still a mile to go and another small peak between here and there.

Mark frowned up at the mountain, his lips curled in contemplation of our multiple bad options. "We have to try."

I didn't have a better idea, so we pressed through the worsening weather. Gusts of wind blasted wet, thick snow into our faces. We could hear it pelting our jackets like raindrops on a roof. There had been only a dusting of snow on the ground when we broke camp this morning. Now it covered our toes and showed no signs of slowing.

Eventually we reached the summit of the next mountain. The wind at the top was so strong, it felt like walking through water. Worried that Lily would be blown over, Mark shuffled her behind him and had her cling to his pack. Even Bear had a hard time, trudging through with his ears pinned back in displeasure.

We should have been able to see the hut from the summit, but I could barely see Mark. A swirling haze hung over everything, making the ground seem to blur together with the sky. In minutes, we couldn't see the path ahead, and I knew we were in real trouble.

CHAPTER 74

WHITEOUT. I'D HEARD THE TERM, but I'd never experienced it first-hand before. Fear twisted my insides.

"Daddy, I'm scared!" Lily wailed. "I can't see you."

"Hold onto me, Lil," Mark's disembodied voice floated back to me.

"Mark, how the hell are we going to get down from here? We can't even see the trail." I had to shout for him to hear me. The wind blasted our ears, sounding like a freight train. Icy tendrils stung my cheeks and cut through my jacket, pants, and gloves. I walked hunched over, trying to make myself a smaller target for the wind.

"We're almost there," he called back. "We just need to follow the ridge."

"Can you even see the ridge?" I couldn't. I held up my hand to shield my face, but it didn't help.

"We can do it." Which didn't actually answer the question.

We pressed on, methodically placing one foot in front of the other and praying we didn't wander off the side of a cliff. We'd only gone a few dozen yards when Lily let out a piercing scream.

Feeling like my stomach had gone into free-fall, I rushed forward. Through the white haze, I could barely see Lily's feet dangling over the edge of a steep embankment. Mark's grip on her hand was the only thing saving her from a dangerous fall. He pulled her up with an arm curl, and I crouched down to help guide her back to solid ground.

Lily clung to Mark, crying hysterically. I patted her back, and glanced up to see a stricken look on his face. He shook it off with effort, and slipped his pack off his shoulders. Fishing out a length of rope, he tied one end around his waist and fed the other end back to Lily and I. "Wrap this around yourselves."

I helped secure the rope, then clipped Bear's leash to his collar. He whined at me in complaint, not used to being on a tether, but I ignored him. Keeping one hand on the rope, I fell into step behind Lily. The storm assaulted us with cold and noise, but we fought our way through. Time blurred, every effort consumed by our desperate attempt to reach shelter. Every step felt treacherous, threatening a tumble down the mountain, until finally Mark let out a triumphant shout, "I see it!"

I squinted into the swirling snow. How Mark could see anything in this mess was beyond me, but he sounded confident. Lily and I followed blindly.

The blocky shape of the "hut"—which looked more like a big lodge building once we could see it clearly— finally came into view, standing out against the lonely, barren hillside. My breath puffed in a sob of relief. *Thank God.*

After pounding on the door to make sure we didn't surprise anyone, Mark found it unlocked. We went inside. Bear sniffed around, exploring, and I surmised from his relaxed demeanor that we were the only ones here. Past the foyer, there was a kitchen, and a big dining room filled with picnic benches. The lacquered wood decor gave the lodge a rustic summer camp feel. Giant bay windows probably would have given a great view on a clear day, but now were blanketed in white.

Closing the door on the howling wind, we dropped our packs by the door. "Daddy, I'm cold," Lily complained, her teeth chattering fiercely.

"I know, princess. I'll get a fire started." Mark moved off to the central fireplace, while I helped Lily get out of her wet coat and snow-caked snowpants. In short order, she had on a dry sweater and socks, and was sitting on my lap under a blanket to warm up.

Once Mark got the fire going—thankfully whoever managed the lodge had left behind a bin of firewood—feeling returned to my fingers and toes. "We're lucky nobody got frostbite," I remarked. Mark just grunted a somber agreement.

After supper, Lily curled up beside Mark and fell asleep using his leg as her pillow. All the furniture in the main room was wooden and uncomfortable, but Mark had dragged out a pair of mattresses from the back bunkroom and set them in front of the fireplace.

As I sat back down after laying another log on the fire, Mark stared at Lily with an oddly distant frown on his face.

"What's wrong?" I wondered.

He didn't answer at first, but then said softly, "I almost lost her again."

I reached out and squeezed his arm. "But you didn't."

Mark acted like he hadn't heard me. "I could feel her slipping." His voice sounded haunted. "If I hadn't been holding her hand…"

Keeping my hand there as a paltry gesture of comfort, I said, "Mark, you'll drive yourself nuts over what might have been. Everyone's safe."

After a stretch of silence, he asked, "Am I doing the right thing?"

The question, heavy with doubt, surprised me. I cocked my head. "What?"

"This trip. All of this." Mark waved a hand vaguely. "You said from the start that this was a crazy idea." I squinted at him, shaking my head. "Maybe you were right. Maybe we're past the point where I should say 'enough is enough' before I get us all killed." Guilt-stricken eyes searched my face for validation.

After months of watching him act so confident and certain, hearing him say that felt like emotional whiplash. I was speechless. Some part of me wanted to let him off the hook. To agree that it wasn't sensible to trek another hundred miles through the mountains, risking bandits and winter weather and God-knew-what-else, for a woman who may not even be there when we arrived. But as I stood there, watching his agonized indecision, I couldn't do that to him.

"It *is* crazy," I began. His frown deepened. "That doesn't mean it's wrong. Everybody told me I was crazy too, the first time I went on a mission for MSF. Jess would've said I was nuts for agreeing to hike a thousand miles with a guy I just met." His lips twitched at that, almost a smile, but the shadow of doubt lingered on his face. "But those turned out to be two of the best decisions of my life. Some things are worth the risk."

I watched him quietly for a long moment before prompting, "It's your family, Mark. Do you think we should stop?"

The silence stretched on as he mulled it over, the frown lingering on his face. "I've asked myself that question a thousand times since this started. I know we're taking more risks by traveling, but we'll be in danger no matter where we are. Here, the Williams Farm, even once we get to Maine." He looked at me. "Lily needs her mother, and when I think of what Lauren must be going through…"

"You need your family together," I interjected softly as he trailed off. "Mark, ever since I met you, you've been a man on a mission. If we stop now, when we're this close, it'll eat away at you. That doubt. That guilt. Always wondering—what if she was there waiting for you? You'll never be able to let it go."

He nodded, relief lighting up his eyes. "So we keep going?"

I smiled faintly back. "Yeah. We keep going. Crazy pair of fools that we are."

CHAPTER 75

"WELCOME TO MAINE. THE WAY life should be." Lily haltingly read the sign aloud, squinting at the weather-beaten letters. It was a blue hand-painted slab of wood nailed to a tree next to the trail, the top bordered with last night's snowfall. It took a moment for the words to register, and then she started jumping up and down. "We got to Maine! We got to Maine!"

Mark grinned. "Just about two weeks to go."

Lily's arms flopped to her side, pouting. "Weeks?" Despite looking at Mark's maps, it hadn't sunk in that our destination wasn't just over the state line. Maine was a big place.

Ruffling her woolen hat with a gloved hand, Mark kept his upbeat tone. "I know, but we'll be there before you know it." He caught my eye and we exchanged smiles.

What had seemed an impossible goal when we started now lay just under a hundred miles away. It felt surreal to be here, having come so far. We all just stood and soaked it in for a minute.

It had been a few days since we left the lodge near the lake. One mountain range had bled into another, trading the rocky ridges of the Whites for the evergreen-carpeted slopes of the Mahoosucs. The snow clung to the pine branches around us, forming a beautiful tunnel of white as we made our way through a narrow valley. Following a curving path down a wooded hill, we came upon a place that looked like a giant had broken the mountain apart and strewn the pieces everywhere. Huge boulders, some as big as school buses, covered the trail, with tree roots snaking through the gaps between them. High granite walls hemmed us in on either side.

"Where's the trail?" Lily said what we all were thinking.

"Was there a landslide or something?" I wondered aloud.

Mark gestured to a white arrow etched into the side of a pile of rocks nearby. "There, I guess."

"Wait—through this mess?" I eyed the field of boulders skeptically.

"Looks like." Mark stepped tentatively up onto one of the lower boulders, testing his footing.

An impatient Bear wove past Mark into a gap between two car-sized boulders, picking his way over the rubble like a mountain goat. He stopped at the top of the pile, looking back at us as if to say: *You guys coming or what?*

Mark and I looked at each other and shrugged. "Seems like we've got a guide."

Scrambling over giant boulders would have been difficult even in dry weather. With them covered in snow and ice it felt like some kind of insane obstacle course challenge. After just an hour, Mark and I each had bruised knees and shins, and our fingers were numb from finding purchase in icy crevasses. I tried curling my hands into fists, keeping the fingers in to rewarm them, but the warmth never lasted.

Mark worked his way up on top of one cabin-sized boulder and then extended a hand down. "Can you lift Lil up to me?"

Lily made a face. "I can climb up myself," she declared, and then she proceeded to do so, scaling the rock as nimbly as a monkey. "Come on, Bear."

Bear took a windy route up the side, while I got about halfway up and then let Mark give me a hand. While my arm grew stronger each day, I didn't want to test it too much.

Minutes blurred into hours as we moved through the valley, carefully picking our way over, around, and under the slabs of rock. Bear seemed to be having a ball, always eagerly charging ahead and waiting for us. Lily, having conquered the first tunnel, viewed the boulder obstacles as her own personal playground. Their enthusiasm buoyed Mark and I along, even as our muscles burned from the constant exertion.

Finally, the rocks began to thin and the hills around us became dotted once more with evergreens. We breathed a sigh of relief. "Thank God that's behind us," I murmured.

"I wish we could come back and do it again when it's warm out," Lily declared, her grin a sharp contrast to my disbelieving stare.

"Should we camp here?" I wondered. My arms ached from the exertion, especially my weak one.

Mark surveyed the area. "It's going to be cold as hell here tonight in the valley." He pointed to the mountain that lay before us. "We should be able to make it up and over to the next shelter before dark."

Remembering the sharp dip in temperature we felt entering the valley, I wasn't eager to see how low it got overnight. Much as I wanted to rest, Mark was right. "Makes sense. Let's go."

Heading out of the valley, the forest floor gave way to steep, rocky slopes. We found ourselves on all fours, like trying to scramble up an icy, stone escalator. Bear found his own path as usual, switch-backing up some sketchy-looking terrain beside the main trail. He made it to the top first and waited impatiently for his slow-poke humans to finish our ascent. At one point the trail went vertical, our passage aided by iron rungs pounded into the side of the mountain.

We crested the rise, and started down the other side. Patches of ice and loose rocks made it a treacherous descent. On one side of the mountain face was a ledge that must have been at least a twenty foot drop.

"Careful, it's slippery here." Mark, in the lead, pointed out a spot he'd just passed. I held Lily's hand as she navigated across it.

Up ahead of us, Mark planted his boot on a rocky outcropping. I heard a crunching sound, and saw a rock slab give way beneath his foot. He lurched sideways. One arm shot out to catch himself, but found only open air. There was a heart-stopping moment where he seemed to be frozen in mid-air, and then he fell.

CHAPTER 76

"MARK!" THE HOARSE SCREAM ESCAPED my lips as Mark dropped away from me. He was too far for me to reach, but that didn't stop me from extending an arm towards him instinctively, as if through sheer force of will I could somehow stop his fall.

I crawled to the ledge and peered over. Mark was sprawled on the rocks at the bottom of the cliff, almost two stories below me. A vice of anxiety squeezed my chest. I just stared, struck dumb, for several long seconds.

Lily had heard me shout, and scooted close enough to the edge on hands and knees to stick her head over. "Daddy! Daddy, are you okay?" When he didn't answer, her voice pitched up in alarm. "Daddy!"

He wasn't moving. "God, no," I gasped. From this distance, I couldn't tell if he was breathing. That desperate thought snapped me out of my shock with a jolt of adrenaline.

"Why isn't he answering?" Lily cried.

Hands on both her shoulders, I looked into those wet eyes. "He probably got knocked out. We're going to help him, but we have to get down there safely first, okay? Hold my hand and stay close." She gave me a shocked, tear-filled nod.

Hands trembling, I wanted nothing more than to race down the hillside to Mark's side. I resisted the urge. It wouldn't do anybody any good if we all fell. Carefully and methodically, Lily and I continued down over the boulders. "Mark, we're coming!" I shouted, not knowing if could hear me.

After what felt like an eternity, we reached the bottom and picked our way over the rocky ground to Mark. He had fallen on his side, so I crouched down facing him. A frantic Lily hovered just over my shoulder. I rubbed a knuckle against his sternum, and let out a relieved sob when he groaned softly in response. He was alive. *Thank God.* "Mark, can you hear me? Mark?"

As I stripped off my gloves, I sucked in a sharp breath at the red stain spreading across the snow under his head. Gently palpating the side of his skull, my fingers felt the edges of a deep gash and came away slick with blood. I couldn't feel any obvious cracks in the bone, but my gut clenched at the possibility of a skull fracture.

"Is Daddy okay?" Lily asked in a hushed whisper, clinging to Bear.

"I'm going to take care of him." I wished I had more assurances to offer her.

Carefully extricating him from his backpack, I rolled him onto his back and resumed my brisk exam. I didn't find any other immediately life-threatening injuries, but wouldn't know the full extent until he woke up.

Rubbing knuckles against his sternum, I tried once more to rouse him. "Mark. Hey. Open your eyes, Mark." Once again he tried to shift away from the uncomfortable pressure, but remained unconscious. "Damn it."

I wrapped a dressing around his head wound, applying pressure for a minute to slow the bleeding. After tugging his bloodstained knit cap carefully over the bandages to keep him warm, I tried once more to wake him. Only silence answered me.

My brain started running through all sorts of worst-case scenarios. Skull fracture. Brain bleed. Things that I could potentially treat in the ER, but not here in the shadow of a damn mountain. Fighting back a tide of helplessness, I took a breath to steady myself. The sun was going down, and we still needed shelter and a fire. Mark might have other injuries I could treat. These things, at least, I could do.

I got the tent up while Lily gathered wood for a fire from around our campsite. Examining Mark more thoroughly, I discovered a couple cracked ribs, a badly swollen knee, and too many bruises to count. I supposed it could have been worse, but it was still pretty awful. I tended his injuries as best I could and got him bundled up inside his sleeping bag. Bear watched Mark from nearby, head on his paws.

Lily and I had a solemn supper, unable to enjoy the amazing view of the fading sun painting the rolling evergreen forests a brilliant orange. As the sky grew dark, we sat together outside the tent, watching the fire crackle. I tried to stick to our routines as much as possible, reading a few chapters of her battered Frozen novelization to her before she went to bed. I winced as we got to the part of the story where the sisters' parents were lost in a shipwreck. Lily didn't call me out when I glossed over that section, skipping the words she knew by heart. "Do you want another chapter?" I asked.

"No, that's okay," she mumbled, tucking her head against my arm.

I closed the book and slipped my arm around her. "You did really good today, helping me and your dad," I said softly. "He's going to be really proud of you. And I am too."

She said nothing, then after a few moments I heard a waif-like, fearful voice. "Is Daddy going to be okay?"

It was the same question I'd been asking myself all evening. I swallowed past the sudden lump in my throat, my own fears feeding off hers. In medicine, you had to strike a balance with children. Tell them too much, you'd scare the shit out of them. Hold back too much, you'd lose their trust. Earnest hazel eyes searched mine. Part of me wanted desperately to lie to her, to promise that Mark would be fine and wake up any minute. But she'd seen more death and destruction than any seven-year-old should, and she deserved an honest answer.

"I don't know, sweetheart," I whispered. "He hit his head really hard."

"Can't you fix him?"

The question was like a dagger in my heart. "I wish I could. But some things even doctors can't fix." Tears spilled over onto her cheeks, and I shifted position and drew her into a protective hug. "I know. It's okay. I'm scared too. But we've done everything we can to help him. Hopefully he'll wake up soon. The best thing we can do now is just pray for him."

"That's what Daddy always says about getting home to Mommy," Lily said with a tiny sniffle, muffled against my shoulder.

"Well he's right." One hand patted her back while the other wiped at my eyes, glad she couldn't see them.

She was silent for a long time, just clinging to me. Finally she looked up at me, watching my face with an undisguised need. "If Daddy goes to Heaven, will you still take me home to find Mommy?"

"Of course I will," I assured her. "I promised I would, didn't I?"

She nodded, but then her lips turned down in a pensive frown. "But what if she's not there? What if we can't find her?"

"We will." There was only so much honesty I could lay on the kid at once. And truth be told, I wanted to believe it as much as she did.

Lily's anxiety was not put down by my stubborn insistence. "But what if we don't?"

The answer came easily. "Then I'll take care of you."

"Forever?"

I hugged her tighter, pressing a soft kiss to the top of her head. "Forever."

CHAPTER 77

I SAT VIGIL OVER MARK that night, even after exhaustion made my eyes scratchy and heavy. Our battery-powered lantern cast a dim glow over the tent. Lily slept beside me, using my thigh as her pillow. She'd resolved to stay up with me, but after a full day of scrambling over rocks and up cliffs, she conked out in minutes. Tired and sore as I was, I longed to join her, but I couldn't. If Mark woke up, I wanted to be there for him. And if he didn't... I couldn't let Lily wake up to that alone. This wouldn't be the first time I'd pulled an all-nighter. I'd stay awake for as long as it took.

I pulled my blanket more tightly around my shoulders, shivering as the frigid night air invaded our tent. The wind howled, battering the tent walls. Some loose flap fluttered in the breeze. Untucking Mark's hand from the sleeping bag, I cradled it gently in mine. "You know, you're really starting to scare me," I told him. I felt silly talking to myself, but the silence was oppressive. "We just need you to wake up, okay?"

My voice cracked. I had run out of ways to explain Mark's prolonged unconsciousness that didn't involve some kind of dire prognosis, and despair threatened to swallow me. Bear edged closer, nudging my elbow with his head. I bent down to touch my forehead to his. Scratching his ears, the soft warmth of his fur brought some small measure of comfort. Throat tight, I straightened back up after a minute and rambled on to Mark.

"I promised Lil I'd get her back to Lauren no matter what happens. You know she'll be safe with me—as safe as anything is these days, anyway. But she still needs you, Mark." My voice dropped quieter. "And I need you, too." I gulped, the words I really wanted to say catching in my throat. "Just... come back to me. Don't make me do this on my own."

He didn't answer, of course. Impassioned pleas didn't cure brain injuries. My shoulders sagged, defeated.

One hour blurred into another as the night wore on. I tried to read by lamplight, but after reading the same passage three times without registering the words, I gave it up for a lost cause. Next thing I knew, my chin touched my chest and then snapped back in a rebound, making me feel like a whiplash patient. I'd only dozed off for a moment, but scolded myself like a soldier who'd abandoned her post.

I rubbed my face, as if that could banish the exhaustion that hung like an anchor around my neck. "What I'd give for some coffee," I mumbled.

I hadn't expected a response, but Mark lifted his hand, holding it up off the ground as if not certain what to do with it. I sat bolt upright, sliding Lily's head gently off my leg so I could rock up onto my knees beside Mark. "Mark?"

He opened his eyes, blinking at me with an unfocused gaze. "Anna?"

His weak groan brought tears to my eyes. "Oh, thank God." I caught his hand to keep it from touching the side of his head, and just clung to it in mine. "Take it easy. You've got some stitches there."

Mark grimaced. "What happened?"

"You fell and hit your head pretty hard," I explained, smiling and crying at the same time. "Can you count my fingers okay?" I moved the lantern and held up a couple fingers in front of his face.

"Three." He got up on his elbows. Wincing, he cradled his side.

"Easy," I repeated, helping him sit up. "I think you cracked some ribs, and your knee's bruised all to hell. Does anything else hurt?"

He winced. "What doesn't?" After a moment of taking stock, he said, "That seems to be the worst of it." Squinting at the tent, he wondered, "Where are we?"

"At the bottom of the hill. What's the last thing you remember?"

Mark's face scrunched up as he puzzled over that one.. "I remember going through all those boulders." He frowned, started to shake his head, then stopped and grimaced. "What happened?"

"You fell off the mountain and hit your head," I repeated patiently. "It's normal to have some memory blanks." He was showing the classic concussion memory loss. Hopefully it wasn't anything worse than that. At least he was awake. Talking. Sitting up and moving all his limbs. Worry remained, but it felt as though an unbearable weight had been lifted from my shoulders. Overcome with relief, I held up a hand to my mouth.

"Anna?" Concerned, he leaned in and gripped my upper arm in a light, supportive touch. "What's wrong?"

"I thought I'd lost you," I whispered brokenly, tears spilling over my cheeks.

"Hey, it's all right." His voice was gentle as he drew me into his arms. He held me while all the emotions I'd been holding back for Lily's sake spilled out. My tears wet his shoulder. "I'm not going anywhere."

We both knew he couldn't really promise that, but it felt good to hear him say it anyway. I tilted my head up to see his face. His tender gaze met mine, and there were enough sparks between us to set the tent on fire. Yet neither of us acted on the simmering desire. We sat unmoving, spellbound, for a long moment before finally Mark slowly and deliberately planted a kiss on my forehead and released me.

I sat back, a torrent of conflicting emotions rushing in. Relief, worry, guilt, love, and exhaustion all dueled for prominence in my mind. Needing a diversion, I gently shook Lily's shoulder. "Lil, sweetie." She opened her eyes, squinting and still half-asleep. I smiled. "Look who's awake."

She turned her head and gasped. "Daddy!" Up in a flash, wriggling out of her sleeping bag, she rushed into Mark's arms with a force that couldn't have been kind to his injured ribs. He smiled through it, holding her tightly and murmuring soft reassurances.

"Everything's going to be all right, princess."

For the first time all night, I actually believed that.

CHAPTER 78

MY HOPEFUL ATTITUDE LASTED UNTIL we started breaking camp the next morning and discovered that Mark couldn't walk. His knee had swollen up like a grapefruit, and the bruises on his foot and ankle had turned nasty shades of purple overnight.

"I'll be fine," Mark said through gritted teeth as he leaned with one hand against a big boulder, keeping the weight off his injured leg.

"Seriously? You can barely stand."

"I'll manage."

I heaved a sigh, my breath puffing in the cold morning air. "Mark…"

"We can't stay here," he snapped, waving his free hand. "We can't waste any more time." He fixed me with a determined stare. "So wrap it, splint it, whatever you need to do, but we need to keep going."

It was nothing short of a miracle that the concussion had left him with just a headache and an irritable disposition. It could have been so much worse. I didn't want to press our luck, but I could see he wasn't budging. And he did have a point.

I huffed again. "Fine, but please just… be careful. I just don't want you to fall and crack your head open again." Sending a patient with that kind of leg injury and a head wound out to scramble over icy hills felt like malpractice.

When we finally broke camp, the flexible orange splint I'd worn for so long on my arm now hugged the sides of Mark's leg as a knee brace. An athletic wrap and his boot braced his ankle. Not ideal, but it would have to do. We transferred as much as we could to my pack to lighten his load, but it didn't feel like enough. I could still see the strain in his jaw, and the pinched look around his eyes as we set off.

Even with his trekking poles for balance, Mark's braced knee and ankle didn't have the flexibility to navigate the rocky terrain. He stumbled several times that morning, each one drawing a grimace as it put undue pressure on his knee. Once he fell and stayed down long enough to worry me. I crouched by his side and saw his face twisted in agony. He pounded a fist into the ground, swearing as he stamped down the scant inches of snow dusting the forest.

"Let me see." I reached for his leg, but he waved me away. Bear and Lily hung back, watching us quietly.

"It's fine." He rolled himself up into a sitting position, still grimacing.

"It's not fine, Mark." Frowning, I collected the trekking poles he'd dropped and put them within reach. "We should just camp here."

"No. I can manage."

"Mark…"

"I said I'll manage," he snapped. "We've only gone, what, five miles today? We can't camp yet. We'll never get there."

"We'll never get there if you fall and break your neck, either. Or hurt your leg worse and can't walk. It's not like I can carry you." Ignoring his frown, I held his eyes with a pointed gaze. "You've been toughing it out all day—you've made your point. You don't have to crawl the rest of the way just to prove your devotion."

"Maybe I do," he mumbled, lips drawing together in an unhappy line. He grabbed the poles and pushed himself back up to his feet.

I sighed. Shaking my head, I stepped in closer. "Give me your arm, then. Lean on me for a bit." After a brief flicker of surprise, he gave me a grateful nod. Settling his arm across my shoulders, we set off once more.

Mile after grueling mile, we trudged through ice and snow. The mountains weren't as rugged or steep as the ones we'd already crossed, but Mark's injury turned them into an exhausting slog. The beautiful snow-capped Mahoosuc range barely got a second glance as we continued moving north, our gaze so focused on where to put our feet.

It was Lily who spotted the cabin as we skirted around the edge of a frozen lake. "What's that over there?"

I followed the line of her finger, squinting into the white-dusted trees. "A building maybe?"

Mark paused, leaning on his trekking poles, his breath puffing from exertion. He pulled out his binoculars and took a closer look. "Looks like a cabin. No smoke; no light — probably abandoned. We should go check it out."

I wasn't keen on the long trek around the lake, but the prospect of sleeping indoors was too tempting to pass up. Any break from the freezing weather was a welcome one. I nodded, and we set off.

The cabin showed no signs of activity as we approached—no smoke from the chimney, no footprints in the snow, nothing. Bear hadn't given any sign of smelling anyone either, but that didn't stop my nerves from setting themselves on edge as we neared the building. Sensing my tension, Bear tucked his ears back and walked close beside me.

"Hello?" Mark called from the front yard. "Anyone home?"

No one answered. Stepping up onto the porch, I brushed away the frost and peered through the front window into the living room. Sparsely furnished, its centerpiece couch looked like something my grandmother might have owned. The fireplace stood empty, despite a stack of logs on a rack nearby. "Looks like nobody's here." I checked the door, mostly out of habit, and did a double-take when it opened.

Mark and I exchanged surprised glances. We were about to investigate further when Bear barked. Then Lily, standing near him, let out a startled shriek.

My rifle was off my shoulder and in my hands in an instant, my blood running cold. Mark was just a tiny bit slower, dropping his trekking poles. Gun in hand, he limped over toward his daughter. "Lil?" he asked, an alarmed edge to his voice. "What is it?"

Mutely, Lily pointed. She and Bear stood in the yard, near the corner of the porch. Just ahead of her, half-buried in snow, lay a man's body. Unlike many of the corpses we had encountered on our journey, this one showed no outward sign of trauma. His skin was white and waxy. If it weren't for the ice crystals on his face, he might have looked asleep. Near his right hand, an axe handle poked out from beneath the snow. He'd probably been on his way to the woodpile.

Mark hugged Lily with one arm, comforting her softly. "Is he frozen?" she asked timidly.

I nodded. Crouching down to get a better look, I studied the man's features. "I don't think that's what killed him, though. A stroke, maybe. Heart attack. Something like that."

We all stayed there solemnly for a long moment, before Mark said, "We should cover him up."

In ground this frozen we couldn't give him a proper burial, but we could at least do that much. "I'll look around. Maybe there's a tarp or something. You guys go on inside; get the fire started."

I could tell from his frown that Mark wanted to help. Between his injury and not wanting to leave Lily alone, though, it was a clear choice. Nodding, he led her into the cabin. Bear stayed outside with me. Around the back of the cabin, I found an exterior garage. A keychain in the dead man's jacket pocket got me inside. There I found a battered old pickup truck, and a hodgepodge of lawn tools and fishing gear. Buried among boxes on a shelf was a plastic tarp. My eyes drifted over the rest of the stuff, looking for anything that might be useful. Maybe we could fashion Mark a better splint.

I was still mulling over that possibility when I stopped suddenly and peered at the pickup truck. We'd passed so many derelict vehicles on the trip, my brain tended to dismiss them as part of the scenery, but something stuck out about this one. It looked ancient, and I remembered what Mark had said about some older vehicles still working. Ones that didn't have fancy electronics in them. What if this guy had driven out to his cabin *after* the blackout?

The truck, like the cabin, was unlocked. After a quick search through the keychain, I slipped the likely key into the ignition and turned it.

I honestly didn't expect it to work. An old truck, sitting idle for who-knew-how-long… what were the odds? The initial attempt wasn't promising—just a whirring noise and a few clicks. But I reset the key and tried again, and this time the engine flared to life. I flopped back in the seat, stunned.

"Well I'll be damned."

CHAPTER 79

"NO WAY. IT'S TOO DANGEROUS."

For a guy who could barely walk, I had expected a bit more enthusiasm for my discovery of a working vehicle. "Mark, I know it's a risk. We've avoided the roads this far…"

"For good reason," he interjected. We had all gathered in the living room of the cabin, the roaring fireplace casting a blissful warmth throughout the room.

"I know. And that was the right call then. Now, though?" I leaned forward, resting elbows on knees. "The weather's bad. Food's sparse. You're hurt. We're, what—eighty, ninety miles away? That's a solid ten days away the way we're going. Maybe longer if we run into more storms or something else goes wrong. In that truck…"

"We could be there tomorrow," Mark finished, his eyes dancing with the realization.

Lily perked up. She and Bear were snuggling right in front of the fireplace, half-paying attention to Mark and I talking. "Tomorrow? Really?"

"*If* we didn't run into trouble," Mark amended, dampening her enthusiasm slightly. "That's a big damn 'if', Anna."

"Going on foot isn't exactly trouble-free either." I gave his leg a pointed look, lips thinning as I remembered how close we'd come to losing him. "We've seen that enough times already."

He leaned back in his chair, letting out a long sigh. "Five hours."

"We could see Mommy tomorrow," Lily said, wide hazel eyes practically begging him.

Mark looked to me. I tilted my head, shrugging to leave the decision up to him. His jaw worked, mulling it over. Finally Mark nodded. "All right. We'll leave at dark."

Lily let out a whoop, raising her hands in the air triumphantly. That got a grin from Mark, and even Bear seemed to pick up on the excitement, his tail thumping against the wooden floor. I smiled, too, but at the same time felt an anxious knot forming in my stomach.

Not just because of the potential risks on the road, but of what we might—or might not—find when we got there.

CHAPTER 80

IT WAS STRANGE BEING BEHIND the wheel again. Stranger still driving on snow, which I'd never done. Mark would have been the better driver, but with his gas-pedal leg in a splint, it fell to me. Lily sat between us on the padded bench, and Bear had the back seat to himself, curled up with our backpacks and a pile of blankets.

"You're driving like my grandma," Mark chided playfully.

I slanted him a scowl. "Seriously? There's snow and I can barely see the road." Mark just snickered.

Leaving after dark had seemed like a good idea when we left the cabin: fewer travelers on the road, less chance of running into bandits. But it also made it nigh-impossible to see the edges of the ill-marked, snow-covered path connecting the lakefront cabins to the main road. All I could do was aim for the gap between the trees and hope for the best.

Things got easier once we hit the highway. Two lanes gave me room to maneuver around the occasional deserted vehicle, and the guardrails and markers helped me find the road. Lily started off the trip practically bouncing off the walls, but soon got bored and fell asleep. Even with the heater off to save gas, and the cold creeping into the cab, the comparative comfort of the drive was both a treat and a somber reminder of all the blackout had stolen from us.

After a few hours, the blocky shapes of buildings rose out of the dark ahead of us, derelict structures illuminated by the truck's headlights.

I glanced over and saw that Mark had also dozed off. I nudged him awake with a gentle elbow. He sat up, carefully adjusting Lily's head, and rubbed his face. "Didn't mean to fall asleep on you."

"Don't worry about it. You needed it."

He stifled a yawn. "Where are we?"

"Little over halfway, I think. Coming up on a town. I thought it'd be good to have another set of eyes out." Driving through the deserted forest hadn't been too bad, but approaching the town I felt a knot of anxiety forming in the back of my neck. Mark nodded readily, his frown betraying his own worry.

The area by the main road was mostly old businesses—offices, diners, and mom-and-pop shops, their windows smashed during some long-ago rioting. "It's weird seeing everything like this," he observed quietly as we passed by a darkened gas station. "No lights; no people. I wonder how many even stayed."

I thought I caught the soft glow of firelight down a side street, but we were past it before I could be sure. "People stay put more than you'd think. Even through disasters, wars… it's hard to leave behind everything you know." A sign heralded an urgent-care one mile east. Part of me wanted to go check it out on the off chance we might find something useful, but we didn't dare stop. The truck put a target on our backs, and our best chance was to get through as fast as we could. Despite the slick, snowy roads, I gave the truck some more gas. At least the temperatures and late hour might also work against anyone who would give us grief.

Wishful thinking.

We'd just turned a corner near a big white church when I caught motion out of the corner of my eye. I barely had time to register the shapes of people and the light of a torch before one of them hurled something at us. I jerked the steering wheel to avoid it, but the brick struck the edge of the windshield on my side. Cracks spider-webbed out from the impact.

The rear end of the truck fish-tailed from the sudden swerve. We skidded sideways up the road. I pumped the brakes and tried to steer away from it, but we ended up in a flat spin.

"Watch out!" Mark yelled, but I had no control. The truck whipped around and slammed into another parked car with a crash of shattered glass and metal on metal.

One down-side of stealing an ancient truck? No airbags. I realized this an instant before my head smacked into the steering wheel.

Everything went black for a few seconds. Sensations came at me, muffled like I was underwater. Bear barking; Mark yelling; angry voices.

"Anna! Anna, wake up!" Lily's shrill cry cut through the fog in my brain as she frantically shook my shoulder.

The fog parted. I jerked upright, bracing myself against the steering wheel as the world tilted wildly.

Mark stood by the truck, leveling his rifle at a pack of people approaching with clubs and torches. The dangerous, determined look in his eye gave the would-be assailants pause. "Stay the hell back!" He fired a warning shot in the air that made everyone jump. "Anna, can you drive?"

"I think so." The engine was still running. Hand shaking, I shifted the truck into reverse and gave it the tiniest bit of gas. We edged away from the car we'd hit. The steering felt off—maybe something had gotten knocked out of alignment—but it drove.

"Get in!" I called back to Mark. Without a word, he climbed up into the truck bed and knelt down, rifle still leveled at the mob. As soon as he was settled, I swung the truck around the wreck and got us the hell out of there.

CHAPTER 81

IT WASN'T UNTIL WE'D PUT several miles between us and the town that my breathing started to return to normal. I let us coast to a halt in the middle of the road and finally released the white-knuckled death grip I'd had on the steering wheel. Mark climbed out of the truck bed and limped around to the passenger side door. "Everyone okay?"

Lily gave a somber, wide-eyed nod, and scooted over to hug him. He held her tightly, his chin resting against the top of her head. Eventually he lifted his eyes to mine, and we shared a sad, pained look. He reached a hand over to me silently. I took it, my fingers intertwining with his, and squeezed gently in return.

"Are the mean people going to come after us?" Lily asked, her voice small and scared.

"No, princess, they can't catch up without a car," Mark assured her.

I glanced up at the rear-view mirror anyway. Silly as it was, I half-expected to see a mob with torches and pitchforks chasing after us. "We should get going anyway. Put some more distance between us."

"Let me see your forehead," Mark said. Gentle fingers brushed the hair away from my face.

I swallowed my protest, knowing it wouldn't deter him. I could feel the sticky blood drying on the side of my face, all the way down to my jacket collar. I just sighed and sank back against the bench, letting him work.

"It's still bleeding. Let's take care of it, then we can go." He reached into the back seat and fished out my medical kit. Gingerly dabbing some antiseptic on the wound, he murmured a quiet, "Sorry," when I winced. His brow furrowed in soft concern.

"Going to make a medic out of you yet," I murmured.

"Quit getting hurt and you won't have to. I swear, you're the most accident-prone doctor I've ever met."

I made a face. "Most of them weren't accidents."

Mark finished taping a dressing over my eyebrow. "There. Why don't you let me drive for a bit."

"What about your leg?" I asked.

"I'll manage. It's no worse off than your head. Besides, one crash a night is my limit." Seeing his twinkle of amusement, I jabbed him lightly in the arm. He mock-winced.

Scooting across the bench, I vacated the driver's seat without argument. My head throbbed so much it left me on the edge of dizziness. It probably was best that he drove for a while. Lily moved to the middle, then contorted around the bounds of her old-school lap seat belt to lean into me. Poor thing still had that spooked look in her eyes. I slipped my free arm around her, holding her close. Mark draped a blanket over us both, tucking Lily in so just her head and the top of her stuffed cat peeked out. As he bent down to kiss her hair, he caught my eye and we exchanged a strained smile.

Mark got Bear settled in the back seat, and off we went. Between the quiet monotony of deserted country roads, the comfortable warmth of Lily and the blanket, and the dull pounding behind my eyes, I soon drifted off.

Some time later, I jolted awake. I blinked around blearily for a minute before realizing that the truck had stopped. Just enough moonlight seeped into the cab for me to see Mark's frown. "Damn it," he mumbled.

"What's wrong?"

"Gas." He let out a sigh, his breath fogging in the cold cab air. "Thought we'd make it farther."

"How close are we?"

"Maybe six, seven miles?" He banged a gloved hand on the steering wheel. "So damn close."

I reached past Lily to touch his arm. "It's okay, Mark. We're almost there."

His head bobbed. "Yeah. Yeah, you're right. We can make it there tomorrow." He rubbed his face, looking somewhat amazed. "Tomorrow."

I didn't want to think about that, so I changed the subject. "Should we set up the tent?"

Mark considered a moment, then shook his head. "Nah, I think it'll be just as warm in here. Besides, you two look comfy."

I rubbed at my stiff neck then glanced down at Lily, a wistful smile creeping across my face. "Well, one of us is, at least. I'm amazed she was able to sleep after all that."

"She always fell asleep in the car. Ever since she was a baby."

I adjusted the blanket near her face, a pang of sadness causing my smile to dim. Tomorrow it could be Lauren holding her, comforting her. That's how it was supposed to be; I just wasn't ready for it. Maybe I never would be.

Mark must have seen my expression change. "You okay?"

I shrugged. "Still have a headache. It'll be fine."

"Anna…" He started with a tentative frown, then paused. Debating how much he wanted to push. "You don't have to pretend. I know this must be hard for you. It's been just the three of us for a long time."

Eyes locked on Lily, I tried to reason away the ache in my heart. "We knew this day was coming. It's the whole reason we're here."

"Knowing it's coming doesn't make it easier." He watched me for a minute. "I can't ever thank you enough for everything you've done for us."

"Mark, you don't have to…"

He cut me off gently. "Yeah, I do. All the times you saved us. The way you stuck by us through everything. We wouldn't have made it this far without you."

The gentle conviction in his face touched my heart. My throat tightened, overcome with emotion and the words I'd left unsaid for too long. I looked away from him, blinking rapidly to keep the threatening tears at bay.

"What's wrong?" Mark's brows knitted in concern. When I didn't answer, he prompted softly, "Anna? Whatever it is, you can tell me."

That nudge was enough. If I kept it in any longer I'd never have another chance. "I'm in love with you." Somehow it came out sounding more like an apology. Maybe it was.

His forehead creased, caught somewhere between surprise and confusion. It couldn't have been a shock to him, but maybe he just didn't expect me to say it out loud. "I know. I mean… I guessed." It looked like he wanted to say something else, but instead a pained look settled on his face.

I winced, too. "It's okay. I know you don't feel the same." I shook my head, sighing. "I don't know why I even told you. I guess…I just wanted you to hear it. Just once. So you know what you mean to me."

"No, I'm glad you did." Mark reached for my hand, curling his fingers over mine. He studied my face in the dim light of the cab. The tenderness in his eyes stood in contrast to the conflicted furrow across his forehead. "You're an amazing woman, Anna. You mean so much to me, too. And to Lil. It's just… different. I'm sorry."

"You don't have to apologize for being faithful to your wife," I chided, slanting him a strained smile. "You're my friend, and that's enough. All I really want is for you and Lil to be happy. Tomorrow, God willing, you'll have your family back."

He squeezed my hand. "You're part of our family now too. Whatever happens tomorrow, that's not going to change."

I shot him a grateful look, too choked up to say anything more. We both fell quiet for a long time before finally I found my voice again. "Mark? I want you to know… I really do hope she's there."

He smiled softly. "I know you do."

But there was a small, traitorous part of me that still imagined what it would be like if she wasn't.

CHAPTER 82

LILY SHOCKED ME BY WAKING up at the crack of dawn, bouncing off the walls despite getting to sleep so late. Never have I seen her volunteer so readily for camp chores to get us on the road faster. I'd barely gotten any sleep either, squashed into the corner of the pickup's front seat. Seeing her enthusiasm, I felt even more guilty for thinking—even for a second—that maybe we wouldn't find Lauren.

"It's weird to think this might be the last time we pack up camp," I mused. My breath fogged in the cold morning air as I tucked the breakfast gear into my backpack.

"With any luck we'll be sleeping in real beds tonight," Mark agreed. His voice mirrored Lily's childish glee.

We left the truck behind and ventured up the road on foot, the bright, clear skies allowing the sun to reflect off the ankle-deep snow. Lily spent the morning babbling about the cabin. I gave non-committal mmm-hmms as she related every detail—the rooms, the lake, the toys and books she hoped would be there. And, of course, Lauren.

We ate lunch on-the-go, and I could hardly blame them when we were so close. I caught Mark looking at me a couple of times as we walked, concern tugging at his lips. I tried to reassure him with a faint smile, but I didn't think he bought it.

When we caught sight of water through the trees, Lily let out an excited shout. "Look, Daddy! It's the lake! We're almost there."

I think she would have run the rest of the way if Mark had let her. We skirted around the edge of the lake. Small drifts of snow sat on the icy surface, which stretched out for at least a mile. In the background, a mountain towered. Even in my glum mood, I had to admit it was beautiful. We passed by another cabin. "That's the Phillips' place," Mark commented as we passed. Seeing the dark windows and unbroken snow around it, he said, "Looks like they didn't come."

He frowned, wondering if we'd find the same at his cabin. Anticipation mingled with dread as we quickened our pace, Lily practically bounding through the snow. "Come on, come on," she urged.

At last we came to a break in the trees, a wide clearing with a cabin at the far end. White smoke drifted up from the chimney. "Daddy! Someone's home!" Lily squealed.

"We don't know who it is, princess," Mark cautioned, but I could see the hope lighting up his eyes.

The cabin door opened, and someone stepped out. From this distance we couldn't see their face, but with the feminine cut of the powder-blue winter jacket and the errant blonde curls peeking out from under the knit cap, I knew.

"Mommy!" Lily shouted.

PART FOUR

CHAPTER 83

"LILY?" THE WOMAN'S SHOCKED VOICE floated back to us.

Lily pulled free from Mark's hand and ran towards her mother. "Mommy! Mommy!"

Lauren rushed towards us and they met halfway, Lily taking a running leap up into her mother's arms. Mark limped over as fast as he could manage, drawing them both into a tight hug. Lauren's words dissolved into unintelligible babbles, laughing and crying at the same time.

I hung back, watching their reunion with happy tears in my eyes. Whatever else I felt, I would have walked another thousand miles just to see that look of unbridled joy on Mark and Lily's faces. Even Bear got into the action, weaving around their legs, barking, and panting happily. I just continued to stand off to the side with my hands stuffed into my pockets.

"Oh God—I thought I'd never see you again," Lauren's tearful happiness made her voice quaver. She touched Mark's cheek, frowning at the remnants of bruises on his face from the fall. "Are you okay? What happened?"

"I'm fine, it's nothing," Mark demurred, punctuating the sentiment with a kiss.

Finally the tears and laughter and group hug eased off enough for Lauren to finally register my presence. Her brow furled in a perplexed expression, and then she slanted a questioning look Mark's way.

"Lauren, this is our friend Anna." Mark kept an arm around Lauren's shoulder, beaming like a kid who'd just unwrapped the best present in the world.

"She helped us find you," Lily provided helpfully, tugging on my hand to pull me closer. "And this is Bear. We found him and now he's our dog."

I tried to swallow past the lump in my throat and smiled. I hoped it didn't seem forced; I really was happy for them. I just needed to shove aside that little piece of me that was being a selfish, jealous jerk. "Hi. It's really great to finally meet you." Despite her uncertain look back, I withdrew a hand from my pocket to offer it to her.

Lauren shook it tentatively, then looked back at the cabin and smiled. "Let's go inside. You must be freezing."

The inside of the cabin was just as Lily had described it—small but cozy, decorated in bargain furniture with a few personal knick-knacks on the walls and mantle. We dumped our packs in an alcove by the door and spread out to start removing winter gear. A fire roared in the fireplace, and for several seconds I just basked in its warmth. Bear had the same idea. He let out a happy bark and shook off the snow before sprawling on the rug right in front of the fire.

As Lauren hung up her coat, it revealed something that had been hidden by all the layers of outerwear. Mark saw it, a hand touching Lauren's stomach. He tilted his face up at her, eyes wide with the unspoken question.

"Yes," she laughed, "We're going to have another baby."

As Mark engulfed his wife in an ecstatic hug, Lily's mouth dropped open. "I get to have a baby brother or sister?" She shrieked. "This is the best. Day. Ever!"

I just stood there with a strained smile plastered to my face.

"When?" Mark asked, sounding dazed.

"Early March."

I did the math in my head, and realized she probably figured it out right after the blackout. That must have been a hell of a thing, on top of being separated from Mark and Lily. I offered a polite, "Congratulations." She gave me a brief glance of acknowledgement, still not sure what to make of me being here.

"Sit down, sit down," Lauren urged. The Ryans settled on the couch. Lily snuggled up on her mother's lap, and Mark sat beside them with his arm around his wife. I found a chair nearby. Their smiles lit up the room, though Lauren's was tinged with a tearful, overwhelmed amazement. "My parents?" A timid hope shone through in her voice.

"They went to stay with your Aunt Ruth," Mark explained, and Lauren let out a relieved breath. "They were fine. They sent their love, of course."

Lauren sniffled and nodded, nuzzling Lily's hair with her cheek. She seemed too choked up to say anything more for a long minute before she finally asked, "How on earth did you get here?"

"We walked," Mark said, pride creeping into his smile.

"You walked." Lauren chuckled, as if waiting for the punchline. When none came, her eyebrows lifted in disbelief. "You *walked*—all the way from Pennsylvania?"

Mark nodded, chuckling, and Lily chimed in excitedly. "We totally did, Mommy. We rode in a boat and a truck for a little bit, but mostly we walked. It was super far. And we got to camp out, and we picked berries and me and Anna learned what plants we could eat, and Daddy caught lots of fish."

Lauren shook her head. "That's… amazing. I can't wait to hear all about it." All that talk of food must have made Lauren realize it was almost supper time. "Have you eaten yet? You both look like skin and bones."

Mark shook his head, "Not yet, but it can wait."

"I can make something," I offered tentatively. "Let you guys get caught up. We still have that venison on ice." Well, on bagged snow, technically. Winter did have some advantages.

Lauren looked between me and Mark, her brow creasing. Mark gave her an encouraging shrug, leaving it up to her, and then finally she nodded my way. "Okay, thanks. Let me know if you have trouble finding anything."

"Sure." I gave her a weak smile and fled to the kitchen. Once around the corner, out of sight, I leaned heavily against the kitchen counter and took a minute to gather the tattered threads of my composure. Tears stung my eyes—unfair tears I had no right to feel.

I hadn't expected it to be this hard.

CHAPTER 84

SNATCHES OF CONVERSATION AND LAUGHTER filtered through the thin wall as I busied myself in the kitchen, preparing the meat and some canned green beans. Bear went with me, sitting at my feet hoping for scraps to fall. The cabin's propane stove still worked after the EMP, saving me from having to venture out to the living room to cook on the fireplace. I didn't want to intrude on their reunion. For almost six months I had spent every day with Mark and Lily, but now in an instant I felt like an interloper.

Once supper was ready, Lauren insisted on helping me bring everything out. We crammed ourselves around their tiny kitchen table, and Mark said a heartfelt grace thanking God for reuniting his family and keeping everyone safe. The sun was already going down, painting the frozen lake with shades of orange and pink through the window.

"This is great," Lauren commented after tasting the steak. "It's been awhile since I got a deer. I've been sticking closer to the cabin, now that the weather's gotten worse."

She looked better fed than we were, though, which made me wonder aloud, "Must be hard. What have you been eating?"

"I'd get some birds or small game sometimes with the shotgun, but mostly the supplies we had stored here." Lauren gave an embarrassed shrug. "I went through a sort of mini-prepper phase after Lily was born, and we started bringing stuff up here when we visited: canned goods, bottled water, that sort of thing. We had enough for the three of us for a couple months, so I was able to stretch it."

I nodded, impressed. Chopping wood and hunting in the snow was hard enough without being pregnant. "How long have you been here on your own?" I asked tentatively, afraid of poking at a sore subject.

"It took me about a month to make it up here from Boston, after everything crashed." Lauren's lips pressed together, the strain of what she'd been through surfacing for a moment. Mark saw it, too; he reached over to pat her hand. She managed a wan smile and then poked her fork at her plate. After a bite, she changed the subject, "Mark said you've been with them since this all started?"

I nodded. "Yeah, we met at the airport."

"She saved Daddy after the ceiling fell on him," Lily chimed in, entirely too brightly.

Lauren gasped, "My God, what?"

"He was fine," I felt obliged to clarify. "Just got caught in some debris."

"One of the planes crashed into the terminal," Mark added grimly. "It was a mess. After things got sorted out there, Anna didn't have anywhere to go, so she came with us to your parents' place."

"Your parents are wonderful people," I offered, smiling faintly as I remembered the short time I'd spent with them. I hoped they'd made it to Ruth's farm all right.

Lauren's lips curled upward at the compliment to her parents, but then she shook her head. "So what made you decide to walk all the way here?"

Not really knowing how to answer, I just gave a weak chuckle. "Temporary insanity?"

"Temporary?" Mark teased. Then, glancing to Lauren, he explained, "I asked her to come with us. Figured it would be safer for all of us if we stuck together. And it was. I've lost track of how many times Anna saved our as…butts."

Lily giggled at his averted curse, then said, "Like when she saved me in the river. And made my foot all better."

I poked at my steak, shifting awkwardly. "Mark's not giving himself enough credit. It was more of a team effort. Even you, Lil… you ran to get help at the airport."

"And I warned Daddy about those bad guys at the ski place." Despite her pride, her smile flickered, bad memories resurfacing. I felt it, too, and laid a comforting hand on her arm.

Lauren scooted her chair over close to Lily, drawing her into a protective hug. I let my hand fall away as Lauren murmured, "My poor baby. You've had to be so brave." Lauren's eyes glistened, pain written all over her face.

Mark's mouth tightened in a somber half-frown, and he reached across the small table to squeeze Lauren's shoulder. "We're all here now. That's what matters." Lauren caught his eye and gave a tearful nod. She pressed her lips to the top of Lily's hair, then scooted her chair back.

I averted my eyes while Lauren sniffed and wiped at her face, focusing on my plate. Silence fell, until finally Lauren stabbed at some greens and ventured, "So Anna—what are your plans now?"

That dialed the awkward up to 11. My fork stopped halfway to my mouth. I looked to Mark, hoping for a lifeline. He cleared his throat. "Actually, I told Anna she could stay with us."

"She's gonna stay forever!" Lily declared, smiling at me.

Lauren wasn't smiling. Her expression bland, she shot Mark a look that could only be interpreted as *we'll talk about this later*. "Oh. I see."

"Mark's very generous," I demurred, "But I don't want to impose on your family."

"But you're our family too, Anna," Lily protested. Lauren's mouth twitched.

"Thanks sweetheart." I smiled faintly, touched by the assertion. "I'm sure we'll figure it out."

Lauren made a soft 'mmm' of acknowledgement.

Strained pleasantries filled out the rest of supper. I asked Lauren questions that I already knew the answers to just to be polite, and she probed my background in return. The questions were innocent enough, but somehow there remained an undercurrent of someone scoping out a potential threat. I felt a wave of relief when Lily asked, "Mommy, do you want to see my pictures?"

"I'll get the dishes," Mark said, freeing Lauren up for an impromptu art exhibit in the living room.

I got up to help him. As soon as we were alone in the kitchen, I mumbled, "That went well."

Mark slanted me a sympathetic smile, nudging me with an elbow. "She doesn't know you yet," he said softly, his voice hopeful. "Give it time."

"Yeah." I tried to keep the doubt out of my voice.

Bedtime brought a different kind of drama, when Lauren offered to make up the couch for me. "Sorry, we don't have a guest room or anything."

"It's fine, thank you," I assured her.

"But I want Anna and Bear to sleep in my room," Lily protested, wearing actual pajamas for the first time since I'd met her. Apparently they kept some spare clothes here for their getaways.

Lauren's brow creased, casting an uncertain look to Mark then back at her daughter. "I don't know, sweetie."

Undaunted, Lily was already problem-solving. "It's kinda crowded, but Anna's sleeping bag will fit on the floor. It'll be like a sleepover!" Then her lip curled under. "I don't wanna be all by myself."

I shrugged to Lauren, leaving it up to her. "Anything's a step up from being outside in the tent, really."

Understandably not wanting to be the bad guy on Lily's first day home, Lauren caved. "Okay. Why don't you help Anna get her stuff all set up?"

Lily let out a happy whoop. "Come on, Anna. I'll show you my room." She took my hand, leading me toward the back. I glanced back over my shoulder, catching just a glimpse of a pained look on Lauren's face before she turned away.

Shit.

CHAPTER 85

MARK AND LAUREN TRIED TO keep their voices down that night, but through the thin cabin walls I could hear snatches of them arguing.

Arguing about me.

"…without even talking to me?" Lauren accused.

Mark mumbled something conciliatory, then protested, "…no idea what she's done for us, Lauren."

"…having a stranger in our home—in our lives…"

I found myself holding my breath, but the conversation became too muffled for me to make out until Mark's indignant exclamation, "Of course not! How can you even…"

I didn't blame her. I'd be suspicious too if my husband had turned up on our doorstep after almost six months with some strange woman in tow. And it wasn't like I was completely innocent, either. When I closed my eyes, I would dream about that night in the ski resort. His arms around me, his mouth on mine… I pushed those thoughts to the back of my mind, but they'd return. They always did. I stared up at the ceiling, the guilt weighing on me as I tried not to eavesdrop.

Listening to them kiss and make up was almost worse than hearing them argue. Heart in my throat, I rolled over, tucked an arm over my head, and tried vainly to chase sleep.

A restless night meant I was the first up the next morning. Not feeling comfortable enough to rummage around Lauren's kitchen uninvited, I dug through my pack for a baggie of cereal I'd been saving. Bear joined me once I got the fire going, camping out in his favorite spot in front of the fireplace. I sat down on the couch, a blanket wrapped around my shoulders as the water boiled for coffee.

I stared into the fire, feeling vaguely unsettled. We'd been breaking into peoples' houses for months, but somehow I felt more like an intruder sitting here than I had in any of them.

Lily wandered out, mussed bed-head poking out from the blanket swaddling her. "Hey Anna," she said with a sleepy yawn.

I smiled. "Morning, sweetheart."

"I'm hungry. Can we use that pancake mix we found?"

We'd pilfered food from the cabin where we'd found the truck, and a box of just-add-water pancake mix had immediately caught Lily's eye. "Sure. We can make some for your mom and dad too." Lily bobbed her head enthusiastically, grinning at the idea of surprising them.

After we'd finished breakfast—and had a stack of pancakes set aside for Mark and Lauren—I said, "Why don't you go get your hairbrush; we can get those tangles out."

"Okay!"

A little while later, her hair was brushed and I was halfway through braiding it when I heard a jubilant, "Mommy!"

Braid strands in hand, I glanced up to see Lauren paused at the mouth of the rear hallway. Her brow creased for just a split second when she saw us, then she smiled. "Morning, baby girl. You sleep okay?" Lily nodded. "Are you hungry?"

I got the last hair tie in place. As soon as the braid slapped against her shoulder, Lily was up off my lap and running over to greet her mom with a hug. I stamped down an irrational pang of jealousy.

"Me and Anna made me pancakes already," Lily said brightly.

"Did you?" Lauren cast a bland glance my way.

"And there's some for you and Daddy too. I'll get you a plate!"

As Lily bounded off to the kitchen, Lauren came over to the living room. Seeing her heading for one of the side chairs, I waved her off and stood up. "I'll sit there. You take the couch with Lil."

She paused. "Thanks."

Lily returned with a plate a moment later. "We had some extra syrup packs too," she announced proudly.

I watched quietly as they sat together on the couch. Lauren's face transformed, relaxed and smiling as she cuddled with her daughter and ate her pancakes. Lily grinned up at her. However I felt, she was exactly where she was supposed to be. With her mother.

Our days were filled with chores, things we once took for granted now turned into elaborate productions. I pitched in where I could, though Lauren often demurred my offers to help. She treated me with a distant politeness, making me feel like a guest at a bed-and-breakfast who'd already overstayed her welcome. Lily became her mother's shadow, and it left me twiddling my thumbs for large stretches of the day. Crazy as it seemed, I found myself pining for the trail. I could do without the endless days out in the freezing cold, but there was something comforting about the routine—being on the move, marching towards a goal.

By the third day of walking on eggshells and being bored out of my skull, I needed a break from the claustrophobic cabin. As Mark and Lauren cleared away the breakfast dishes, Bear nudged my hand, hoping for some scraps. He contented himself with some distracted ear scratches instead. "You want to go out, buddy?" Hearing the magic word 'out', Bear hopped up with a happy tail wag. I rose as well, heading for the door to grab my coat.

"Where are you going?" Lily wondered.

"Just going to take Bear out and explore a bit. Set some traps, maybe get something for supper."

"Can I come?" she asked brightly. "I can show you the lake and the treehouse and everything."

I nodded. "Sure. Get your stuff on." I checked my rifle over and slung it over my shoulder.

I was heading into the kitchen to tell Mark the plan when Lauren came out. Her eyes landed on Lily pulling her boots on, and her brow creased. "What's going on?"

"We're gonna go set up the traps and show Anna the lake and stuff," Lily announced.

Lauren rested a hand on the back of a dining chair, her lips curling downward. "I don't want you going that far from the cabin, Lil."

"Oh, we won't go far," I assured her. "Just scouting for game trails. Maybe see a deer if we're lucky."

Lauren's frown didn't ease. "I'd rather she stay close to the house."

Lily looked from her mother to me, uncertainly. "But I usually always go out with Anna. I want to show her grandpa's treehouse."

"Not today, sweetie." Lauren's voice had a tone of finality to it.

Scowling, Lily tugged her boots back off and slammed them down on the ground. "Not fair," she grumped, stomping off to her room.

"Lily…" Lauren's call trailed off with an exasperated sigh as Lily disappeared into the back of the cabin. She fixed her frown on me, then. "You should've asked me first."

Meeting her glare head-on, my lips thinned in displeasure. A dozen angry retorts sprang to mind, but I held them back and said flatly, "I'm not going to let anything happen to her. I've been taking her hunting for months."

"That's not the point," she fired back, "You're not her mother, Anna. You don't get to make those decisions."

My fingers tightened around the door handle, channeling tension into the grip. Mark emerged from the kitchen, dish towel in hand, and disrupted the brewing explosion. He glanced between us, brow creasing in concern. "Everything okay?"

I shot him a fiery look, then pulled the door open. "Come on, Bear." We escaped out into the cold.

CHAPTER 86

MARK FOUND ME OUT BY the shed hours later. Bear's bark alerted me to his approach, and he left my side to go say hello. Mark petted the dog briefly, then stuffed his hands into the pockets of his fleece sweater. He hadn't bothered bundling up, and I felt colder just looking at him. After spending a couple days mostly indoors, it seemed like I'd already lost what little climate acclimatization I had. My hands were pink and numb.

Bear and I had bagged a pair of pheasants while we were out. I'd already plucked and cleaned them, and was wrapping the meat up to place in a snow-packed cooler for later. "I would've done that, you know," Mark offered. "You kill it, I clean it, right?" He flashed me a smile.

I shrugged, closing the cooler. "It's fine. I wanted some air anyway." I'd put some water over a small fire to take the chill off, and used it to scrub my hands and knife clean. Then I held my hands over the fire, letting the warmth penetrate my tingling fingers.

"Lauren told me what happened," Mark said. I didn't respond, and he just arched his eyebrows. "Don't you think you're overreacting?"

My head snapped up. "Seriously? You're taking her side?" It hit harder than it probably should have. She was his wife, after all.

Scowling, Mark protested, "I'm not taking sides. Look, I know things have been a little awkward…"

"A little awkward?" Rising, I turned to face him fully. "I've spent the last six months helping you take care of Lily. Protecting her. Now I can't even take her out of sight of the cabin? That's bullshit, Mark."

"So what if it is?" Mark fired back, stepping closer and gesturing towards the cabin. "Lauren's been through a lot, too. She's been out here all alone. She thought we were dead! Don't you think she's entitled to be overprotective? This is her daughter we're talking about."

I scowled at his words, but then a pained grimace took over. I paced back and forth a few steps, hugging myself. I didn't want to admit he was right, but deep down I knew I'd overstepped my bounds.

Mark watched me pace for a minute before venturing, "Anna, what's going on? I know you're not this upset over a hunting trip."

The nudge caused my simmering discomfort to finally boil over. "Lauren doesn't want me here."

Mark squinted at me. "What are you talking about? When did she say that?"

I rolled my eyes. "She doesn't have to *say* it. It's obvious."

He made a face, then said in a patient voice that bordered on patronizing, "Anna, I think you're jumping to conclusions."

"Oh, for the love of…" I sighed in exasperation. "You saw her reaction when you and Lil talked about me staying here. And I heard you two arguing that night."

Mark ducked his head. A flash of surprised embarrassment that I had overheard their argument—and the making-up that followed— quickly turned to a frown.

"The only way she could make it any plainer is by throwing my backpack out in the snow." I let that sink in for a moment. "She thinks there's something going on between us."

"No," Mark shook his head. "I told her we were just friends."

"And did she believe you?" His silence revealed his doubts. Arching my eyebrow, I asked pointedly, "Did you tell her about that night at the resort?"

Mark rubbed at his jaw, wincing. "I was going to." My face called him out without me saying a word. "I will. It just… it wasn't a good time."

I snorted. "Yeah, good luck sliding that one into a conversation." We both fell quiet, the awkwardness thick enough to swim through. "Saying we're 'just friends' doesn't make it true, Mark. We crossed a line."

"That's not going to happen again." He drew himself up defensively.

"Of course not, but how's she supposed to know that? How would you feel if it were the other way around? If she had turned up with some guy she'd spent the last six months with?"

Mark frowned. "I'd trust her."

"But would you trust *him*?" He didn't have an answer for that, and once again I let out a sigh that fogged the air. "Maybe she's right." My throat tightened painfully, a stubborn knot remaining even after I tried to gulp past it. "Maybe I should go."

"What are you talking about?" Mark waved a hand at the forest that surrounded us. "Go where?"

I shook my head, nudging some snow with the toe of my boot. "I don't know. I'm sure someone somewhere needs a doctor."

Mark stared at me for a moment, then his mouth curled downward. "So that's it, huh? Mission's over. Time to move on? Is that all we are to you?"

His sharp words took me aback. "What? Of course not!" Despite my denial, he had hit closer than I wanted to admit. I loved them, but I'd spent most of my adult life moving from one crisis to another.

"Then what, Anna? After everything we've been through, this is where you throw in the towel? What about Lily? How do you think she's going to feel if you leave?" The question needled me, causing me to dip my head and frown. He pressed on, "What are you so damn afraid of?"

"I'm not afraid." The protest sounded weak even to my own ears.

"Bullshit," Mark snapped. "You've been running your whole life. What are you running from?"

Tears stung my eyes, and I blinked up at the gray sky. I didn't say anything for a long minute. I didn't want to answer, to open that door, but he deserved an explanation. "Everyone leaves, Mark."

His brow furrowed, trying to understand. "Like your dad?"

"Not just him, though. Friends rotating in and out of the naval bases we were stationed at when I was a kid. Staff on the aid missions. My fiancee."

"Nikolai," Mark added, realization showing on his face.

I shrugged. "Sometimes…it's easier to leave first."

Boots crunched on the snow as Mark came closer. He laid his hands on my shoulders, his expression softening. "We're not going anywhere. Don't run from us." He pulled me in gently for a hug. I stiffened at first, not wanting to add fuel to the smoldering embers between us. But even as I felt the soft fleece of his jacket against my cheek, I found it more comfortable than awkward. Relaxing, I hugged him back.

He held me for a minute before taking a step back. "Anna, listen. All this is an adjustment for everyone, but I know Lauren. She'll come around. Trust me." Earnest eyes bored into me, pleading with me to believe him.

The silence hung in the air until finally I let out a sigh. "All right. I'll try. At least until spring—until the baby comes." I wouldn't leave before I knew they were okay, and traveling in the middle of winter would just be stupid. "But Mark, if she doesn't—"

"She will."

"But if she doesn't, I can't stay. I can't be something that comes between you." My voice was adamant. "I won't be that person. I won't be my stepmom."

Mark nodded. "I get it. It'll be fine. I'll talk to Lauren…"

"No," I interrupted gently. "I'll talk to her. You need to be on her side."

He gave me a puzzled squint. "Weren't you just pissed at me for taking her side a minute ago?" I hitched one shoulder in an embarrassed shrug, which got a chuckle out of him. "Okay. I'll leave it to you, then." He blew into his hands. "It's freezing out here. Let's go inside."

Mark kicked snow on the fire and picked up the cooler of meat. Stuffing my hands in my pockets, I followed.

I desperately hoped that he was right, because for the first time in as long as I could remember, the pull to stay was stronger than the one to go.

CHAPTER 87

TALKING WITH LAUREN PROVED MORE difficult than I'd thought it would be. The dark winter days dragged on, and plummeting temperatures kept us all close to the cabin. Mark and I made sure we had plenty of wood to keep the fire going, and we mostly just hibernated. In the cramped quarters of the cabin, I never had a chance to catch her alone for more than a few minutes at a stretch.

Meanwhile, Lauren's cold-shoulder treatment continued, and any hope of reconciliation seemed to move further and further from my grasp. I braced myself for the inevitable—leaving them for their own sake. The idea sat like a rock in the pit of my stomach, but I resolved to wall off my heart and do the right thing.

After a few days of bitter cold, it warmed up enough for the snow to return. The skies dumped a solid six inches through the day, and showed no signs of slowing.

"Thank God you're not still out in that," Lauren said, frowning out the window.

"I'll second that." Mark grinned, coming up to hug her from behind. She leaned back, nuzzling her head against his chin, and smiled softly. I looked away, back to the book I'd read three times already on the way here.

"Do you think there'll be snow for Christmas?" Lily asked. She and Lauren had made an Advent calendar out of an old cardboard box, and she'd been anxiously counting down the days. Just two weeks to go.

"Maybe," Mark mused.

Lily grinned. "Can we still get a tree?" Seeing Mark start to hedge, she whined accusingly, "You promised."

"That was before we got half a foot of snow," Mark protested. Between dueling pointed looks from Lauren and Lily, he held up his hands and relented. "All right, all right. When the weather lets up, we'll see."

The weather didn't let up that day, or the day after. By the weekend —not that the days of the week mattered much any more—the clouds had cleared and the sun started chipping away at the snow that blanketed everything.

I left mid-morning to go hunting. There were four of us now instead of three, and the cold snap had put a dent in our meat supply. Bear walked beside me, bounding joyfully in the snow that reached his shoulders. We trekked out past the lake and into the forest beyond. Despite the cold and the awkwardness of walking on snowshoes, it felt good to be out of the house for a change. I paused at the crest of a rise to just take in the forest ahead, watching the sunlight glisten off the snow-crusted branches. Even though I'd rather spend my days on a nice tropical beach somewhere, I had to confess this land had a certain beauty to it. I just still had a hard time imagining it as home.

Hours later, with only a squirrel and rabbit to show for my trouble, I rubbed my hands and sighed. "Not our day, apparently," I said to Bear. He just panted at me expectantly, and I ruffled his fur with my gloved hand. "Good boy. Let's head back." Bear fell in beside me as we started back.

Emerging from the trees into the clearing by the cabin, I saw Lauren sitting on the bench by the front door, struggling to clip on her snowshoes. A stuffed backpack sat on the bench beside her. I approached with a puzzled frown. "Lauren? What's going on?"

Her head jerked toward me, the worry in her eyes obvious even from a distance. "Did you see Mark and Lily on the way back?"

"No, why?" I closed the distance between us, her worry causing my own to flare up like gasoline dumped on a fire. "Where'd they go?"

"They went to get a tree," Lauren replied tightly, waving her arm northward. Grimacing in frustration, she finally got the first snowshoe attached. She contorted her leg to an angle that let her reach her foot despite her pregnant belly and fluffy jacket, and started on the other. "Mark said they'd be gone an hour, two tops. It's been almost twice that and it's starting to get dark."

I frowned in the direction she'd indicated. It wasn't like Mark to be late like that. I could see two sets of grooves in the snow, one narrower than the other. "Well, the tracks are still there. Shouldn't be too hard to follow them." Turning back to her, I said, "I'll go. You should probably stay here."

"No."

The sharp reply didn't invite argument, but I sighed and tried anyway. "Lauren, I know you want to help, but you need to think about the baby."

She got the second snowshoe on. "I have two babies to think about. One of them's out there." Lauren jerked a gloved hand in the direction of the tracks.

"Lauren…"

"I'm going." Her eyes held a look of almost frenzied determination, and nothing I said would matter.

"All right," I said, my sigh misting in the cold. "Let me get some things and then we'll go together." She said nothing, but was still fussing with her snowshoe. I wondered if she'd wait for me.

Tucking the carcasses of the animals into the cooler to deal with later, I stepped inside the cabin. Lauren had already doused the fire in the fireplace, but the warmth lingered, a blissful reprieve from the weather. Anxiety hit me full-force, assaulting me with unwelcome memories: Lily held at knifepoint; Mark laying on the rocks with blood pooling beneath his head. If something had happened to them…

I shook off the thought with effort. First things first—we had to find them.

Normally I carried my smaller daypack with survival essentials on my hunting excursions, but this time was different. I dumped the contents of my big backpack on the floor of Lily's bedroom and then hastily collected what we might need for a rescue: dry clothes for Lily and Mark, rope, our tent, my medical kit, and a few other odds and ends. I settled the pack across my shoulders and grabbed my rifle, hoping I wasn't forgetting anything.

When I emerged from the cabin, Lauren was already most of the way across the clearing. Huffing a sigh, I called to Bear and hurried after her.

A brief glance my way when I reached her showed that she had registered my presence, but she said nothing. "You could have waited," I pointed out dryly.

"I knew you'd catch up." Her bland voice gave no apology, but I just frowned and let it go.

We marched on in silence, following the tracks through the forest. The sun dipped closer to the horizon, but the sunlight evaporated faster than I anticipated. I didn't realize why at first, but then Lauren mumbled, "Damn it. Storm's rolling in." She was right. Clouds had begun to obscure the sun, an ominous gray line stretching west. The temperature dipped noticeably.

"Better hurry, then." I lifted our binoculars to my eyes and scanned the forest ahead of us. The snowshoe tracks disappeared over the next rise, but still no sign of Mark or Lily. "For God's sake, how far do they need to go for a tree?"

"Mark always made a big production out of finding just the right one," Lauren answered, absently chewing her lip.

Lowering the binoculars, I shot her a sympathetic look. She didn't seem to notice, and we started moving again with increased urgency. "Mark had his rifle with him, didn't he?" I wondered.

"What?" Her blank look suggested she hadn't actually heard my question.

"Mark's rifle. I didn't see it by the door. I assume he took it with him?"

She scrunched up her forehead in thought. "I think so, why?"

"We had a system—if there was ever any danger, we'd fire three shots. Kind of our own S.O.S. I didn't hear any shots besides my own. That's probably a good sign."

A frown settled on her lips. "Maybe he just didn't have a chance to."

"Maybe," I admitted with a frown of my own. "But it doesn't help to jump to worst-case scenarios." I felt like a hypocrite for saying so after all the doom and gloom that had been running through my mind.

She made a light scoffing sound. "Easy for you to say," she mumbled, barely loud enough for me to hear.

Gritting my teeth, I said, "You know, I want to find them as much as you do."

Lauren stopped. She half-turned back toward me, a baleful look on her face. "Really. As much as I do." She jabbed a gloved hand in the direction of the tracks we were following. "That's my *family* out there. My little girl. You can't *possibly* fathom how much I want to find them." Her chin trembled, and for a moment her eyes revealed the anguish behind the anger.

I sighed and took a conciliatory tone. "Lauren, I didn't mean…"

"No," she cut me off. "Just who do you think you are?" I drew back, startled by her vehemence. "You travel with them for a few months, and you think—what? That gives you the right to parent my child? To make eyes at my husband?"

"That's not…"

"This isn't your family!" she roared.

We stared at each other for a long moment, her shout hanging in the air. I'd suspected how much she resented my presence here, but the words still landed like a punch. My jaw tightened, and it was only the thought of how much she meant to Mark and Lily that kept me from saying something I'd really regret.

"Who do I think I am?" I echoed in a clipped tone, mouth twisting. "I think I'm the person who helped your family get back to you. I think I'm the person your husband invited to stay." That reminder got me a sour look. "You have a problem with that? We can have a conversation —*after* we find Mark and Lily."

I didn't wait for her to answer, but just started walking. Storming off as much as one could in snowshoes. After a moment, with a grudging shuffle I didn't need to look back to see, she followed.

CHAPTER 88

THE SNOW BEGAN TO FALL, slowly at first then more persistently. Wet flakes caked Bear's fur and our jackets, and it wasn't long before we realized that it was obscuring the tracks as well. Standing at the top of a little rise, we stared ahead and realized with dismay that we had lost the trail altogether.

"Shit," I mumbled. Then I considered for a moment. "They couldn't have gone that much further though, right?"

Lauren, who hadn't spoken to me since our argument, shook her head. "Probably not. Would've taken forever to get the tree back." She cupped her hands around her mouth. "Mark! Lily!" She repeated the calls a few times, but we heard nothing back.

I unslung my rifle, dusting the snow off it. "I'll try signaling them." I'd been reluctant to draw attention to ourselves before, in case Mark and Lily had run into trouble of the human variety. Now it seemed worth the risk. I aimed at an angle up into the air, like a soldier performing a salute, then squeezed off two rounds in quick succession. The gunshots reverberated through the forest, startling some birds, but still nothing answered us.

Bear had laid down in the snow while we paused, but suddenly stood up and barked. I peered at him curiously. Lauren watched him, too. "What is it?" she wondered.

I gripped the rifle tighter, alert for danger. Bear paced forward a few steps and looked back at me expectantly. "Maybe he smells something." I waved him on. "Okay, Bear, go. Let's go find Lily." I didn't know if he'd understand her name, but it couldn't hurt.

We set off again, Bear taking the lead. Twenty minutes later, clouds had blanketed the sky in gray and a biting wind began to swirl the snow. It cut through our clothes, but neither of us talked of turning back.

"Lily!" Lauren yelled, her voice growing hoarse. We had taken turns shouting. She frowned at Bear. "I don't see how he can smell anything in this wind."

I shrugged and gestured toward the dog, who was still out in front of us. "He seems to be onto something."

"Can he find them?"

The gnawing worry in my stomach had eroded my patience. "I don't know, Lauren. He's not fucking Lassie. He could be tracking a rabbit for all I know." I sighed. "At least we're still going in vaguely the direction they were before we lost the trail." I glanced back when she didn't respond, and saw that she had stopped. "Do you have a better idea?"

"Be quiet," she hissed.

"What?" Indignant annoyance reared its head, and I almost snapped something else before the look on her face stopped me. Scrunched with concentration, her head tilted, she seemed to be listening intently for something. "What is it?"

"Do you hear that?" She didn't wait for an answer before calling again, "Lily! Mark!"

This time I heard it, faint but unmistakable. "Lauren!"

Lauren gasped, covering her mouth, and we exchanged a relieved smile. Bear barked, and I ruffled his fur. "Good boy." He bounded forward, and we followed. Mark's voice grew louder, and we heard Lily as well. "Mommy! Anna!"

We met up with them in a copse of trees. Lily rushed forward into Lauren's arms. Mark trailed behind, dragging a leg that was bound up in a makeshift splint of branches.

"Are you all right, baby?" Lauren asked, looking Lily over for signs of injury.

Lily bobbed her head. "Yeah but Daddy hurt his leg." Bear danced around their feet.

I went to Mark, helping him to sit down on a fallen log. Mark stretched his leg out with a groan, a pinched look of pain weighing on his face. "I think it's broken," he grumbled, jaw tight.

"What happened?" I wondered, examining the limb.

"Slipped down a hill on some ice a ways back. My snowshoe caught on something and then I felt it pop." He sucked in a sharp breath as my gentle fingers probed his leg.

I mumbled an apology. "Why didn't you signal us?"

Mark shrugged. "I thought we could make it back." I shook my head, mumbling something under my breath about stubborn men.

His knee was swollen, the tip of his shinbone clearly out of place. "Same one you hurt before." With all the walking he did on that injury, it occurred to me he might have weakened the ligaments and made it more prone to being re-injured. "The good news? I don't think it's broken."

"It's not?" A disbelieving furrow formed in his brow.

"It's dislocated."

Mark scowled. "That's better somehow?"

"It should feel better after I reduce it," I explained. Mark's face stilled.

Lauren asked, "You mean set it?"

"Like when your arm broke?" Lily's timid voice chimed in from behind me.

I nodded. Opening my medical bag, I dumped a couple pain pills into my hand. I'd been saving them since we scavenged the bottle from someone's medicine cabinet last month. "Take these. It'll take awhile to kick in, but it'll help." He washed them down with a gulp of water from my canteen. I watched him in concern. "Sorry I don't have anything to put you under."

"Just do it." Mark took a deep breath, steeling himself.

With one palm on his knee, I pulled on his ankle. Mark let out a pained howl, and Lily buried her face in Lauren's jacket. Wincing in sympathy, I struggled to maintain focus as I guided the errant bone back into place. Once I'd checked that the knee was back in its proper alignment, I clasped his hand for a moment. "I'm sorry. It'll get better soon." He just bobbed his head, too overcome to answer.

I fitted the familiar orange padded splint around his knee. "Not that damn thing again," Mark complained through gritted teeth.

I glanced up at Lauren. "I'm worried about moving him in all this. The storm's getting worse, and it's a long way back to the cabin."

"What's the alternative?" she wondered.

"I brought the tent, but it'll be rough without sleeping bags. We could all stay, or you could take Lil back…"

Lauren frowned, not liking either of the possibilities. Then a lightbulb went off. "The Baldwin place." I gave her a quizzical look, and she elaborated, "Another cabin. Hasn't been anyone living there for years. It's not far from here." She frowned up at the swirling snow, then looked to Mark. "Do you think we can make it before the storm gets too bad?"

I figured that was code for asking Mark if he could manage. He drew himself up straighter and nodded. "Yeah, I think so." I zipped my backpack up and slipped my arms through the straps.

Lauren took Mark's arm, ready to help him up, but he shook his head and clapped her lightly on the forearm. "Hon, let Anna do that," he said gently. "You should take it easy."

She didn't argue, probably realizing he was right, but I glanced over just in time to catch some side-eye as chilly as the weather. Lauren scooped up his rifle and motioned for Lily to join her. "We should get moving," she said flatly, starting to walk.

Mark sighed. "I can't win," he mumbled, barely loud enough for me to hear.

"No comment," I whispered back.

Clasping both my hands around his arm, I hauled him up onto his good leg. He leaned against me, hands on my shoulders to steady his balance. I ducked under his arm so he could lean on me like a crutch. "So all that, and you didn't even find a tree, huh?"

"Don't you even start," he groaned, but I could hear the tiniest hint of amusement in his voice.

I just smiled as we set off through the blowing snow.

CHAPTER 89

THE STORM INTENSIFIED, FORCING US all to cluster together to avoid losing sight of each other. Every step filled me with trepidation, remembering the last time we'd stumbled through a storm like this. All I could do was hope that Lauren knew where she was going.

Eventually the boxy shape of another cabin became visible through the snow. We hurried inside, a gust of wind sending a cloud of powder in with us. As Lauren had said, the place looked like nobody had been there in years. The door was unlocked and the furniture all gone. A thin layer of dust mingled with the snow on the floor. Bear added to it by shaking off the snow caked all over him, sending wet clumps flying everywhere.

I eased Mark down against a wall near the fireplace. Lauren was at his side in an instant, offering him some water from her canteen and just generally fretting over him. I guess concern had overcome her irritation from earlier. I slid my backpack over to her. "There's some clothes and blankets and stuff in there. I'll get some firewood." I ducked out to give them some time alone.

By the time the sun had gone down, we were all lounging in front of the crackling fireplace. Canned ravioli and stale trail mix wasn't much of a supper, but the best we could manage on the supplies I'd hastily packed. I found myself wishing I'd brought along the rabbit I'd hunted earlier.

Mark fell into a painkiller-induced slumber, his leg propped up on my backpack. Lily soon followed suit, exhausted after the stress of their misadventure. Lauren stroked Lily's hair as the girl lay snuggled up against her side.

I checked on Mark's leg again, making sure the splint wasn't cutting off circulation and that no other concerning signs had developed. "He's pretty lucky, everything considered," I mused quietly. "No vascular compromise. Doesn't look like anything's broken. If we can get him to take it easy, he should be fine." I folded the blanket back down over his foot, and unconsciously gave his leg a comforting pat.

"How long have you and Mark been having an affair?"

Lauren's question, completely flat in tone, came so far out of left field that my head snapped her way and did a double-take. For a moment I was convinced I must have imagined it. Lauren watched me with an accusing frown, and all I could muster back was a stunned, "What?"

"You heard me." Brown eyes bored into me, glinting in the firelight. "How long?"

Flustered, I shook my head. "We're not…"

"Oh, please." Lauren interrupted my denial with a bitter bark of a chuckle. "Don't play me for a fool, Anna. You think I can't see what's going on?"

I didn't know what to say. Sensing the pain beneath her anger, guilt gnawed at me. I may not have done what she was accusing, but I still felt responsible.

The angry facade cracked into a more plaintive plea. "I could forgive him," Lauren said. "I know how lonely it was here, thinking the worst." Her voice broke. "If you ended it…"

This time I cut her off. "Lauren, stop. There's nothing to end. I told you, we're not having an affair."

Doubt creased her forehead, thrown by my sincerity. "I don't believe you." She wanted to, though. That was clear in her eyes. "I know him too well. And I see the way you are together. I know there's something."

I glanced at the sleeping Mark, my lips curling downward. If he hadn't told her everything, what right did I have to? Seeing her face, though, I knew Mark wouldn't want her to go on suffering. "It's not what you think."

Still Lauren stiffened, expecting the worst. "I just want the truth."

I nodded. Tucking an errant strand of hair back behind my ear, I took a moment to figure out what the hell I was going to tell her. Finally I sighed, waving a hand. "Out there on the trail… we went through so much together. Sometimes it felt like it was just us against the world. The three of us? We were like a family." Her jaw tightened unhappily at that claim, but she held her tongue and let me continue. "I know it's not the same as what you have with them. You're his wife; you're her mother. I know that. But what we had was something too. Call it what you like—family, friends, partners, I don't know. It was something—it *is* something—but it's not an affair."

Still frowning like she'd eaten something sour, Lauren challenged, "So all those months, just the two of you…you're telling me nothing happened?"

I wanted to snap back that lots had happened—all the near-death experiences, the hardships, the violence—but that would have been a cop-out. I knew what she meant. And something *had* happened. Something that now made it hard to look her in the eye. My head dipped. "I kissed him once."

"I fucking knew it," she muttered, her anger subdued and tinged with resignation.

I winced at her reaction. I'd seen that look before on my mom's face. The anger. The pain. The betrayal. Shame flooded through me. "It wasn't something I planned."

"Oh, well, that's a relief," Lauren snarked, and I deserved every bit of her biting sarcasm.

I sighed. I didn't want to dredge it all up again, but I felt like I owed her more of an explanation. "The night it happened… Lil and I were in a cabin at this ski lodge, and these two guys kicked the door in. One of them had a gun." Lauren's eyes widened in alarm. "Mark was off getting supplies. They were going to kill him when he came back, but we managed to warn him. There was a fight." I whispered hollowly, "Mark and I killed them."

Lauren's eyes flicked to Mark. "My God. Did Lily see…?"

"No. She was hiding. She didn't see anything until after." Though I would never forget the petrified look on her face when Mark carried her out of the bathroom. "Anyway, later that night… Lil was asleep. Mark was trying to comfort me, and I kissed him." I shook my head, lips thinning. "We were a mess, Lauren. Neither one of us was thinking clearly. I know that doesn't make it okay. It was a stupid, selfish, inexcusable thing to do." Her frown obviously agreed with me. "But whatever you think of me, you have to know—Mark stayed faithful to you. I swear, it never went any further."

Lauren let out a slow breath, studying my face with a scrutiny so intense I wanted to look away. I forced myself to hold her gaze. "But you're still in love with him," she accused flatly.

My throat bobbed. "Yes." I felt like an ass for telling her, but I figured the only path forward for us was to lay all the cards on the table. "And I love Lily too, but they love you."

"They love you, too, though. That's the problem."

"It's not the same." I insisted. She shot me a skeptical look. "It's not. They're your family, Lauren. They were with me for almost six months, but that whole time all they cared about was getting back to *you*."

She said nothing. My eyes settled on Lily's sleeping form. "Lily was such a trooper. Not just that night, but through all of it. You would've been so proud of her. Helping to cook; taking care of Bear; she even taught me how to clean a fish. When there was trouble, she was so brave... braver than a seven-year-old had any right to be." I found myself getting choked up, and cleared my throat. "This one time, Mark got hurt pretty bad. We weren't sure if he'd make it." Lauren's expression shifted subtly, concern mingling with the tiniest hint of sympathy. "Lil asked me if I'd still help her find you if anything happened to him. I promised I would. In her hardest moments, it was you she cried for."

Lauren looked down at the girl curled up against her, tears glistening in her eyes. It must hurt to hear how much Lily had missed her, but I still thought she needed to hear it.

Heart in my throat, I went on, "And Mark? He risked everything to find you. Your mother *begged* him to go with them to your aunt's place. For a minute I thought she might hog-tie him and take them along." That got a ghost of a smile out of her. "Everyone thought he was crazy for doing this—me included. I figured he'd give up after a couple weeks. There were plenty of chances to stop along the way...friends we'd made, places that weren't so bad. We ran into bandits, blizzards, floods, but he never lost hope. He kept going long after anyone else would have called it quits."

I took a breath. "They walked a thousand miles to get back to you, Lauren. And if you hadn't been here? They wouldn't have stopped looking."

Lauren wiped at her face, a few tears leaking from her eyes. "I just can't lose them again," she whispered brokenly.

"I'm not going to let that happen," I said earnestly. "I know I screwed up. Sorry doesn't fix it, but I *am* sorry. I promise you nothing like that is going to happen again. And I'm sorry about the thing with taking Lily hunting the other day. You were right—I should've asked you first." I couldn't fault her for the skeptical frown she leveled at me. Swallowing hard, I asked, "Do you want me to leave?"

"I can't ask you to go," Lauren said. "Not after everything you've done for them. It'd break Lily's heart."

It wasn't exactly a 'no', but I'd take it. "We can make this work for all of us. I'll prove it to you."

"And if you can't?"

"Then I'll go. I already said as much to Mark. I swear, the very last thing I want to do is screw up your family."

The silence stretched on before she finally nodded. "I believe you."

The soft acknowledgement brought a wave of relief. Thanking her felt a bit weird, so I just gave her a grateful nod in return. We both fell quiet again after that. Drawing the blanket more tightly around my shoulders, I settled back against the wall to rest.

Lauren's voice broke the stillness again, surprising me. "Anna?" I glanced over. "Thank you for what you did today."

Knowing how much it took for her to say that, I smiled. "You're welcome."

It wasn't a lot, but it was a start.

CHAPTER 90

MARK RUBBED HIS FACE, WINCING. "When you said you'd talk to her, I didn't know that's what you had in mind."

"It wasn't," I protested, lifting his injured leg to slide a pillow underneath. The storm had blown itself out during the night, dumping an extra six inches on top of the old layer. Limping back to the cabin had taken the better part of the morning, but we'd finally made it. Lauren and Lily were in the living room taking care of the gear, leaving me to get Mark settled in the bedroom. I figured I owed him a head's up. "But I had to. Mark, you didn't see how upset she was."

"And telling her about the time I kissed you made her feel better?" Incredulous eyebrows arched at me.

I shrugged. "Kind of, yeah? I think we reached an understanding. For the record, I told her I kissed you. I didn't exactly go into details."

"Thank God for that," Mark mumbled.

Sighing, I stepped back from the bed and folded my arms. "You'd rather I let her go on thinking we're having an affair? Or had one?"

He let his hand flop on the bed and mirrored my sigh. "No. You did the right thing." He grimaced as he shifted his leg. "I should have told her myself, before all this. It was just hard to find the right way—the right time."

"I don't think there's ever a right time for something like that." I knew that much from my experience delivering bad news. "Mark, I'm really sorry about all this. I never should have let that happen in the first place." I had to pause, tearful and overcome with regret.

Mark shook his head, a concerned crease across his brow. "It's not all on you," he said firmly. "I'll make things right with her." He glanced to the door, where we both heard Lauren's voice growing closer. "Time to grovel," he whispered.

Mark's groveling must have worked, or maybe it was his injury, or the holiday spirit. Maybe Lauren was just relieved after fearing the worst for so long, or he got some grace for having gone through hell to get back to her. Whatever the reason, I counted our blessings that the explosion I feared between them never materialized.

Days passed, and despite the last quest for the perfect tree ending so disastrously, it didn't take Lily long to start begging to go out again. "Anna, can we go get a Christmas tree?"

"I have to go hunting today, sweetheart." With Mark laid up, it fell to me to pick up his share of the chores.

"Well, we could go hunting for a Christmas tree too?" Lily flashed those puppy dog eyes I had such a hard time saying 'no' to. "Please?"

I chuckled, willpower faltering. "Ask your mom." It had become my go-to phrase lately, a peace offering to Lauren.

"Okay!" Lily said brightly, charging off to the kitchen to pester Lauren. I couldn't hear their entire conversation, but there was at least one 'pleeeeeease' involved. Finally Lily emerged, grinning. "She said I can go!"

Lauren trailed after her, a slight furrow across her brow. "Don't go too far, though, okay?"

"Sure thing." I glanced at Lily then. "Well, go get your stuff on." As she rushed off to start putting on layers, I glanced to Lauren. "We'll just check the game trails over by the lake. There are some pine trees over that way too."

Lauren nodded. She watched us get ready, and I could see the anxiety brewing in her eyes. As I shrugged on my jacket, I said offhand, "You could come with us, you know."

I didn't really expect her to do it, but before she could politely decline, Lily's face lit up. "Oooh, please, Mommy? We could do like a girls hunting day!"

I could almost see the excuses running through her head, but then abruptly Lauren relented. "All right. Let's go."

Soon enough, the three of us and Bear were tracking across the fresh, untouched snow. Lily's cheerful chatter proved a helpful buffer against an awkward silence. "Are you sure Santa's going to be able to find the cabin?" she wondered. Even if she was on the verge of aging out of the whole Santa thing, I couldn't blame her for clinging to it after these last few months.

Lauren smiled. "Sure. How else would he know if you've been naughty or nice?"

Lily thought that over for a minute, then said, "But we don't have cookies! Or milk!"

"We can save him something from dinner instead," Lauren agreed. "I'm sure Santa will understand."

"I wonder if he likes venison," I offered dryly.

"The invisible lightning won't hurt his sleigh, will it?" Lily wondered next.

"Of course not," Lauren assured her. "It's magic, isn't it?" That seemed to appease her. I caught Lauren's eye, and we actually shared an amused smile.

The conversation veered off into the post-EMP logistics of Santa's workshop, with Lauren cautiously trying to temper Lily's expectations about what presents she might be getting. As we neared the lake, Lily pointed to a big fir tree. "Oooh what about that one?"

"That one won't even fit in the door!" I told her, chuckling.

"How about that one over there?" Lauren pointed out a smaller one closer to the lake, and Lily clapped her hands in excited approval. I headed for it, saw in hand.

Helping them decorate the tree that evening, I saw a glimpse into their old lives. Happy and smiling, improvising ornaments out of everything from construction paper to old hair ribbons. The tree may not have had any lights, but it certainly had enough joyful color to spare.

Later that night, after checking that Lily was sound asleep, Lauren rejoined us in the living room and leaned forward. "We need to finish planning the presents," she said with an intensity more suited to the emergency room than the living room.

I set my book aside, arching my eyebrows. It didn't surprise me that they'd been planning something special for Lily; what surprised me was Lauren including me on it.

Mark, it turned out, was close to finishing a sled he'd started before hurting his leg. Lauren pulled out a pioneer-style doll she was crafting from odds and ends around the cabin. I volunteered a hat and mittens set I was trying to make out of some rabbit skins ("trying" being the operative word, given that all I knew about tanning came from a survival book). Lauren seemed pleasantly surprised that I had something underway. We also surveyed our food stores to see if we could cobble together some treats for the day. At the end of the discussion, Lauren sat back, her inner project manager satisfied. She and I exchanged a little smile, and for the first time there was something approaching acceptance in her eyes.

CHAPTER 91

CHRISTMAS CAME AND WENT, MARKED by carols (it turned out Lily got her lovely singing voice from Lauren) and Lily bouncing off the walls. She rejoiced that Santa had found the cabin, and didn't seem to mind the hand-crafted gifts.

Without parties or a ball drop in Times Square, New Years passed as just another day in what would prove to be a long, dreary winter. Mark's leg healed enough to bear weight, and I improvised a physical therapy routine for him. Rehab wasn't really in my wheelhouse as an emergency room doctor, but what other options did we have? Day by day, he built his strength back up until finally he could venture out on snowshoes again to help with the chores.

And not a moment too soon—our food reserves were starting to run low and we really needed his ice-fishing skills. We rationed everything, hunted, trapped, and scavenged what we could from neighboring houses. It amounted to barely enough for the four of us. At least with Kayla's pine needle tea recipe we wouldn't get scurvy.

Bad dreams had always been an occupational hazard for me, and the peril and violence we'd experienced since the blackout certainly hadn't helped. Trauma is a funny thing, though. It can fade into the background for a while, fooling you into thinking you've moved past it, only to ambush you again when you least expected it. Talking to Lauren about the ski lodge had cracked open a door, inviting the bandits to once again invade my dreams. Sometimes they were joined by the sniper from New York, or faceless assailants of my own imagining.

One such nightmare had me jerking awake so sharply I almost upended the simple cot Mark had crafted for me. Lily slept on, oblivious, but Bear stirred at the foot of her bed and lifted his head. Alone in the darkness, gulping down air and sweating like I'd run several miles in my sleep, I anchored myself with the now-familiar fixtures of Lily's room. She was okay. Mark was in the next room over. We were safe now.

My breathing slowed, but the dream had left me shaken. I wouldn't get back to sleep any time soon, and honestly was afraid to even try. Slipping a blanket around my shoulders, I went out to the living room. The fireplace lay dark, and my lantern cast eerie shadows across the floor. My eyes drifted to the window. The heavy curtains cut down the chill, but kept me from seeing out. I imagined an unseen threat lurking just beyond them.

"Anna?"

I jerked in fright and fumbled the lantern. The plastic thudded against the wood floor, but fortunately didn't break. Lauren stood at the mouth of the hall. "Lauren. God, you scared me." My pulse pounded in my ears, slow to acknowledge the lack of threat.

"Didn't mean to startle you," she murmured. She regarded me with concern in her eyes. "Couldn't sleep?"

"Just a bad dream. I'm fine," I lied. The slight tremble in my hands betrayed me as I crouched down to retrieve the lantern.

Lauren didn't challenge my denial. She just said, "I'll get you a drink."

"Oh, you don't have to…"

"I don't mind." The bobbing glow from her flashlight was already halfway to the kitchen, so I didn't fight her on it. I sat down heavily on the couch, tightening my blanket. She returned with two small juice glasses in her hands and her trusty water bottle tucked under one arm.

When she handed the two glasses to me, my nose swiftly realized that one wasn't water. I sipped the whiskey first, hoping its burn might settle my nerves.

Lauren took the chair nearby, and we sat in silence for a bit before she ventured, "When I first came up here, the nights were the worst. So quiet. So empty."

"It must've been awful, being here on your own," I murmured, grateful for the distraction. "Not knowing where Mark and Lily were; if they were okay."

Lips thinning, she nodded. "It was hard. Impossibly hard, some days," she admitted, a catch in her voice. "I knew it would take them longer to get here than it took me, but every day I woke up hoping that today would be the day. And then it wasn't." She frowned. "It got to be a kind of torture—that constant hope and disappointment. I had to resign myself to the idea that they weren't coming. That maybe their plane had crashed."

Tears glistened in her eyes, and my heart broke for her. I worried about my family, but this had to be a million times worse. "I'm sorry," I whispered. It felt inadequate.

Her head bobbed in acknowledgement, then she patted her belly. "This little one gave me reason to hold out hope." She smiled. "I just wish she'd stop kicking my bladder while I slept. I could do without waking up three times a night."

I tilted a head at her pronoun choice. "She? Hoping it's another girl?"

"Oh, I'll be happy either way, though I think Mark's secretly hoping for a boy. He's feeling a bit outnumbered." Lauren flashed a wistful smile. "She just feels like a girl. Mother's intuition."

The physician in me was skeptical of her conclusion, but I let it go. "Well, boy or girl, Lil is going to be thrilled to be a big sister."

Lauren gave a soft mmm-hmm of acknowledgement. After watching me quietly for a moment, she said, "I heard you before... calling out in your sleep."

"Oh." I hadn't realized I had made any noise. Embarrassed, I ducked my head and mumbled, "Sorry."

"Don't be." Her assurance had a gentle tone I wasn't used to. She looked thoughtful, weighing how much she wanted to pry. "Was it those men you told me about? At that ski place?"

I nodded. She waited, a patient silence letting me decide if I wanted to share more. What the hell. It wasn't like she could think any less of me than she already did.

"Sometimes I just see it happening all over again," I admitted softly. "Or flashes, like when I pulled the trigger." I winced. "But sometimes it's different. Worse. Imagining the way things could've gone. Like we can't warn Mark before they shoot him. Or Lily..." My voice faltered, and I spared Lauren the details of how that particular nightmare had ended. All the feelings from the dream resurfaced—the fear, the helplessness. With the back of my hand, I wiped at the tears that spilled over. I stared down at the glass and then downed the rest of my drink. "I know it was just a dream..."

"But the feelings are real," Lauren finished for me. "Believe me, I know."

I tilted my head to peer at her, and saw the distant expression on her face. "You have them too," I realized. "What happened?"

She didn't answer at first, but I suppose my honesty had earned the same in return. She sighed. "It was about a month after the blackout," she explained, her voice hushed. "I met a woman at one of the trail shelters. We shared some food with each other; talked some. She seemed friendly enough. As soon as my back was turned, she came after me with a knife. We fought, and… I stabbed her."

I remembered the couple we'd met on the trail back in Pennsylvania, who had tried to steal our gear. How easily it could have ended the same. My brow creased in sympathy, impressed again by her resilience. "That's awful."

"You can tell yourself a million times that you didn't have a choice," Lauren said, her voice somber, "But it still eats at you. A hole in your soul."

"Yeah," I agreed solemnly. "I guess that's the price we pay for having a conscience." Twisting the glass around in my hand, I stared into its empty bottom. My eyes were locked on a memory miles away, though—the sniper in New York, his brains splattered across the foliage in the forest. I had a choice that day, but it wasn't much of one. Would I ever stop wondering if I'd made the right decision? Would Lauren?

Lauren's voice brought me back. "I imagine it's even harder, being a doctor."

I shrugged. "Maybe in some ways. But at least I didn't have to go through it alone like you did."

"That's true. Though we're not alone now." She leaned forward and picked up a deck of cards on the coffee table. "Uno?"

My eyebrows lifted. "I appreciate the gesture, but you don't have to wait up. I'll be fine."

"I know." A corner of her mouth quirked up in a half-smile. "You want to deal first?"

I chuckled softly. "Sure." I took the deck and started to shuffle.

CHAPTER 92

AS THE WEEKS PASSED, THE weather grew even more bitterly cold. Sometimes we'd be snowed in for days at a time. The days started to blur together, routines growing monotonous. Six months ago we could have solved so much in minutes with technology or a quick trip to the store. Now just surviving was a full-time job. Gather food. Gather water (or snow to melt). Prepare the meals. Check the traps. Chop wood. Mend the gear. Clean the weapons. Supper and the scant hours afterward were the only thing I looked forward to—reading, playing games with Lily, and chatting with Mark and Lauren. Then our exhausted heads would hit the pillows, only to repeat it all again the next day.

Though I didn't miss the wind rustling the tent all night, or waking up to frozen socks, I found myself missing the trail. At least there the view changed and there was some promise of adventure. Here I knew every individual tree along my usual circuit, and it all felt a bit like the movie *Groundhog Day*. Every day I forced myself to take a minute and think about our blessings to counteract the malaise.

One day in late February, I wandered out to my favorite spot and took a breather on a wooden stool Mark had made me some weeks ago. Bear accompanied me, as always. From this vantage point, I had a great view overlooking the lake, with the mountain in the background. I liked to come up here sometimes to just sit and think and escape the cabin for a while.

Today my thoughts drifted to our friends in New York. Was everyone all right? Had Anthony's arm healed up? Would Kayla's garden help them weather the winter better than we were? Was Nikolai still with them? Did he ever think about me?

A gunshot echoed through the valley, jolting me out of my thoughts. Two shots. Three. Our SOS signal. My heart skipped a beat, and I was off the stool so fast I almost tripped over my snowshoes.

Fearing the worst, I clutched my rifle in white-knuckled hands and raced home as fast as I could. After what felt like an eternity, the cabin came into view. Nothing looked amiss from the outside. Someone must have been watching for my approach, though, for the front door flew open and Mark called out, "Anna, thank God."

Ditching my snowshoes at the porch, I rushed inside. "What happened?"

"It's the baby. It's too soon, though, isn't it?"

I heard Lauren cry out in pain from the bedroom and beelined that way, past a wide-eyed Lily sitting on the couch. Lauren lay on their bed, her face scrunched up in a grimace and glistening with sweat.

Over my shoulder, I answered Mark's question, "It's a little early, but you said first week of March, right?" Lauren nodded. "Close enough. How far apart are the contractions?"

"Five minutes or so? My water broke right before Mark signaled you." She grimaced. "Everything's going so fast—faster than it was with Lily." The amniotic fluid soaking the sheets was clear, so that was one less thing to worry about.

"That's not uncommon after the first," I replied calmly. "Any complications with Lily?"

Mark chimed in, "No, everything was fine. What can I do?"

"Just stay with her, I'll be right back." I returned to the living room to get my medical kit and wash my hands.

As I did so, Lily's frightened voice called to me from the couch. "Is Mommy okay?"

I smiled over at her. "Yeah, sweetheart, she's just getting ready to have your baby brother or sister."

Her eyes widened even further, but it was like a switch flipped from dread to glee. "Today?!"

"Looks like. Though maybe not for a while. You chill here with Bear for now." I ducked back into the bedroom and grabbed my stethoscope and exam gloves from my kit. "I'll just have a look, see how things are progressing, okay?" Lauren had only allowed me to examine her a couple times, so I wasn't exactly following her progress as closely as a regular OB would have. I placed my stethoscope on her belly and listened to the baby's heart rate. Then I pressed gently on her abdomen to check the baby's position, and my face stilled.

Mark saw through my poker face instantly. "What is it?"

I double-checked to be sure. "The baby's still breech."

Lauren frowned in alarm. "I thought you said she would turn?"

"Usually they do, but this one decided to come before she made it all the way around."

Mark looked between us, a blank look on his face. "What's that mean? Is the baby okay?"

"It means the baby's still upside down, positioned to come out bottom first instead of head first," I explained as I finished my exam. "Everything's fine right now, but it's just something we need to keep an eye on." Mark took Lauren's hand in his, giving it a reassuring squeeze.

"Can't you do something?" Lauren wondered. "Isn't there a way to turn her around?"

I shook my head. "I don't want to risk it with the water broken."

"But she's going to be all right?" she asked.

I perched carefully on the edge of the bed, so I wasn't looming over her. "Lauren, there's always a chance of complications with any birth. With a breech baby, there's a greater risk that the labor won't progress, or that the umbilical cord will become compressed." I didn't tell her that in a hospital we'd be sending her over already for a preemptive C-section; we didn't have that option here and I didn't want to scare her needlessly.

"She could die," Lauren realized, voice hushed in fear.

I looked between the two worried faces, offering a gentle smile. "That's very unlikely. The majority of breech babies are delivered without a hitch. Right now your baby is active and has a great heart rate, and everything's progressing normally. There's no reason to panic."

Two hours later, during a routine check of the labor's progress, I started to panic.

CHAPTER 93

"WHAT'S WRONG?" MARK ASKED, NOTICING the sudden tension in my shoulders and jaw.

I listened with my stethoscope for a little longer to be sure before answering grimly, "The baby's in trouble."

"What do you mean, in trouble?" Lauren's voice pitched up in alarm. Mark picked up her hand, wrapping both his hands around it in a protective cocoon.

I frowned. "The baby's heart rate is down. It's a sign of fetal distress."

"What can you do?" Mark asked, his face stricken.

I was asking myself the same question, frantically digging through memories from a too-long-ago obstetrics rotation. "Roll over on your left side. Mark, give me those pillows."

Lauren started to move, and I shoved the pillows under her to raise her hips up. "What are you doing?"

"It can help take some pressure off the umbilical cord. I'm going to take another look." I crouched down at the foot of the bed to perform another pelvic exam, then checked the baby's heart rate again.

"Anna, what's happening?" Mark shifted from foot to foot nervously beside the bed.

Dread swirled within me, but I took a breath and forced a calm facade. I rose and faced them both. "It looks like the baby is compressing the cord. It's one of those complications we talked about."

"The ones you said were unlikely?" I couldn't really fault Lauren for the harshness of the question.

"They are, but it's impossible to predict." I exhaled sharply. "If we could get you to a hospital, an emergency C-section would be the definitive treatment, but obviously we're not set up for that here." I waved a hand to encompass the bedroom.

Lauren's face contorted as another contraction hit. "What else can you do?" she asked once it had passed.

They both looked up at me, searching my face for reassurances I couldn't give. This part would've been hard enough with strangers, but remembering the way Mark and Lily's face lit up when Lauren told them about the baby made it even more heart-wrenching. Throat tight, I said as gently I could, "There are some things we can try, but they're meant to be stopgaps for a C-section or an immediate delivery. You're not even fully dilated yet. I'll do everything I can, but..." My voice cracked. "The baby's chances are very slim."

Mark looked as though I had sucker-punched him, turning away and rubbing a hand over his mouth. Lauren closed her eyes, holding back tears, and I felt my own eyes start to water. It wasn't my fault we were stuck in the middle of nowhere without a hospital, but it still felt like I was letting them down somehow. "I'm so sorry."

Lauren lifted her head and fixed her gaze on me. "The C-section would give the baby a chance, though, wouldn't it?"

"Yes, but…" My stomach flip-flopped as I registered the expression of resigned determination on her face. "No."

Slower to catch up, Mark looked between us. "No what?"

"You have to," Lauren told me, ignoring him.

"Like hell I do!" When Mark continued to look confused, I laid it out for him. "She wants me to do the C-section."

All the color drained from Mark's face. "What? Lauren, no, it's too dangerous."

"If we don't, the baby will die," she said flatly.

"You don't know that for sure," Mark protested.

Lauren shook her head, tearful but determined. "I can't lose her," she whispered.

"And we can't lose you." The desperate pain in Mark's voice tore at me. The last time I'd seen him this overcome was when Lily had been near death's door. He clasped Lauren's hand again and pressed it to his lips. "You have to think about Lily too. She needs you. I need you. We just found you again, damn it."

"You don't understand," Lauren cried, tears leaking from her eyes. "She's what kept me going all this time, thinking you and Lil were gone. We have to save her."

I perched on the edge of the bed again, so Mark and I were bracketing Lauren. "Lauren, I know this is horrible. I can't imagine what you must be going through. But Mark's right—your family needs you here. Even with a C-section, there's no guarantee that the baby would survive, and there are a million things that could go wrong. We don't have a proper operating room, or anesthesia, or a surgical team…" I paused and leveled a grave look at her. "The most likely outcome is that you would die."

"But she would at least have a chance." Lauren turned her tear-streaked face toward me. "What would you do if it were your child?"

The words skewered my heart. Lauren must have seen the crack in my resolve. "Please, Anna. Do this for her."

I looked to Mark, my face scrunched up with turmoil. Hoping somehow he could rescue me from an impossible decision. He frowned at me "You can't seriously be considering this. It'll kill her!"

Lauren squeezed his hand. "Mark, it'll be all right. Whatever happens, you'll be all right."

Mark shook his head violently, denying her plea. "No. No, I can't believe I'm hearing this. This is insane."

I stood up. "Look, you guys need to talk about this. I'll give you a minute. If we're going to do something, we don't have much time." Leaving them staring shell-shocked at each other, I stepped out of the bedroom. I closed the door behind me, sagging against it for a moment.

"Is the baby here yet?" Lily asked brightly from the couch, oblivious to the catastrophe unfolding in the other room.

Shoving down my feelings, I straightened and shook my head. "No, not yet. I'm just getting some things." I started some water boiling, then gathered some towels and washcloths. Despite my preparations, the doubts still hammered at me. Could I really go through with this?

It wasn't long before the bedroom door opened again. One glance over my shoulder at Mark's face told me the verdict, even before he said, "Lil, go to your room for a minute. I need to talk to Anna." Lily looked between us, bewildered, but the tone in Mark's stern voice didn't invite argument. She scurried off to the bedroom we shared.

Mark waited until she was gone, then growled, "You can't do this."

I sighed. "It's what she wants, Mark."

"Fuck what she wants," Mark hissed, coming into the kitchen area to keep his voice low. "You know this is wrong. It's written all over your face. You're the doctor. Just tell her no!"

"It's not that simple, Mark. Are you even listening to yourself? This is your *wife*, begging me to save *your child*. Lauren understands the risks."

Mark made a face. "Does she? I remember you said that same 'desperate measures' shit to that ganger at the hospital, too, and we both know how that turned out."

Ouch. I folded my arms across my chest, glaring at him. "Yeah, well, 'desperate measures shit' is all we've got right now, since I'm the only doctor for a hundred miles. It's her life. Her choice."

"This is my life, too, damn it!" Mark swept an arm across the counter, sending pots clattering. His expression immediately crumpled, the burst of anger giving way to a tearful desperation. "Please, Anna, I'm begging you. If you have any feelings for me, please… don't do this."

Even recognizing that he was just saying anything to save his wife, it still stung. "That's a low blow," I snapped back. "You think I *want* to do this? You think I haven't wracked my brain trying to come up with something else that would give them both a better chance?" I held up two hands like a scale, weighing the options. "If I do the C-section, Lauren's at risk. If I don't, the baby is. The kicker is that we could trial the labor and then end up having to do a section anyway, *after* it's too late to help the baby. Then we could lose them both." He frowned, not having considered that possibility.

"There are no good options here. I know how much she means to you, Mark, but what the hell kind of doctor would I be if I ignored a patient's wishes because of what I felt for her husband? I can't do that. Not even for you."

Mark hung his head in resignation. Fists clenched at his sides, he said nothing.

I stepped closer and touched his arm. In a gentler tone, I said, "Mark, I remember when you were ready to go charging off into a nest of psychos to get the medicine Lily needed. You wouldn't hesitate to trade your life for hers. This isn't any different. I know you love Lauren. But right now? I think you need to trust her."

"Even if that means losing her," he said hollowly.

"We just have to pray that doesn't happen." I paused. "I can't do this without you. You've assisted before, and I need your help." I watched his jaw muscles blanche. "I know it's a shitty thing to ask of you, but it's her best chance of making it through this. Are you with me?"

Seconds ticked by in silence before finally he nodded. "We have to save her. Whatever it takes."

"We'll do everything we possibly can. I promise you that."

I just wished I could promise him that would be enough.

CHAPTER 94

THE MORE THINGS WE PREPARED, the more I was reminded of all the things we *didn't* have. No general anesthesia or ventilator? Make do with a local anesthetic. No surgical garb? Improvise some face masks. No abdominal gauze pads? Boil some washcloths. We opened up the doors, lower temperatures reducing the chance of infection. A shower curtain, hastily bleached clean, covered the bed as the closest thing we could get to a sterile operating surface. Time was of the essence—the gold standard was thirty minutes from diagnosis to delivery—so we didn't have the luxury of shooting for perfection. The whole thing was one big Hail Mary from start to finish.

The biggest thing we were missing? A doctor who knew what the hell she was doing.

I suppose that wasn't entirely fair. I had assisted on several C-sections during residency and in the ER. I'd even led one overseas, though admittedly the senior OB nurse on our team had carried me through. None of that made me comfortable to do one solo, let alone under these insane circumstances. Knowing how far in over my head I was, sweat soaked my shirt despite the chill in the air.

I stood by the bedside, scalpel in hand. "Lauren, are you really sure?" I asked her for the dozenth time, part of me still hoping she would change her mind.

Lauren nodded resolutely. "I'm sure. Thank you, Anna." With a lump in my throat, I bobbed my head in return. She shifted her gaze to Mark, who knelt on the bed opposite me. "I love you," she murmured.

"I love you, too, honey," Mark whispered brokenly. "I love you so much."

A silent prayer ran on repeat in my mind. *Please please please…* Taking a deep breath to steel myself, I made the first incision.

Mark sucked in a breath. My gaze flicked up to him briefly. Over the mask, I could see his brow knitting, his eyes hooded in agony. I deepened the incision, down through the layers of fat and fascia, working as fast as I could without cutting anything important. The field clouded with blood, which I dabbed away with the washcloths. "I'm through," I said breathlessly. "Mark, hands here and here." He applied manual retraction with trembling hands, sweat beading on his forehead.

I glanced up at Lauren's face. Her face was scrunched up in discomfort, but the local anesthesia seemed to be working. I found the baby's head by feel and started to maneuver it out through the incision.

"I feel nauseous," Lauren groaned.

"Baby's almost out. Hang in there," I assured her. Then, as much to myself as to the slippery baby I was tugging on, I whispered, "Come on, come on." Finally, triumph. "Baby's out. Mark, suction."

Even with the shell-shocked look in his eyes, Mark remembered the instructions I'd given him. He used a mini turkey baster thing to suction the gook out of the baby's mouth and nose. "It's a girl, honey," he announced to Lauren, taking the baby from me into a towel.

"I knew it," she murmured tiredly, a faint smile touching her lips. "Is she okay?"

Mark's brow creased again. Alarm bubbled up into his voice. "Anna, she's not crying."

"Dry her off and get her bundled up in the blanket," I told him, while I dealt with the umbilical cord and placenta. "You're doing great, Lauren." Undercutting my calm words, an alarming amount of blood soaked through the towels.

"Come on, baby girl, give us a cry," Mark murmured desperately as he toweled off the newborn. "She's not breathing."

Shit. I buried my dismay and said, "Put your mouth over her mouth and nose and give two breaths."

"You do it," Mark begged, his eyes wide over his mask.

"I have to stop this bleeding," I snapped. I refrained from adding *or your wife is going to bleed to death.* "You can do it, Mark. Just take a breath, and breathe out over her mouth and nose." He tugged down his mask, revealing a panic-stricken look. He did what I asked, bending his face down over the swaddled baby. "That's it," I said distractedly while I continued to work inside Lauren's abdomen. "Two breaths, then press on the middle of her chest with two fingers. Yeah, like that, just harder."

"I don't want to hurt her," Mark pleaded.

"It's fine. You have to push hard enough to pump the blood." I multi-tasked like a mad-woman, talking Mark through newborn resuscitation while frantically trying to sew up the bleeding cavity I had created.

"Mark, is she okay?" Lauren sobbed.

"We're taking care of both of you," I assured her. "How are you doing?"

"Woozy," she admitted, her voice weak.

I glanced between baby and mother, torn. I knew Lauren wanted me to prioritize the newborn, but Mark was doing a good job. Right now, Lauren needed me more. "That's great, Mark, keep at it." I tried to keep my voice level, even as my heart was trying to hammer its way out of my chest. I tied off another knot, using my shoulder to wipe the sweat out of my eyes. Fear threatened to consume my thoughts. *Please, I can't lose both of them.*

The sudden peal of a baby's cry split the air, and both mother and father dissolved into happy tears.

"Oh, thank God," I breathed shakily, letting out a little laugh.

Mark brought the baby closer to Lauren's face. "Look at her, honey, she's perfect." Stripping off his exam gloves, he brushed the hair back from Lauren's forehead tenderly. His joy was tempered when he looked into his wife's face. "Anna, she's really pale."

"I know. Damn it, she's losing too much blood." I packed off the uterus to apply pressure from within, hoping to clamp down on the bleeding. Lauren's eyes drifted closed. "Lauren?"

She didn't answer, and I mumbled a curse. Clamping and packing off what I could, I grabbed some IV tubing and catheters from my medical kit. "Roll up your sleeve," I told Mark.

He did so. "What are you doing?"

"Direct transfusion. She needs blood now." It couldn't keep up with her current rate of lost volume, but it might buy time for me to get the bleeding under control and get everything closed up. I knelt next to Mark on the bed, glancing down at the baby cradled between him and Lauren. At least one of them was okay.

Mark's mouth was set in a frazzled frown as he watched me work. "Anna…" His voice faltered.

"I know," I murmured, a painful tightness in my throat. "I'm doing everything I can."

Once the transfusion was going, I checked on Lauren. She was still breathing, but had drifted unconscious. "Lauren, can you hear me?" I rubbed on her sternum, and got only a groan in response.

Damn. Damn. Damn. I'm losing her.

Working with renewed desperation, I donned new gloves and picked up the needle once more. What I would have given for some proper suction and a cautery tool. Methodically, I removed the blood-soaked pads and sewed up the damage. Sweat stung my eyes. My hand cramped up, still weaker than it used to be before I broke my arm. Slowly but surely, though, I was making progress. Once I was confident the inner bleeding was under control, I could close up the external incision.

Finally, the job done, I stepped back. The fact that she still had a pulse after all that was a miracle. I pulled off my mask and gloves. With a long, shaky breath, I leaned heavily against the dresser.

"Now what?" Mark asked, looking afraid to hear my answer.

"We'll let the transfusion run for a bit longer. Other than that…" I shook my head. "All we can do is wait and pray."

I stood there, watching Mark's worried face and replaying every detail. Wondering what I could have done differently. After a few minutes, driven by nervous energy, I started cleaning up.

When the room no longer looked like a crime scene, I said in a hollow voice, "I'm going to bring Lily in. She can meet her little sister and be with Lauren." *Just in case.* Mark didn't answer, his gaze locked on the little one.

Lily had curled up on the couch under a pile of blankets, using Bear like a pillow. She sat up when she saw me emerge. "I heard a baby crying," she said excitedly. "Is it here?"

I crouched down next to the couch, nodding. "She is."

Lily flapped her arms in excitement. "I have a baby sister?!"

I tried to smile at her reaction, but it came out stiff. "That's right. And you can go see her in a minute. But I have to tell you something first." I took a breath. "Your little sister had some trouble being born, so I had to help her by operating on your mom's tummy."

Lily's brow furled, knowing me well enough to read between the lines. "Is Mommy sick?"

I nodded, keeping my tone gentle. "Yeah, sweetheart, she's very sick. She's sleeping right now, but hopefully she'll wake up soon. We just need to help her get better and be really gentle around her tummy."

Lily took me at my word, and I was too much of a coward to tell her just how dire things really were. "Okay. Can I go see her now?"

I nodded. She threw her arms around my neck for a quick hug, and then darted off to the bedroom.

I watched her go, then slumped down to the floor. The stress and despair washed over me all at once, a tidal wave I'd been keeping at bay all evening. Clamping a hand over my mouth to stifle the sound, I let the tears fall. Hoping and praying that I hadn't just killed her mother.

CHAPTER 95

MARK AND I SAT VIGIL that night. Lauren's vitals stabilized (more or less) after the transfusion, but she still hadn't regained consciousness. With some careful maneuvering, we changed the sheets, and Lily had fallen asleep beside her mother. The baby also slept for the moment, swaddled inside a makeshift bassinet fashioned out of a dresser drawer.

"I'll need to finish the crib." Mark's strained voice broke the silence. "I thought I had more time."

"She'll be fine in the drawer until she outgrows it," I said absently. "Did you guys pick a name?"

He shook his head. "We talked about it some. I'll wait till she wakes up." Fearful eyes fixed on Lauren, he whispered, "Will she wake up?"

I swallowed past a painful tightness in my throat. "I don't know, Mark. She lost a lot of blood." He didn't respond.

We both fell quiet for a few minutes, then I rose from my chair, "I'm going to go make some coffee. You want some? Or anything else?"

Mark shook his head. I was almost to the door when he called after me, "Anna? I'm sorry about earlier." When I squinted at him in confusion, he clarified. "In the kitchen."

"Oh." I shrugged. The argument already felt like forever ago. "It's okay."

"No, it isn't okay," he argued, unsatisfied by how easily I let him off the hook. "It wasn't fair to put you between me and Lauren like that. Especially knowing what it's been like for you here."

"You were overwhelmed. It's fine. Really." He nodded in relief. I paused, hand on the door jamb. "Mark, I know how hard this must be. If there's anything I can do…"

Following my gaze, Mark's face crumpled. "I can't lose her, Anna." He rubbed at his eyes, so I wouldn't see the tears that threatened.

I moved behind his chair and wrapped my arms around his shoulders from behind. Mark wasn't the sort for an open breakdown, but he leaned into the crook of my arm, his hand coming to rest atop my forearm.

I murmured near his ear. "I know. Don't give up hope. Lauren's a strong woman. She's going to fight for you and the girls."

I stood there for a while, just holding him. Eventually, the baby's cry broke the silence.

Mark straightened up. Clearing his throat, he said softly, "I'll get her. I think I would like that coffee now, if that's okay."

"Sure." I released him and stepped back.

He went to the makeshift bassinet, lifting the swaddled baby. "Hey, precious," he cooed at her.

Smiling faintly, I ducked out to the kitchen to start some water boiling for coffee. I had just put the kettle over the fire when I heard Mark's excited call, "Anna, she's awake!"

I rushed back into the bedroom and saw him gingerly handing Lauren the baby. "Lauren," I greeted in relief. She turned her smile from the infant up to me. Even though there were still risks, seeing her awake and alert was a two ton weight lifted off my shoulders.

Mark sat beside them, perched on the edge of the bed. He scooted closer to Lauren's feet when I approached, giving me room to examine the patient. "How are you feeling? I'll get you something more for the pain." The anesthetic must have worn off by now.

"Thanks," Lauren replied, the strain evident in her voice. "I'm tired. Look at her, though." The smile lit up her face. "I think she's hungry. Can I nurse her?"

"Sure. You just don't want her resting on the incision. Here, like this." I helped her maneuver the baby around into a more sideways position, and the crying ceased as soon as the newborn latched on. "You're an old pro," I observed. Lauren just quirked a little smile.

The kettle howled in the other room. Mark offered to get it, along with some water for Lauren.

Lauren barely noticed him go, her eyes still locked on the baby. "She's really okay?"

I smiled. "Everything looks great. No sign of trauma. Got a good set of lungs on her."

Lauren nodded, tearing up in relief. "Thank God." She looked up at me, her voice tentative, "And the surgery?"

I took up Mark's position on the edge of the bed so I could be on her level. "You gave us quite a scare there for a few minutes," I said gently. "You lost a lot of blood, and I had to give you a transfusion from Mark." A worried furrow marred her brow as she listened intently to my words. "You're not out of the woods yet. We'll have to keep a close eye on you for the next few days—make sure there's no infection or other complications. But given how well you're doing now, and how tough I know you are? I'm optimistic." Lauren bobbed her head again, letting out a shaky breath.

I went on, "Your part is to get lots of rest, and let Mark play mother hen," I told her. She made a face, and I stressed with a smile, "Doctor's orders."

"I'll try," she pledged. The baby had nursed herself to sleep already, and Lauren just held her quietly for a few moments before saying, "Thank you, Anna."

I shrugged, my lips tugging up in a small smile. "You're welcome. Just doing my job."

Lauren shook her head. "No. You could've said no. I know Mark asked you to."

"He told you that?" I peered at her, hoping she hadn't heard us arguing in the kitchen.

With a tiny, knowing smile, Lauren shook her head again. "He didn't have to. I know him."

"Oh." I felt a tug of guilt for inadvertently confirming her suspicion. "He was just afraid of losing you."

"I know," she murmured. She fixed her eyes on me. "But I knew if something happened, they'd be in good hands."

Having become so used to borderline hostility from her, the reversal caught me off-guard. "Lauren, I…" I didn't know what to say.

Lauren went on as if I hadn't said anything. "I resented you for being there when it should have been me. I thought you wanted to drive us apart." I shook my head in an unnecessary denial. "I misjudged you, Anna. Watching you today… I saw how much you care. You saved all of us. You saved my girls." Her eyes went to them, and her voice got choked up. "I can never repay you for that."

Seeing the tears trace down her cheeks, I cupped her hand between mine. "You don't have to." I found myself tearing up as well. Seconds ticked by, neither of us having the words. Finally I spoke, "You know, back when all this started, your mother asked me why I agreed to walk a thousand miles with some man I'd just met. I had my rationalizations, but the truth is—it was just a feeling. An instinct. And when I think of everything that lined up to bring me here… I know this is where I was meant to be. Not for Mark, but for all of you. You've all given me so much." I quirked a tearful little smile. "I'm the lucky one."

Lauren sniffled, too overcome for words.

I patted her hand. "You just focus on getting well. We need you here. Especially this little one." I smoothed out a crease on the blanket swaddling the infant.

Mark chose that moment to return, a pair of coffee mugs and a cup of water balanced carefully in his hands. He saw Lauren's tear-streaked face and his face grew alarmed. "What's wrong?"

"Nothing," Lauren assured him, smiling. She glanced at me briefly, then back at him. "We're fine."

Feeling more hopeful than I had all evening, I affirmed, "We are."

CHAPTER 96

I WATCHED LAUREN LIKE A hawk over the next few days for any signs of infection or complications. At one point, she spiked a low-grade fever and gave me a heart attack, but some antibiotics we'd looted awhile back managed to keep the infection in check. Every day she grew stronger, and by the second week I decided she was out of the woods.

When I told him, Mark hugged me tearfully and whispered, "Thank you."

I squeezed him back, shaking my head against his shoulder. "This wasn't me, Mark. Both of them surviving that, under these conditions? It's nothing short of a miracle."

"Well, miracle or not, I don't know what we would've done without you here. So thank you all the same." He pressed a light kiss to my temple and then released me.

I smiled self-consciously. "Fine. You're welcome." He grinned.

My prayers knew who to really thank.

A couple days later, the girls were all in the living room while Mark was out fishing. I watched Lauren trudge back from the kitchen, pushing through her exhaustion. Nursing a baby around the clock while recovering from surgery would knock anyone down. Mark and I helped as much as she'd let us, but she always put her girls first.

Lauren had just sat down on the couch and closed her eyes for a second when baby Grace let out a cry from her drawer on the coffee table. Lauren pinched the bridge of her nose, gathering herself.

"Want me to get her?" I offered tentatively from my chair.

"Thanks," Lauren said with a weary smile. "She probably just needs to be changed."

Lily bounded over from some craft she had been working on at the dining table. "I can help! I'll get the diaper ready." She dashed over and grabbed one of the squares of fabric from the stack of makeshift cloth diapers. Never had I seen anyone more excited about being a big sister. Babysitter material for sure.

I couldn't match Mark or Lauren's experienced efficiency at diapering, but eventually Lily and I had the infant changed and re-dressed. Lacking any real sleepers or onesies, Lauren had made Grace a few simple nightgowns out of old pillowcases. I carried her over to the blanket laid out in the warm zone by the fireplace. Bear moved from his favorite spot to lay nearby, wagging his tail. Like Lily, he was quite taken with the newest human. He kept watch over her in his usual gentle way.

"Here's her toy!" Lily offered, plopping down beside us with the wooden rings Mark had carved. She jangled them near Grace's head, but the baby was focused on me. Curious tiny hands reached for my hair, her mothers' blue eyes intent on the red strands.

Lily giggled. "You're supposed to play with the toy, silly, not Auntie Anna's hair."

I looked up, blinking at her. It was the first time she'd ever called me anything but just "Anna". My heart swelled, but then I felt a tug of worry. I slanted a glance to Lauren, seeing if she had heard. The last thing I wanted was to rock the tentative foundation we'd built.

Seeing the anxious crease across my brow, Lauren smiled softly. She didn't address me directly, but looked to Lily. "Maybe you and Auntie Anna can keep an eye on Gracie for a bit while I go take a quick nap?"

"Sure!" Lily agreed brightly.

I couldn't find my voice, too choked up to answer, but I gave Lauren a tearful nod. "Thank you," I mouthed silently. She just smiled and trudged off to the bedroom, leaving me with the girls. My honorary nieces.

CHAPTER 97

THE WEEKS PASSED AND THE snow began to melt. Snowshoes were discarded, replaced with muddy boots and a muddy dog. Mark traded his fleece sweaters for shirtsleeves, teasing me for continuing to wear my coat. I thought I wasn't doing bad for a girl from Hawaii stuck in the tail end of a northeastern winter. I had begun to despair of ever feeling warm again.

Part of me felt content. I loved the girls, and seeing Lily settle into "big sister" mode brought back fond memories of me and Jess when we were kids. Seeing Mark and Lauren's affection every day still felt like a smack in the gut sometimes, but I forced myself to focus on how happy they were. What they had was special, and in time things would get easier.

And yet, something was missing. A vague discontent, festering just beneath the surface.

One clear day in April, I sat on a log near the lake shore, watching the water lap against the rocks. It was a far cry from the sandy beach at home, but I still found it soothing.

A crunch of rock announced Mark's presence even before Bear started thumping his tail against the ground. Resting after the morning's work, the dog was too lazy to get up to greet him. "Thought I might find you here," Mark said amiably.

I offered a wan smile. "Just taking a break." I let my eyes drift back to the lake and the still-snow-capped mountains rising beyond it. "It is beautiful here, I'll give you that."

"Always struck me like something out of a postcard," Mark agreed. We admired the view in silence for a bit before finally a sad frown settled on his lips, "It's not enough, though. Is it?"

The question caught me off guard. "What?"

He waved a hand back toward the cabin, a sad frown touching his lips. "This. Us. You're not happy here."

"I'm not *unhappy*," I protested. "I love you guys. This is the first time in a long time I felt like I belong." Brow creasing, I looked down at Bear by my feet and sighed. "It's just..."

"You're a doctor without any patients," Mark finished for me. I shot him a grateful look, relieved that he understood. "You don't have to feel bad about that. It's baked into who you are."

"It didn't bother me on the way here," I admitted. "I mean, a little at the beginning, after the airport, but we had our mission. There were people I could help along the way. But now? I can't help but think of everyone out there who still needs help. It feels like I'm taking a vacation while the world burns."

"I think you've already done more than your share of putting out fires, but I get it." Holding up a hand palm-up, he said, "So I guess we need to find you some patients."

"Where?" I held out both my arms in an expansive gesture to the emptiness surrounding us. "I can't just leave you guys, Mark. You need me, too. If something happened and I wasn't here…" I couldn't find the words to articulate that gnawing worry. I'd never forgive myself.

Mark sat down on the edge of the log beside me, and I scooted over to give him some more room. Elbows on his knees, he looked at me sidelong. "Anna, you know we all want you here, but I don't want you to stay out of some sense of obligation, or fear. You don't owe us anything. If you wanted to strike out on your own, we'd manage. I'd worry myself sick—" I snorted lightly at that. "But I'd understand."

"Thanks, Mark. I appreciate that." We sat in silence for a while as I considered what he'd said, both watching the lake. "But I want to stay. I would miss it too much. Hanging out with you. Watching the girls grow up. Lauren and I just found our footing. I don't want to give all that up." I sighed again. "Maybe it's selfish, but I just wish there was a way to do both."

He bobbed his head, relief flitting across his face. Another minute ticked by, then he said, "Well, we'll just have to go with you, then."

From the off-hand way he said it, I assumed he was joking. "Ha ha, very funny." Then I saw the look in his eyes, and his inscrutable grin. I squinted at him. "Wait. Why do I feel like this another Crazy Mark Ryan Scheme?"

"Actually it was her idea." He nodded past me, and I turned to see Lauren walking up the path from the cabin. The girls must still be inside, close enough to be within earshot if Lily called or Grace started crying.

Seeing the baffled look on my face, Lauren grinned and looked to Mark. "You told her?" she asked.

"I started to. I don't think she believes this was your plan." He smiled. "She's used to me being the one with all the crazy ideas."

"She still doesn't know me that well." Lauren offered a bland shrug.

I looked between the two of them. "You're serious." It didn't compute. "Why? Where would we even go?"

Lauren answered my second question first. "Well, we were thinking New York."

"Back to the Williams farm," Mark added.

My jaw hung open, stunned that they would even consider it. "But why?" My brain still tripped over that question. "You have everything you need here."

They shared a private smile, then Mark said, "But you don't. Anna, we know how much being a doctor means to you."

"You have a gift," Lauren threw in, her voice gentle. "It would be selfish to keep you from sharing that with others."

They had tag-teamed me, but in a good way. "I don't know what to say," I finally stammered. "Obviously I'm grateful, but… I can't ask you to do that. To leave all this behind? Trek through the mountains with an infant?"

"Well, like you told me once," Mark said with a grin, "You don't have to ask."

My lips curled up at the memory, but logic still resisted. "We don't even know what things are like out there now. They were bad enough even before winter."

Lauren, ever the pragmatic one, pointed out, "If this past winter showed us anything, it's how hard it is to make it on our own. Even here. In New York we have a chance of finding a community. That's good for you, good for us, good for the girls…" She smiled. "It'll be worth it."

I thought of the trail between here and the farm. The mountains. The dangers. Whatever they may say about the other benefits, they wouldn't even be considering this if it weren't for me. I was touched. Humbled. But also scared. I didn't mind shouldering risks for them, but it felt wrong for it to be the other way around.

Still, Lauren made sense. We'd all be better off with a village around us, and I could think of nowhere better than with the Williamses and their neighbors. Mark and Lauren waited patiently while they watched the gears turn behind my eyes.

Finally, I squinted at them. "You guys are sure about this?" They exchanged a knowing glance and nodded, no sign of reservation on either face. "All right. I guess we've got another crazy plan."

Mark grinned. "Like we'd have it any other way?"

I glanced down at Bear, my mouth quirking upward. "What do you say, buddy? You up for walking another couple hundred miles?" Hearing only the word 'walk', Bear cheerfully thumped his tail against the ground. He had no idea what he was in for.

Did we?

CHAPTER 98

IT DIDN'T MAKE SENSE TO leave immediately. In another month or two, the weather would be better, the rivers would settle down after the spring ice melts, and it would be easier to hunt and forage along the way. Waiting also gave Lauren more time to recover from the C-section. Still, just knowing that plans were underway helped me shake the angst that I'd been feeling. I had a new mission.

We started preparing. The camping equipment had barely had enough time to gather dust, but everything needed to be cleaned, checked, and sometimes repaired.

Sitting in front of the fireplace one evening, sewing up a frayed corner of my sleeping bag, I mused aloud, "I never thought I'd say it, but I'll actually miss this place."

"I don't think I will," Lauren replied. She sat nearby on the couch, nursing Grace, while Mark and Lily played with Bear outside, taking advantage of the longer days and warmer weather.

"Suppose it's a little bittersweet." Thinking of all the time she'd spent here alone and bereft, I couldn't really blame her. To say nothing of when she'd nearly died.

"Change of scenery would be nice," Lauren admitted. A short stretch of silence passed before she asked, "Mark said you and Kayla were pretty close. You must be looking forward to seeing her again."

"Yeah," I agreed with a ready smile. "Lil can't wait to see Jaden, too." She had let out a whoop of excitement when we told her, over the moon at the prospect of reuniting with her friend. "And the farm animals. Especially the llama."

"She's been going on about it," Lauren agreed, chuckling softly. "The horses, too." Lauren looked up from the baby's face to watch mine. "What about Nikolai?"

Smile dimming, I hitched a shoulder. "I don't even know if he'll still be there. Sticking around wasn't exactly his strong suit." I tried not to sound bitter about it.

"Do you want to see him again?"

I hesitated a moment before answering. "I mean, I'd like to at least know that he's all right. But I'm not looking to just pick up where we left off or anything." Lauren gave a quiet mmm-hmm to that, just listening. "I haven't really thought about him much. It wasn't serious."

Grace had fallen asleep, so Lauren rearranged her sweater, cradling the baby in the crook of one arm. "Of course not. You were in love with someone else."

The matter-of-fact way she said it, glossing over the fact that her husband was that someone, made my brows lift. She wasn't wrong, but I brushed past that subject quickly. "It wasn't just that, though." I pushed the needle through the nylon shell of the sleeping bag a few more times while I gathered my thoughts. "I went into it thinking he was only going with us to the next town. 'Happily ever after' never really entered my mind, but it still sucked when he bailed on us. We really could've used his help. It's hard to get past that. To think about trusting him again." I was conscious of the irony of me, the lifelong nomad, being angry about him leaving. It didn't change what he'd done, or how I felt about it.

"Trust takes time." Rising gingerly, Lauren started toward their bedroom to take the sleeping baby back to her crib. She paused to glance back at me. "I don't know Nikolai, but I do know that sometimes people can surprise you if you give them a chance." The pointed stare and twinkle in her eye made it clear she was talking about me. I quirked a brief smile in return, and she went on, "There's no need to rush into anything. You'll have plenty of time to sort things out."

"If he's even there."

She tilted her head. "You really think he'd move on?"

I remembered how well he got along with Kayla's husband and the boys; how anxious he'd been to find somewhere better than the devastated city the gang had taken over; how readily he'd taken to helping out on the farm. "No. I don't." More than that, I realized I didn't want to think that he'd run out on the Williamses as easily as he had me. I wanted him to be better than that. With a brief smile, I said, "You think it's too much to wish he's been pining away there this whole time?"

Lauren chuckled. "Nah. Not at all."

CHAPTER 99

SPRING ARRIVED IN FULL FORCE, and the forest around the cabin came back to life. Leaves returned to the trees, their blossoms sending Mark's allergies into overdrive. I saw fawns on my hunting excursions, which led to a stern admonishment from Lily to be careful not to shoot any of their families. One day, I even saw a moose. I just sat and watched it for a while, marveling at its size.

We began finalizing our plans to leave, stockpiling travel-ready food and other supplies. Bear and I were smoking some venison jerky over a fire in the yard one afternoon when he surprised me with a barking fit. I peered at him. He knew better than to bark at the wildlife and scare them off, and humans he regarded with more curiosity than alarm.

"What is it?" I wondered aloud, despite his inability to answer. I waved a hand at him. "Quiet."

He stopped barking, but paced beside me restlessly. I retrieved my rifle from its resting place against the cabin porch and held it in a loose grip as I scanned the forest. Squinting, I spied shapes moving through the trees. People.

My knuckles tightened around the rifle, heart thudding. I counted three—no, at least four forms. I leapt up the stairs and pounded on the door. "Guys! Someone's coming!"

Mark abandoned the pile of gear he'd been arranging on the kitchen table and rushed to grab his own rifle. Lauren ushered Lily into the bedroom with the baby.

Bear barked again, and that's when I realized his tail was wagging. I looked from the dog to the tree line. What the hell? He looked up at me, panting happily. Whatever it was, he didn't consider it a threat. "Okay, go." At the release command, Bear darted across the yard, just as the first figure came into clear view through the trees.

My rifle dipped down to the ground, and I stared in disbelief at young Jaden Williams riding atop Nikolai's shoulders, both grimy and sweaty, both wearing backpacks. "Holy shit," I breathed.

Nikolai swung Jaden down, grinning as Bear came over to circle their legs like he was greeting long-lost pack members. The rest of their party came into view behind them: Kayla; her older son Anthony; more people I remembered as their neighbors whose baby I'd treated; and Joshua bringing up the rear.

Behind me, Mark rushed out onto the porch. He saw the smile break across my face and then looked from me to the new arrivals. "Well, I'll be damned. Lauren! It's okay—it's the Williamses."

I heard a surprised reply, but didn't catch the details because I had already set aside my rifle and was hurrying across the clearing to greet them. "My God, what are you guys doing here?" I asked, grinning through my shock. Kayla greeted me with open arms, tears in her eyes, as I rushed in for a fierce hug.

"It's good to see you, lovey," she murmured close to my ear. She'd traded some weight for muscle on the journey, her long hair tamed by a ponytail.

I glanced past the other smiling faces. The teen boys, uncertain what kind of greeting to offer, settled for cheerful waves. Anthony's shoulder seemed to have healed up just fine. Joshua had put on a good ten pounds of muscle from all the farm work, and a hint of stubble on his jaw made him look older than I remembered.

Then my gaze landed on Nikolai. He smiled.

"Anechka." Just the Ukrainian diminutive of my name, nothing else. That simple greeting and the warmth reaching his eyes conveyed his joy at seeing me. I hesitated just a moment before hugging him, too.

"Jaden!" Lily's excited cry echoed from the yard, and she ran over to meet her friend. Mark and Lauren trailed behind her, the latter carrying baby Grace.

Jaden had sat down to say hi to Bear, and didn't get up when Lily got closer. It was then I noticed a makeshift splint on his left ankle. I was about to ask what happened when my brain also registered something else. Releasing Nikolai and taking a half-step back, I scanned the group again, but saw no sign of Kayla's husband. "Where's Stephen?"

I had my answer as soon as the words left my lips, dimming the mood like someone flipping a light switch. Kayla's lip trembled, her brows knitting in a pained expression. Neither of the boys would meet my gaze. "Oh, Kayla, I'm so sorry."

"Bandits," Nikolai explained, his jaw tight. "They came over the winter for the food and the animals."

"We drove them off, but..." Joshua added grimly. "They shot Mr. Williams."

Guilt socked me in the stomach. Nikolai must have seen it in my face, for he touched my arm. "It was quick. Nothing you could have done." Lips tight, I gave him a solemn nod.

Lauren watched Kayla in sympathy. Shifting the baby to her shoulder, she said, "I'm sorry for your loss. Mark and Anna told me how you and your husband helped them."

Kayla nodded. She was putting on a brave face for her kids, holding back the tears. We'd talk later. For now, she was studying Lauren. "You must be Lauren." When Lauren nodded, offering a slight smile, Kayla clapped her hands. "Oh, praise be. I'm so glad they found you."

Grace turned her head to regard the newcomers, her forehead wrinkled in serious consideration. Waving a hand to everyone, Lauren took their arrival in stride and took charge, "Come on inside. You all look exhausted."

The group began shuffling forward, conversation buzzing. Joshua nudged Anthony's arm, sharing a quiet remark I didn't catch. It earned him a grateful half-smile from the other teen, and I could sense the brotherly bond between them.

Kayla hung back, glancing at Nikolai and Jaden.

"I will bring him," Nikolai assured her, getting a quick nod. He bent down to scoop up the injured boy.

"What happened to you?" I asked, checking out his ankle. Two sticks braced each side of his shoe with what looked like strips of a dirty T-shirt.

"I fell off a boulder," Jaden admitted with a lamenting sigh.

"Today?"

"No, a couple days ago."

Nikolai chimed in as we started toward the house, "Kayla thinks it is maybe broken."

"Okay. I'll check it out when we get inside." I slanted Nikolai a glance as we walked back to the cabin. The cut by his ear had left a scar, but otherwise he looked the same. A little leaner, maybe. "How did you guys even find us?"

"Nikolai knew the way," Jaden explained. "He knew how to hunt and do traps and stuff, too."

My eyebrows arched at that, and Nikolai flashed a little smile. "I paid attention to your lessons. And Mark's map." He jerked his head towards the lake. "The lake for a landmark helps." He held my gaze for a moment. "It was too dangerous to stay, so we thought to find you."

Maybe later I'd tell him of our plans to do just the opposite. "Well, I'm glad you guys made it here safe." We shared a smile, and then he carried Jaden inside.

Mark had gone out into the yard to retrieve a few lawn chairs for our unexpected guests. I held open the door for him as he reached the porch, but he paused in the doorway. "Guess the community came to us, huh?"

"Yeah, I guess it did. Good thing there are some other cabins around." My brain was already sifting through the logistics, making a task list to get everyone taken care of.

"Anechka, where should I put him down?" Nikolai's voice filtered out through the doorway.

Mark looked amused. "Sounds like you're being paged, Dr. Hastings."

I grinned and followed him inside to take care of my patient.

Your Review Matters

Thank you for reading! If you enjoyed this book, please take a moment to provide a review at the point of purchase. Your reviews are extremely helpful for independent authors, and I'm always thrilled to read them.

Stay Up to Date

Visit my website (www.lindanaughton.com) to learn about my other books, or join the newsletter for blog posts and updates (www.lindanaughton.com/newsletter.html).

Acknowledgements

For a software engineer who's never been on more than a tourist's day-hike, writing a novel about people hiking cross-country and living off the land was far outside my comfort zone. It would not have been possible without the support of a great many authors and content creators, whose work helped me to research what it might be like to walk a thousand miles in the middle of a disaster.

Any errors, omissions, or excessive use of creative license are my own, and no fault of the sources here.

The North Country Trail Association website (https://northcountrytrail.org/) was invaluable for learning about the trail that Anna and Mark follow across Pennsylvania and New York. The CNY Hiking website (https://cnyhiking.com) has amazing mile-by-mile descriptions of the trail, including landmarks and photos.

YouTube's wonderful community of thru-hikers has shared many wonderful anecdotes of trail life, gear recommendations, and even videos of them hiking some of the actual trail sections featured in this story. My favorite hiking YouTuber is Dixie, who has shares her journey on her channel "Homemade Wanderlust" (https://www.youtube.com/c/HomemadeWanderlust). Her uplifting videos are entertaining and educational.

Many authors have also written about their experiences thru-hiking the major trails. The two I found most helpful were *Wild: From Lost to Found on the Pacific Crest Trail* by Cheryl Strayed (also a great movie), and *AWOL on the Appalachian Trail* by David Miller.

For research on surviving the apocalypse, the prepper community provided a wealth of information on everything from food preservation to what kinds of vehicles might run after an EMP. City Prepping (https://www.cityprepping.com/) and The Survival Mom (https://thesurvivalmom.com/) have a lot of practical tips for preparing for disasters. Les Stroud's book *Survive!: Essential Skills and Tactics to Get You Out of Anywhere - Alive* and his YouTube channel are filled with great details about surviving in the wild. *The Survival Medicine Handbook: A guide for when help is NOT on the way* by Joseph Alton, M.D., and Amy Alton, A.R.N.P. helped to inform some of the medical situations in the story.

Speaking of medicine, I'm grateful to my friend Doctor Joska for patiently answering my medical questions. I also wanted to give a shout-out to Médecins Sans Frontières (aka Doctors Without Borders). The overseas missions described by Anna are based on real MSF projects, where staff far more heroic than my fictional doctor save lives in conflict and disaster zones around the world.

I'd also like to thank my friend Marisette and our guide Nate from the Three Rivers Rowing Association (http://threeriversrowing.org/) for taking me on a tour of the river route used in the story. Also my friends Glen and Lynne, for their encouragement and countless lunches spent chatting about upstate New York and "grid down" scenarios.

Fellow science enthusiasts will probably realize that the EMP depicted in this story is a "Super EMP", exaggerated for dramatic effect. In reality, there are important differences between EMP effects caused by high-altitude nuclear blasts and solar storms, and subtleties in how each of those affects different kinds of electronics. These pesky details were glossed over to engineer a collapse of society so hard and fast that it resulted in the social isolation central to the story. A real EMP, while it would play out differently, would still be catastrophic. Global supply chains are fragile, and most cities do not have the local resources necessary to sustain their populations for more than a few days. The novel *One Second After* by William R. Forstchen arguably kicked off the "EMP disaster" genre, and its depiction of society's collapse is so well-regarded that it's even been mentioned on the floor of Congress.

I am grateful for the coaching and insight of Katie McCoach (https:// katiemccoach.com/) in fine-tuning some character arcs. The awesome cover art is from Deranged Doctor Design (https:// www.derangeddoctordesign.com/), who brought my three precious characters to life even better than I could have imagined. Elena Anderson is an awesome narrator that brought the characters to life in the audiobook.

Last but certainly not least, I am grateful for my family. My mom is my biggest cheerleader, first reader, and copy editor. My dad fostered my love of sci-fi, and is my resident science and military advisor. My kids are not only the collective inspiration behind Lily, but also my inspiration every day.

About the Author

Linda Naughton has been writing stories for as long as she can remember. She is the author of several novels, children's books, and the blog Self-Rescuing Princesses. A proud geek and gamer girl, she enjoys sci-fi, disaster movies, and role-playing games. She is a software engineer, paramedic, and mother of two.

Also by Linda Naughton

Blackout Trail Series

(post-apocalyptic EMP thrillers)

Blackout Trail

Dustoff Down (novella spinoff)

Other Sci-Fi

Another Man's Freedom Fighter - dystopian thriller

www.ingramcontent.com/pod-product-compliance
Lightning Source LLC
Chambersburg PA
CBHW021328310726
48971CB00001B/23